WOLF TECH 1

WOLF TECH 1

New
Beginning

ADAM WEBSTER

Self-Published by Adam Webster

CONTENTS

AUTHOR NOTE

While the first draft was made available on Wattpad, this story contains a great many corrections, expansions, and other changes to make it ready for publishing. There is 30,000 additional words, or about 24% more content! While those who have read the story already on Wattpad, I do hope there is enough new content to make it well worth the purchasing of this story.

This is a work of fiction. All the characters and events portrayed in this novel are either fictitious or are used fictitiously. Any relation to reality is completely coincidence.

Prologue

Brook moved her staff at half her usual speed but was still able to block the staff of her opponent. Her return strike was at her controlled half-speed, with little of her strength, and they barely blocked… this time. The pup she was training was covered in bruises, which would be gone before morning, from the moves they hadn't blocked: the pain would remind him he needed to block them. The pup was missing basic moves now but had let him stop with a successful block.

Grounding her staff, "You need to get your high blocks up faster, Jake, if you want to be good enough to do patrols."

Jake couldn't speak, he was so out of breath. He nodded he heard, as he went to get a drink of water from his water bottle beside his seat on the bench at the side of the workout-circle. It was the same size as a challenge circle, but rather than just bare ground packed hard, it was padded well to absorb hits and the young pups appreciated it.

Brook nodded at the next pup, and repeated the exercise, while the rest watched. Her group of five pups were the ones who the instructors thought had potential, even though they were just beginning their second decade of life. If they survived the decade, they would be trained and have the skills to enter the Enforcers and be able to help defend and protect the pack.

She was a little surprised there were three she-pups this year who had been offered and decided to take the class, as usually the majority interested were he-pups. She treated them the same, as it didn't matter the gender to her, she taught them all equally. If the girls—or boys—needed extra help to succeed, they would ask or drop out. Most who were offered the training took it, as it usually meant a senior wolf thought they could get a high rank in the pack. Likely to be a Patrol leader before they were a century old, and they might even reach Beta rank. All were wearing matching close-fitted shorts and tank top, which were now sweat-soaked from their hard morning with her.

The few who dropped out either found it to not be for them or were not willing to put in the effort needed to succeed. The pack knew it wasn't for everyone, as it was one of the hardest positions in the pack, thus it was also one of the most respected. Even these pups who were mostly just starting their training would be role models for the younger, so knew they had higher standards they had to meet; if they broke a rule, they would be punished as an example too.

"Showers!" Brook eventually called out, dismissing the pups for the morning. In the afternoon, the Elders worked with them on their class learning skills. They had to meet the human provincial learning skills, but with even only having half the time of the humans, they were able to generally meet the average grades. Some didn't bother with anything past high school, but for those who had the marks to make them in, the pack paid for them to go to their choice, provided they continued to pass. If they failed, they–or their parents–had to pay for them to retake the class. All were expected to at least graduate high school unless they had an exception from the Alpha. There were a few of those, who the Alpha had permitted, but had discussed it with the human education board, and they had agreed with it. Often it was exceptions for classes, so they could still graduate.

She headed up to her room on the second floor, so she could wash up without anyone bothering her. She did share the bathroom with her friends Evan and Kuri, who had the bedroom on the opposite side of the bathroom, but they were out on patrol, and wouldn't be back until late afternoon at the earliest. Stripping off her bike shorts and thong underwear, along with her sport bra, all of which were soaked from her training, as she had tossed her tank aside mid-morning, dumping them into the laundry hamper, she hopped into the shower.

After pulling on some fresh clothes of a soft capris and matching tank top in blue, over a clean sports bra and panties, Brook headed down to lunch as her stomach complained about the delay to shower. The pack generally did a buffet line of food, and each picked out what they wanted and served themselves. It made it easy for the pack chef and their helpers, as they had only to bring out to one place and could easily refill the trays. Making her choices, she headed for her usual spot.

Dropping in her seat with her plate of food in the dining hall, Aurora and Nikki smiled a greeting, "Tiring morning?" They could see Brook drooping a little. Aurora and Nikki were the ones who dealt with the little tech the pack had and helped with the building maintenance. Most of their work was finding ways for them to acquire technology without the humans being aware, and it was getting hard, as most expected high-speed internet, which they still hadn't found a way to get it out to the pack house, without having a human come out to hook it up, and the Alpha refused to let them do that. Brook helped where she could, as she had learned how to blend in fairly well with humans.

Brook nodded and started to eat, *It takes a lot out of me to not use my strength. The pups are advancing. Can we not talk about work?* She told them silently over their shared pack bonds since her mouth was full of food.

Well, you are an excellent trainer. Most of those who don't drop out of your class go on to good positions. Was the response from Aurora. Almost half of the pups who went to Brook didn't finish the first year of training. *Did you hear about...* she said as she told them about a new tech which had just hit market. It was another item she would only drool over—figuratively—as it needed high speed internet to work.

The others nodded, and they started to talk about the latest tech they knew was out, and some thoughts on getting the Alphas to give permission to bring it here. *Mostly, Alpha Gareth's resistance is he can't really see enough of a need for it, which counteracts the risks of our discovery.* and they knew for such a change, they would need the Elder's consent as well, as the Alpha listened to the Elders on most ideas, even if there were times he overruled their objections. Unlike some Alphas, he never used 'because I say so' but had a reason for it.

After finishing her second helping, "Well, I need a good run. I should be back for supper." Brook told the others, as she picked up her used dishes and took them to the tubs which were beside the door to the kitchen. Some of the pack just left the used dishes on the table for the Thetas to deal with but had found if she took the little work to help them, they generally were friendly about her requests for assistance of any sort. She knew the Thetas just had to drop off the clothes to her bed, for her to fold and put away, but since she helped them with putting her dishes away, and with whatever task they asked of her, usually lifting and carrying something heavy, her clothes were always just found folded in her drawers or hung up. Even if it was like this morning's top, dumped in the common hamper in the training area with the used towels, which they only had to put in the clean hamper out there for her to collect.

Brook generally had only a morning or afternoon to work, but at times, she did one-on-one training in her off time, if she found some-one who needed the assistance or deserved punishment, or those she felt would excel better from some one-on-one attention. Or if they asked for it. Right now, she didn't have anyone, so the time was her own.

*****

Brook was a half hour into her run, enjoying the wind going through her fur as she used the long run trail, which wrapped around several mountains and went through a couple passes, which was designed to take a few hours to run. Usually, it took her two to three hours, depending on the trail conditions, and she wasn't pushing it today, as it was a nice day, so would be to the three-hour side. She was thinking if she wanted a hot soak or to run another trail when she finished this run, letting her wolf to be forward and mostly in control to set their paws so they didn't make a misstep and she could think on what to do.

A delicious smell crossed her nose which nearly made her trip. **Mate!** her wolf said, yanking control from the human half, and heading into the wind trying to track it down. It seemed to fade, then come back even stronger. There was a scent of human mixed in, but her wolf still had control and ignored that part of the scent. She didn't care if their mate was human; she just wanted her mate. He could be Turned once they were mated.

They bounded across a valley, heedless of the possibility there could be humans around to see her, it being in the part with less cover; Wolf-Brook was firmly in control and wasn't going to let their mate get away! He was their other half, and both halves of Brook had waited since she came of age and learned his scent to meet him. She didn't want to wait for even another day!

The elders told of a story where a wolf was lazy and when they smelled their mate, just waited for them to be found, instead of going to them. Lazy Jack smelled them for a week every summer, then nothing until the next year. This went on for several decades, with a different story for each year for the excuse why they never went to their mate, just expected them to come to find him, but then they stopped smelling them. They lived on waiting for their mate for the rest of their lazy life, never having their mate find them... They were *not* going to be such a wolf; they *were* going to find their mate!

Reaching a scree-filled slope, she started bounding on the rocks, Wolf-Brook was heedless of her safety and refused to give control back to the human mind; their mate was close! Jumping on a log about halfway up, it dislodged, levering a boulder up and starting a rockslide. Scampering, she tried to evade the tumbling rocks. It seemed the boulder was supporting much of the slope above it, and when it was released much more moved above!

She nearly made it out, dodging the boulders bouncing around her, turning trees into kindling, but then a rock bounced off her head and knocked her out...

CHAPTER 1

The Rescue

Adam was taking pictures deep in the mountains from a lookout he hadn't been to before and had just heard about, although he had been in the area many times. Reaching it, you had to take an unmarked road which most didn't even see and go up a steep winding road. He thought it may have been abandoned and forgotten many years before, as there looked to be no maintenance done, unlike his usual lookouts.

The garbage can was gone, the signs were missing, just the posts were there to show where there had been signs. The parking pad had deep ruts and runoff eroded spots. In a couple places, the trees made it hard to see much of anything. The road wasn't in any better condition and looked almost washed out in a couple places. He had been glad for having all-wheel drive on his Chevy Traverse. It was the first vehicle he had bought new and was quite happy with the fact he could afford it. It had enough cargo room to fit all his stuff when camping, and taking others with him, while still handling well.

Movement down in the valley caught his eye; he turned the camera seeing a wild wolf for the first time in his life! He had only ever seen wolves in the zoo before now. It was a beautiful dark brown wolf, with a slightly lighter belly and it seemed to be running towards him across the valley. He started taking some nice shots, a smile on his face, and he couldn't seem to take his eyes off it.

He was glad he had his longer lens already on his camera. He was getting some good shots which made it seem he was much closer to the wolf than he was, even if he kept having to zoom out as they came closer.

When the wolf came to his end of the valley and left his sight, right below the ridge he was on, he kept looking for them to reappear. After a bit, he heard a rockslide rumble down near him, it sounded like it was sending rocks directly where the wolf had been last seen!

Not considering why he had the urge, Adam abandoned his expensive camera and just as pricey lens and started racing down to where he last saw the wolf. He nearly ran down the hill, heedless of his own safety, or the fact he could be facing an injured wolf who might bite him or cause the rocks to move more.

When he finally reached the wolf, he found it was caught in the edge of the slide and was knocked out. Looking at it, there it had been tossed out of the main slide path, luckily, with only smaller rocks on it, he worked quickly to free it totally, looking for injuries. Noticing a couple of broken limbs, he felt the need to help it. Picking the wolf up, and draping it across his shoulders with a grunt, he felt an unusual tingling sensation moving through his body, centring where her body touched him. He thought nothing of it—nor of the fact he could move such a large animal, nor why he had the *need* to personally see to their help. The only thought in his mind was to get the wolf some help, with something urging him on and lending him strength. He stood and started to slowly make his way back up the ridge to the lookout and his vehicle.

As he eventually reached the lookout, he could feel the wolf starting to stir. Not knowing what it would do, he put the wolf down on some soft grass gently and stepped back. Trying to stay busy and not hover, he tore his eyes away and went back to pack up his camera gear, tossing it all quickly in the back of his SUV, not bothering packing it back into the camera bag or retracting the legs of the tripod. More wanting to get back to the wolf.

Once done, he looked back over at where he laid the wolf down and the wolf was gone! In the exact place was a battered, naked young woman, who wasn't quite awake. She looked beautiful to his eyes, she wasn't tall, but neither was he. She seemed to not have much in the way of breasts, but again, he preferred that. Many times, he had heard from females who had large breasts who complained about them being sore or getting back pain from them. She did seem to be very fit and had a good selection of muscles visible on her. He had started to get flabby, with his tech job, and hoped she could help him with getting more fit...

Shaking his head, not sure he could believe—yet—what had happened. Thinking logically, he realised there was *nothing* to explain it, except to accept the fact the wolf and the human were the same creature, as he had read in lots of werewolf fiction. He grabbed his first aid kit and a survival blanket and rushed over. He decided no matter *what* she was, he'd do as much as he could for her; it was the right thing to do. Something in him would not let him think of anything else and kept urging him back to her, not that he wanted to fight it, anyways.

"Lay still," Adam gently told her, as he gently tried to clean the largest injuries of any dirt with some alcohol wipes and wrap them up in gauze, then covered her up in a blanket. He quickly realised he couldn't help her other than setting her two broken limbs. He quickly had them immobilised with a couple of fallen branches and the triangle bandages from his first aid kit. The scratches and bruises already looked like his did after a few days and were fading before his eyes. He didn't know if what he had in his kit could hurt her worse than doing nothing. Holding her hand, so she knew she is not alone, he felt those strange tingles run up his arm as she woke and started wondering about what was causing it and hoped it was something like what he had read about. It never crossed his mind she could harm him when she woke up, but just *knew* she would never harm him.

Her eyes looked feral, and she let out a growl as she awoke but fell back with a whimper when she tried to sit up, as he lightly pressed her shoulder back down. Her eyes turned to look more human, but again the feelings of alarm were soothed away, "Lay still, and I'll move you in a minute to something more comfortable," he told her, and getting a nod in response, he reluctantly released her hand. He quickly set to work clearing his passenger seat of his lunch bag, snacks, and electronics for her to sit in, as well as getting an emergency plastic seat cover for it, to keep the blood off his new-looking seat.

He started to grab a spare shirt and shorts, but he stopped for a moment, as he realized it would be hard to dress her with couple of broken limbs, deciding to just leave them and just stick with the Mylar blanket for now, moving back to her when she moaned, as her injuries start to make themselves known.

She started to move her arms to sit up but relaxed back down when her broken arm made itself known, and she realised it already was bound up tight. She did turn her head to watch him.

Adam decided quickly, as he moved back to her, he was going to need to move her because the nearest cell service was forty-five minutes away, and the nearest help was much farther. Looking down as he crouched beside her, and realised she was still awake and aware, suddenly aware he didn't know if he could even take her to any medical centre he knew, deciding perhaps she would know the best care she needed, and for speed, he needed to be blunt and not hide what he had already figured out on his own.

"I know you are some sort of werewolf or shifter, as I carried a wolf up the ridge, from where it had been caught in the rockslide. When I turned away, it disappeared, and you were exactly where it had been. The only explanation is the wolf was also *you*," Seeing the fear and alarm in her eyes, he tried to reassure her, "I am not going to hurt you, or send you to anywhere you don't want to go. I *was* going to rush to the nearest place I could get cell service, and call for medical help, but I doubt you want to go to one of the human medical centres, right?" He lightly touched her cheek, hoping in a way she would find comforting and again felt some tingling.

She nodded in agreement and tilted her head into the touch, closing her eyes as the skin tingled nicely where he touched. She decided to trust him with the truth, in hopes of keeping him close till she was well enough to stake her claim on her mate, "Medical centres would ask too many questions about how fast I heal. I don't think I know the packs near here. I need you to call my Alpha, and he'll know where to go and who to trust."

"OK, first is to get you into my vehicle and get to the cell service. I hope I don't hurt you." Adam picked her up with a grunt of surprise, as she weighed much more than he expected, and again feeling the tingles. He heard her take a sharp intake of air, before she relaxed in his arms, thinking she was in pain, he moved her gently and carefully to the waiting passenger seat. Buckling her in, before racing around the vehicle and getting in, to take them as fast as he could safely, which for the winding roads, and the weather, which was closing in fast, was the speed limit.

Watching his phone in its mount attached to the dash, he was hoping for a little bit of service—he didn't need data, just a basic service. Deciding to try to find out more and hoping for confirmation of what he was hoping the tingles meant, "My name is Adam, what's yours?"
*****

When he picked her up, the pain hit first and then the warmth and tingles started. As they grew, the pain Brook was feeling seemed to fade and she turned her head into his neck. Though he probably didn't realize it, she inhaled, filling her nose with confirmation, and wanted to bite him then and there. If it wasn't for the pain, she might have really considered it, even though it would have been against their laws, **Ours, our mate.** her wolf commented in wonder and love, as she moved back in trust; their mate wouldn't try to hurt them.

Feeling the tingles when he had picked her up, had Brook's wolf bouncing a bit in her mind. Both realised she had been rescued by her Mate and he was carrying her. It left her nearly gasping in surprise, before relaxing in his arms. She now knew he wouldn't harm her intentionally, and she could trust him. He smelled of clean honest sweat, and not of the rancid-smelling chemicals many humans covered themselves in was a nice bonus.

Once on the road and fighting to stay awake now she felt safe; knowing, with her probable head injury, which she suspected was a concussion from the pounding head and feeling dizzy. She knew she needed to stay awake till they reached the Healer, was grateful for him trying to speak with her, as it helped to take her mind of the pain, "My name is Brook. I guess there is no reason to hide it, since you have already realised it; yes, I am a werewolf. I'm not sure if you noticed the tingles, but we are Mates. We—well my wolf—had smelled you from the other side of the valley on the wind and was racing to find you." Giving a little wry smile, "It didn't go too well, as the rocks started moving as my wolf tried to climb them. A boulder hit us. The next thing I remember was waking up with your beautiful face above me."

Nearly forgetting he was driving when she said 'Mates', Adam had to calm himself down, but he couldn't get rid of the big grin, and nearly missed her description of what happened, "I knew it! I knew it! Not sure why, but I was driven to climb down the ridge, and go after you." Taking a deep breath as his mind went to what *could* have happened and he could had lost his *mate*, "You are very lucky the rocks didn't land on you, as you were right on the edge and had only some small rocks on you, which I could lift. I am very glad I did it, now! Most of what I know about werewolves is from stories online and other fictional stories but have read some non-fiction information about the history of the myths. I never knew how much was real, but always hoped the bit of fact hiding in the fiction would let you be real. Can you tell me what's fact or fiction? I am glad mates are something real."

Returning a bit of a smile, before wincing as the broken leg moved with a bump and sent a spear of pain up her leg, "I love reading the fictional stories humans put out, as it is usually very funny on what they think we are like. Especially the idea an eighteen-year-old has the skills and ability to run the pack successfully!" She snickered at the idea before calming down a bit and continuing, "Well, we can shift at any time; not just on a full moon being the biggest myth. You already saw our wolf form; we have a third shape, the 'monster' werewolf, is us in a shape we call a hybrid or Were; we stand on hind paws like a human but have fur and a general wolfish look. We have a wolf in our mind, who has separate thoughts and personality, but in most cases, mesh well with our human minds, although for some it is nearly their polar opposite."

Smiling shyly at Adam, Brook continued, "As you have already discovered, Mates are real, and even humans can tell when they find theirs, if they know what to look for. We mate for life, but if rejected or a mate dies, you can sometimes find another, but it's rare. We try to stay hidden, and not tell too many about what we are. We do tell our mates, and they are allowed to tell their closest family, but we try to limit how many know about us, as it is believed humans in general are not ready to openly know about us." She did think the majority would accept them, but the fact there would be some who would refuse to and would start attacking them. It was a decision only the Alpha could make and had to ask for permission beyond immediate family.

Thinking of one more part, she continued, "Mating is done by biting the shoulder hard enough to draw some blood, and both have to do it to the other to complete the mating. It leaves a mark for as long as the Mates both live as a visible sign of the bond they share. Once mated, each other take on a trace of the other's scent to tell others they are taken, and if they know the mate, can tell who it is as well. When a mate is a human, the Were bites first, which starts the process, and will cause you to grow fangs to allow you to complete the process, at which point they fade away. If the process is started but not completed in a week, both will get sick and eventually die."

Realising he needed to know, as she couldn't leave him ignorant; mates had to be totally willing and not coerced, she spoke softly, her wolf whimpering at the thought, "It's uncommon, but Mates can reject each other, but if it is a reason which the wolf-half doesn't agree with, they may turn away from their other half, and if they don't reconcile quickly, both sides will fade into death; we cannot survive without the other."

Adam listened closely, and refused to think about giving her up, even if he didn't really know her yet, and would have interrupted her if she had said anything farther on it, "I am *not* going to reject you. I'm already falling in love with you. I saw your beautiful wolf running across the valley, and I couldn't take my eyes off you at all! I accept you as my mate and want to be with you." Realising she hadn't said anything about *becoming* a wolf, "Is it possible to make me a werewolf, too?"

Brook's wolf was nearly out of her mind in happiness, when he said he accepted her, letting out a very joyful howl into their mind, nearly missing his next question, "Yes, once we are mated, you can be Turned. We can discuss it later, as there is a fair amount you need to know before you make a final decision to do it." Her wolf was bouncing around in her mind, chanting, **He accepted! He accepted!** Making her smile, even through the pain, "You made my wolf very happy with your acceptance of us. She's bouncing around in my head." She sighed, "I've heard stories of humans who can't accept us and run from their mate or even try to kill them." The stories had her upset, and half-expecting to be rejected.

Adam grinned back, "Not me! I have always loved wolves and have always wanted to be with them." Pulling off at the side of the road as he had noticed they had cell service, "We can call from here. I think you should speak first; I'll just have it on the speaker so we both can hear, what's his number?"

Brook rattled off the number all pack members had to memorise at a young age, so if they were in trouble, they could get help fast and Adam entered it into his smartphone, putting it on Speaker mode.

A deep voice answered on the second ring, sounding a little annoyed, "Gareth speaking. Who's calling?"

"Hi Alpha, its Brook: I got caught in a rockslide out at the east edge of the territory," she said tentatively; it sounded like he had been in a meeting, to sound *so* annoyed. Taking a breath, she continued with much happiness, "My Mate was able to get me free. We need directions for the nearest Healer, as I don't know where they are over here." She winced as an injury twinged.

The Alpha's voice changes to one of concern, "Where are you now?"

Brook looked to Adam with a pleading look; she didn't know the area at all, she tended to stay away from the road, as it wasn't too safe near it.

Adam spoke up to pass on the location with as much details as possible. He could hear a rustling of a map over the phone, along with another voice, as they worked out where he should go.

"Head to Longview and wait by the Fire Hall," Was the eventual reply, "I'll get Grant to send some pack members to meet up with you there. What are you driving?"

Brook sighed in relief, as she knew the pack, but didn't realise they were so close. When they visited, they drove vehicles. The way the roads were to get through the mountain passes took them several hours. Looking at the directions of the trip as Adam put them into the map, it seemed they could run as wolves in less time, as they could go a much straighter route, although it included crossing several creeks and had a fair amount of up and down.

"I'm driving a white Chevy Traverse," Adam replied, giving some of the identify details so whoever Grant was would know what to look for.

"Congratulations you two, on finding your mate." Gareth told them, sounding happy, "Make sure you come see me in person, as soon as you can." He ordered, before disconnecting.

As soon as the call ended, Adam pulled out and started heading down the road towards the town of Longview, still over a half hour away. He didn't think too much on the welcome to the pack, or the congratulations. He was more worried about his injured mate. She already meant a great deal to him. He had to work hard not to speed. If he had emergency lights and siren, he'd be using them! As it was, he was having to fight himself to not speed; every time he looked down, he was having to slow down. If an officer caught them, it would only delay her getting help even more—or worse.

Brook relaxed back into the slightly reclined seat, many of her smaller cuts having already closed up, but still feeling battered, nor was the pounding in her head getting better, and she was still too dizzy to think she could stand on her own, even if her leg wasn't broken. To pass the time, she wanted to learn about her mate, "Adam, tell me more about yourself?" she asked gently, wanting to find out more about her beautiful mate and to pass the time.

"I'm thirty-two. I was born in a town in the mountains, but my parents moved back to the big city when I was only three; lived there ever since. I work in IT, as a computer tech. I work for a company which is contracted by other companies, or the governments. My current job is to do the support which their helpdesk can't fix, or they don't have a specific software support group for. Mostly, I fix issues where the computer doesn't start, or they need a tech to be at the desk to solve it. Been doing this job for over five years, and it is starting to be a bit boring!" he smiled at his mate, "I love taking nature pictures, and going out to the mountains—I got some nice ones of you running across the valley, too! My favourite animal has always been the Wolf. I love to read, especially stories which have werewolves in them, and not the savage killer type." Adam finished, "How about you?"

Brook smiled, "Well, I was born a wolf, haven't moved out of the pack territory, but I moved into my own room when I turned fifteen. I'm thirty now. I work as a Beta in the pack, and train the pups in many skills, including hunting, tracking, and some fighting." She looked at her mate shyly, "If you become a wolf, I'll teach you. I love running and being out in nature, but it describes almost all wolves. Never really thought about a favourite animal, as I love my wolf." Shaking her head—which was a mistake, as it made it pound harder, "Right now, the pack doesn't have much technology, since nobody has ever done too much to get it to work, and there are a few who don't want any at all. Mostly those who are my age and younger are thinking if we don't change, it is going to make it harder for us to blend in, when we go out."

Adam was surprised she was just a little younger, as she looked much younger than him. He had issues telling ages, but thought she looked what he thought of being just 18 or so. Just then they come into the town and pulled into the nearly empty lot. Just as Adam started to wonder how long they would be, three big black SUVs pull up around his mid-sized one. He turned to Brook, "I hope this is them..." he said, a little nervously.

Brook looked at those stepping out, saw one of the Betas she knew was a member of Longview Pack, "Yes, it's them." She confirmed with happy relief.

One went to Adam's door and opened it, "Adam, I presume?" he said with a slight growl.

Nodding respectfully, "Yes, I hope you can help my Mate." Adam was a bit nervous, since he had never learned to fight, and he felt he needed to protect his mate, even if he didn't know how to do it. For his mate, he realised he would do anything to keep her safe, even if he barely knew her.

The wolf nodded, "If you two will hop into the one over there, we will get you to our healer right away, and I'll drive your vehicle there." He knew not to try to separate them, or to try to get too close to the hurt one, as it would be asking for him to be lacerated when Brook's wolf took over to protect her mate; it would be worse than getting between a momma grizzly and their cub, as even the wolf half was smarter than an average animal and knew *where* to attack. Likely, it would make her injuries much worse, too. He could smell the blood.

Quickly unbuckling his seatbelt, Adam hopped out in wordless agreement. As fast as he could, went around and slid Brook carefully out and over into the back seat of one of the black SUVs, and followed her in. Again, not realising how much weight he was moving. As soon as the door was closed behind him, the engine roared as the driver took off fast, the inertia pushing them into the seat. He heard Brook take a sharp breath but didn't say anything. One SUV moved ahead of them, then his was driven behind them, then the last one. He quickly helped Brook with a seatbelt before he did his up, and then cuddled against his mate, wrapping an arm around her, and relaxing a bit. He then noticed they all had flashing lights and a siren going, even though the siren could barely be heard inside. He smiled; they were getting to help as soon as they could. Both just quietly relaxed, each with their own thoughts.

Sooner than he thought possible, they were climbing up into a forested hill. The convoy was waved through a gate without stopping, before skidding to a stop outside what looked like an emergency room door, as it had a red cross and MEDICAL above it. A couple of women dressed in scrubs raced a gurney to the door. Almost before he could get the door open, they were there, not giving him any chance to look around.

Trying not to jostle his new mate, Adam lifted her gently onto the gurney. Holding her hand, he stayed right by her side, refusing to let her out of his sight. He couldn't understand his protectiveness at all, just feeling it was right as they wheeled her into a room. It must have been normal, as they hadn't said a word, just made room for him. Brook was gently moved to a bed before the woman he took for the doctor motioned to a chair beside the bed, "You can sit there; I'm a Healer. If you are touching her while I work to heal her, I may miss something."

Nodding, he sat in the chair, resisting the urge to pick up Brook's hand, as they worked on healing her injuries.

"Nice job on the bindings of the broken limbs. It held them in the right spots, and they have already fused; I don't need to re-break them." The Healer commented, as she continued to use her abilities to speed the already fast healing and checking she didn't need to redo anything.

Adam smiled at the complement, but tried to stay out of the way, and watched his mate. It was taking lots of work to not reach out and grab her hand and not let go.

Once the Healer finished, "She had some head trauma and some other internal injuries but will fully recover. She needs to stay here tonight, but will be fine to head out tomorrow," She told them both before turning to Adam, "I presume you want to stay with her?" Getting a nod in reply from both as neither was willing to let the other out of their sight. The healer sighed, "I'll arrange to have her moved to a larger bed so you both can get some rest, and some food soon," before heading out the door to arrange it.

Smiling, Adam quickly grabbed Brook's hand, feeling the tingles against his skin again, he felt relief at her touch, "What are we doing after today? Does your pack have a need for a computer tech? I would be quite willing to move in and join you and your pack to keep you with me." While she was being cared for, he had decided he'd make the big concession, and move to the pack, giving up his life. From what he had heard, he would be quite happy staying with the pack. He had always wanted to move out of the city but lacked the means to do it.

Turning to him, with a grin on her face, already feeling better, "Well, my pack doesn't do too much with humans right now. Many of the younger generation is wanting to get more connected, which does mean more involvement with humans, so we definitely need someone to do the work to connect the pack. But we also need to keep ourselves secret. We definitely need some help in learning it, too."

Thinking hard, "Hmm, I'll have to think on it." Adam said, thinking it would be a very fun challenge. He wasn't sure on how he could lead, as he'd never had a leadership position which was over more than three others.

An orderly walked in pushing a wheelchair, "Your room is ready for you to move to, and there has been food ordered for both of you."

Nodding, Adam thanked the nurse before he helped Brook get off the bed and into the wheelchair. They knew to not help, as she had been warned they were unbonded mates, and none of the staff wanted to stress either of them, or cause Brook to shift. Adam moved to push his mate in the wheelchair as the orderly led them to a private room. The bed was large enough to fit them both, and there was already a nice spread of food on two side tables for them.

Adam helped Brook get into the bed and brought over the table with the food for her. Afterwards, he climbed up beside her and pulling the other tray of food he assumed was for him, as it was much smaller. Even though his was much smaller, both finished about the same time, and pushed the tables out of the way, almost at the same time, "I like the idea of keeping the Mate with you while you are recovering, instead of separating them." Adam commented, as he laid back, "Although it seemed everyone was making sure not to come between us at all." A couple of times he had seen them slide behind him, instead of going in front of him, which at the time he hadn't really noticed.

Brook laughed outright, "Newly found mates, especially where one is hurt, and before they complete the mating, has the Were very protective." Calming down a bit, "Some have been killed, because they momentarily stepped between the two, or caused the injured one some pain the other didn't like. Even worse for those who touched or even picked them up! If the Were is the one hurt, they could shift, and especially in my case, it would likely have made the broken bones worse." She grinned, "I've noticed you are feeling the mating pull. If I was human, I would be considered extremely clingy, but us Weres are much more tactile creatures. I hope you enjoy touching and hugs." She leaned into his side and put her head on his shoulder and enjoyed as she breathed in his scent, which helped to relax her. If he didn't now, he would get used to close contact, and eventually enjoy hugs and cuddles.

Enjoying her laugh, Adam smiled, wrapping an arm around her as she leaned on him, holding her close, "I have always loved touching, and cuddling." He said as he moved closer until he was against her side, "I am glad it doesn't have to stop." Thinking on his life, "I do have to be at my job on Monday to start my work week, but tomorrow, I think we should talk to your Alpha, and see if I should just turn in my notice and start packing to move to the pack. When should we do the Mating, and what should I know about it before we go through it?"

Yawning, Brook replied, "We'll talk further, tomorrow. I just want to curl up and sleep the healing off." It was early, but she was feeling very tired. She knew it was her body relaxing, and taking her energy to deal with her injuries, and the healing she had.

Slipping down, Brook curled up as Adam moved over to turn off the lights for the room, before stripping down to his underwear and climbing into the bed, and snuggling up against his mate, with a smile on his face. He fell asleep faster than he had in a long time without having to exhaust his body first. Both had felt the loss of contact and sighed happily when Adam climbed back in and snuggled down.

When the nurse checked on them a little later, she grinned at the two snuggled tightly together. They looked very peaceful, but knew not to approach, as Brook's wolf would be on guard with being injured and having a human mate to protect. The two curled up would help her heal faster anyways, and if there was a change, Adam would feel it, even with only the barest hint of a bond between them.

She put a Do Not Disturb note on the door as she left, as Brook was just being watched for any complications from the concussion. Sleep, especially together, was the best remedy for them right now, anyways.

CHAPTER 2

Mating and Changes Start

The next morning, Adam woke up first, feeling very much refreshed and better rested than he had in a long time. He smiled when he realised his mate was snuggled down in his arms, her head tucked under his chin, and a leg thrown over his and his arms around her. He gave her a squeeze before rubbing her back gently, enjoying the feeling of someone curled up with him, it was a feeling he very rarely had, and almost never with a female, up till now.

Slowly, Brook woke up, and it took her mind a bit to start working, and for her to remember the day before; she was glad it wasn't just a dream. She smiled as she stretched out and then smiled up at her Mate; *'Her Mate,' it has a nice ring to it*, she thought, and was glad she wasn't going to be alone for most of her life, unlike some she knew, who had the misfortune to wait for much of their life to find their mate.

"Good morning, Cutie" Brook said as she looked at Adam happily. All her injuries felt, if not already mended, most of the way there, and less than times when she had been training.

"Good morning to you too, Love" Adam replied, "How are you feeling today?"

"I'm feeling great! Being with you helped speed the healing up," At a chuckle of disbelief from her mate, Brook continued, "It's true; we heal faster when we are in contact with our mate, even if the bond hasn't been completed. Usually, injuries like I had would have taken two or three days to heal."

A nurse poked their head in, "Oh, you're awake. I'll get a Healer, so you can find out if you can leave." She ignored Brook's growl of warning since she wasn't going to even try to enter their room.

It was only a few minutes later when the Healer knocked and entered slowly. "Good morning." He said with a smile of greeting. "I need to just check on Brook, to see if she has healed enough to leave."

Both nodded and Brook grinned in reply, "OK. I feel much better now." She said, as Adam moved to not be touching her.

The healer placed a gentle hand on her shoulder and closed his eyes for a long moment. Opening them, he blinked a few times, "You are mostly healed, and just may be slightly tender for a few days." He told them, "You can leave at any time you wish. Brook, I want you to rest over the next few days, so no hard workouts or training for five days." He paused for a moment before grinning and added with a wink, "I don't see you two having fun being a problem..." before leaving the room.

Getting, up, Brook realised she had no clothes; they were back in her pack's territory. She didn't really care, as growing up as a wolf, she was not body-shy at all, since casual nudity was normal. They were in a pack's compound, so no human who wasn't used to it, apart from her mate, would see her to frown on the walking around without anything on. She knew she needed to get some clothes before they left, but it shouldn't be too hard. Her feet were used to running around without shoes, as even in human form, it was rare to wear anything, unless they were out in human areas.

Adam looked at his clothes and sighed, they were covered with some blood; he hoped the blood would come out when he washed them. Bundling them up, he looked at Brook, and grinned as he realised she still has no clothes, and he was just in his underwear, "I wonder where my SUV got parked; I have a couple of changes of clothes in it." He didn't bother trying to hide the fact he was looking over Brook's body, she was good looking.

Laughing, Brook just posed for him, as she could see in his eyes, he liked what he saw. She answered, "They probably either left it near the doors here or parked it near the other vehicles. We need to speak to Alpha Grant before we leave, anyways. Let's get checked out of here and he should know either who has your keys and where the vehicle is, or who to ask."

Brook took Adam's hand, and both were feeling the tingles again, pulled him out the door of the room and over to the nurse's station to start the paperwork to check them out, not worrying about any cost being charged, as the two packs were allies and would deal with it. Adam stood protectively at her shoulder, making a mental list of what he needed to do to wrap up his human life. First, to talk to Alpha Gareth, to confirm about having work or some income to deal with his expenses, and he would need to turn in his resignation letter to his boss, and let his roommates know he was moving...

Waving a hand in front of his face to get his attention, Brook's eyes were dancing in mirth, "What had you so distracted?" She asked as she pulled him out of the door and headed off to the Alpha's area. They didn't have a mental bond—yet—so she couldn't follow his thoughts directly.

Adam blushed slightly, "Just thinking about what I need to change in my life to stay with you. First is to confirm about the job in your pack since I have some debt which I need to make sure to pay. Then I'll need to quit my current job, which will take three weeks' notice, and need to start packing up to move," He gives a shudder at the last one; not wanting the work to pack up all his stuff. He had an entire storage room of stuff including camping gear, old computers, and parts; he warned Brook, "I hate moving, as I have a fair amount of stuff. Some, I'm going to see if my roommates might be interested in it."

Snickering at him, "Well, we can get a moving truck from the pack to take it and have them bring some packmates when they bring it, to move it all at once." Brook replied, not worried at all. "We have storage, and what you don't want, you can give to the pack."

Reaching the building, Adam noticed his vehicle was parked beside it, and commented, "One less thing to find. Not sure about you, but I prefer to be wearing something more than my underwear when meeting with the Alpha!"

Brook noticed the doors were locked, "It's locked. Don't we need to get the keys first?" Brook asked.

Adam shook his head, and let go of her hand reluctantly, before digging in his bundle of clothes for the vehicle remote he had attached to his belt, and tapped the button to unlock the vehicle, making it chirp twice, "Nope; I still had the remote for the security system. To drive away, I'd either need to get into the console to get the spare key or get my keys back." Reaching into the back seat, he tossed in the old clothes, and pulled out some shorts, and jeans, and a couple of shirts, "Shorts or jeans?" he asked Brook, having already noticed they were fairly close in size.

Looking at him shrewdly, as he passed her some woman's panties she asked, "Why do you have woman's underwear? Shorts." She replied decisively to answer his question. She knew he'd feel the cold more than she would. She could see him shivering, even though the weather was quite balmy for this time of year.

Blushing hard in embarrassment under her scrutiny, "I wear them; usually I find them more comfortable than men's underwear" Adam replied, not mentioning his current underwear was also female panties, as he passed her the shorts and shirt, as he pulled on the other shirt and jeans.

She just pulled on the clothes, as she shook her head at the quirkiness of her mate, but thought it was cute and not really caring about what he wanted to wear; it was just clothes. Thinking on how the panties he had passed her were more comfortable than the ones she often got, thought she might need to borrow more of his clothes in the future. Her wolf was nearly purring with the fact of wearing something which smelled of their Mate. She wondered about wrapping their mate in clothes smelling of them...

Dressed, they headed up to the door and before they could knock, it opened to a beautiful woman who looked not much older, but the way werewolves aged, she would be much older, "I wondered if it was you two making noise outside, I'm Louise, the Alpha female here. Come in, Grant is just finishing some paperwork." Leading them to the kitchen, "I bet you wanted to get out of Medical as soon as you could so didn't even wait for breakfast, let me whip up some pancakes for you."

To their embarrassment, Adam and Brook's stomachs answered in unison for them, agreeing with her. Sitting down at the breakfast table, they sat as close together as they could.

Louise just smiled and busied herself as she made the food, "I can smell you two haven't yet completed the Mating, did you want a room to do it before you headed out?"

Adam and Brook looked at each other. Brook looked at her mate with clear lust in her eyes. He spoke respectfully and thankfully, "I think it would be best. I share a house with a couple of roommates, and I would rather they don't know what I am up to, and I'm definitely not sharing the wolf-side with them."

Louise smiled and nodded, "That is probably best; we have room here you can use." Smirking, "It's insulated to our standards, so nobody will hear you." She replied as she placed the food on the table. She loved to cook, so on the weekends, her Thetas got to sleep in, and didn't have any duties till noon. It was one compromise she had made when she was not even an adult with the two Thetas who had decided they were taking care of her. It was to let them take care of cleaning of her room generally, which she hadn't wanted anyone else to be doing.

With a quiet thank you, the two quickly dug into the food and ate ravenously. When they were nearly done eating the breakfast, Louise commented, "I'll go get Grant." As she headed out the door to pull him away from the endless paperwork of running the pack.

Almost immediately, both walk back in, as Grant had already been heading their way, needing a break from sitting at a desk. Grant walked over to give them both a hug and sniffing their neck in a wolf greeting,

"Welcome, Adam. It's nice to see you again, Brook, and congratulations on finding your mate. He seems to be very much a keeper!"

Brook blushed as Adam smiled at the comment, not exactly sure how to respond, but decided to just give a simple, "Thank you." As it seemed to be a genuine thought.

Passing the keys back to Adam, Grant commented, "It's a nice vehicle. 2014 Traverse?"

Adam nodded in agreement with a smile and thanked him, as he took the keys and put them in a pocket. "How much do we owe you?" he asked, not sure on how Packs did it.

Grant shook his head, "I have already arranged everything with Gareth." He assured Adam, "It's all handled. It's our pleasure to help you two new mates out."

"You should have enough time to complete the mating today, if you hop to it," Louise advised, "First door on the right, up the stairs."

Brook quickly gave a thanks as she hopped out of the chair, grabbed Adam's hand, and pulled him up out of the chair, and headed to the room, not needing any more suggestions to mark her mate; he wasn't going to get away, since he had already said he accepted. Opening the door, what was clearly a guest room, from the lack of personal scents or items, with a king-sized bed in it.

*****

Brook began by sitting Adam down beside her, "Now, I need to tell you exactly what happens with the Mating, because once we start, we cannot stop. I'm a little foggy on what we discussed on the drive here, so I'll cover it all. First, it must be done by informed consent between adults, as it is permanent, and till one of us dies, and when one dies the breaking of the bond can send the other into a deep depression, and even into suicide." She wanted to get it all out, as she could be in very big trouble if she missed something, "Our law is fixed, if I didn't tell you it all, and let you decide while knowing all the facts, you could decide to put me to death for taking the decision away from you. Also, once we start, if we don't complete it within a week of the first bite, we will both fall sick and eventually die."

Taking a deep breath, knowing she had Adam's undivided attention, and moved onto how the Mating happened, "Both of us must bite the other hard enough to draw blood and scar. Traditionally, it is on the shoulder, at the base of the neck. The mark is a visual sign and stays as long as both live. Traditionally, we bite during sex at climax, as it helps speed the changes, and reduces the perception of pain of it happening. As you are human, I have to bite first, as it will cause your teeth to temporarily become sharp and very canine-like, to help the bite to happen; this change usually takes an hour or two to form. Once you bite and the bond is complete, your teeth will return to normal. You will feel a little sick for a few days, and symptoms may persist for a week or two." She clearly was reciting what she had been told, not what she knew from experience.

Getting a nod from Adam, showing he was still with her, Brook continued, "Over the next couple of weeks, you will gain some new abilities: you will be able to speak with me telepathically, even at great distances, and we both will know what the other is feeling at all times, and even a bit of what the other is thinking about; I will teach you how to ignore it a bit. Your senses will be enhanced, not quite as much as a Werewolf, but much more than a human; you will see better both at a distance and up close, you will be able to hear much better, and be able to smell much better. Your sense of taste will also increase, as will your sense of touch. You will need to watch your strength, as you will get to have the strength and speed of a professional athlete. Your ability to heal will be much faster than a human; you'll heal broken bones in a week or so, and minor scratches and bruises will heal in about a day. You'll become immune to most human illnesses, and you will age at half that of a human, and probably seem to appear younger over the next couple of months." Right now, he looked like a wolf who was into their late second century or early third to Brook.

Taking a breath, "Downside, if you take it as one, your metabolism will increase, and you will need to eat much more. Another is some werewolf illnesses you will become susceptible to, but they are very rare." She hadn't ever had one, but when she was young, she had asked their healer, and it sounded unpleasant; fever, cold and/or hot flashes, sneezing, coughing, headache, no energy, were the main ones. With the fact it could last for a week or two and could infect others made her very much not wanting to catch them. If the healer didn't isolate those who were sick, some werewolf-illnesses could take out an entire pack and leave nobody well enough to do any patrols.

Her questions must have been passed on to her history instructor, as the next assignment was one of looking up for where illness happened. The one she was assigned, one pack had many ill and during a fight, the other pack who had attacked had been infected, as they had no choice but to have the sick enforcers fight. Once their pack recovered a bit from the illness, even though they had lost many enforcers in the first attack, they had decimated the other pack, as they were very ill, with the leaders near death before the attack, so had no real leadership. Since they had recovered, they were immune to the illness. In the end, the pack which seemed initially victorious over the other, died out, as the illness and the counterattack removed most of the leaders, and the rest moved to other packs. She shook her head from the memory.

Remembering she forgot one thing, "Right, our scents will pick up a trace of the other, which will show we are mated, and those who know me will know you are mated to me without either saying a word. By tradition, we Mate before turning, as it will also speed the turning, when you decide to do it, as the Mating is like a gentler, partial Turn." Smiling at Adam, seeing him open his mouth to asked about it, "Right now, you don't have enough information to go through the Turning. Ask me later about it."

Adam nodded and closed his mouth, letting her continue. He did have a question about the Mating, about something she didn't discuss so far, "So, Mating is considered your version of a wedding?"

Nodding her head, "Yes, but is much more binding, and is done in private. Nothing at all can break a Mating, except death. Some still do a wedding ceremony, to appease their human family. Normally we don't do rings, as they can be easily lost, and can either be broken or hurt a paw if you shift while wearing it. Some do matching tattoos, to show their commitment. I have heard of one who did tattoos on their ring fingers in the place of a wedding ring."

Smiling brightly, Adam answered, "I had decided when we talked a little on our way here, I wouldn't reject you. I have loved you since I first saw your wolf. Nothing you said has made me want you less or made me change my mind at all. Yes, I want to be your Mate, and I accept you as mine. I may not know you well, yet, but I would be happy to spend my life with you and we can work through any problems."

Both Brook and her wolf were ecstatic at his reply, as they felt the same. She pounced on him ferally, as her wolf tried to take over a little and smashed her lips to his face and kissed him deeply. She started to pull his shirt off, and realised he was doing the same for her. The rest of their clothes quickly followed.

Pushing Adam to lay on his back on the bed, her wolf was forward, and showing in her eyes, as they had changed, which was something he learned later. Brook told him gently, pushing him to lay on his back, "Let us do the work, you just relax for this part."

Adam was quite happy with letting Brook take the lead, as he wasn't too experienced with girls, so being able to just lay back and enjoy was nice. He did let his hands roam her nice smooth body, not showing any body hair, even in her crotch. He didn't know if she shaved, or it was a difference she hadn't said anything about. Her eyes had changed from the normal brown to a glowing gold, which looked good on her. He didn't know yet it was a sign her wolf was forward. He was already aroused.

Brook was moving more on instinct than experience, as she too had very few experiences, more of wanting to keep herself for her mate, well outside of Heat. Her wolf was in the front of her mind as they enjoyed the activity. She bent down to kiss him well, then trailed kisses down his face to the neck, kissing the place on his shoulder where she would soon be biting.

Both were quickly rising and were soon spiralling over the edge, and just as they went over, Brook's wolf took over and lunged forward, to bite Adam's shoulder, breaking the skin easily with her sharp teeth.

Releasing the bite, she lapped at the wound, stopping the bleeding. Smiling, as she watched it scab over well, like it should, as she lay on Adam's chest, and both enjoyed the afterglow. Brook was already starting to feel the start of the Mating bonds, and relaxed, getting used to them.

Adam wrapped his arms around her and enjoyed the close contact and let his mind wander as he enjoyed the euphoria roll over him, as he cuddled his mate—His Mate; he still was ecstatic about the fact he wasn't going to be alone any longer.

Both ended up drifting off to a nap.
*****

Waking up a bit later, Adam enjoyed waking up with his mate curled up on his chest. Testing, he ran his tongue along his teeth, and realised they have done their changes, and they could complete the Mating. Giving Brook a good hug, he felt her stir, and smiled, as he waited for her to wake fully so they could finish the Mating.

When Brook woke up, she stretched, and enjoying the feeling of her mate against her. Kissing him deeply, she ran her own tongue over his now distinctly canine-ish, sharp teeth, and wanted to finish the bond, "Ready for round two, Lover?"

Rolling them both over so he was above her, Adam startled a squeal out of her, he grinned, "I was just waiting for you wake up to start!" he told her with a laugh, "I am ready and willing!" His speech had a bit of a lisp, due to the changed teeth, but the meaning was clear.

He followed her example and kisses down her neck, finding her spot, nibbled it gently, making her nearly melt as she moaned, before moving to kiss her lips again as he started to make love to her, taking control.

Both quickly spiral up, and just before Adam moved his head and got ready to bite. Again, they both went over together, and Adam almost instinctively bit down, and was a bit startled at the taste of his mate's blood in his mouth. Releasing the bite, he licked it a bit, following her example, as it stopped bleeding.

Starting to feel the aches he was warned about, and feeling like he had a slight headache, Adam rolled onto his back beside his mate and commented, "I do hope I can get into work tomorrow, so I can tell them I'm quitting! I do have a couple of vacation weeks on the books; I wonder what they'll do for it or make me work all three weeks."

Brook rolled over and snuggled into his side, "I don't care if it takes a year, as long as we get to be together!" Remembering one thing, "We need to talk to Alpha Gareth soon, too."

Adam smiled and cuddled Brook for a bit, "I guess we'd better call him now, then. The sooner we get it all arranged, the sooner we can get to the Pack." He could already feel how much her pack meant to her. Reaching down he grabbed his phone and pulled up the number they had used previously.

Gareth answered the phone just as quick as last time, but without the growl, seemed to not be interrupting anything this time. "Adam and Brook, I presume?" he asked. He had just learned about adding contacts from incoming calls, so he could know names when they called in.

"Yes, Alpha," Brook answered for them both, "The healer released us already this morning, and we have Mated." She told him the happy news.

"Congratulations, you two. You need to come back to see me soon." Gareth replied. Matings were always a happy thing, even if it was with a Human, and always brought some issues.

"Alpha," Adam spoke up, respectfully, feeling how much respect Brook had for him. "We will need to go back to my house in the city, as I have to be at work tomorrow. I would prefer to quit, and work for the pack."

"What sort of work do you do?" Gareth asked. It sounded like they were going to get a nice, diligent worker, and one who wasn't going to be clinging to his existing human life, which would minimize the issues. He would do what he could to keep Brook around, as he had ideas for her skills. Being he was willing to leave his human life made him like her mate already, and willing to help find him a place with the pack.

"He works with computer and technology," Brook replied before Adam could, knowing their Alpha wouldn't know what 'IT' was. She could already sense her mate's thoughts, "He seems fairly skilled, and would be able to help bring the pack's tech up." Adam smiled and let her say what she wanted. He didn't know where it came from but felt Gareth was one who didn't use much technology.

"Excellent!" Gareth said, deciding the time was right to remove some of his objections for the tech, "Right now we have nobody who knows enough to bring us more in line with what the humans have, and we need to catch up. Would you be able to manage it and provide the support?"

"Yes, I think I could, but I would need help." Adam replied, "I can teach the computer skills, they just need to be able to be problem solvers."

Gareth laughed, "It's fine. I have plenty of young wolves who would enjoy the challenge. You can have the job as soon as you can get here." He decided, as they definitely could use his skills. There were many young adults and older pups who they had no work for, so new roles would deal with several of his issues.

"Can we get permission to use the large truck, and borrow a couple of packmates to help move my mate?" Brook asked, already able to get the picture in his mind of the amount of stuff. "My mate seems to have a fair number of possessions." As did many humans.

"Granted," was the quick reply, as Gareth had expected the request. "Adam, we will cover any costs you need dealt with, so don't worry about it."

"I have nothing booked next weekend," Adam said, "We'll be out there so Brook can introduce me. I'll call you when I know when my last day of work is."

"Sounds fine." Gareth said, "Plan to be here the whole weekend. I'll see you both then." He told them. Getting a new member was a reason to party, add on the celebrating the Mating, and it would be a major party. Brook didn't realise it, but this would be something big, with how senior she was within the pack.

Hanging up the phone, Adam sighed, "Well, I think I will need to get going, so I can start packing."

Brook looked at him strange, "*We* can; I'm going with you. Once Mated, it is rare for us to be separated more than we must be. I understand work, but for now, I am living with you in the human world." It was a sacrifice she would make. Her duties would be covered. "Remember, the Healer told me to take it easy and no training, so I would be idle at the pack, anyways."

Sharing a last kissing session, they climbed out of the bed and took a shared shower at her insistence before they got dressed. They headed down to give their goodbyes to Alphas Grant and Louise and were shortly on their way out and back to his place. They chatted on the way back about their lives. Although Adam had been living in the city since he was three, the mountains always called to him, and he was always sad to leave them. Brook had always lived in the pack and didn't ever plan to leave it. She worked as a trainer for the pups and had only high school education, since the pack expected everyone to get their diploma, where Adam had a college diploma, and worked with computers, and was looking for a new challenge so was excited to help the pack. Both loved to read, and had very similar tastes in books, although there were many books both hadn't read, each having found different favourite authors, the descriptions each gave sounded interesting to the other.

Hearing Brook's basic description of the pack's territory and how they lived, Adam sighed in bliss. It sounded perfect; live and work out in nature, far away from the hustle and bustle of city life.

It lasted the whole way to his place, and he grinned, when he noticed his roommates were both out, as their cars were missing, "Guess we have the house to ourselves as both of them are out. I'll show you the place." Adam gave Brook a quick tour she smiled as he brought her to his messy room, a little embarrassed at the mess.

Brook gave Adam a stern look, "You have some work to do, I see; Our space is to be kept *tidy*." She did notice it was mostly just clothes; it wasn't like there were piles of old food or garbage laying around, nor did it smell, "Clothes are to be folded and put away right after they are cleaned!" His desk was full of papers she noticed too. "As are any papers!"

Nodding, Adam agreed it was the best, "I'm just horrible at wanting to fold my clothes, so I usually don't. I do the laundry weekly. Feel free to make sure I do it." He started to fold the clothes while Brook flopped on his twin-sized bed and watched, pulling one of his stuffed wolves into her arms. She could smell he cuddled this one a great deal, and it was nice and soft, grinning at Adam's possessive look.

Adam smiled and shook his head before commenting, "Since I've never been in a relationship before, the stuffed wolves were what I cuddled at night with." He grinned as she hugged his large stuffed wolf tighter. He stopped to just watch her.

Brook glared and made her mate clean the room. He kept at it and had the room mostly clean by the time the lasagna he put in for dinner was ready. Together, they each ate more than he usually ate, nearly finishing off the tray which normally gave him several meals of leftovers. For the evening, they cuddled and talked some more.

Looking at the clock beside the bed, he sighed, as the way he was feeling wasn't even as bad as some colds he had worked through, and it was starting to get late, "Almost time to get to bed, I have to be up at five to get ready for work."

Leading her to the bathroom, he handed her a new toothbrush to do their teeth. Finishing first, Adam moved to evict most of his stuffed animals and pillows from the bed to make room for a second body to be in the bed. He stripped before crawling into the bed to wait for Brook to come. Before he could even roll over, Brook pounced him playfully, before climbing under the covers, and curling up with Adam, "This is nice and cozy warm, but I think we need some fewer blankets; wolves have a higher body temperature."

Using a single arm, Adam pulled three of the blankets open, so they were pushed against the wall, "Better?" he asked as he turned off the last lamp.

Brook nodded in answer, and both snuggled down for a good night sleep.

*****

Adam grinned as he looked at his watch, as he loaded the last of his belongings from work into his vehicle Friday afternoon. He was free! His boss was surprised when he turned in his resignation first thing Monday morning and had tried to find out what he had been offered to see if they could match it, which the business didn't even have anything which was close to it. Since he did have several weeks of vacation time to take, they had arranged to have him work the week out, and then vacation for the rest of his notice and then forward the papers to his new address.

He was glad the changes meant he didn't need glasses or contacts anymore. He had kept them with him, but after Tuesday, he hadn't touched them. Brook had arranged the pack doctor to give him a record saying his eyesight had been corrected, since his license said he needed corrective lenses. Once moved, they would get the updated license made.

With the sudden change of plans, they had been packing up in the evenings during the week, and were taking a load tonight, spending the weekend meeting with the pack then coming back Monday to finish packing up to move the rest on Tuesday. The truck had been arranged to be there towards the middle of the day on Tuesday.

Monday night, he was going to be introducing his mate to his mother, and the whole idea of being a werewolf, and letting her know he was moving six hours away. He was not looking forward to it. He had no idea how she would take it; he had met her only a week ago and was already moving in with her!

Heading inside, Adam handed in his ID, phone, and a few last things which were the company's, before shaking hands and saying his good-byes to a place he had worked at the last seven years, in several positions and jobs. He was fully ready to turn the page and have a completely new challenge with his life. He had left a forwarding address for the last paperwork and stuff to be sent to, along with the main contact number for the pack, and a personal e-mail address.

He had arranged with the company to be a supplier for many of the changes he had ideas planning in his head; it was nice to be able to use his contacts for something. He had to just figure out how to do it without tipping anyone off as to the whole werewolf thing.

Hopping into his vehicle, Adam mentally called to his mate *Leaving work now, be there in a bit.* Getting her reply nearly instantly in acknowledgement and feeling her love, he had to really watch his speed as he went home to his Mate; he still loved the sound of it.

Brook's meeting of his roommates while he was at work couldn't be helped; one was unemployed—again—and other had a night shift; neither was awake when he had to be out for work. The roommates had loved Brook but were sad when she told them they were losing a roommate, as she had let them know both would be there for less than a month. They had decided to pay rent for another month after to help them out with finding another roommate, which they were fine with. He had already set up a forwarding of the mail to the pack and left his roommates an e-mail to let him know if there was any mail which was missed redirecting and arrived at the house.

When he got to the house, growly due to many inconsiderate drivers, Brook was already waiting outside. He had noticed his temper had gotten much shorter, and it took more work to keep calm; Brook had just grinned and told him it was part of the changes. After a kiss, they worked together to fill up a pile of items he wanted to be moved first; some were bulkier or heavy. Some were delicate and had sentimental memories. Once loaded up, they stopped for some food on the way out of town. He was both nervous and looking forward to meeting everyone, including the first face-to-face with the Alpha.

"You'll do fine," Brook reassured, "He already likes you, as you are bringing some skills the pack is sorely lacking. You have nothing to worry about." She didn't tell him mates were always celebrated, and there would be a welcoming party. Nor did she tell him how many of the pack had called and thanked her for the changes it seemed the Alpha was now permitting.

It was both a long drive, and one which was over way too soon for Adam. He was glad he had Brook drive the second half of the way in, as he would have missed the turns several times, especially since it had gotten dark while they drove. While he could see better, her eyes were much better than his. Pulling into a hidden, covered parking space, they used for temporary parking of vehicles which did not have assigned spots in their parkade, especially since she didn't have her ID to get into it, they stepped out and stretched.

It was a fifteen-minute walk to the pack house, as they tried to keep the vehicles from going up the steep access road, if they could, and almost never used it in the dark. They would get the stuff from the vehicle in the morning. The parking area was one of the areas which had constant monitoring by the pack. It was one of the jobs of the older pups who wanted to be Enforcers, they had a rotation of shifts they did them, each being six hours long. Those who fell asleep or missed something often didn't join the Enforcers, and it worked well to weed out those who decided it wasn't for them.

Adam grabbed Brook's hand, as they started to walk into a new chapter of their lives for both of them.

CHAPTER 3

Joining the Pack

Adam was quietly thinking on the walk to the pack house, about the discussions they had on the drive and while at his place regarding what being 'Turned', as they called becoming a werewolf meant. He was starting to get used to his enhanced senses and could tell they were being watched; it didn't alarm him, as he was new and expected he would be. Even if it was just to make sure nothing happened to him from someone thinking he was trespassing or from a wild animal. He really loved the changes to his sight: no more need for glasses or contacts, and even though to a human it was a dark and cloudy night, to him it was about as bright as an overcast day; bright enough he could travel without worrying about tripping, running into trees, or falling over roots without using a flashlight, so it stayed in his pocket. He not only could hear the wolves rustling through the bushes, but he could also smell the ones who were upwind: two females, three males.

Neither had grabbed a jacket, even though it was fairly cool. Adam had found his tolerance for cold weather had greatly increased, to the point the crisp weather, which was just above freezing, felt nice for a walk, where before he would have wanted more layers and definitely would have wanted a jacket. For November, it was very warm, and the path they followed was clear of snow, which surprised him, even if there was snow in patches in the trees.

Adam had found out they traditionally only turned Mates, as they had the support in the form of their mate during the transition, and in learning the skills needed. If a human learned about them, and decided to join the pack, they might Turn them after they were settled in the pack and understood what the changes would mean to them. In that case, they would need a sponsor to be with them, and help them through the process of becoming a werewolf and would be their mentor for as long as they needed one.

For the rare Forced Turn, the law was the person who was turned was given a say for the punishment, and they could call for the death of the one who'd turned them, or to be given no punishment at all, as generally happened in the case of an accidental turn, or one to save the former-human's life. Generally, the wolf would be responsible to support and teach the new wolf their ways. If they didn't fit, another was found who suited them better to mentor them in their new life.

Given the average lifespan of a Werewolf was four centuries, he could see why they didn't jail their offenders. Brook had also told him generally, if a wolf was totally confined for a long period—usually counted as a month—they would likely go Rogue, and be insane, and need to be put down. It was generally better to just get it over with without the pain on both sides for having them go insane. Rogues had no morals and would even attack family members.

Adam was mostly over the changes the Mating had caused, but he had another week or so before he could have Brook bite him to start the Turning. He had told her when it was first brought up if it would save his life, he'd want to be turned. Everything so far which he had been told and all the answers to his questions had led him to feel being turned was the right thing for him. Even Brook had commented he had a bit of a wolfish nature, even as a human. His roommates hadn't noticed any changes, which him and Brook had chuckled over on the way up, nor those at work, other than he brought a much larger lunch, and a couple of snacks with him every day. The first day he didn't and had been grateful there was a cafeteria he could go to for snacks and a second lunch. After that, he made sure his bag had them.

He remembered the details Brook had described about the Mate-Turn he would have; *The bite heals to a scar within a couple of hours, showing the 'infection' has taken hold, and are changing. The mark disappears once they are fully Turned, at which point there is no physical way to tell a turned-wolf from a born-wolf. You will be down for about a week to two weeks, and a human doctor would say they are having an auto-immune attack, as their human DNA is re-written to be that of a werewolf.* He wasn't sure he liked that part, as there is a slight chance of someone getting a bad reaction and dying, but he was willing to accept the risk, but being Mated first reduced the risk of death to nearly non-existent, when they waited for the mating changes to complete before the Turning. It was due to the fact the Mating caused minor changes, which accepted the Turning better, and helped ease the person into the changes. He wasn't willing to wait years to let the Mating slowly enhance him further, he wanted to be able to get out and run as wolves with his mate! Brook had promised she would take care of him through the Turning and would help him learn their ways. Since being Mated, he had a dream nearly each night of running with her as wolves. Each morning at awaking it saddened him he couldn't yet.

Once recovered from the DNA re-write and enhancements to their body, their wolf will make themselves known in their mind, usually before they are strong enough to change, to let both sides get used to the other mentally, before they first shift forms. Usually, the Turn took anywhere from two to eight weeks before the first shift, but if they felt threatened, their wolf may take over and cause them to shift early, which could cause complications. Especially with control and discipline. During this time, their metabolism increases to one of a werewolf. He was already surprised how much food he could eat, and he was not gaining a pound; he was getting more fit at the urging of his mate. He was learning to run more, for one thing. He was looking forward to having a wolf to talk to, as occasionally Brook's wolf would pass a comment on to him through their mind link.

When the first shift happens, it would take two to three more months for the body to settle down to the new normal of being a wolf. At which point, it was impossible physically to tell if a person was born or turned. Seven to Twenty-one weeks to be Turned; it was going to be a rough time but would be a passing pain to get what he has wanted all his life: to be able to run as a wolf.

The two times they had a chance to let Brook's wolf out for a run, he marvelled at her sleek form. He had many pictures of her in various poses and activities now. Once they had moved out, she would be free to be a wolf whenever she wished; his landlord strictly forbade pets, 'not even to visit' was his answer when asking about them when he had moved in, which irked him badly. They had no right to decide who he had visit, let alone what species. But since it was their house, he hadn't bothered doing anything about it, and he had followed their rules. Having some wolf-fur in the house may have caused issues, so they went out to parks, and she shifted in the trees.

Adam had told Brook once they had discussed the details, he still wanted to be turned, and she said to think on it, and his final decision couldn't be made lightly or quickly, and he'd have to finish the changes the Mating had on him before he would be asked about his decision. She had commented the Mating changes did help with the speed of the changes, so likely looking to the shorter time, and may be less out of it on the worst part. He had been thinking on it for years; ever since he had first read about werewolves as a kid and had come to the decision which as long as he wasn't going to become a raving, mindless beast; he would take all risks and issues to the fact of becoming a wolf, if he got the chance. Well, he was getting the chance now, and he hadn't seen anything which would make him change his mind.

Brook had shared some of their beliefs. One was when they died, their spirit was released by cremation and would be reincarnated. So only their worst offenders were buried, as it trapped the spirit in the bones, so they could contemplate the offences they had made in their life, and hopefully when they came back, didn't repeat them. He gave a mental smile at an idea: trapping the spirit in the bones was incarceration with no chance of escape, and there needed to be no guards, just contemplating your heinous crimes for a long time. The only parole was when the bones broke down, to release their spirit, to be reincarnated.

Another spiritual belief they had, was the soul was split, with part in the human, part in their animal, and a last part in their Mate. Once someone was turned, they would usually be reincarnated as a born-were, as if they were born human, they would feel a part of them was missing, even if they found their Mate. He had felt that way for a long time, so after the discovery, he suspected he *had* been a were in a previous life, they might get an answer to that thought when his wolf started speaking to him. Or at least, he would feel whole.

Both beliefs felt right to him, deep inside. He wanted to find out more, but they could wait for a while, as there were many items he knew he couldn't be told till he was fully joined to the pack, and more they didn't say till they were Turned.

Brook had also described the pack's structure to him, with the Alpha pair leading, although a single Alpha—gender didn't matter—could be in control. To help them, they had Seconds. The Seconds took over if the Alphas were not available for any reason, and usually did a fair amount of the day-to-day decisions with the Alphas or elaborations to the Alpha's orders to give tasks to complete. When the Alphas had pups, once they entered their third decade, they would then be more who would help lead, as needed. They could be given some of the Seconds' or the Alpha duties as well. Gareth and Maria's pups, John and Bri, were currently at an elite training school, simply called *The Academy*, and only made it down at the solstices and equinoxes, which was when they had short breaks. They weren't going to be down, as they were spending the break at a friend's Pack in Germany. She did comment for Next-Alphas, they were often the offspring of the Alphas, who were learning to lead, either their own pack, or to wait for the Alphas to pass the pack over to them. At the moment, John and Bri were 'presumptive' till they were done their training, as per Alpha order, and they would be confirmed, once they passed all the pack's tests to show they had the skills they required of the leaders.

Brook had told him her name was on the list to hopefully go for the training at some point, but not till they moved to a new location, as the current pack wasn't very nice to females, and she didn't want to have the hassles Bri had to deal with. When she told him since they were mated, generally both went together, which made Adam happy, as the descriptions of the training offered sounded like it was well worth the very high costs. Nor did he want to be separated from her for the two years the training lasted, only seeing her on the breaks.

Betas were the next rank, who were the managers for the Alphas. They were the ones to make sure the will of the leaders was carried out by those under them. There was a bit of a pecking order of seniority for them, but generally their duties didn't overlap. Typically, there was only one Beta—or mated pair—for 50-100 members. For smaller packs, they didn't even have an official 'Second', instead one of the Betas took the duties of leading when the Alpha was away.

Gamma rank was below them and were the main enforcers who filled the bulk of the pack. They were also the pack's Enforcers, as they were the ones who generally monitored for pack discipline of the lower ranks, and made sure the pack's rules were enforced, especially for security. Often, they were called Enforcers instead of Gamma.

Delta ranked below and were generally the reserve forces and day-to-day administrators who protected the Thetas and the inner pack territory from attack and directed the Thetas in their duties. Thetas, if they wished to learn the fighting skills and worked hard could aspire to a Delta ranking, even if they wished to stay at their normal duties, although they generally were given some leadership duties as well, like leading a team to do a specific task and report to the Beta or a more senior Delta.

Thetas filled much of the pack. They were the regular workers who supported the pack; some worked outside the pack or worked in support roles within the pack. Usually, they would run before fighting, but Brook had told him they also were expected to have basic self-defence skills within this pack.

Omega was used as a punitive rank and would follow them around for their life. If a wolf was made Omega, the Pack Law was even if they made it to their fifth century, they could not join the Elders, and they would never be trusted with a role higher than a Delta, even if they ever had the Omega removed. Brook had told him some who had been given the rank decided to kill themselves instead of living in shame. Suicide was not considered bad for a wolf, as there were times living came to be too much and looking forward to their next life was preferable.

Within many packs, the pups didn't move more than a single rank up or down from their parents, with most staying the same rank, but within their pack, they had Spring Trials which the Elders and selected helpers who were not competing, ran. This allowed for anyone to try out for a rank, and if they qualified, could apply for the positions, and all were expected to re-qualify once a decade, but they could do so more often. Mates were expected to qualify separately, but new mates from another pack were given status equal to their mate, and then had three years to pass the qualifications, but with Alpha approval could have it extended farther. Humans were not expected to enter in the trials and the Alpha could assign them a rank, although they would still be considered a non-combatant, and if/when they were Turned, they were given a decade to qualify to maintain their assigned rank.

The pack currently didn't interact much with the humans beyond those in the nearest town, where they were mostly an open secret, but there was a push from the younger ones just getting into the leadership positions to integrate more, especially since the humans were starting to push into their territory the last few decades. Adam already knew they were just using a single mostly-reliable satellite connection, although in bad weather it tended to go down, and the ones who wanted to use the newer gaming systems were having trouble with any of the network games as the latency—the time delay of the communication of the computer and the server—was too high.

He had already started working on a proposal with some help from Brook to have them upgrade to a much faster and reliable connection. This weekend would allow him to find out how tough it would be to bring the pack into the 21st century. It was likely the Elders, who needed to be convinced as he already knew the Alpha was for it, since he now had someone who knew how to do it correctly.

From the couple of times, he mentioned it to the Alpha, he seemed to be willing to go along with it, and commented, "Those who don't change with the times at best are left behind, at worst are run over by those who embrace change." He wasn't sure he wanted to know the reasoning behind the last part, as when he had first heard it, it sent shudders down his spine. For the werewolves, likely it would mean them being outed to the humans, and the packs being forced to break up.

The biggest block to doing upgrades was they didn't want the humans coming out to do it. With Adam already being trained in doing so, they didn't need to have someone who didn't know about them coming out now.

His research had shown there was fibre optic cable at the mouth of the long valley, about 50 km away, which they could connect to and using a fixed wireless signal the rest of the way would work. Running fibre would be best, but not only was it pricey, would have a bunch of machinery which would bring attention to it. If they didn't have property near the fibre they could tie into, they would need to buy it, the rest of the links he could then have wolves deal with, and minimise the exposure, although they needed to hide the traffic to the territory.

Once he had full approval, he would figure out the questions and turn his goals and basic ideas into workable plans he could present to the leadership for approval.

*****

Shaking his head to clear his thoughts, as he realised the lights weren't stars, but was the large pack house hiding in the trees, and it wasn't a campfire he was smelling, but some wood burning fireplaces from the little bit of smoke he could see coming out of the chimneys. It was a three-story building with steep roof, made to look like a stone lodge, but was blended into the trees and the nearby ridge, so humans were unlikely to see it, and the roof was also made to blend in, to hide it from the air. He grinned as he loved the look. Some rooms had a soft glow of light, while many others were dark. Even with his enhanced eyesight, he would have missed it, without the lights, if he wasn't looking for it.

There were people—werewolves according to his nose—and wolves—although some smelled a little more like dogs—moving about, and looking at him curiously, before going on their way. Those downwind, took a good sniff to catch his scent as well.

Brook grinned at him, "I'm glad you like it," she had felt his pleasure and awe through the bonds, "Come on, the Alpha is waiting," she commented as she tugged on his hand, heading for the front door. There was a stone wolf, laying down with its head held high on one side, and another sitting tall on the other. Both were carved so well they almost seemed alive. The doors were a heavy metal, with wolves in various poses engraved on them. A little bit of dim light was on the steps, but the rest was dark.

The lever handles opened with a click, and the door opened without a sound, stepping into a large entryway, the inside looking like a cabin on a grand scale, with varnished warm pine pillars and mouldings. More carvings, this time mostly in different woods, of wolves in various poses and activities were hung on the walls. Pictures and paintings nestled in between them as well, some of nature and others of people, who he assumed were past and present pack members.

The lights were low, but he could read by it, if he wanted. If he had the full Were-sight, it probably would be as bright as day. Which was understandable; why light the building to the level humans were accustomed to, when most were at least Mated and had somewhat enhanced skills. The roof was higher than was normal, but he just shrugged it off.

Turning to the left, they went through a door marked with a big stylized "A" on it made up of several wolves when he looked closely at it; he assumed it was the Alpha's suite. He was right when a very tall man came up and Brook introduced him as Alpha Gareth; he bowed his head in respect, and greeted him, "Alpha, it is good to finally meet you." As Brook had instructed, after meeting his eyes for a moment, let them settle on his chin. Unlike humans who expected you to stare at their eyes, for a wolf it was a challenge.

As was the wolf way, Alpha Gareth pulled him in for a good hug, and a sniff of the neck, as werewolves put much more emphasis on scent and were much more tactile. Hugging also exposed the neck to attack, so it showed you trusted the other to not attack you.

"As I am sure Brook told you, you need to be formally accepted into the pack, and introduced. We have scheduled a Pack Meeting for tomorrow at lunch to introduce you. Come, I will induct you to the pack tonight." Turning, Gareth headed to a door past a fairly large meeting room, currently dark, and having steel shutters over what he assumed was a window to the outside. Entering the room, Adam could see it was his office, with a couple of couches, a fireplace cheerfully burning a log on one wall, and an ancient computer with a CRT screen taking over one side of his desk.

Adam cringed inwardly and added probably getting new PCs and laptops for the pack to the list of work he would need to do. Brook caught his feelings, and chuckled at him over the link, already knowing him enough to know what the cringe was for. She had enjoyed playing on his PC and laptop while he was working over the last week. She had chuckled, since he had a "Fursona" of a wolf and hung out with others who were into that sort of thing. She had teased him he would finally be able to become his fursona a couple times. They had decided he should try to distance himself from the human world, and the easiest was to fade away online, and just not enter discussions, or start conversations. To do so, he had started to leave groups on his IM systems, and transfer ownership of any online communities he managed. They had discussed it with the Alpha, and he didn't need to leave everything, and others, since they were just online and didn't include any real view of him, could slowly leave them.

Brook stepped to the side silently, she couldn't interfere or be involved at this point; she was the witness, as Gareth stood up straight and looked right at Adam, putting both his hands on Adam's shoulders, starting the ritual to join the pack, "Do you wish to join the Pack?"

"Yes, I do," Adam replied, standing straight. He realised this would be one the most important events in his life. Pack was a family and friends, ones who would know when he was hurting. He already knew all he had to do was ask if he wanted or needed comfort or cuddles. He had already found they were totally willing to help with his costs and expenses. His debts had been cleared, although he would have to pay them back, it had been an interest free loan. The salary Gareth had given him was enough he was returning half of it to pay for his outstanding debts, which would only take three or four months! The rest was his and was much more than he had made at his last job, too!

"Will you uphold the Pack Laws?" Alpha Gareth asked.

"Yes, I will." Adam agreed, formally. Brook had taught those to him over the week. They made sense, when you looked at them in context of the fact werewolves were not human and had different morals and different customs. There were much fewer laws which had to be followed than the complex system of the humans which most didn't understand and had a great many laws which were not even enforced regularly.

"Will you protect all those who are weaker than you, even if it means laying down your life for them?"

"Yes, I will." Brook was a Beta, he had been told until he tested, he would get his rank from her. He would do all he could. Being human still, he was considered a 'non-combatant', and thus to be protected. If there were any weaker, maybe a small pup, he would totally give his life to protect them, if needed.

"Will you guard the pack secrets which are entrusted to you with your life?"

"Yes, I will." Protect the secrets of this new life? No way he wouldn't. He knew if his old friends found out about this, most would demand to be Turned, regardless of what it would require or the risks. Not many he would want as packmates, as they rarely cared for anyone outside of their close friends and he had been snubbed many times.

"Will you obey those in the pack who are senior to you to the best of your abilities?"

"Yes, I will." He didn't like it; he preferred not to have others over him, and knew Brook felt the same. It was one thing she had told him about when she was growing up, some of the things which now were a bit silly which had got her punished. As she got older, and her skills showed, it gained her the Beta rank, and lately, one which was fairly highly ranked. He had teased her when he realised how high she was, she did it to not have many to tell her what to do.

"Will you help your packmates to the best of your ability, whenever possible?"

"Yes, I will." He *liked* helping others, and whenever he could. It was one reason he had gone into working as a computer technician. Fixing the same issue over and over, and for the same person? Not so much.

Now smiling, Gareth walked up to Adam, and place a hand on each of his shoulders, "Then welcome to the MacLaren Pack, Adam."

Gareth placed his forehead against Adam's, causing Adam to gasp as he felt his mind open up to the pack, and able to sense a feeling of joyful welcome from his new packmates, making him smile as the Pack-link filled an empty spot in his mind which he didn't even know he had, giving him a warm feeling of belonging. Even he could faintly hear the joyful howl which rang out from everyone in the pack, welcoming him. Then his happiness was overwhelmed as a splitting headache started, causing him to wince.

Brook was beside Adam immediately, as Gareth released him, wrapping an arm around him to help support him as his legs threatened to not hold him; joining a pack did that even to wolves, if they changed packs, as when they were born, the pack bonds formed slowly over the first days to a month as they grew.

"I think it is time to take him to bed, so he can sleep it off. I have assigned you a nice suite on this floor. I'll take you to it." Gareth commented, before heading out of the office, and out of the Alpha area. Leading them through a door which was just on the other side of the stairs to the second floor, led them to the first door, and opening it, he tapped a light switch, turning on some more gentle lighting, "This suite is yours now, I hope you like it. I'll see you in the morning."

Brook nodded, with a surprised look on her face while Adam was nearly asleep on his feet, and not really hearing anything other than the throbbing of his head, as Gareth quietly closed the door behind him.

With her wolf in full Mate-Protection mode, Brook moved Adam to the king-sized bed, and quickly undressed him and slid him into the bed before quietly padded over to the bathroom and wet a cloth for Adam's headache.

No drugs could touch the headache, as it was just the new connection settling in, and could slow the mind's acceptance, causing the pain to be extended or worse; could cause mental damage or even death, it would also weaken the bonds, making it easier to damage or cause further harm if not allowed to heal first. The healing could take several years to resolve.

He would be fine after a night's rest. Padding over to the bed, turning off the lights as she went, she placed the cloth on his forehead, getting a sigh of relief from Adam, before stripping and climbing in. She snuggled up tight against her mate, as had become normal for them, before both drifting off to a deep sleep.

Brook's wolf prowled forward in her mind and sniffed at her mate. She growled happily, as her mate was already having the pack-scent, showing to anyone with a nose he was protected by a pack; if he was attacked, he wasn't alone, and the pack would deal with them. She relaxed, but stayed alert to protect her mate, since he didn't have a wolf to do it for himself.

*****

The next morning dawned bright and sunny, and they were serenaded awake by bird song. Adam stretched his stiff body with a groan, having barely moved all night, waking Brook. His headache just a nasty memory now. Getting a morning kiss from Brook, Adam sat up, looking around the room in awe. It looked like they had a king-sized bed, a nice TV and sitting area with a couple of couches, and a wood fireplace. Beside it was a nice table with seats around it. There were some movies and books in one of the bookcases there. He also saw a couple of desks; one had a few items and an old-looking laptop on it. There was a door he could see, which opened onto a deck or patio, and the view was great too; it was overlooking a nice slope of trees, with a mountain rising above them. It made him smile, loving the view.

He saw two closed doors on one wall, and being curious, got up to check them out. One was a large walk-in closet; half had clothes in it, Brook's scent hung around them. The other half he assumed was for his, when they got the boxes from the vehicle, either later today or the next day.

Opening the other door, he froze. It was a beautiful full bathroom, with a shower stall which was big enough they could fit four people in, and with multiple heads. There was a large soaker tub which looked the size of a hot tub and would fit several. Then there was the standard toilet, although it was hiding in a stall, and a sink with a reasonable counter around it.

Brook wrapped her arms around him from the back, "From the fact all my personal stuff is here, not in my other room, I'm assuming they moved it here for us during the week. This suite is typically for one of the most senior Beta pair; one who need to be close, as they are constantly in contact with the Alphas. I think the idea you gave Gareth to upgrade the pack, he accepted." Giving a bit of a sniff, "I think it would be best for us to have a shower before going to breakfast." After the long drive, and the stress from the forming of the pack bonds, their normal scent was a little strong.

Wrapping his arms around Brook's he started to slowly walk forward, "I like that idea!" Pulling her along, closing the bathroom door when they were in the room, Adam walked to the shower. Turning it on and warm, he sighed as they walked in and started to wash each other, "If this is respective to what's here, I am not surprised you didn't want to leave it!"

Brook giggled, "Well, the pack does try to give members the comforts to make it a home. I know you didn't really enjoy cooking; there are several here who have gone to school to do it, and they trade off shifts cooking for the pack, others who like cooking generally work under them in the kitchen. We try to not overwork members, and give them time to relax and have fun, as well as doing training." Brook gave Adam and evil grin, "Since I am a trainer, and we need to get you up to speed as fast as possible, I have you all to myself. Once the mating changes are completely settled, you can decide if you want to still be Turned right away or hold off. We will be doing some running and weight training to get your strength and endurance up when we can."

Adam nodded and smiled, "I wondered if you would do it, or if they would choose someone not involved to train me," He commented as he finished washing her back and hair, turning so she could do the same for him; he really enjoyed this part. Showering alone was so much more work and much less enjoyable!

Brook replied, "It's easier for me, as I am qualified, and makes less chance of my wolf wanting to tear into a packmate for leaving bruises on your lovely body. I also have a vested interest in making sure you are trained to the best of my ability; you are my mate, if you get hurt, it will hurt me!"

All clean, Adam dried off wondered what he would wear, as his nearest clothes were a 15-minute walk away, in his vehicle, till Brook piped up, "I was looking forward to this; I have been wearing your clothes all week, this weekend you get to wear mine for a change!" Adam shrugged with a smile, "Fine with me, having your scent all over me is great. What should I wear?"

Laughing, she didn't want to embarrass him at his pack party, even though she wondered what he would look like in one of her dresses, she pulled out a soft thong and some bike shorts, and a nice t-shirt, "Here," pulling out something similar for herself, she smiled as he just pulled the clothes on without making a comment. She had learned over the last week he liked wearing female clothes, and she was quite happy to help him out with it, and she too actually enjoyed being wrapped in clothes which smelled of their mate. He did look cute in the outfit; the shirt saying, 'I'm only available to my mate' and was one of her favourites. Hers said, 'Don't bother asking, unless you're my mate'.

Holding hands, they walked out of the room following the mouth-watering food smells which met them as they reached the entryway. Filling her plate at the buffet table with food, Adam followed and filled his with hot pancakes, bacon, sausage, and drizzled Maple Syrup over them and grabbed cutlery from the trays before following his mate. Brook led him into a large dining room and walked him to a table with several females and a few males about their age. Taking a pair of empty seats, Brook introduced Adam to her friends: Erin, Nikki, Aurora, Shana, Kuri, were the girls and Martin, Peter, and Evan were the boys. He was warmly greeted and welcomed as they congratulated them both on the mating; nothing needed to be said, they could smell it on them. Adam felt he probably could become good friends with all of them. Jugs of juice sat on the table, as did bowls with fruit.

As they ate and chatted, both got a bit of teasing about how they met. Finding out he had a tech background, they started asking some questions about it, having not had much chance at the pack to learn much. Answers about him being tentatively accepted to work on the pack's technology, were met with great enthusiasm, and he even found out several who would be quite happy working with him to teach the rest of the pack the new devices once they learned it.

Once they were done eating, Brook took him on a tour of the pack house's public areas, showing them the games room, several living rooms, and a large meeting room. He almost drooled over the large library, and she had to drag him away saying he could look more later.

Heading outside, she showed him the greenhouse which not only had nearly a forest of fruit trees, but it also had a large hot tub and a cooler soaking pool in it and some grassed area to lounge on. She told him there was an underground tunnel which linked into the main building, so in bad weather, they could still get to the greenhouse.

Brook also showed him the kennels, where they kept some wolf hybrids. Which explained why his nose was telling him some of the furred wolves were not werewolves, but were more dog, even though they acted very intelligent, "I was saving this as a surprise. I had talked to Gareth, and he approved us taking over one. They help hide the fact of all the fur around from us, and they make good guard dogs for those humans who might be in danger from their association with us or who are dear to us."

Adam was ecstatic, having always wanted a dog but something always prevented him from having one, "I would love to get one today, but let's wait till I'm all moved in here. My landlord would not be happy if I brought one in." He didn't really care what they thought but didn't want to mess it up for the others he was leaving behind.

Brook nodded, "It would probably be the best, even if my wolf is all for having you protected, even if they are rated as 'service animals' and they would have no way of denying him access. It would not be fair, to bond then immediately stay away for a couple of days." It was unlikely but it could even harm the bonds which would form between them.

All too soon, it was time to head to the back porch of the house for the introduction to the pack. Everyone seemed generally happy, and welcoming, but Adam still was getting nervous. He could hear everyone heading in the same direction. He clung to Brook's hand tighter for reassurance as they made their way there, trying to hide it, to put on a good impression for his introduction, but knowing everyone would be able to smell his nervous sweat.

Brook leaned over and nuzzled him, trying to calm him a bit, "They expect you to be nervous, they won't think badly of you being a bit nervous, if you don't allow it to stop you. Not showing any nerves makes them think you are trying to hide something. They have already accepted your bond to them. This is so they know your face and scent, and for some to get to know you." It was also an excuse to have a party, which the wolves liked to do.

Several near them heard her comments, and when they caught Adam's eye, they nodded with a smile, showing they agreed with Brook's thoughts.

Smiling his thanks, they arrived at the deck, and climbed up to wait at the side of the deck for the Alphas to arrive, so the formal part could be started. Everyone else was down on the grass in front of it.

CHAPTER 4

The Introduction

The Alpha's mate, Maria, who had been out at a meeting with another pack had rushed back just to make it for the introduction. Normally, she would have been at the Joining of a new member. Both Alphas walked out of the house right on time, seeing what looked like everyone was there, gave a short howl to call the attention of the about 300 werewolves to order.

"We are here to celebrate a Mating and to welcome a new member to the pack!" Gareth started before pausing.

The wolves howled their pleasure and welcome, grins on their faces.

Motioning Adam and Brook forward, he continued, "This is Adam—" he introduced, and had to stop as there was a long, loud welcoming howl, which set a warm grin on Adam's face as he could feel the welcome over the pack bonds as well. When it quieted down, he continued, "He is mated to Beta Brook!" An even louder howl was heard in celebration, as Brook was liked by almost everyone, as she had helped train many of them over the last decade.

Once everyone was quiet again, Gareth formally introduce the computer upgrades idea to the pack, "Adam had an interesting idea, which since he is trained and experienced in computers and networking, he is planning on working to upgrade our technology to something much more current and much more in line with what the humans have. He, and his mate, will be working on it as soon as they get moved and settled in. We will be starting a box on the first floor atrium for any needs, wants, requests, and nice-to-haves. I do know he has ideas for upgrading the internet feed here—"

Gareth had to stop, as another howl broke out, from most of the wolves under forty, and some of the older ones too, in support of a better network connection. "We will also need to find those who are interested in learning, so they can be instructors for the rest of the pack. As with all other skills, I will not push it on anyone, but some senior positions will require at least some skills going forward. As is normal, those already doing the duties will get training or be permitted to move to other duties within the pack. Details have to be worked out, and plans approved by me and my mate, at which point if help is needed, it will be posted on the help board to be arranged."

The pack howled their pleasure again, and once they calmed down, Gareth grinned and shouted, "And now it's time to party!" The loudest howl yet as the wolves loved to have their parties, as those on the deck stepped off it and joined the rest of the pack as they broke up and started to talk.

Adam let out his breath in a sigh and smiled, *That wasn't so bad*, he thought to himself. He heard someone turn on the music, but smiled when it was kept it fairly quiet, and those who wanted to dance stayed near the stereo and those who wanted to chat moved farther away to where they could hear each other.

We don't blare the music, Brook told him, as she could feel his relief, *Our ears are already fairly sensitive, and we understand not everyone wants to do nothing but listen to it. Many want to chat, so we let them, without driving those people away.* She elaborated, as they mingled with the pack.

The barbeques were lit, and some venison and elk meat were placed on them to cook. As most wolves preferred them rare, most was cooked quickly. The rest was medium rare, and the occasional forgotten piece was medium.

Once everyone was well fed, some started to break off having their own plans for the day, while others stuck around to chat, especially to meet the newest member. Adam and Brook had been in the middle of most of it, with the Alpha introducing them to the Elder Council who advised him; everyone on the Elder Council was over 400 years old, so were a wealth of wisdom through experience; they looked like healthy seniors, and still moved without any trouble. Most were looking forward to having a better connection, as they had found the wealth of information the internet had, and the ability to connect with other Elders from other packs without having to make the big production of going for a visit, as it required major security for them to travel. There were a few who grumbled about not needing it so far, and not really wanting to learn something so new.

Don't worry about them, they never want to do anything new, they grumble, if not actually oppose, just about every change and decision, if they didn't bring it forward. Brook linked to Adam, as an aside, as the moved away from the Elders. She knew those Elders didn't like changes for any reason.

Most of the older pack decided to wait until the changes happened to see how much they affected them, but most were looking forward to better communication with those they knew in other packs. Some just shrugged and since the Alpha had ruled, their opinion didn't matter any further. Since Adam was mated to a Beta-ranked wolf, he was considered Beta as well. After meeting the Elders, Brook took him to meet with the other Betas, including her parents.

Adam wasn't quite dragging his feet as Brook pulled him to meet her parents. He was hoping they liked him.

"Adam, these are my parents, David and Marilyn." She said in introduction, "Mom, Dad, this is my Mate, Adam." She nearly glared at them, sensing Adam's nerves. She'd be growling at her parents if they said anything about her mate not being a wolf.

Marilyn smiled and hugged Adam tight. "You're going to have your work cut out with training him." She told her daughter, grinning. She didn't care her daughter mated a human.

Brook smiled, "I love doing the initial training, which is why I take on the pups." She said, relieved. "I don't see a problem, and he's actually progressing well." She had known her parents never enjoyed the beginner training, instead preferred doing the advanced Enforcer training. When Brook had gained the Beta rank about a decade before, soon after coming of age and being permitted to take the testing, she had taken over the initial training, which generally was done between six and fifteen, depending on the pup's parents, with her parent's blessing. They now dealt with the more senior training for the pups.

"We're happy you found your mate so young," David told Brook, who blushed with pleasure. He laughed, "What? Did you think we would care he was born human?" He shrugged at her look, "Fresh blood is always good, as it makes for much stronger pups."

Adam and Brook turned red at the idea while her parents laughed, and wandered off, so to not monopolise all their time and not let others greet them.

Adam sighed as Brook led them as they wandered off to another group, as he felt the meeting had gone well; her parents were good. He wasn't really looking forward to telling his mother about the whole werewolf thing, and the fact he was already Mated.

Very few people drank any alcohol, and any which was there, was very light, and they drank it for the flavour, not to get drunk. It was not a custom of the werewolves to get drunk, as it usually caused problems with uncontrolled shifting or aggression. It also took a very large amount to get a wolf drunk, and the effects didn't last long, but their headaches were magnified, as it lowered the mental barriers, leaving them open to the thoughts of others around them. Adam liked the idea, as he avoided alcohol completely, which surprised Brook for a moment, as most young humans liked to get drunk; she too avoided the alcoholic drinks for the most part, but did introduce him to one, not telling him it had a little bit of alcohol till after he agreed it was good.

Adam's head was spinning with all the names of the packmates he had met, which he would not be able to remember at all, but he gamely went on, and continued to mingle with the pack, to at least be known to many. All who came to say hello, gave him a welcoming hug and sniff to catch his scent, as he had been told was a normal greeting between those who were friendly. Others came wanting to see if they could find out more, or give suggestions, some were eager to learn and wanted to help. Those who were looking for information, were told he would need to figure out what was needed before he could do anything, as he didn't even know much about what the current condition was, although he was starting to think he'd need to start from scratch. He would keep the satellite connection as a backup link.

Those with suggestions were told to drop notes in the box when it was set out, and those wanting to help, were asked to put a note with their name on it in the box, so he could keep track of them. He was already feeling overwhelmed and wouldn't remember the names of those who were wanting to help.

Towards evening, those who had stuck around started to head in one direction, and Brook urged Adam to follow. Wandering down a short forest path among the crowd, they reached a large fire pit, which rather than a circle, was more of a strip, which allowed for using less wood, but gave more seating space for people. Adam was crammed in between Brook and Erin, with their other friends from breakfast around them. They munched on fire roasted hot dogs, smores, and other stuff, while chatting, and some sang songs, with some shifting to their Were shape or wolves and howling in harmony to the songs.

Those in wolf shape, Adam was amused to see, acted like dogs, and were flopped generally with their bellies to the fire, across the feet of those in the first row of benches.

Adam just enjoyed the easy acceptance and welcome he had received from the pack, and the warm feeling of belonging. Many had offered to help them move. Brook had already arranged with friends to head out on Tuesday with the truck to move. Most would be ready to help when they got back if they didn't have duties to attend to. A fair amount of his stuff was going to be placed in storage, and he had already been assigned a large storage locker for it all, be given away to other members who needed it or sent for someone less fortunate if it wasn't something the pack needed. Living in the Pack house, he didn't need his freezer, bar fridge, dishes, and many other items which he had accumulated over the years of living mostly independently.

Late in the evening, Adam was yawning, and ready to sleep. His head rested on Brook's shoulder for a bit, with an arm around each other, before he started nodding off. Catching himself, he noticed Brook was also tired and nearly asleep.

Think we should head to bed before we fall asleep here? He sent over their bond, not wanting to disturb the singing which was happening around them.

Mmmm? Came Brook's sleepy reply, *Uhhh, yea, that would probably be good.* She replied, her mind catching up with what he said. It wouldn't be the first time she had fallen asleep at the fire. There were generally some who would sleep here, and there were always a couple who were awake till the fire was out cold and everyone who fell asleep had awoken.

Getting up at the end of the song, they said a goodnight to everyone, getting many calls of "sleep well" back, before trudging back to their room. After opening a window to allow the nice cool fresh air in, they both just stripped off their clothes, tossed them in the hamper, and crawled into the bed, wrapping their arms around each other, and falling asleep almost immediately.

*****

Adam awoke as a click startled him awake. Looking up he saw Erin and Aurora with a camera, grinning at them. Nudging Brook to wake her up, he sat up, "What's with the early morning wake up?" Adam asked.

"Early? It's already after nine!" Aurora exclaimed, "When you didn't make it to breakfast, we wondered where you were, and came looking. When we found you two snuggled so cutely together, we couldn't resist and just had to take a picture! See, you two are adorable!" As she turned the camera to show the picture on the back screen.

Adam smiled and had to agree with the thought it was very cute, "I agree, it is. I want a copy!" Stretching, he decided it was time to get up, "We were out at the fire for a couple more hours after you left, and almost fell asleep sitting there!" Kissing Brook as she stretched, "Morning!"

"Morning," She greeted the other two, "Since you are already here, you can help us move the load we brought out already. Go grab a couple Argo's from the shed and meet us at the west garage." They groaned and glared, but they had no duties today, and had said they would help, nodding they headed for the door to grab the eight-wheeled Argo's to carry the stuff. Not to mention since Brook was more senior, they almost had to obey her, since they had no other orders which would be impacted.

Heading to the closet, Brook selected another thong for Adam with a grin, then some stretchy bike shorts and a fitted tank, handing them to him. She selected a similar shorts and underwear, but pulled on a crop top, as they'd be moving and sweating for a while, "I want to see the muscles you are starting to have," She commented cheekily, teasing him. For humans, they would have needed pants, and a jacket, as while it was above freezing, it still was cool out.

Adam just grinned at his mate, and smiled at her lean body, which had well defined muscles, "Only if I can do the same for you!" He teased back. He again felt like he had won the lottery and had a big smile on his face. He wondered about being cold but shrugged it off and decided he'd just have to move more. The mating changes he had realised did make it, so he liked cooler temperatures.

Holding hands, they headed out the door, they walked out to his SUV, the other two already there, waiting for him to unlock it and the U-Haul trailer so they could start unloading. Noticing a trailer hitch on one of the Argos, they decided they'd just haul it all the way there instead of unloading here. With the strength of the three werewolves, they were able to move the trailer and get it connected for the last leg without any trouble. Opening his rear hatch, they start unloading the vehicle, filling up the back of the Argos.

"What's in these boxes, Rocks?" Aurora commented, lifting a small but very heavy box. From the size, she hadn't expected the weight it had.

"No; textbooks," Adam commented, with a grin, "For a while there, I was able to get really good prices for some computer books, some are on photography as well. The others that size are all books!" Many were not going to be opened, as they still needed to move the bookcase, but it was for when they had the big truck on Tuesday.

There were some boxes which were very light, full of his stuffed animals, and seeing his larger ones, the two girls aww'd and commented they would steal them. Adam glared at them sharply, and asked, "Did you want to piss off a Beta?" He commented a bit teasing, but a bit possessive. They shook their heads 'no' while smiling and continued. He did pass on where he had got them, and both commented they might go buy one for themselves, which had Brook nearly dropping her box as she was laughing very hard at the idea.

When they reached his computer gear, they were nearly drooling over his setup. Adam grinned, "This is already a few years old, and I have been considering replacing it." There were offers to accept it from him, but he shook his head and refused to commit to anything; he thought he might offer it to Brook first.

They continued to have playful banter as they unloaded the vehicle. Soon, the vehicle was empty, and everything was ready to go. Brook and Adam climbed into the one with the trailer, while the other two took the other. Brook was driving, as Adam had yet to learn how to handle one. Started it up, Brook pulled out slowly, taking the access trail at walking pace, not wanting to jar the precarious load which was perched in the back. Reaching the back porch, and their own door, they hopped out and started to unload the stuff. Their other friends were there waiting to help and make light work, and more pack members kept coming over to help as well.

Adam smiled when he realised the entire load had been unloaded and unpacked in under thirty minutes and it wasn't even lunch time. "Thanks everyone! Like the saying: many hands make light work!" He told those who had helped.

*****

Adam used the day to have longer chats with some of the pack, to start to get to know them. Brook took him on a tour of parts of the inner territory, outside of the pack house. He got to see where the storage units were, and where the Argo garage was. He liked the fact they had some workshops for creative work, as it was something he was interested in learning, even if he had not done anything since way back when he was in school.

A couple of hours before dinner, he had a private meeting with Alpha Gareth to go over the initial scope of his work. Brook decided she was giving herself a nice long run and would meet him for dinner.

Adam nervously knocked on the Alpha's Office door, working to hide his nerves, or at least not let him be stopped by it.

Gareth grumbled at his computer, "I am just about to toss this thing!" He commented, as Adam came in and closed the door.

Adam smiled and held in his laughter, along with his wince at the sound from the CRT monitor.

"Not only does it seem the internet connection needs to be upgraded, but I am also thinking the computers need to be replaced too." He said, as from what he heard from others, there was very little which was even usable, to his mind.

Gareth sighed, "Most are a decade old, and some are from the turn of the century." He acknowledged. "I think it would be for the best."

Adam smiled, "Having everyone at the same level of equipment is much easier from a support standpoint." He stated. "I am thinking a standard PC and a laptop, or two configurations would be best. The pack is not likely to need the power of a PC, for the most part, but would enjoy the portability of a laptop." He nodded at the monitor, "And all CRT monitors will be replaced with LCD screens." He knew some likely would want to make their own computer or want to dictate the specifications. Within reason, he would help them get what they want and how they wanted, but they would be the one to pay for it.

Gareth nodded, "Yes, that seems to be a good idea. We also have a room of broken computers. I haven't had them out to have them repaired, as can't be found..." He stopped as Adam grinned.

"Well, we'll just hang onto the hard drives, test and find out what the issues are, and replace the drives with new ones, and get rid of them." Adam stated, shrugging, "Easy as that. Likely, there are plenty of systems we can donate out for those who can't afford one and don't need much. The broken parts, we can have e-cycled."

"That works." Gareth agreed, surprised nobody else had thought about just removing the drives and clearing out the rest; likely it would not take anywhere as much space.

Adam nodded, "It is something easy, which I can have the pups interested to learn first. It would be good experience, and if they break anything, it's not really a big deal. It's not too hard to learn how to do it."

"Great." Gareth said in approval, "I'll leave it to you. How are you going to get the internet connection?" Asked, turning to the main part of this meeting.

"I am thinking we will need something nearby to have an internet feed to connect to, and enough facility to run their end of the connection. We can then deal with it ourselves to get it from there to the pack house." Adam stated, not sure on exactly how or what was needed for the connection. While he had experience with wireless connections, nothing at the scale he needed. "Maybe buy or lease a place in the town?"

Gareth smiled, "The pack already has a warehouse in town, along with some other buildings. In the warehouse, we don't even use half the building, so we could easily set it up with what you need. It is often where we have deliveries and the mail arrive, and the pack deals with it past there. That should work for you, as we can have the equipment there and the pack bring it further from there. There is always someone there."

Adam grinned, "It works perfectly. All the service provider needs to know is the feed is going to the building in town, and we can deal with it from there." No need for them to deal with their internal network, no need to come out. "We will just need to work it from there." He looked Gareth in the face, but didn't stare at his eyes, as it could be taken as a challenge. "I have never done anything like that, so would need to learn how to do it as I get it going. I have studied how to do it, and have done some stuff much smaller, but nothing on this scale."

Gareth nodded, "You are way beyond anyone else at the pack for skills. I am sure you are going to be able to do it. Whatever you get done will be much better than anything we have now." He leaned forward, "In that, I am placing you in charge of the technology for the pack and it is why you and Brook were moved to the senior Beta's room. You, and Brook, will be in charge of setting up the connection at the warehouse, getting a link to here, and anything further which is needed here."

Gareth passed Adam several sheets of paper, the first with his new title, *Chief Information Officer, MacLaren Technologies Inc.* with the tasks to *1) Set up a faster, more reliable internet connection, 2) Upgrade/replace existing computers, 3) Upgrade/replace internet access within the properties, 4) disposal of old systems, while maintaining data security.* It stated a salary higher than they had initially discussed, but the scope of the work had increased. It was more than three times what he made in his last job, too! It listed that day as the start date, with some other details, like coverage of all travel, cellphone bill, the nominal deduction for housing and unlimited access to the food services, access to all on-site facilities at no charge.

Another sheet had a list of people who worked in construction, with a contact who worked as a foreman for the pack, for if he needed help building anything.

Adam was shocked but stammered out his thanks for the role, which was more than he thought he was getting. He signed off on both copies before handing them back to the Alpha, who signed off too, and returned one to Adam. There were no budget numbers listed on the work, just *Reasonable costs to be billed directly to the company.* He was basically being given signing authority to do all the work!

"I also have the idea for once they are finished with our old equip-ment, we could set up a small computer sales and service shop at the warehouse, to have some income from all the tech work. It would also allow the younger wolves a controlled interaction with humans, so they can learn the skills to handle the tech." He suggested.

Gareth leaned back and thought it over. "Not going to give any sort of approval right now." He stated. "I will want to discuss it with others first, and they need to get through our old stuff anyways. It won't be till after the pack is done."

Adam nodded in acceptance. It was more in line with what he planned anyways.

"What does the pack have for security?" Adam asked, as he had seen a couple of old cameras, which seemed to have seen better days.

Gareth smiled, "Mostly, it is actual patrols by the enforcers. We do have a few cameras which monitor key points and are watched down in the security centre. Have Brook tell you more."

Adam nodded, "From what we have already discussed, in bad weather, the patrols are basically suspended, so you have no security. Can I look into getting some electronic sensors and for replacing the existing camera systems with something better?"

Gareth again had to think on it. He asked several questions about it. "You can see what it costs, and can get quotes, but it is all. Nothing to be done beyond without further approval." Was the final answer for now. He could see how it would enhance the security of the pack, but not require any more wolves to deal with it.

"For the pack house, do we want networking everywhere or just key areas?" Adam asked.

This was a short discussion about what he meant, and what it would entail. Adam was surprised on the fact the building was made so changes and upgrades could be done, so would be much less work than he thought. It ended up being decided for the most part, there would be both network ports, and wireless network.

"I do want to see how the pack wants it done, before we start with this." Gareth said, as it was always better to discuss before changes were made."

Adam smiled, "Is fine with me. I want to get the internet connection done first." He planned on maybe seeing about a Fixed Point-to-Point wireless link, and then maybe making their own fibre link to the pack house, at which point the wireless would be a backup.

It was arranged for a look at the warehouse before they did anything else, so he could get the planning for it first.

Adam started tentative plans on the warehouse in his head, as it had to be done before many other parts as both he and Alpha Gareth headed to the dining room to meet with their mates.

Adam snuck up on Brook, and wrapped his arms around her, and gave her a kiss to the side of the neck, "I missed you!"

Brook could hear and smell him as he came up to her and let him seem to catch her. She giggled at his comment, "We were only separate for about an hour, silly." Her wolf was much more relaxed after a good run, and especially now with their mate against them. He was enjoying the time with his mate.

Pouting, he replied playfully, "I don't like being away from you."

Brook kissed his pouting lips, before they joined the mass of pack-mates heading for the large dining room and joined their friends for a well-earned meal. It was a dinner of some large slabs of roast beef, heaps of mashed potatoes, and some steamed veggies and fresh buns. Everything was done well. Adam decided to skip the steamed veggies, and grabbed some salad, and fresh vegies and dip, which was his preference.

Adam shared what he could about what was decided during his meeting with the Alpha. Most were just happy some work being done, but when he described how much work still was needed, their eyes got big. "We are going to need plenty of help." He commented, "But I need to check out what sort of space there is at the warehouse on my way back to the city." The warehouse, he kept expecting to be tiny, and not have much room for more than a rack of networking gear. It would be the first thing needed to be ready, as it would be how everything was connecting.

Following dinner, Adam and Brook decided to just spend some time together, as it had been a busy weekend, and they were needing to leave at dawn to get back to do the packing, and for the evening to introduce

Brook to his mother. Both were glad they didn't either need to leave tonight so Adam could get to work.

They curled up together in their bed, and Adam kissed Brook deeply, and rubbed along her body. Eventually they finished having their fun and went to sleep. Both were happy with the mating, and the few issues they had, they talked through and were able to solve.

CHAPTER 5

Moving and Talking to Adam's Mom

The next morning, Brook agreed, since they were heading back to his other place, he should wear some of the clothes he packed, to not offend the humans. After a hearty breakfast they had with the early wolves just before dawn, they walked back to the SUV, pulled it out of the parking, and reattached the U-Haul trailer for the trip back.

They stopped off down at the warehouse in town, and Adam was quite happy with what he found: lots of room for storage of pallets of equipment, an empty room seemed to be just waiting for a raised floor and to be turned into a data centre. He would just need to figure out how the internet feed was coming in and enough power to the location. Measuring it, he decided to order the raised floor and a couple of racks and other basic equipment he needed to get ready to feed the internet. He decided one rack would be dedicated to internet feed or feeds, and the other to the pack's internal network.

Accessing the roof was easy, as the building had an interior ladder which went to a roof hatch. Standing up on the roof, Adam realised he had a straight shot view to the ridge over the pack house, which made running the initial link easy; he even had most of the mounting hardware, the rest could be picked up at a quick stop at a building supplies store. He could just anchor a cord directly to the cliff and run it down near the pack house, as a temporary measure. Permanent, he would want to install a ladder up the cliff or use a tower, to make the emergency servicing of it easy. The Alpha may know a spot which had a bit of a trail to it which could see it. This was something they could check when they got back.

Smiling he wrote a quick note to be run back to the Alpha with the findings when they finished their shift and let them know what he was having delivered. The Alpha had given him a Pack credit card, which had no limit on it. He was going to be getting his thoughts together, and the orders ready on the drive back, when he wasn't the one driving. He was going to need some help installing the equipment on the ridge, but it would be easy to do off a rope.

He also now had the information he needed to contact the fibre company to arrange to get the connection installed as well. Once the feed was to the warehouse, he should already have the wireless link up and running, as it would take only a day or two. He hoped the fibre company wasn't too busy and could move on to at least planning the connection immediately.

*****

Brook had taken over the driving as they left, leaving him the time to work on getting the orders and details in. By the time they had arrived back in the city, to do as much packing that afternoon as they could, Adam had already arranged the fibre link details, and they would be investigating what they needed to get there, including the costs. He had ordered in the equipment to be shipped to the warehouse for what he needed to set up the raised floor, and a couple of racks, and arranged for some specific networking equipment he needed for the fibre link to the wireless one, and all the supplies for the wireless link. All the equipment should be there before the end of the week for him to get installed. The floor should be there in a couple days, and he could gather some help to do it. He also ordered some equipment for wireless networking some of the common areas in the pack house. He had gotten enough agreement to do it, even if he couldn't turn it on for general use.

Moving everything around to the living room, to make it easy to take out when the moving truck arrived in the morning, took the hours till it was time to get ready for the dinner with his mother. Both Adam and Brook took a good time to get ready, wanting to look good.

*****

Arriving at his mother's house, Adam parked, and took a deep breath, letting it out slowly to calm his nerves, as Brook sent him some love over their link before stepping out.

Holding Brook's hand, Adam smiled at his mother, who was waiting for them at the door to her half of the duplex, "About time you got yourself a girlfriend! Come on in. I'm Mary."

Brook smiled in reply, "Hi, I'm Brook. I'm so happy to meet you."

Leading them to the living room, with a loveseat and a chair, Mary took the chair, "So how long have you two been together?"

Adam and Brook looking at each other, Adam answering for them both, "A couple of weeks." Cutting off her exclamation, he continued, "Before you say anything, I am going to need to tell you some things."

Mary nodded, waiting for him to continue, her attention riveted, as she would have thought they had been together for months, if not years from the way they acted.

Taking a deep breath, Adam started, "You can't tell anyone about what we are going to tell you, it would put many people's lives at risk, ours included. Not even family."

Getting a nod in agreement from Mary, Adam continued, "Brook is a werewolf. I first saw her as she was running in a field in the mountains, towards me. I saw a rockslide right near where I last saw her and headed down the slope. I found her hurt and unconscious as a wolf. I brought her up to the lookout where I was parked, where she started to wake up, and shifted back to human. I figured out what she was at that point. I helped her as best I could, and once she was fully awake, told me what I was feeling when I touched her was because we were mates. I felt a connection from the first time I saw her and saw no reason to disbelieve her."

Taking a breath, Adam asked his mother, "You still with me?"

Mary stared at them, incredulous, "Why do have to make up such an unbelievable story? Werewolves don't exist."

Adam turned to Brook and nodded; he wasn't sure she'd believe them without showing her. Brook stood up, and started to undress, "I guess we'll have to show you we are not making it up,"

She quickly shifted into her brown wolf. Mary just stared disbelieving that the large wolf now standing in her living room was her son's girlfriend. Brook moved forward and nuzzled Mary's hand. She jerked it away before returning it to rub her soft head fur a couple times before Brook backed up, and shifted back to her human form, and dressed.

Mary sat there shocked, blinking at them for a bit, and they just watched her, as she tried to process what just happened.

At least she didn't scream, that would have really hurt, Brook commented silently to Adam. Some people screamed loudly, and a few continued till they passed out.

*Or just continued to deny it. She seems to be accepting it, although slowly, * Adam replied.

Giving her head a final shake, and shaky deep breath, Mary commented, "I guess werewolves do exist, and you are one."

Nodding, Adam continued, "I am her mate – or Soulmate, I guess – which makes living separately very difficult. I have already started moving in with Brook's pack, and I'm very much enjoying the friends I have already met. The moving truck will be here tomorrow to move out everything left. I have changed jobs, and I am now in charge of IT for the pack."

Mary blinked at how suddenly her son had changed his life, but it being his life, she knew if she didn't accept it, she would lose him, "I'm surprised, but you seem happy with the changes." The wonder in his voice is what sold her, he was wanting this.

Adam nodded as the timer for the oven beeped, "I guess dinner is ready," The smell had been driving him to distraction since they arrived.

Adam headed into the kitchen, and knowing his mother's setup, he pulled out the tray of chicken, and started serving everyone, motioning for Mary and Brook to just sit down. He served up the sides as well.

Brook looked at him in surprise, *I guess you do have some domestic skills, after all* she teased.

Yup, learned enough to survive; I may not like folding clothes or cleaning, but I do know how to do them! Adam commented back.

Sitting down, Mary did grace before they ate. Brook may not follow the beliefs, but when you are in someone's home, you need to have the good manners to show respect to their beliefs, even if they are not your own. She just would not allow them to try to force her to follow them.

Mary smiled as both ate neatly but fast, "I guess you are both hungry?"

Adam laughed, "As a werewolf's mate, I had some changes from the mating steps, to be able to somewhat keep up with my Brook. One side effect is an increased metabolism. I do intend to be Turned and become a werewolf as soon as I can."

Mary blinked, "I take it, to other werewolves, you two are basically considered married?"

Both Adam and Brook nodded their heads yes.

Looking down, Mary noticed no rings, "Where's the rings?"

Brook answered, "We don't wear rings often, as if we shift while wearing one, they will either snap the ring, or hurt the paw. We do sometimes wear bracelets. Personally, I don't like bracelets, so don't wear any."

Looking sad, Mary commented with a sigh, "I so wanted to see Adam married,"

"Well, nobody said we couldn't do a marriage, to be joined to human standards." Brook replied, "Would have to be six months to a year from now. You'd be able to organise it, along with my parents, if you wanted?"

Mary's face lit up, "You would let me do that for you?"

Nodding, Brook smiled, "I have got the part I wanted, to me the wedding is just a pain,"

Adam spoke up, "But not tonight. I have some other stuff we need to tell you,"

Mary continues to smile, "Fine. You found your werewolf mate, you are moving tomorrow, and you are changing jobs. What else is there?"

"First, the pack is in Eastern BC. We have a warehouse and a mail drop," Pulling out a card, Adam handed it to her, it had 'Adam Wolfe/CIO, MacLaren Technologies Inc.' on it, along with contact information and a mailing address, "You can get me there, day or night. Whoever answers for me would be able to get a message to me in an emergency."

"Second, the reason the wedding needs to be put off for a while is I am planning on becoming a werewolf, we call it being Turned, fairly soon, and I need to be comfortable with my new 'normal' and completely in control of myself before I could do something like that."

Mary smiled, "You have always loved wolves, so I guess it is a big dream of yours, to be able to *be* a wolf?

Adam smiled and nodded in agreement, as he stacked the dishes in the sink and started to wash them, *See, I'm even doing the dishes, and without even being asked!* he commented teasingly to Brook, as a response to the earlier teasing.

Following dinner, they moved back to the living room, Mary having thought up some questions to ask them, asked her first one, "So where exactly are you living now?"

Adam smiled, "We have a suite in the pack house, and the pack house is about a thirty-minute walk from the nearest road." He gave her longer times, as it would take her longer to walk it, "We do have all-terrain vehicles to bring bulky items from the parking area to the buildings. The pack house is hidden near the end of a ridge and designed to blend into the ridge."

Brook added, "We also try to discourage hikers from the area, so there is some signage to keep them away, we deal with the few nosy ones with inventive ways."

Mary smiled sweetly, "Sounds like a nice place. Would I be permitted to visit at some point?"

Brook nodded, "Family of members are always welcome to come stay. It is a six-hour drive there, so you may want to spend a few days.

Let us know when you want to come, and we'll arrange a guest room for you, and an escort in if we couldn't do it."

Mary glared at Adam, "Have you told your sister?"

Shaking his head, Adam responded, "No, I haven't told her. We will have to do it at another time. I did tell her I was moving, and since she is a sales rep, we could meet up out close to where we are. I will tell her more later when I have time. I will see about some time next week."

Looking at Adam shrewdly, "Since you're mated, when will I see grandchildren?"

Adam laughed out loud, "I thought would be your first question. They will happen when they happen, and I hope not for a while."

Brook commented, a blush on her face, "Female werewolves only go into heat once a year, like wolves, and only if they are not nursing and are in good health. Also, typically only Mated ones get pregnant. We will know if it will happen early winter. Also, we are only pregnant for four months." Werewolves had a much faster gestation period, but it was much harder on their bodies, which many thought the reason they wouldn't go into heat if they weren't in good health and why they generally had a higher miscarriage rate.

As an aside to Adam, Brook commented, *Not sure why, but my heat was early, and was just before we met, so no pups this year. I get you to myself for a year!* Adam worked hard to keep his blush from deepening at the silent comment. Brook just sent her amusement.

Mary commented with a sigh, "Lucky; no monthly periods, and short pregnancies."

Brook laughed, "Well our heat is about a week long, and during the time it is hard to think about anything but sex. Our pregnancies are harder on the body, and we can have litters with up to four pups." The more senior, the more likely the pregnancies would be smaller, and Betas and above typically had only single births.

Getting off the heavy topics, they discussed some lighter things, with Mary getting more into Brook's background, wanting to get to know her new daughter-in-law.

Eventually, Adam and Brook were ready to call it a night, and after a bit of a chat at the door as they left with hugs and kisses all around, they promised Mary they would arrange a time for her to come over and see the place. As they started the vehicle and drove off, Adam let out a sigh, "I'm glad it is over! Although it went better than I expected."

Brook smiled, "I don't know, the visit was enjoyable. Your Mom is nice. The food was good, but not enough to fill us up. Don't know about you, but I'm already hungry again!"

Adam's stomach answered for him, and they both laughed, "I think there are still some frozen chicken breasts we could have." As they were not going to be there after the next morning, they had decided they were leaving all the food for the other roommates, instead of trying to bring along food, as keeping the frozen items cold would be hard, and the pack already had their own food supplies, and didn't need extras.

After the second dinner, they decided to head to bed, so they could get the last things packed before the truck arrived the next day. After some quiet fun, they curled up together to sleep.

*****

The next morning, Brook made a breakfast of pancakes and bacon, and they quickly washed, dried, and packed the dishes. The last of the bedding was run through the laundry machines, then was folded and packed. Everything was ready to go when they had Rein send a text message to them and give them a heads up they were only an hour away.

Adam commented, "They're earlier than I was expecting. Let's get the furniture outside, so they can put it in first."

"Sure" Brook agreed.

Together they moved the bookshelf, desk, bed, recliner, and the other larger items out onto the front grass. They were starting to move boxes out when the truck pulled up, smiling they waved at Rein, his mate Mikan, and their friend Peter.

"I can see why you want to move," Rein winced as a firetruck raced by on the main road across a thin strip of grass.

Adam gave him a hug in greeting, "It's one reason. The company is a big reason. Space a third." He gave hugs to the other two as well, thanking them for helping, "Lunch is on me, on the way out."

A short cheer was given as they started moving the furniture into the truck. The werewolves making the heavy items look like they were made of Styrofoam. Everything was packed up quickly. They did a last cleaning of the bedroom, leaving it sparkling clean, and even did a scrub of the common areas to surprise the other roommates.

Leaving the key in the mailbox, he sent a quick message letting them know him and his stuff was all gone. Looking at his watch, he was astonished how fast they did it, "Guess it's time for some food. Arby's sounds good?" He laughed at the four hungry growls which was his only reply of agreement.

Agreeing that it was going to be easier if they didn't try to take the cube truck through the drive-through, they gave their orders to Adam to write down. Rein and Mikan agreed to meet them at a rest area just outside the city while they got the food.

Peter hopped in the back while Brook and Adam were in the front. The rest was full of boxes and a couple of bags.

Arriving at the drive-through, after the usual greeting, Adam rattled off the long order of four large roast beefs for each, several fries, and various other items. Asking for just waters with the meals, as pop to wolves didn't taste good; they were able to taste the individual ingredients, and the amount of chemicals made it not taste good. Even to Adam, it didn't taste good anymore. They were astonished at the large order, and exclaimed "What are you feeding, a Wolf Pack?" and commented it would take them a bit to organise it. Driving up to the window, trying to keep a straight face, Adam paid for it, then waited for the several bags of food. Once they pulled away to catch up with Rein and Mikan, they burst out laughing at their comment basically being correct: feeding several hungry wolves.

Adam munched on his curly fries on the way to the meeting, as eating a beef sandwich while driving was a recipe for an accident, or for at least a spill down his front. Arriving quickly at the spot, he pulled in behind the truck.

"Finally!" Quickly pulling his bag close he stepped out to use the hood as a table, he smeared some barbeque sauce on the beef and started to eat. The other two laughed, as Brook walked the two bags to the wolves hungrily looking at Adam eating.

"Here's yours," Brook commented handing them over, sending a glare at her mate.

What? You try to keep from starving while the smell fills the vehicle! I just about pulled over early just to eat one! You're up for driving so I can eat. He sent, eating his food.

Catching Rein's eye, Adam asked, "Meet in Frank in two and half hours?"

Rein nods in agreement, "Gives us a few minutes to each eat one, and to stop to swap drivers."

Hopping into the passenger seat after finishing the first sandwich, still clutching the bag with three other sandwiches and a couple turnovers, the other two slid in. They decided to stay right behind the truck and cruise along chatting.

*****

Arriving in Frank, they took a half hour break and scrambled over the rocks from the major rockslide about a century before.

I'm glad the slide I got caught in was a baby compared to this one! Brook commented silently to Adam, in awe of the house-sized boulders thrown up a fair distance the far side of the valley.

I'm very glad too, I doubt you'd have survived it! Adam agreed, pulling her close, not even really liking the thought.

"OK, break it up you two! It's time we got going again." Peter commented, looking forward to getting back to the Pack, his wolf antsy for a good run.

*****

Arriving at the parking area, there was a fair crowd waiting for them to help move them in. They parked the truck as close to the storage locker as possible as most of the stuff was going there, at least for now.

Adam directed the items as they were taken off the truck, the items which were to go to his room were loaded on the Argos for the last leg of the journey.

Once they were all done, Adam called everyone's attention, "Thank you all! Many hands do make light work of a big job, and fast too!" He got a laugh and a cheer, as they broke up, with a few following them with the Argos to their suite, to move in the last items. He was amused about how much they could lift as well. Usually it was bulk, not weight which they had to use multiple people for.

Once they were unpacked and homes found for them, Adam flopped on the bed with a heavy groan, "I don't want to move again! It's too much work!"

Brook giggled, "Well, if you had less *stuff*, it would be much easier to move!"

"Don't remind me! I plan on talking to the Alphas and figuring out places for most of it. I don't need a 40-inch TV, we have a nice one here," he motioned to the one over the fireplace, "I don't need my desk or bookcase, as we have plenty here. Although, I am going to see about the bookcase in a computer room, for all the tech books, and I'll get some more at lower levels than what I have now." Changing his mind, he had decided there was no need to have the computer books in their room.

Stripping off his clothes and for once dumping them on the floor, Adam didn't want to get off the comfortable bed, "For tonight, I just want to sleep. Some items should start arriving tomorrow which I ordered, and I want to get the internet going at least minimally within a week."

Brook stripped off her clothes, thought about it for a moment, then shifted to her wolf, before jumping up on the bed. Adam blinked in surprise, as she hadn't done it before, before holding the blanket open, so she could climb under. Once she laid down, head on the pillow, Adam wrapped his arm around her and snuggled into her back fur, "You're so soft, love. Goodnight."

Goodnight, my mate. She sent back, before they both drifted off to sleep; tomorrow was going to be another busy day, even if nothing bad happened.

CHAPTER 6

Meeting with the Alpha and Elders

Waking up the next morning, Adam's face was buried in some soft fur, and he smiled before stretching. The movement woke Brook up, and she yawned, before licking Adam's face with her wet tongue.

"I don't need a tongue bath! I do need a good long shower though. Care to join me?" Adam commented, as he started to get up.

Brook barked her agreement and jumped off the bed, heading into the bathroom before shifting and starting the shower. Adam quickly followed and as they had started doing, washed each other's body; it being not just a way to get clean, but a way for them to bond and enjoy the other's company in a non-sexual way.

Heading out of the shower, they both dressed well, as they had an appointment with the Elders and the Alphas to agree on the first stages. Brook decided against putting Adam in a dress, as to a couple of the elders thinking negatively about him.

*****

Walking into the Alpha Wing's meeting room after an enjoyable breakfast with their friends, Adam smiled at the relaxed feeling in the room, and exchanged greeting hugs with everyone.

Brook sat back, and just listened, as she was Adam's Mate. Although she knew what Adam wanted to do, and what he was proposing, didn't have the background to have the elders understand it. She would just listen, and make sure all the points Adam wanted to make were hit.

"OK, I am calling this meeting to order." Alpha Gareth announced, once everyone was there, from his seat at the head of the table. "Beta Adam has come up with several really good ideas, which I think will help us integrate more with the humans and will help keep us hidden from discovery by blending into what is considered normal and common." It was something he had been trying to do for several years. "I am for these changes, so we will be implementing the ones which are approved, over the next few months to a couple of years."

Looking around the table, the Alpha noticed he had everyone's full attention, "The first change is to bring a better internet connection to here. Adam, you have the floor."

Adam stood, "First part, is to start the work on getting a larger and faster connection, one which doesn't go out in bad weather. The concern about having humans knowing about us was a real concern. For this, with the Alpha's approval, the plan is only to have them access the warehouse in town and run a fast fibre link into a room which is being set up as a data centre there. The work to do the connection from there to here, we will handle, internally by the pack."

Just as they were speaking, Shana, who was working at the warehouse sent a quick mental link to let Adam know the floor items had arrived. He gave a quick thanks and turned back to the meeting.

Adam smiled, "I have just been informed the first part needed, the items to make a raised floor, have arrived. Talk about timing!" He got the wanted chuckles from them and relieved some of the tension.

Adam then sobered, and continued, "The raised floor allows for better cooling, and organising of cables in the room. I am planning to eventually use it as a backup data centre, and for backing up data, for in a worst-case scenario of this building burns to the ground, and we lose everything here."

Getting nods about following, as the Elders all knew of issues like it and doing so was a prudent move. Adam moved on, "Once the fibre is installed to there, the rest of the work will be done by the pack. I have the skills needed to train others to help me. I will be using some long-range wireless equipment to set up a link from the roof of the warehouse to the side of the ridge here. I still need to figure out exact placement, and how best to hide it. I won't bore you with the details on it, as it is very technical and isn't needed."

Going to the last part, Adam was looking forward to discussing it, "Once the connection is connected in the house, I am not sure how we want to have everyone connected. I was thinking of setting up wireless connections, but did we also want to set up wired network ports?"

One elder spoke up, "Wireless networks, where?"

"At least in key areas but was thinking of having them set up throughout the building, and even some outside."

Another commented, "We don't have many laptops which are new enough to have wireless in them."

Alpha Gareth replied, "After discussing it with Adam, we are planning on doing a sweeping upgrade of the current pack devices and implement an upgrade schedule of every four to five years, to keep us more up to date. Currently, we are looking at what sort of work someone is going to be using them for to figure out what to get, and what sort of costs there will be."

A third elder, "With a new laptop, we'd be able to work wherever we wanted in or around the house?"

Adam nodded, "Yes, and not just laptops, but smart phones or other electronics would be able to use it, too."

"What about security?" was asked.

Adam grinned, "I have a multiple stage security system planned. Any new device would need to be registered before they would be able to connect. It is much higher security than just having a simple password on it, which someone can steal, but will also do some authentication. I am currently learning the industry standards on how to do it correctly and will finish the course before I install the equipment outside the building."

Discussing the wireless more, they decided having it everywhere would allow for a much easier time and all could see the benefits.

Deciding to install them over the building would be best. The actual equipment and layout decisions were being deferred to Adam, as they didn't need to be involved with it at all.

"Back to the wired network, did we want to have ports installed? They look like large phone line holes. At the same time, we could upgrade or install phones which use the network to talk out, so we don't need separate cables. They would also be able to send calls to other phones or call others within the building. The same faceplate on the wall can do both. Rooms which don't have TV, I could also run a line for it as well."

Nodding, they quickly agreed the phone system could be upgraded, and although it would cause disruption to the rooms, it could be scheduled to minimise the amount it disrupted everyone. They would put a network in the rooms, one for each desk, and lines for the phone upgrades, and the changes to make it more reliable as well.

As usual, several of the Elders didn't like the changes, and didn't want to support it. Alpha Gareth overruled them, and approved the changes as stated, especially since the majority did approve of it. The few who rarely supported any of the changes, even when they had lots of effort to show how it would positively affect them. Finished up with the tech, the Alpha excused Adam and Brook from the meeting, as they had some other items to discuss, as this was their weekly meeting.

*****

Getting back to their room was a relief to Adam, "I am not used to making the big decisions, this is going to take me a long time to get used to it!" He said with a sigh, as he pulled off his clothes, the back of his shirt damp with sweat.

Pulling hers off, Brook commented, "You will have to; you are responsible for it, and everyone will be there to help you with it. I will help you as much as I can." Remembering about the mental interruption they had, "Lets go see what goodies we had delivered!"

Adam smiled, "It's just the floor parts. But let's also bring those I know are into tech with us."

Nodding in agreement, Brook gave a mental summons to Erin, Aurora, and Nikki to meet them at their vehicle, and getting their reply passed it to Adam, "The trio will meet us at your vehicle."

Smiling they walked out of their suite when they had changed into something which could handle some dirt, and started walking down the path to the garage, holding hands.

*****

Arriving at the warehouse, he smiled as he already had a designated spot up close. Walking up to the door, he smiled and used his ID and code he had just been given to get in with the other four following quickly.

"I guess the Solstice came early," Nikki commented, seeing the several pallets of gear to build the raised floor for the small room which was going to be the network feed. They had been placed out of the way of the other items; near the room they were working on.

The room seemed to have been designed for a raised floor, or one had been there previously, as the room had a couple of steps down into it from the rest of the building. They had used it for containment if they had any chemical spills, but they had a better system now, and it would work great for the server room. For right now, the door was keyed, and very few had the keys to get in: The Alpha (who had keys for every door), Rein (who was the pack's maintenance manager so also had keys for all the doors), and both himself and Brook.

Unpacking one box, he smiled at the heavy-duty Hilti concrete drill he had ordered, "Yup! Christmas came early!" He knew this was one of the best tools for drilling into concrete, so with control of the budget, decided getting good quality tools would be an investment. The tool would get other use, and he could hand it over to Rein, who Brook had checked with first. He hadn't needed to drill into concrete enough, so a small hammer drill would have been enough to do the job. This meant he hadn't purchased the more powerful tool.

Seeing the several pallets of floor panels, the one of pedestals, and one of stringer sections to link the pedestals, he directed, "Don't move the pallets of panels, we don't need them yet. Move the two others beside the door, as we need to set them first."

Working together, they laid out the pedestals and stringers to get the correct layout. They took their time and were finished around lunch.

Taking a lunch break, they went to a small restaurant in town, everyone but him being well known to the staff. Adam was surprised to learn many people in the town, like the owners of the restaurant, knew what they were, and protected their secret. They smiled and greeted Adam like an old friend, especially when they heard what he was doing. They commented that they hoped there could be some spinoff for the town, Adam commented, "Maybe, I hadn't thought about that; it's a possibility but I would need to talk to the big boss first. It would be easy to do something for the town and would hide the data use even better." They chatted about other ideas and what other plans were in the works, as the three with Brook and Adam would probably be the people who would make the changes happen for him and would be the people who provided support.

When they were ready to start making noise, he handed out earplugs to everyone. They spent the afternoon bolting down the pedestals to the subfloor, and attaching the stringers, and having a good time making lots of noise. They chatted over the mind links, continuing the lunch discussion, as it was too loud to do otherwise. Adam warned them the work could get tedious and very boring.

Later in the day, just as they were starting to fit the tiles in, they had a surprise visitor in the rep from the company doing the fibre link. Adam had them slow down when he showed them the room, and the rep smiled seeing the work they were doing. "This looks perfect." He told them, "The installers are just finishing up the last job, and we should be able to have the link in by the end of the week."

Adam smiled and agreed, "That is perfect. I would prefer to get it in as soon as possible. Do you have the equipment to bore a hole in the concrete?" he asked.

The rep nodded, "Yes, and the installers have done it before. All we will need is a small section of rack space to put the equipment."

Adam nodded, "I have racks on order, and they will be here in a few days." He had also ordered UPS equipment for each rack as well. The room had adequate heating and cooling for what they were installing, so he wasn't doing anything with it.

The rep nodded, "Everything looks in order, so if you will sign here..." he told Adam, passing his clipboard with the agreement for the services. Adam reviewed the documents to make sure there wasn't anything hiding in them, then signed off on them. He personally showed them out the door when they were done.

When he returned, it was almost a party atmosphere. They drilled a pilot hole, to locate where the bigger hole would go, and left the tiles open in that area, then finished most of the rest of the floor.

Next, since they still had a few hours left of the afternoon, they started getting everything ready for the wireless link. They ran a new conduit up onto the roof to a service box and ran a network cable up to it. They left plenty of slack at the end of the line, as they weren't sure of the exact placement yet.

Brook smiled at Shana, as they finished up, "All done with what we have here." She told her friend. "Let us know when the other stuff arrives, so we can open those presents!"

Shana chuckled, "Will do!"

The five climbed into the vehicle, Nikki called driver, and Adam just chuckled and handed her the keys. "Meet at breakfast tomorrow to look at the cliff for what to do?" Adam asked, slipping into the back seat, beside Brook.

There were several calls of agreement from the others to the plan. "Evan and Kuri like to do climbing," Brook commented, "I'll have them join us."

They got back to the pack house just in time for dinner. Sitting down with their friends, Brook smiled at Kuri and Evan, "I know tomorrow is your day off, but would you like to do some climbing?"

Both perked up, as Brook knew they would; both loved to climb. Brook agreed with her wolf, who preferred to have her paws firmly on the ground. Well, other than when she was pouncing!

Adam grinned, "I need to find out if there's an easy way to put this side of the radio link up."

Evan laughed. "I know of a nice cave, a bit above the top of the trees, and with a clear view of the town, too."

"Perfect!" Adam exclaimed, "That would work well! We can look at it tomorrow."

Brook shuddered, "I'm staying on the ground." She stated, firmly. "I'll start figuring out what people want for computers."

Several of those at the table called out what they wanted, as well. Most just wanted laptops, but beyond that didn't really care. The dinner chat turned to what sort of stuff they wanted it for, mostly for getting onto websites, and seeing what was there.

Once Brook was done, she stood and stretched, "I feel like a run, who's with me?"

Everyone clamoured to go; most wolves loved running. It not only was good exercise but was also a good way to run off extra energy or stress. Adam looked on wistfully, "I'll catch you later!" He knew he would not be able to keep up with them on a run. Brook gave him a good kiss, "I'll see you soon," she told him.

Adam held in his sigh as he went back to their room and relaxed for a bit, and double checked the wireless link calculations, making sure the link appeared to be correct, and the gear would be correct.

*****

Brook felt sorry Adam couldn't join them for the enjoyable run and play time. Her wolf kept pushing her to cut the time short and return to her mate.

She could smell that his changes following the mating were nearly complete. She was going to wait to tell him, till he got the network link done, as they had talked about getting that project done first. From what she had seen, he had gotten used to always having an internet connection at hand and was trying to get it out at the pack house. She was surprised he had decided to move before it was ready and it showed her that she and her happiness were more important to him than any other contacts; it really warmed her heart, and all his little touches just made her love him more.

Snorting, she decided to give into the pleading of her wolf and head back. She padded in the main door silently and headed into their suite. Brook snuck up behind Adam, as he sat on the couch reading a book. Getting close she gave the side of his face a good lick, startling him. His book went flying, and he fell off the couch. She wagged her tail in silent laughter, as she padded around the couch to nuzzle him on the face.

*****

Adam thought he heard the door, but was too engrossed in his book, having had no quiet time to read in the last week. Suddenly he was getting a lick, and he had an automatic reaction. When he saw Brook's beautiful wolf walking around the couch, he glared at her. When she nuzzled him, he wrapped his arms around her neck and wrestled her a bit, before just cuddling into her fur as she won, and she laid down across him—as was normal; she was stronger and had much more stability with four paws.

Kissing her nose, he just relaxed, enjoying the warm attention, "I thought you would be out much longer," he commented.

My wolf wasn't happy about leaving you and whined the entire time to go back to you. I finally gave in and returned.

Smiling at the growl in the sending, he kissed her nose again, "Thank you my wolf. I knew she really loved me too." Sighing, he commented, "I can't wait till we can go on runs together. By my calculations, I should be ready by Monday. I'm going to get the internet working and show our friends how to do the wireless access points and let them deal with the tedious work of getting it installed." He would do the basic organization, but not the actual installs.

Both ended up just cuddling together for the rest of the evening, laying before the fire, listening to the crackles, before heading to bed, banking the fire, and continuing the snuggles for the night.

*****

Brook and Adam ate the usual excellent breakfast with their friends, before splitting up to their tasks. Adam told Shana to contact Brook, as he was going to be on the cliffs, and they agreed it was safer.

Giving a last kiss, he followed Kuri and Evan, to get geared up and head to the cliff, hanging onto his binoculars to confirm his eyes.

Climbing up the side of the cliff was hard, and exhausting, as he had never done it; his climbing had been on indoor climbing walls. Reaching the cave made it all worthwhile. It was large enough to fit all the gear they could want, with a nearby fissure which ran vertically almost right down to the pack house. It was convenient and made for some different plans for it.

*Shana, have a minute?** Adam called, pretty sure he had the right place in direct view.

Sure, what do you need?

Can you go on the roof; I think I'll be able to see you.

Getting a silent agreement, even if she was confused as to why he was asking her, he waited and saw the roof hatch open and Shana climb out, *Yup! Got the right place. Thanks!*

Hearing her a bit confused, *I thought you were climbing the cliff this morning, where are you?*

Adam sends a chuckle, *I am up on the cliff sitting in a small cave and can see you with binoculars. I was checking the building I thought I saw was correct and was completely clear from here. Look North-east, and a bit above the trees. I'm the dark spot.*

Ah! I think I see you; wave?

Adam gave a big wave, wondering if her eyes were that much better than his.

Yup, I see you. That is funny, the pack house is right near there? Could almost do a zip line from there!

Adam laughed outright to that *Almost but would be hard to hide it. I'm done with what I needed you for, thanks!*

Welcome. Oh, here's a delivery truck. Might be your stuff. If it is, I'll let Brook know and have them put it beside the data room.

Adam smiled and let her go, turning to Evan and Kuri, "This cave is perfect for what I need; high enough to have clear sight, but low enough to ease access. We'll need to make a ladder, bolt it to the cliff, and do something for the wiring." Measuring the cave, he had about seven feet across, and about four tall at the opening, but it was over seven tall a bit farther back and was about fifteen feet deep. He considered getting a larger cabinet up here, and what exactly he wanted to do. Seeing a small hole in the side, he smiled as it went straight to the fissure which ran down the side of the cliff to the ground, and near the pack house, "I have the hidden wiring way; it's going to be much more work to install, but once installed it will be much, much easier to work with. It's almost like this was made for this!"

He quickly gave his findings to the Alpha, who was very happy and gave approval. As it happened, Rein was about to leave to pick up some building supplies to fix a railing which was damaged from a fight, and got him to wait till after lunch, while he figured out what exactly he needed.

*****

By the time he was down on the ground, they had worked out the cave was seventy meters above the ground, so they needed twenty-three 10-foot lengths of conduit. It was about fifty to the house. Shaking his head at the luck, he quickly worked out to get 30 pipes and decided to go with 2-inch aluminum. It was many connectors, and they'd need to seal them as well, so added a case of silicone and a couple caulking guns. Added a pipe bender, and a case of liquid nails, as it would be impossible to get the strapping in to secure it in the crack. He added on a couple cases of Tapcon screws, as he could use them directly into the rock with only needing to pre-drill the holes. Next, he added a couple of large fall-arrest anchor loops, so he could mount them in the cave, and a spool of heavy aircraft wire, which was rated for a fall-arrest line. He could make an ascender route easily, till they had the time to manufacture a wire and steel ladder, at which point the ascender lines would be just fall-arrest cables. He added on a spool of 12/2 Armoured Outdoor rated cable, an Outdoor box for the top, some clips to secure it all. Realising the length of his order, he decided he should just go with Rein. He grabbed Brook on the way to help as well.

Rein grumbled but accepted the help when he saw the length of the order, "They may not have the amount of stuff you need in stock." He warned.

Adam shrugged and climbed into the truck and helped Brook up, "That's fine. I can deal without most and set up a tacky temporary link to get it running if I need to."

*****

Coming out of the hardware store laughing, all three pushing a heavy carts full of gear. Adam commented after they had loaded it up, "That sure was funny! Can you believe our luck, one order was cancelled so they were overstocked on the conduit and connectors, and another for the cables we needed? We have everything we need to get it going." The manager had even given them an extra box of network cable for free, as it had also been part of the cancelled order, and they needed to get rid of it.

They had let the Alpha know they were going to need plenty of help but had everything they needed and were going to get the link done by the weekend.

Shana had let them know the wireless gear was there, so they could get it ready and prep the side at the warehouse first and try to get the spot aligned first, before returning to help get the conduit in place. A temporary link of network cable was going in, even though it was pushing the limits by spec, for 100 metres between devices, but Adam wasn't too worried. He had at one point just used an entire 500-foot spool of cable as a temporary link, and it had worked correctly. The fibre had to be ordered in but could be done later.

They were all still smiling when they got back to the parking area with all the supplies. A couple of Argos with long trailers were waiting to haul the gear. Adam's was going to just stay on the trailers overnight and be dealt with in the morning. Rein's was going to the woodshop to be dealt with as they had time, since it needed painting first and it was too cold to do it outside and have the wood seal correctly.

Heading in, word had already spread that the link would be ready by the end of the weekend, at least where there was existing internet.

*****

The next morning, after the now usual good breakfast, Adam and Brook, along with the trio of helpers quickly got down to the warehouse to start working on that end of the link, while some helpers started working on the low-tech parts of the link; the conduit and the safety systems and getting everything prepped for them. There were several who wanted to do the work and knew what was needed to be done. Every joint in the conduit line needed to be waterproofed.

It took very little time to unpack the equipment and show how the gear worked. They programmed the radio to the settings and turned as much stealth on it they could and the basic security, as the infrastructure needed for the more advanced configuration was not available, yet. The technology needed some servers up and running to be able to handle it. Hopefully, the security he used would be enough.

After only a couple hours, the link was all ready, and they had also configured the other half of the link, and tested it in the parking lot, so it was just needing to be installed in the cave.

Getting back to the pack house, Adam was astonished how much was done. The conduit was fully installed, and the liquid nails were curing it into place, the network and power cords had been run. They just needed the drill they brought back from the warehouse to punch into the house and connect up the power and network.

Passing the Hilti Drill with a smile, the hole was quickly drilled, as Adam got geared up to get up the cliff. He smiled as some wolves just used the rope to pull him up the face, so all he had to do was basically walk up the cliff, carrying the gear he needed.

Getting to the top, they had already connected the power inside, so he plugged in a UPS—basically a power bar with a built-in backup battery, and with the wiring fault light out when he turned it on, knew it was working right, they quickly drilled holes in the cave floor at the front, for the antenna's mount. Attaching the mount was easy, the Tapcon bolts biting right into the rock, self-tapping the holes, and the size and length would hold them in permanently—or till they decided to remove them. The antenna and radio were quickly installed and powered up. Adam took more time than he absolutely needed, as he was showing Aurora and Nikki how and what to do as well.

They planned on some camouflage for the front of the cave, but to get some which wouldn't interfere with the radios was going to take a few days.

Can you see the connection? Adam called to Brook, who had stayed at the warehouse.

Yup, and the signal strength and quality are excellent. I did turn down the power a bit, and still going solid. We just need to get the house online to test the speed, but the test you showed me was great between the two radios. See you in an hour or so. By the way, they came by to drill the hole for the fibre, and the conduit for it is ready. The fibre team will be by mid-morning to get it completed. Even she was getting excited, as the last major piece was the connecting the Wi-Fi in the building once the fibre link was completed the next day. She was just going to run back as a wolf, since she then could be back early in the morning, to wait while Adam showed Erin, Aurora, and Nikki how to start getting the Wi-Fi installed.

Adam had been informed his Mating had completed and got the all-clear from the Pack Healer to be turned the night before, while Brook was out on her run. They had to get the formal approval from the Alpha to let him be turned, but when between mates, it was more a formality.

When Brook got back, they tested the link from his laptop to the small router in the warehouse's room and were pleased with the link.

At lunch, Adam stood up, and at a howl from Brook, the pack quieted down. "I have an announcement to make! With everyone's help, the work to get the wireless link is done; we are waiting on the fibre line to connect the internet here. Those places which have internet, will have a much faster connection soon. We are hoping to switch over within a couple of days!" The cheer and howls which greeted his announcement,

Adam thought it must have been heard back in town, it was so loud. It did affix a grin to his face, though.

After lunch, Brook took Adam back down to the kennels, "I think this is the time to pick one out. We have all afternoon free to bond. The trio are dealing with getting the server rack and the parts in the room ready for tomorrow."

Smiling, Adam responded, "Delegating already, I see. I think so, too," as they wandered off to the kennels.

CHAPTER 7

Pet Choosing

Adam and Brook wandered around looking at all the wolf hybrids, most giving them their deference, able to sense they were dominant. Many did come up to sniff, but then went off to do their own thing.

Over an hour later, one large male, which at a glance looked like a wolf in his fur colour with a mix of greys with black highlights and well-muscled though somewhat lean body shape, came up, sniffed them both. Unlike all the others, then nuzzled and whined at Adam, wagging his tail. He was clearly on the large side, although not as big as Brook, he was bigger than all the others which had come to sniff at them.

Brook smiled, "I was hoping this would happen. Many decide themselves who they want to be with. This one has decided he wants to be with you. His name is Charlie."

Adam had started absently giving him a good scratch behind the ears, and smiled, "I like him too. How trained is he?"

"He's Two, so basic commands, how to open doors to get outside. He's also had some self-defence and protection training. Since he's bonded to you, he won't want to go too far away, but if he needs to run, he will take himself for one then come back. They do accept mental commands, and he's one of the smartest around. Largest, too."

Looking down, Adam commanded, "Charlie, sit."

Charlie sat and watched him, wagging his tail. The look in his eyes was one of intelligence. Adam knelt beside him, and Charlie nuzzled his face. As Brook had told him, he, touched his forehead to Charlie's. The bond was near instantaneous. It left Adam stunned for a moment, as he felt the warmth of Charlie's care and love for him. He grinned up at his mate, "He's perfect." He told her, as he hugged Charlie tightly around the neck, sending him his own love. Charlie leaned into Adam gently, whining slightly.

"Let's take him for a jog for a bit," Brook offered. It would help them bond.

Nodding in reply, Adam called for Charlie to come. They picked up a nice collar on the way out, and a leash for when they were in Human areas. The caretakers promised the rest of his supplies and his papers would be put in his room soon.

Charlie padded beside Adam, enjoying the run. He acted as if he was leashed, even though he wasn't.

Coming back, Adam noticed they already had a bowl of water for Charlie beside the bathroom, with a soft pad by the couch. They had been told they had some Thetas assigned to them, but so far hadn't caught a glimpse of them; just doors closing after them.

After a shower with Brook, Adam went to talk to the Alpha to get formal approval for being turned. Brook had said for mates, it really wasn't required, but was better to have it, as then the Alpha could make sure you knew what you were getting into. Charlie followed him, keeping close. It took a bit, but he found Gareth relaxing in the pack hot pool in the greenhouse. After being asked some questions to quiz his knowledge of being turned, to make sure he knew what he was getting into, the approval was quickly given.

"But," Gareth added, "Please wait for a couple of days, so we can make sure the network connection is all working, and your helpers know what to do for the next couple of weeks, please."

Adam nodded, "I can do that." He agreed. He didn't say it had been his plan already.

Heading back, he flopped on the couch beside Brook, and wrapped an arm around her, as she put down the book she was reading. Both enjoyed some downtime before dinner. Charlie climbed on the couch, and dropped his head in Adam's lap, begging for attention.

As he started to stroke Charlie's head with his other hand, he told his mate the result, "Well, we have approval, but were asked to wait a couple of days, so Monday I can be turned."

Brook nodded, "Well, you had all the information, and still decided to go for it. Morning on Monday. You need to fast Sunday night then, and no breakfast. The first bit as you know is the hardest on your body and fasting before the change helps prevent any issues."

Cuddling, he kissed her temple, "You know best."
*****

Supper that night, once everyone was there, Adam stood up to say a few words, "I want to thank everyone who helped get the network connection wired into the cliff. Tomorrow, the fibre link should be ready to go. Once it has been tested, we will switch over all the existing links to the new one. At which point we will be starting to install wireless throughout the building, starting on the first floor."

Taking a deep breath, he decided to let everyone know now, "Most of the work will be organised by Erin, with Aurora and Nikki helping, as I am planning on starting my turn on Monday." A very loud howl was heard, as many took years before they decided to turn, his wanting it right away showed he was committed to the Pack and cared for their ways. Some decided to have a betting pool to figure out when, it would happen. Brook put down for three weeks, and many looked at her weird, as it was a very short time, she just smiled sweetly. Other just glared at her, as rarely did they win if she entered, with some deciding to not bet against her, and walked away before placing their bets after learning she had placed a bet.
*****

The next day went without a hitch; the fibre was installed and tested quickly, the installers commenting it was nice to deal with such a short link. As it turned out, they had needed to do only about a block, as another company had recently paid to run fibre into the community for their own connection, with an oil pipeline. By the end of the day, the gamers were almost bouncing off the walls with the connection running so well. Adam, Brook, and their trio of techies, Erin, Aurora, and Nikki installed a few access points, and Adam showed them the way to figure out where to install them. Once the Alpha's suite and the Beta wing had been done, he left the trio to go at it, letting them know there was no rush; he wanted it done right not fast.

The next morning, Adam woke up, snuggled against Brook, but also had a warm body on the other side, taking a breath, he smelled Charlie's slightly musky scent. Just like the night before, he had curled up against him. He smiled, as he had missed having an animal show affection by curling up with him. He smiled, and let himself doze off, not wanting to get up, as it was still early, and neither of the other two seemed to be awake. He had grown up with a cat in the house, and they had regularly cuddled him at night.

He was dozing when he felt Charlie get up, jump off the bed, shake, then open the patio door, and go outside. A short time later, he heard the door open again as he padded back in before jumping back up on the bed to flop down against him again. He smiled at the thoughts of the very smart dog, and how he didn't need to housetrain him; he knew how to let himself out! He was glad the doors were self-closing, too.

Just as he was falling back asleep, a knock at the door got a low growl from Charlie, before Aurora called out, "If you are wanting breakfast, you will need to get up now, they are preparing the late sitting!" Due to the size of the pack, there were three 'sittings' of times which people came, although nothing was official, and they tended to make it to the early one. That they slept through two and are just going to make the third was unusual. It tended to be the teens who went to it, as the next chance for more than the foods which didn't spoil fast which were left out between the meals. Hot food was only served at the regular mealtimes.

Adam groaned and stretched, giving Brook a nudge, "I guess it's much later than I thought it was, time to get up for breakfast."

Brook groaned, but stretched, blinking, "You go, I'll be there shortly."

Adam gave her a kiss, as Charlie jumped off the bed, doing his own stretch as Adam threw some clothes on and followed Aurora out to the dining room. Adam grabbed a bowl with some sausage and bacon putting it down for Charlie; the dogs ate nearly the same food as them, which really cut down on any attempted begging. Charlie could present himself to the kitchen for food, or go off to the kennels, but Adam already enjoyed making sure his buddy got fed himself.

Adam then picked up several slices of French Toast, some eggs, sausage, and bacon. Sitting down in a random spot, he nodded a greeting to those beside him, before grabbing the cut fruit and maple syrup. Brook dropped into the seat next to him as he started to eat, looking a little tired. Her plate was very similar but had pancakes on it.

I guess I wore both of us out last night, Adam teased, as he looked at Brook, out of the corner of his eye, continuing to eat, as he was very hungry this morning. That was one very nice thing about the talking mentally, could have a conversation while eating, and one which nobody else could overhear.

She blushed at the comment, deciding to tease back, *I guess we both had a little too much fun, but we have a day to ourselves today. Nothing is planned, so I want to show you a couple of places deep in the forest.* She sent a couple mental images of what they could do there.

Adam blushed, and sent a wordless agreement, and some love, before picking up his empty plate, and decided on the sourdough pancakes for a second helping. Noticing Charlie was sitting by the empty bowl looking mournful, gave him a nod. Charlie grabbed the bowl in his mouth and brought it over. Adam filled it half full of some more food and held it out. Wagging his tail in thanks, grabbed the bowl, and took it back to the previous spot, before starting to eat his second helping.

Sitting down, Adam playfully bumped Brook's shoulder lightly, she bumped him back as she went to get more, as she glanced over at Charlie, *I guess all three of us were hungry this morning.*

When they finished, Brook and Adam headed out the door, Charlie scampered back the way they came. Adam shrugged, as he'd catch up to them shortly. They had just made it to the forest, when Charlie bounded up, with a pack in his jaws. Brook grabbed it and gave Charlie a scratch to the ears in thanks, "I am surprised that worked already. Usually, it takes some training to get them to listen to a mate of the one they chose. Saved me a trip getting the pack, though."

Adam opened his mouth to ask why she needed his camera bag and what she had added to it, as the top pouches appeared stuffed too, but Brook shook her head as she put the bag on her back, "No asking. It's a surprise. Although I did pack your camera."

After an enjoyable hike through the forest, they reached a ridge. Charlie had been bounding around them, sniffing out various things, and leaving some scent markers behind, but staying within sight of the two. As they stopped at the view, Adam smiled and grabbed his camera from the bag, "I can see why you wanted it. It's a beautiful view." The valley below them was a cupped shape, with a small lake in the middle, some grass and moss clearings, and thick forests around it, and several mountains surrounding it.

Snapping some pictures, he commented, "I love it. One of these is going up on our wall."

Brook grinned, and started down into the valley, enjoying the time with her Mate. She was looking forward to being able to really explore more when he became a wolf too, "I'm glad. Some of my favourite spots are impossible to reach in human form and will have to wait for your wolf."

Nodding in agreement, "I can't wait!" Adam commented, as he followed her down a nearly non-existent path.

Reaching the meadow beside the water, Brook placed the pack down, and stripped, "I'm going for a swim, want to join me?"

Adam grinned, "Sure," as he too took his clothes off and chased her into the water. Adam didn't think about how the mountain-fed lake just felt refreshing, not cold, like it would have been to a human who lacked the changes from the Mating Bite.

They even had Charlie join them for some fun in the water for a bit, before he climbed out, and after a good shake, went by their stuff for a nap.

Eventually, Brook and Adam climbed out of the water, and headed towards the pack. Brook opened one pouch and pulled out a couple of towels, tossing one to Adam.

"Have any food hiding in there? I'm getting hungry!"

Brook looked up at the sun, and estimated it was already near noon, "Sure. I had Jess get some for us while we had breakfast." She tossed some sandwiches and a couple pieces of fruit to Adam.

Grabbing them out of the air, "Thanks!" as he started to eat. He didn't realise his hand-eye coordination was much better than it had ever been. He had never been able to catch something out of the air before.

Brook then tossed a chunk of jerky to Charlie, so he wouldn't be a mooch.

After the food was gone, Brook cuddled up to Adam, as he took some more pictures, some of the mountains, others of the valley, and some of Charlie as he snoozed.

"Need to get some of me?" Brook teased.

"Already got some nice ones!" Adam replied cheekily, "Although I probably won't show them to anyone else..." before sending mental images of what he had taken.

Brook blushed a bit, as there hadn't been a scrap of cloth in them!

"I'll have to get you back!" Brook threatened.

Adam grinned, "Go for it!" He had no problem with her getting pictures of him without his clothes, especially now he was much more fit.

Getting up, Brook offered a hand to Adam, "I have a couple more places to show you today."

Adam grinned, and let her pull him up, "Okay!" He looked around to make sure they had everything packed up, then dressed. Walking nude through the forest was not much fun, even if they could, as they were unlikely to see humans. Even the wolves tended to travel with fur to protect them from thorns and branches.

When Adam had asked about what sort of security the pack had, he had only been told about what he had already seen, and anything else, would have to wait till after he was Turned. From what he saw, it was mostly actual patrols which kept them safe. He had some ideas for changes to make sure they didn't rely solely on the patrols, but anything tech-related could be overcome, so would also have the patrols.

Shaking his head from it, he just wanted to enjoy the day with his mate. Following her, he could hear a waterfall in the distance. Turning a corner at the edge of a ridge, he came to a magical little glade, with a five-metre waterfall, to a small pond, which had ferns and moss around it, and he smiled, "This is very beautiful."

He decided not to take any pictures right now, as it would look good with a long exposure turning the water silky smooth, but he didn't have his tripod to do the picture justice. He'd have to investigate it, as there had to be a way to make the water smooth, without a long exposure.

Brook looked at him curiously, "No pictures?"

Shaking his head, "Need my tripod to do justice to it, so we'll have to come back another time."

She grinned, "Works for me!"

Leading him out the way he came, Brook commented, "This last place I have never scented another wolf at, and want to keep it secret, so please don't tell anyone where it is."

Nodding, "I like it, a place we only know about."

Climbing part of the ridge but staying somewhat near the water, she led him to a hidden tiny pocket valley which had a long series of small waterfalls, filling the air with the gentle babble of water. Not much in the way of grass, the ground was covered in a thick spongy moss layer, with ferns lapping at the water around small pools. Pulling him along around a boulder, they could see a series of several small steaming pools in the rocks, which showed natural hot pools with the water draining off to the cold stream. The highest one seemed to be the hottest, with lots of steam coming off it. The lowest, as he put his hand in, was warm, but would allow for a long soak.

Looking out into the distance, there was a panoramic view overlooking the valley to the east, with lots of mountains all around.

"It's beyond beautiful. I bet sunrises are breathtaking up here with the view."

Brook nodded, "Even a simple one is great from here. We'll have to come up here again. Even in winter, the hot pool keeps this area reasonably warm, for a wolf."

Adam grinned at Brook, "I can see us coming up here for a weekend away from everyone once in a while." Adam smiled and decided a nice warm soak was what he needed to relax, as he was starting to get nervous about the Turning the next morning. After disrobing, he hopped in the third lowest, it being warm, but not too hot for a good soak. Brook joined him almost immediately, cuddling up to his side.

Charlie only stuck a paw in, before pulling it out with a snort, it being too warm for him, with his thick winter fur. He tested the coolest one before climbing into a shallow part and laying his head on the edge.

Both Adam and Brook watched him with some amusement, enjoying his antics. Both felt quite happy with his choice—well, Charlie's choice—as it seemed a very good fit all around.

After a while of meditation, the water was starting to feel too hot for Adam. Looking at the sun, he realised they needed to head back to make it for dinner. Giving Brook a hug, to bring her out of her own meditation, "I think it is time to head back for supper; don't you agree?"

Brook blinked, looking at the sun, "Yes, and we'll need to hurry a bit to make it in time. Good thing it is all downhill."

Looking around, Charlie had climbed out of the water, and was sleeping on a soft bed of moss. Adam gave a low whistle, and Charlie immediately popped his head up, "Time to go," he told him. Charlie stood and gave a stretch, before walking over to them as they dried off and dressed.

The trip back was made at a reasonable pace, not the stroll they did getting there. They made it in time to have dinner with their friends, though they lingered over desert, enjoying the company of the pack now they were refreshed by the alone time.

They chatted about the various ideas Adam had received from the pack, some were so outrageous, like a request for a light sabre, or for a holodeck, having a good laugh over them; no names were mentioned, as it would have been mean. Others were reasonable, as in requests for a computer with specific specs, which he could do, or private phone line to chat with friends outside of the pack, which was one he already had in the works, to several which were basically completed already: asking for internet they could do multi-player gaming with.

Many had just requested specific devices, even to the point of listing models. Some he would accept, others he would ask them to pay for them, as some brand names were pricey for what they offered, and other brands offered better specs at lower prices. Some he wasn't too interested in dealing with, but since he wasn't going to be tech support, he would see if those techs wanted to support them first. A couple of brands he wasn't wanting to deal with due to their policies towards those which made their products, and their environmental policies.

Brook was starting to like overseeing all the tech, as it had already opened her eyes to what was possible. She had grown up with very little tech, but with a bright and inquisitive mind, and the help from picking her mate's mind, she was nearly up to his speed. It helped he had many tech books to learn from; although most were written so dry, she had fallen asleep to them, or had needed to do something else after only a chapter or so. Adam even rated some of them as being sedatives!

It was late in the evening when they broke up and heading off, to get a good night's rest.

Brook decided to take Adam for a hard run to burn off his nervous energy before bed, so he could drop off to sleep quickly. The path she took wove around and through the trees, following cleared paths used for training. To keep it fun, they played tag, with Brook working to stay close and not out distance Adam, although she had to fight her wolf to not do a hard run and make him really work at it. They finally returned when he was dripping with sweat and with slightly rubbery legs, although the last bit she kept it slow with some stretch stops, as a cooldown. Getting back, she had him soak in the tub with an aromatic oil to put him to sleep.

When she checked on him later, after she had a quick shower, he was dozing in the water, so she helped him out, and into bed. Smiling that her plan worked, she crawled in and cuddled against him. Charlie climbed up and curled up on Adam's other side before also going to sleep.

*****

The next morning, Brook was up for the regular breakfast, but Adam was still deeply asleep, silently she got Charlie to come with her for breakfast. He wolfed his food down, and he headed back to curl up with Adam, feeling he needed to guard him. Brook lingered a bit, chatting with their friends, but keeping her mind open to sense when Adam was waking up. When she felt the first stirrings, she excused herself and headed back.

Brook got there in time to be the first thing he saw as he opened his eyes, greeting him warmly with a smile.

"Morning!" Adam replied, as he stretched the kinks from his body, "So when are you going to bite me?" he asked, meaning for the turning.

"Right now," she commented with a giggle at his pun.

"Are you ready to become a Wolf?" She started, the words heavy with tradition. She had been taught the traditional words when she came of age and had the ability to Turn, along with the rules for it, and the consequences if the rules were not followed; many could end in death. It did make sense, as pups could be mouthy, and like to nibble. A few had the ability early, but most of them were Alpha's pups.

"I am." Adam answered soberly, noticing the weight of the traditional words.

"Do you agree to uphold the laws and traditions of the People you are joining, even when they conflict with the laws and traditions of the way you were raised?"

"I do,"

"You have been given what will happen once you are bitten, yet you want to be turned. Do any questions linger?"

"No, I have no questions unanswered."

"Once bitten, the changes are permanent, and will exist beyond the end of this life. Do you wish for this?"

"I do."

Brook smiled at Adam, "Prepare yourself then to be Turned." She intoned, ending the traditional sayings, before she shifted to her hybrid shape, towering over the bed. Adam just gazed at her, having no fear of her, thinking she was very beautiful. She had been taught the best way to make sure to have a mate turn the fastest, and surest, was to do it while in the hybrid Were form and during sex. It was the way that Mate-Turns were always done, from what she had been told, but they still could bite and turn in any form.

Brook slipped forward lapping her wolfish tongue over him, arousing him for the turning. Adam tried to remember more of what happened but could only remember she was to bite when both climaxed, so the endorphins helped with the pain and to speed the changes. His mind didn't want to think beyond that. All he remembered was her warm body. Just as he felt the orgasm hit, he tilted his head, and felt her strike.

CHAPTER 8

The Turning

A searing pain lanced Adam's neck and started to spread till it encircled his neck, feeling like he had poured very hot water on it, as it moved down his body and up to his jaw, and over his head, and down his body. He started gasping, not even having the breath to scream, the feeling moving to cover more of his body. He fought hard to stay conscious, as he didn't want to pass out.

His stomach started to heave, but he barely felt it, as his body was screaming out. He felt like his veins had been filled with fire, and his heart was pumping it around faster and faster, causing the feeling to spread.

He nearly missed hearing Brook talking to him, but not touching, as for the first hour, the lightest touch could be agony, "Ignore your body, it will pass, just listen to my voice. Remember what we did yesterday, and how enjoyable it was. Think about where we were when you first saw me."

As he worked to turn his mind away from his body, the blackness which was trying to engulf him faded a bit, and the feeling of pain receded a bit, till it felt like he had just jumped in a hot pool which was a bit too hot, instead of being boiled alive. His breathing evened out, although his heart and breaths felt like he was running hard while lying still.

*****

Eventually after a couple hours, which felt like weeks to Adam, his skin stopped hurting, and he just felt wrung out, and a bit ill. He didn't even have the energy to lift an arm. He opened his eyes, which took all his energy, to see his lovely mate looking relieved as she smiled at him.

"You made it through the hardest part. The first is basically the injection of the virus, and your body treats it as foreign, so tries to fight it. Right now, we are in isolation, as it basically reduces your immune system to nearly non-existent while it re-writes your DNA. The mildest cold could kill you right now. Your bite has already scarred, so it took correctly."

Adam nodded slightly, not having the energy to speak.

"Once it has re-written the white blood cells and your bone marrow where they are formed, you will get some of your energy back, and it will stop suppressing your immune system." She reminded him. Knowing he was going to be feeling parched, she offered him a little bit of water with a straw. Medical had provided the sterile water and would be providing the food for her.

Adam didn't want to stop when she pulled the cup away and made a tired noise of complaint.

"You can have some more later. Too much and you could be sick, and I would prefer to not need to move you too much."

Nodding slightly, he closes his eyes, to let his body rest as it adjusted. Being told how bad it would be, and now feeling it were two separate things. He told himself it was just a passing pain, to get what he wanted.

He felt Brook slide in beside him and pull the blanket over them. He gave a slight smile as he drifted off, knowing his mate would keep him safe.

*****

Adam woke with a start, nausea rolling through him, as his stomach heaved. Brook placed a clean bin under his head, as he dry-heaved, just a little bit of bile coming up.

After a bit, he collapsed back with a groan, having used up all his energy.

Brook was there with a damp cloth to put on his hot head, "You're almost to the next step; you're going to start feeling better, soon. As soon as your fever is gone, and your temperature is down to that of a wolf, I can let Charlie back in, as your immune system will be back working. He's been guarding the patio door since I made him stay out there. Unfortunately, you will probably have more nausea then."

Adam pulled the cloth down over his eyes, as they were hurting and tried to relax enough to fall asleep, as from the few which had talked to him and who had gone through it, sleeping it off was the best for the first few days. Most passed out with the bite and were out for several days, waking only for some water.

*****

Again, he awoke with nausea, and again Brook was right there with a bin. He sighed as he lay back, his head feeling better.

Brook pulled out an ear thermometer, "Let me check," as she pulled his hair out of the way and checked his temperature, ignoring the indication he was nearly dangerous, as he was down to what was normal for a werewolf, "You are now down to the new normal, thirty-nine-C. I'm going to let Charlie back in, he's been wanting to see you."

Hearing her unlock the patio door, and a scamper of claws across the ground, he could smell him as he entered the door, "Well, my nose is working better." He clapped his hands to his head, as it sounded like it had been highly amplified.

Think about a dial in your head listed as sound, Brook instructed, *Turn the dial down.*

Closing his eyes, he did as she told him, and everything quietened down, he let out a sigh, but then started to smell every little thing, so he did the same with his sense of smell.

Opening his eyes, "That is better. And other than feeling sick to my stomach, and it hurting to move, I'm feeling much better."

Brook smiled at her mate, "That is good; it means the changes are now on your bones and your soft tissue nearly done. If you were to be cut, it would heal fast.

Charlie had jumped on the bed but had stayed away while he had his hands to his face, now laid gently beside him and whined softly, "Good boy, Charlie. I know you wanted to be here, but you couldn't; now you can." Adam commented, his voice going hoarse.

"You need some water," Brook commented, giving him some water, "You have had almost nothing in the two days since I bit you."

He spat out the straw in surprise, "Two *days*?" he repeated.

Brook nodded, "It is nearly noon on Wednesday. We need to get you up to use the bathroom, and a shower. I know I need a shower too."

When she said 'shower', he started to feel how grungy his skin felt, and nodded slightly.

Brook moved to his side and helped him sit up and held him while his body adjusted from two days of laying down. Once he was ready, she moved his legs and helped him stand, wrapping an arm around him, to hold him upright. Once he was steady, she walked him, step by small step into the washroom, letting him sit on the toilet while she warmed up the shower, and gave her body a quick wash; her hair could wait for another time. Charlie followed them into the bathroom, clearly not wanting to be far away.

When he was done with the toilet, she helped him up and into the shower stall.

"It feels cold," Adam complained. It wasn't cold, just cooler than what he liked, but he didn't have the energy to reach up and warm it up. He barely had the energy to stand, with the help of a bar mounted in the wall. He was almost panting with the effort.

Brook just smiled and moved to adjust the temperature dial up a bit, "It's because your body temperature is now higher, you'll feel cooler when it's warm, but you can also stand colder temperatures without needing to bundle up. It also means it is harder for you to get heat exhaustion or hypothermia.

"That makes sense. I hate feeling hot or cold, so it's a bonus. It's probably a good thing for when you are needing to shift outside in winter."

Brook nodded, as she finished washing him, "Now back to bed, so you can rest. There's a day left for your bones, and then three while the changes settle in."

Adam nodded and let her help him walk slowly to the bed, which he noticed their nearly invisible servants, the twins Jess and Joshua, had already changed the sheets for them. He could smell that two had been there. He'd have to think of something very nice to give them in thanks, as Brook helped him lay back down in the middle and covered him with a sheet. Charlie had moved back onto the bed, and now pressed him to one side, as Brook lay on the other while he rested.

Brook had told him Jess and Joshua were Thetas, and being so young, were near the bottom of the pack. They were given the position to care for Adam and Brook, as their first real job, as they were just turning twenty in March. This was a great honour and privilege they didn't want to waste, as if they did a good job, they could be set for life. Since Adam and Brook were not much older than them, they could stay with them for life, if they didn't do something extremely bad, or Adam or Brook didn't ask for them to be reassigned. Adam had already learned if they did, it would be a very bad mark for them, as it would show they didn't trust them to do the work to care for them. He didn't want to get someone sentenced to cleaning common areas for their life.

Adam wasn't aware, but he already treated them better than some members of the pack; some thought the Thetas were there to do whatever they wanted and didn't treat them as people. He had already stopped several of the older pups from high-ranking parents from beating on pups from Theta parents. It was often the pups had similar rankings, but some—like Rein—came from Theta parents. It surprised him, and in some packs, they were not allowed to apply for more than one rank up from their parents. Sadly, some parents also kept their pups from applying higher, and it was harder to change ranks once they became adults and were doing the duties of a rank.

Once he was a Wolf, he'd have the authority and ability to discipline the offenders, and he was looking forward to it. He suspected he'd get some more Thetas under his protection, since he cared about them as a person, not just an object. He had noticed Brook felt the same way, since she had friends more from the senior ranks as she grew up more with them but had no problem with Thetas joining in and knew most by name. Often, as they walked around, she gave quick hugs or even just touches to wolves they passed, often greeting them by name.

Adam winced as a bone twinged sharply but knew painkillers didn't last long, and had to be taken very carefully, as to not become dependent on them. He had been told it was better to just ride it out without anything. Having his mate beside him helped lots; the adage of 'Pain shared is pain halved' at work.

"How long do you expect before my wolf awakens, do you think?" Adam asked, trying to take his mind off the pain.

Brook thought for a moment, "It depends. For you, I sort of expect it to be a short time. Even when I met you, you seemed a bit wolfish. I'm thinking about a week after you are back on your feet, which should be next Monday."

Brook picked up a container of some water, offering the straw to Adam, "You need to drink. You must keep your fluids up."

Adam drank a few sips of water, before stopping, "More later; I don't want to throw up. My stomach is still feeling very sensitive."

"Lay back and rest, the more rest you get, the easier the changes are on your body," Brook soothed, already wanting this tough week to be over. She was glad the hardest parts were behind them, but the shift would be a test, as some had a hard time letting go of their human body. As such, they had a hard time controlling their wolf-side, and some had to be restrained till they learned. She believed Adam wasn't going to be one of those.

Looking over, she noticed Adam had fallen asleep, smiling, she decided to take a nap, but brought her wolf forward, to wake her if he moved ever so slightly. Even though they had two helpers, her wolf growled and wouldn't let them near their mate while he was so vulnerable, not yet trusting them that far. They understood and didn't take it personally. Charlie had taken the hint and was also very protective, which made her wolf love him too.

*****

Over the next two days, as his bones were adjusted, his organs did their own adjustments. He seemed to try to throw up every three to four hours, before his stomach settled down a bit. That made it hard on both, and they were both tired by the time his stomach started settle down.

Once he started to have an appetite, they started him off easy with some broth, but quickly moved to more wholesome foods that which were easy on the stomach. The bit of excess weight he had been carrying on his body was gone from the changes and the not eating. He was starting to eat more, but he was still losing fat, even if they measured it, he wouldn't have been losing much weight. Brook had been concerned, but when she checked and found it to be normal, she stopped worrying. The Healers kept an eye from a distance, letting Brook do the work. Charting the changes, he was following the fastest line, and expected to be mobile during the last three days but he was advised to take it easy and rest in his room.

Once his bones stopped aching, he started having more energy, and not liking being confined to the bed. After the first afternoon, and a long soak cuddled together, then the first full night's restful sleep since the changes started, Adam was getting antsy. He had been shocked when he first looked at himself in the mirror; he was looking younger, and his body much more toned. He looked to be in his twenties again.

"Your body is renewing itself, as it takes the healing ability of the Were. Soon we will look the same age and will be aging about the same."

His hairline had been receding along his widow's peak before he was Turned, was now down farther and there was now short hair growing from what had been forehead skin before. His body also had no noticeable hair. Brook had mentioned, when he asked early on about her not even having pubic hair, getting the answer of 'Werewolves naturally had no body hair' which surprised him. He was glad; his thick body hair was annoying as it itched often, but his clothes felt weird, and he realised it was because his skin wasn't used to having fabric rub against it. He soon got used to the different sensations.

Brook gave up on trying to keep him in bed but told him he had to stay in the room. At his request, and the healer's OK, he was allowed to have visitors, but the healers limited it to one or two at a time.

The first visitors were the Alphas. Brook let them in, knowing they were coming, having let them know personally he was up to visitors.

"How are you feeling, Adam?" Gareth started, as he and Maria sat down on the couch facing Adam and Brook, both wearing soft comfy clothes.

"Glad the aches and pains are mostly over. I'm still feeling a bit under the weather but should pass by the end of the weekend."

Gareth smiled, "You are changing the fastest in my memory, and up there in the memory of the Elders; they have found records of those changing faster, but they are rare."

Adam sighed, "I'm glad, but would like to have it done; I'm already tired of how long the changes are taking. I do understand why they take a while, but it's annoying."

All three wolves chuckled, "It'll take its time, but I think you'll be happy with the results." Maria answered.

Changing the subject, Gareth commented, "I do like the work you went into for the networking so far, the connections which are in, are working much more reliably, with the only issues being either the device needing a reboot, or something outside the network. Although some of the pups had to be ordered to turn off the game to do training or chores."

Adam laughed, "It's the same for humans; time limits for them to game usually is the way to go about it. Right now, the routers are pushing their limits. I am planning on taking some time in the next week to order ones more in line with what is planned, so they can handle the load, while keeping the network secure. They are one of the pricier parts."

Gareth nodded, "Just keep me informed on the spending you are doing."

"Once I have some of the network infrastructure up, I am wanting to set up a couple of data centres here. They would handle the items locally, including email and phones, just to name a couple. The email system would include calendars, so you can know when the boardrooms are booked, or for scheduling patrols. Since the systems are protected here, we wouldn't have a security concern."

Gareth smiled, liking the idea, "Go for it. Any timeline or costs?"

Adam shook his head, "I dabbled in it a while ago, but just on old PCs, it was slow but handled well for just me accessing it. We are wanting to have all the members, along with many positions, so I'd need more resources." Taking a breath, he continued, "I want to contact my previous employer, as they are a full solution provider. When I tell them what I want it to do they would know what we would need for hardware and can even get it set up and tested for us. I would not be using their on-site support; I'll just tell them it is due to the confidential nature of our business and can't go into it. I'll have them point me at the training we need to support it."

Gareth openly grinned, "I love the idea! One stop shopping for our tech needs! I assume they can fulfil the PC orders too?"

Adam nodded, "Yes. They are a major vendor and have ties to companies to supply almost anything. I thought it would be better than doing separate vendors. Only problem I see, is the offices are quite far, so it would either be a courier or us sending someone there. Although with how large of client we could be, we may want to have an employee or two permitted access, and know about us, eventually."

"I agree, having one single vendor would be better. Give me the company name, and I'll investigate to see if any other packs have contacts with them, so we don't need to start from scratch."

Adam passed on the company name but knew it would take a while before they would know anything or before he could set up anything deeper.

They chatted about what he was feeling, being so far from family, what sort of relationship he had with them—close to mother and sister, and father's sister, but not at all close with the others he knew. There were some tears shed when it was learned he had been raised by his mother alone from before his tenth birthday, as his father had died.

"There is a chance my sister could come here, as she is a sales rep for Southern Alberta and the Kootenay's. I completely forgot to make some time after moving to tell her. I am thinking early next week, once the initial changes are complete, and I'm cleared to be out with my Mate?" He made the last a question, making sure he wouldn't be an issue.

"I have no problems, but it would have to be in the town, not hours away. Make sure some other wolves are there too. Use the office at the warehouse, as it would be a secure location to discuss it." Gareth and Maria had concerns, but as it was to meet and tell about them, it shouldn't be a problem.

Adam nodded in agreement.

They discussed a bit more, but Gareth and Maria had other duties to deal with and gave a polite goodbye with some hugs.

With some time, before their friends descended on them, Adam quickly sent off an email to his sister. *I have moved to a place in BC.* Adam wrote, *I would love to meet up with you to have a good chat.* He added the address of the warehouse in town to the e-mail.

Quickly, he had a reply, *Mom had told me you had moved, but refused to say anything else, not even why you moved, saying you would have to give the details!*

They quickly arranged for the next week—him saying he was on bed rest under doctor's orders, but should be back up the next week, pending his doctor's approval.

The next was to start the agreement with his old employer to be their preferred vendor. He mentioned he was building from scratch the corporate network, and he wanted to work with them to design the sort of configuration he would need, and what sort of training he needed to take to support them. He also clearly stated he had no approval to have anyone but their own company within the premise, due to security and confidentiality, and not explaining further. He didn't expect a reply that day, it being Friday afternoon, but he had a basic boiler plate letter back with the terms he wanted, and the sort of costs he was expecting, approximately two to three million for the hardware, software, net-working infrastructure, and getting it all ready. They would deliver it to the warehouse themselves for free.. Adam forwarded it to Gareth, for final approval. Even if it wasn't till Monday before they started working on it, it would be fine. *Some salesperson is going to get a good bonus*, he thought to himself, with how eager they were for this contract.

****

Over the next three days, the agreement for the equipment was signed, and as it would need time to be gathered and built, would take a couple of weeks to be gathered at least, which was what Adam suspected. His trio of their friends were working hard on the wireless networking and would have the building ready by the end of the following week, even though he had expected it to take a month. He did tell them, if they finished early, they would have the rest of the time free, other than supporting it, but they could do it in shifts.

Kuri and Evan stopped in, "The cover over the cave is installed," Kuri told them with a grin, "From the ground it just looks like part of the cliff now, even knowing it's there!" She added.

Evan added, "The conduit was totally secure and can't even be seen up close, after some grey spray paint to match the rocks."

Both waved off the thanks, stating they were happy they got paid to do some fun climbing, instead of just patrolling. Adam grinned and nodded, having had to deal with setting it up for them. Learning the back-end of the payroll system the pack used was interesting. He didn't need to worry about entering time, nor did his regular workers, it was mostly for when he used others, like for the conduit, each of them had been given an entry to put the time against, so it came out of his budget, and so they could track how many hours everyone was working, so nobody got overworked.

Their other friends stopped in to say hi and they missed seeing them.

Between visits, he used the time to talk to some of his online friends who had poked him, being vague on where he now was, as many knew he had moved, and some he told he was working much higher up the IT job ladder. Some he didn't really want to talk to anymore, and hadn't even said hi in months, so had just deleted them from the contact lists. A few, he would have loved to tell them what he was being turned into, but several of them would be begging for contacts in their area or for an address to travel to meet him, to beg to be turned themselves in person. He and Brook had a bit of a chuckle over it.

Monday came around, and he was given the all-clear from their Healer, for his changes were progressing as normal, and he was good. He did get a lecture to stay calm, and not get angry, or really upset, as it may spark his wolf to come early, thinking they needed protection. That could cause problems, although they couldn't say what sort of problems he would have.

Showing up on Monday for lunch, he was given a howl for a cheer, everyone happy to see him, but made sure to give him a bit of room, knowing the changes were still on-going, and would be for at least a couple of months.

That afternoon, he took the three techs aside and showed them how to do wired ports in a couple of empty guest rooms, so when they finished the wireless, they could start running them. They had been using basic network switches to get the wireless online, but he had some better ones on his order, they would just take a while to arrive, so he instructed to test, but to then leave any wired ports, unless they needed them, disconnected.

He was looking forward to talking to his sister, and introducing her to his mate, the next day. He had already updated her everything was a go. They were going to have a lunch; he knew she had several food allergies and had arranged for some hot food with the pack chefs for her, which she could eat.

CHAPTER 9

Talking to the Sister

The next morning, he spent with a tablet, walking around the areas which had the Wi-Fi working, to make sure the coverage was what he was expecting, and the settings were correct. He found a few holes of low signal, but it was to be expected. Where they were located, he doubted someone would really care, and while the level was low, it was still usable. In areas where someone could sit with a laptop, the signals were great. He had sent Brook with another tablet to find areas outside which already had signal, and if it was usable. When they were done, they would plan out where next to install Wi-Fi. They would be continuing to survey and re-survey areas until all the Wi-Fi was installed everywhere.

All too soon, it was time to head down to the warehouse to tell his sister. Since he had told his mother, it didn't bother him as much. His sister was much more open minded than his mother. He headed to the kitchen to pick up the food from the chefs. He smiled and picked up the basket they gave him with the food with a smile, and thanks for the help.

Heading out the door, he smiled at Brook, and taking her hand, they headed down to the parkade for the vehicle.

*****

Sighing, he looked at his watch, *fifteen minutes late*. He thought, *She must have got caught at her last site.* Hearing the ping of a message, he checked his phone: he was exactly right. She was ten minutes away. He messaged back her food was getting cold. He grumbled a little to Brook sitting beside him, and she just laughed.

"We can't all be always on time. Just go with it." Brook replied, amused. She was reading one of the eBooks he had suggested on her tablet and was enjoying it.

When she arrived, he was waiting at the visitor's door near the office he was borrowing.

When she got close, she stopped and stared, "You're looking different. Younger, and what's with the hair?"

Smiling, "All in good time. That is part of what I want to tell you about."

Showing Tara to the office, she looked at all the food, "You made this?" She asked, incredulously; she knew he didn't cook much.

"Actually... I sort of lied about that part. The group I'm with—I'll tell you more after lunch—has chefs; I passed on your allergies and that I needed something for you today. After grumbling and complaining, this is what they whipped up for me." Adam replied truthfully, hoping she would be happy.

Tara sat and took a first bite, and gave a groan of pleasure, "This is really good! We're going to need to do this the next time I am out this way."

Adam introduced Brook as his girlfriend, and they sat down and worked to keep the topics on what his sister did. Once lunch was done, he introduced Tara to Charlie, who was playing shy for some reason, following his nap, since Adam had fed him well before she arrived, to keep him quiet.

Sitting back, he decided now was the right time to start, "Now, I know you have some questions which we have been deflecting since you arrived. Hold onto them, many will be answered by what we are going to tell you." He advised, gathering his courage.

Taking a deep breath, he started, "Tara, Brook is a werewolf. I am her mate. I was out in the mountains and saw her running as a wolf. Long story short, she got caught in the edge of a rockslide, and for some reason I didn't know at that point, I was compelled to help her. She was unconscious and hurt. I ended up laying her by my vehicle when she started to stir before she shifted back. We since figured out her wolf sensed me and was comfortable enough to push the human half forward, causing the shift back."

Tara was looking incredulous again, "Werewolves don't exist. How many times do I have to tell you that?" They had chatted about his fascination about werewolf stories and his research into the myths. They had argued about his belief they existed but were in hiding.

Adam gave Brook a nod, and she started to shift in her clothes. They had decided that was better and had brought her a change of some old stuff she didn't care about to turn to rags and had changed when they arrived. She walked around the table, so there was nothing hiding her before she quickly shifted to her wolf.

Tara had been about to continue her rant, but this was way outside of her even idea of being possible, "What's the trick; people can't become animals." She couldn't look away. Her mind was stuck in a loop, as she was having trouble believing what her eyes were showing. The giant wolf was now shaking off the shreds of what Brook had been wearing.

Adam shook his head, as Brook padded forward, placing her head beside Tara's hand, "It's no trick. Feel her fur."

Tara reluctantly did feel her fur, and it was real, "OK, you have a giant wolf. Where did Brook go?"

Shift back with her hand on your head, love. She's going to be obstinate today. Adam asked Brook with a mental sigh and got a mental affirmative. Sometimes his sister took a fair amount of proof before she was willing to get out of a rut of a thought process, and to accept a change.

"Keep your hand on her head, and she's going to shift back." Adam told his sister.

Slowly this time, Brook shifted under Tara's hand, the fur become hair, and the ears moving from the top of her head to the side and shrinking and changing to become human. Once done, Adam dropped a robe onto Brook, as she was now naked. He knew his sister would have problems with her being nude.

Brook sent mental thanks to her mate as she stood and did the robe up, before returning to her seat.

Tara seemed to be in a state of shock. She was looking from Brook to her hand and back. They sat like that for several minutes. To prevent her from bolting, he had asked Shana to silently keep an eye on the door. Until she had accepted it, he didn't want her leaving.

"Now do you believe?" Adam asked, breaking the silence, after ten minutes.

Tara blinked at him, "I don't understand... how can werewolves exist?" she asked, her mind seemingly disconnected.

Brook shrugged, "I don't either; we just do. Turn it around: how can humans exist? They evolved. Well, as far as we can tell, we evolved too. We don't know what caused it, but when we bite a human intending to Mate or Turn them into a werewolf, it has been proven by our scientists we seem to release a virus into them which re-writes their DNA at a fast enough rate they don't die from an auto-immune attack." The occasional one did, but she had been looking into the records, and it seemed they had been all non-mate turns. She had asked the Elders to find out how often mate-turns had ended in death. So far, there had only been cases where the human mate wasn't healthy and had an underlying health concern which wasn't detected and there wasn't a healer involved to handle it in the past couple centuries.

Tara still couldn't wrap her mind around it but didn't want to cause it to melt down again, "OK, werewolves exist; don't question it if you don't want a massive headache." She said to herself, as she rubbed her head, as she now had a headache.

Adam nodded, "And you can't tell *anyone* about it. It could be very dangerous for us."

Nodding in agreement; some would want to find out the 'how' and 'why' of it, and them not being fully human anymore, would not consider them having rights as a person. "Wait... 'Us'?"

Adam smiled and nodded, taking Brook's hand, "First, Brook is my Mate—or Soul Mate—and since I first saw her, we have barely been separated. Neither of us wants to be separate now." Getting a nod from Tara to continue, "Second, I have had the bite to start turning. I was not sick, but I was on isolation and bedrest last week for the first part of the turn, which I am told is the hardest. I'm now waiting for my wolf-mind to surface, and then shortly after I will shift for the first time."

Tara snorted, still a disbeliever of what she hadn't seen, "I'll believe you can shift when I see it the first time."

Adam smiled, she had always been that way, "OK. I'll let you know when you can see." She rarely believed in things she couldn't see, like Santa. She often asked for proof first.

"Have you told mom?" Tara asked.

"Told her just before we moved. She too was sworn to secrecy. Don't discuss it, as someone could be monitoring communications." Adam advised. He had been warned sometimes the government tried tapping their phones, but most wolves learned to tell when there was the feedback from it.

"So, why did you move way out here?" Tara asked, wanting to know the answer since she found out about the move from their mother almost two weeks before. It had surprised her from how sudden it was, and how he seemed to drop off the map.

Adam smiled, "I joined the pack Brook belongs to." He stated it, as if it was the most logical thing for him to do. "You know how I love to be out in the mountains."

"Pack? How many are there then?"

Adam nodded, "I don't know how many total, but there are about three hundred in our pack, and there are packs all over the globe." He answered, before grinning, "I am considered a Beta, as I mated Brook who has the rank..." He went on to discuss an overview of the top ranks, and how they ranked up just below the Alphas and Seconds and were now in charge of all the technology for the pack, and some of the changes he was now doing. "I shuddered when I saw what the Alpha currently has for a computer. It's older than mom's *old* computer!"

Tara laughed, "I can see you doing that! You keep trying to get mom to upgrade."

Adam grinned and just smiled. Since he had the money, he had arranged to get her a new laptop, as she didn't need a PC for what she did, and they were easier to deal with.

"Here," Adam said, fishing out his new business card, "This is my new contact information. The address is for *here*, which is owned by the pack. Our house is deep in the woods and is where most of the pack lives and would take you about a half hour to walk from the parking lot to it. Let me know on a weekend you want to stay, and I'll arrange a guest room for you."

Tara nodded, "That makes sense, and I'll have to take you up on it at some point. CIO? What does it stand for? Sounds high."

Adam nodded, "Chief *Information* Officer. Basically, like a CFO or Chief Financial Officer oversees the money, the CIO is in charge of all the technology. After the president of a tech company, they are the next most important. So, yea; high. The company is one of many fronts for the pack."

Tara thought for a moment, "Wait—how do you have internet so far out there? I remember you saying something about trees absorbing signal or something." She knew he disliked living without internet; occasionally she absorbed some comments before she tuned him out.

Adam grinned, "I guess you do listen once in a while." He teased, before answering the question, "Well, I had fibre run into a room here, then ran a Wi-Fi link to the cliff near the pack house, where we found the perfect cave, and then ran a cable into the house. That was what I was dealing with the week after moving here. I have three packmates who report to me right now and are working on the wireless and are going quite a bit faster than I expected, so they look like they will be getting a vacation for getting done early."

Shaking her head, Tara didn't care about the *how* for technology; she just wanted it to work. Realising the date, "Wait, Christmas is in under three weeks. Are you going to make it home for it?"

Adam shrugged, "Not sure, but doesn't look good. Until I have shifted fully and show I can control myself to prevent an uncontrolled shift, I am not allowed out of the pack's territory, and even coming here and meeting with you needed approval. At the rate I'm turning, all I can say is 'maybe'. If I get upset, I may change early, 'forcing' the change."

Brook pipped up, "If he shifts before Christmas, *and* if he has control, both of us will be there." She was in the betting pool it was the Solstice party which would pull the change out. He might have the hang enough for the trip by then if she was correct. It did sound likely, though. Plans were in the works for it already, as it was in another pack's territory, they would need to arrange permission for the visit. Especially due to his rank.

Tara replied, "Mom is going to be very disappointed if you don't show up."

Adam shrugged, "Nothing I can do at this point, if the shift is forced, it makes control harder, so it is less likely at that point to making it. If I don't make it, we will make a trip out to see everyone as soon as I am allowed to travel."

One thing clicked in her mind, Tara asked, "Since you are 'mates', does it make you *married*?"

Both Adam and Brook shook their heads, before Brook answered, "No, our bond is soul-deep, and is beyond death. Short form is we believe in reincarnation, and soulmates are linked even beyond death. Our bond is till death, and often if one dies the other will as well. Many do marry to satisfy human legal systems, but its not required."

Adam let out a sigh, "Brook's parents and our mom are planning the wedding. Now I have internet going, they are going at it. I think they are planning for next summer. I am going to insist it be in the mountains. Probably near the Upper Kananaskis Lake, if we can get permission." It was easier and cheaper than having it in the national park, and there were less people out that way.

Tara smiled, "That is a beautiful area." They had shared a few hikes in the area.

Adam smiled his agreement.

"So, when are you having babies?" Tara asked.

"Not you too!" Adam exclaimed. He hadn't thought she would ask that too.

Brook smiled, "No chance till next fall. I had my yearly heat just before I met Adam, so earliest would be March of next year."

Tara smiled at Adam's outburst, "That's goo—wait, *heat*? You mean you don't have to deal with monthly periods?" she asked incredulous.

Brook smiled and nodded in confirmation, "But our heat lasts for a week or two. During that time, it is hard to think about anything but sex." Adam would learn the next year how females got during it, and went after the males, for the most part.

Tara shuddered, "I'm not sure I like that. I'll stick with my monthly period, thank you."

Brook laughed, "Well, I do consider you my sister now, so if you need any help, don't hesitate to call. If needed, I can put you in contact with a pack which is much closer to you." As she handed her card, with the title of 'Assistant CIO, MacLaren Technologies Inc.' A number had been added on the back. Tara glanced at Adam's card and it had the same number with 'For Emergencies' scrawled on it, "The number on the back is a direct number to the pack and is answered no matter what time it is by someone. They will know where we are or how to get a hold of us. If we can't answer, they would have the authority to help you; just tell them you are Adam's sister."

Tara tucked the card in her wallet, but looked at the time, and nearly swore, "I'm late! I'm supposed to be at my next client now!"

Adam and Brook stood, and walked to give her a hug, "Well next time you are coming out this way, let us know."

Tara grinned, "I will, even if it is just for the awesome food!" she commented as they walked her to the door.

Adam laughed, "I'll pass your complements onto the Chefs. Have a safe drive."

After she left, they chatted with Shana for a bit, letting her know she was Adam's sister, to appease her curiosity. After a bit, they dropped a surprise; congratulating her on being promoted to the Warehouse Manager. They had asked the Alpha and Rein, who was her boss, to be the one to tell her. The last manager had decided to move careers just before Adam moved in. Although Rein hadn't said anything to her, he had been seeing how she could handle the work before making it official.

Shana had been very surprised, although the other two warehouse workers were happy for her. They knew the bigger news which would surprise her more, and they weren't telling her now: the position brought her from Delta to a Beta ranking; and the increases which came with it: larger monthly stipend. Pack members had their basic needs covered, but the higher ranks were paid more, since they had more duties and responsibilities. If they were to look at the pay cheque, they would see they were paid similarly to any human job, but a portion was taken off for 'Housing and related' and 'food'. The net pay was for anything other than the basic clothes the pack supplied from their bulk purchases, or any luxuries, like trips outside the pack. The rank increase would also have private instead of shared quarters, with her just sharing a bathroom with another person.

Changing ranks, especially to Beta, was usually an excuse for a party, and this being no different. Rein, as the one she reported to, had booked the large meeting room for a surprise party in the evening for her and had invited many from the pack which were her friends and co-workers. Those who weren't invited were still welcome to show up, as the pack didn't exclude. Brook grinned as she talked about making sure she came up for dinner at the pack, and how they would celebrate after.

*****

At dinner, everyone knew something was up, from the excited chatting, as word got around of the promotion. The Alpha stood and called for everyone's attention, "We have had a change in duties of one of the members. As is usual, we had one who worked under them step forward and take over their duties till a replacement was found. What they didn't realise is they had been groomed to take over permanently and had been given a trial-run by the supervising Beta." He paused to let it sink in before grinning, "Shana, please step up here."

Shana was floored. She knew she had got a promotion today, but not she was getting singled out for it. Adam had sat beside her, and helped her stand, since her mind had gone blank. Giving her a slight push, she walked up to the alpha.

"For her dedication and ability to be the main warehouse manager, I am as Alpha of Pack MacLaren, granting Shana, Beta rank!"

A loud howl was given out, as it was not often they had a Delta move to Beta status, as there were very few top positions. Alpha Maria handed her a plaque with the information on it, before giving her a hug, and telling her she had the next day off to move to her new quarters. She nodded blankly, as she was engulfed in a hug by Alpha Gareth. She quickly moved back to her seat beside Adam with a sigh.

"I hear the chefs caught wind of the changes and outdid themselves tonight! Let's eat!" Everyone knew something was up, as the food was on offer, and there was some elk, moose, and bison meat, items which were harder to get, and more expensive, so were not offered as often as beef.

Adam gave her a side hug, as the rest of the friends around her congratulated her for the major promotion.

After accepting, Shana turned to Adam and Brook, "You knew." She accused.

They both smiled, before Brook said, "We knew yesterday, when we were approached for feedback, since we had been there lots. As your friends, we asked to give you the good news, but the Alpha had already claimed the rank change."

Shana sighed, "At least I don't have much to move. The stairs are going to be a pain."

Adam smiled, "You have access to the freight elevator remember?" The elevator was reserved for hauling cargo, and for when wolves got hurt and couldn't manage the stairs. The Betas all had access, as they might need to help an injured wolf to their room to heal or find themselves needing it. The lower wolves didn't have access, to not abuse it when they were just tired or didn't feel like using the stairs.

Shana looked at Adam blankly, "Only Betas have—"

Adam grinned, "You are now a Beta, although only a low ranked one, so you have access to it. Using it to move is not an abuse of your power."

Shana blinked and smiled, "That makes the move easy! Who's free tomorrow to help me?"

Adam nodded, "I'm there, and I'll have my trio of techs, least I can do for helping me move all my piles of stuff. They will still be on-call for any critical issues, although I don't expect them, every time I try to help to move, they happen." He said, before Erin, Aurora and Nikki could ask to be released to help on his authority. In response they grinned.

Brook commented, "I'll be there too. I just asked, and Jess and Joshua will come help too."

The others wanted to help, but all had too much on their plates at work to request the day to help at such short notice.

After dinner, Adam and Brook distracted her enough with questions as they led her to the meeting room, their friends slipping away to make it to the room first. They kept her distracted enough she didn't notice where they were leading her.

"Surprise!" everyone shouted as Adam opened the door for Shana.

Shana froze, totally not expecting it.

Rein came forward with a grin on his face, "We can't let a little promotion go to waste! You know how we like to party!" He pulled her inside, not giving her a chance to go hide.

*****

The move went without a hitch, although as Adam predicted, an issue did crop up with the technology, it was solved quickly by having Nikki reboot the access point which had locked up. He commented after she returned and reported all was well, he liked being able to just delegate another to do the legwork, while he made the big and tough decisions. He warned that there would be lots of work when they started getting in all the hardware after Christmas, although he expected it just after new years, due to the holidays. Many tech companies mostly shut down between Christmas and New Years'.

Adam spent much of his free time with Brook during the week, going through much of the stuff he had pack-ratted away. Most of it he was giving away. Old computer bits were piled to go to what had been assigned to be the computer lab and join all the others he had found around in various storage areas, and others had found. He was going to have it be a project some older pups could work on; get as much of the old stuff working, so they could donate it to charities. They would find out what parts were broken, and dump them in a bin, and use parts from a similar system which had something else not working to get one working from two broken ones. He also expected many which would need just an operating system reload to get them working. In those cases, he planned to just pull the hard drives and provide new ones, with a freshly loaded operating system. They could deal with them beyond that.

Other cables and related, he was sending to Rein's workshops, along with his tools–although he had kept a list of what he was sending, as he didn't expect to ever leave the pack, he wanted them available for use by any instead of hiding away in storage. The plates and stainless-steel silverware he was sending to the kitchen. The automotive tools he had acquired as he did his own repairs, to save money, were going to their service garage. Once it was done, much of the stuff had been moved. Mostly, it was boxes and boxes of papers and other stuff. He did still have a fair bit of camping gear, and he kept it there, but he did send his sleeping bags to the laundry for a good cleaning.

Adam had taken the time to also learn how to control an Argo while he was making trips to the various shops with his stuff, as he hadn't been in too much of a rush to get everything done. It turned out to be lots of fun to run the Argo.

The technology was mostly supervisory, as there was very little tech to break so far and he had yet to be able to get into the online courses he needed for the training, so he knew the stuff for handling the servers more than the mini-network he had done before. His techs were doing the last few access point installations, and would have nearly two weeks free, right over the holidays, as he planned. He had given them some links to look at for training but wasn't expecting them to start till after the new years, telling them as much, and the server stuff was online.

There was a list of certifications he was expecting them to take, with timelines for passing them. A+ he wanted them to have as soon as they could and included even the pups who were working on the old equipment, as it covered very basic troubleshooting, identifying parts, and how to set up a computer. It was vendor-neutral and required by many vendors as a pre-requisite for their own training.

Next there was Network+, which was another vendor-neutral certification, but this one was on knowing networking. It would allow them to deal with the issues which came up, as they would understand it better. Next, there was a stream for the wireless technology, and which was several exams. The Certified Wireless Network Professional stream he was working on himself, as well. He was taking the time to do the courses too, so he knew what he needed to do. He also planned on taking some on the server side—Server+ was one—as well.

He already had a blanket approval to cover the costs for the exams and the training required, and to be the one to decide which to offer to whom. It was with the same rules of any other learning: flunk out, and would have to pay the money back, or pay to take it again and pass.

Thinking long-term, Adam was considering looking at hosting some networks for other packs, to help discussions between them. He needed to get the plan together before he could do much. Before he could consider it, he needed to have their network up and running first.

As such Adam had started researching what it would take to get the top-level domain '.pack' and host it for all the packs, regardless of if they were on friendly terms. It was going to take agreements hashed out with multiple packs, around the globe. So far, the couple of packs they had discussed it with liked the idea, as then they could limit who could have it, and keep it fairly secure from humans, he hoped anyways.

Brook had also taken him down to the training room in the basement to start his formal physical training. Adam kept grumbling she was ruthless, but she kept smiling. She was keeping it light and at the entry levels the pups did, to not force his wolf early. They had settled into an early morning warmup, breakfast, then spend the morning training, then after lunch, a couple hours on his certification learning, any paperwork, or decisions he needed to do, then work on his storage unit till dinner. After dinner, was a good run, but with snow getting deep, soon it would change. Even Adam noticed he was getting better skills and conditioning.

Some of the training they had involved Charlie, to get even him more trained. The ability to give him mental directions of what they were trying to teach him took training from weeks or months to hours or at most a couple days.

Brook gave Adam Sunday off to relax, partly because she and her wolf could sense his wolf was starting to wake the night before, and it was better to let him rest and just spend time together.

They again went on a hike, this time leaving while it was still dark, arriving at their private spot just as the sky was starting to lose stars. She had made sure to grab his tripod with the camera bag, as he was teaching her the best way to get the pictures. They enjoyed a nice cool morning soaking in the various pools, while Charlie mostly stayed nearby. Although once, he had gone off and returned with a couple of rabbits, dropping one at Adam's feet, before moving to eat the other.

Adam gagged, until Brook kindled a tiny fire, to sear the meat a bit so they could eat it. She also showed him how to properly gut a rabbit, tossing the organs and other bits to Charlie who gobbled them up.

They spent a nice, enjoyable day relaxing and talking together, learning more about each other, and what they wanted from the future. Brook also continued teaching Adam some of the beliefs and traditions they lived by. Some he wouldn't get till his wolf was fully awake, and others till he had shifted. Brook also learned more about the 'why' behind humans. The week she had stayed with him before moving was confusing, and Adam didn't have much basis to compare them. Now he did, he was able to explain them in terms which made sense to her, even if some of the reasons still mystified her.

After the sun had set, so they could take more pictures of it, they trudged back to the pack house to have a late meal then head to bed; Brook expected Adam's wolf to awake in the next few days.

CHAPTER 10

Adam's Wolf Awakes

Monday morning, Adam woke early, as was his habit, and gave a good stretch. Suddenly, a new voice spoke in his head, it was like when he talked to other wolves, but it felt more personal.

Need Mate it begged.

He was a bit startled, which woke his mate when he jumped.

"What is it, Love?" Brook asked.

"Not sure, I seem to have a new voice in my mind, feels... different. It just said 'Need Mate.'"

Blinking a couple of times as she woke, Brook realised what it probably was: his wolf.

"Close your eyes and lay back. Open your mind fully to me, and if it's your wolf, mine will talk to him." Brook directed, before grinning.

Adam laid back and tried to relax the mental barriers Brook had taught him, allowing her wolf to connect to his mind in a very intimate way, and as usual, Brook's wolf had an almost furry feel to his mind, and realised belatedly the other mind did too.

As her wolf usually did, it announced itself with a howl.

This time there was an answering howl, a bit weak, as if it wasn't used to howling, but it was there, which seemed to come from within himself.

In his mind's eye, he could see Brook's beautiful dark brown wolf, and another wolf bounded up, this one black with dark brown and silvery grey highlights and markings, and nuzzled Brook's wolf, **Mate!** he commented, tail a wagging.

Wolf-Brook started wagging her tail, and nuzzling back, commenting, **Mine!**

Mine! Agreed the second wolf, which Adam now realised was *his* wolf!

Adam smiled and approached, laying his hand on his wolf's back, and noticing Brook's human-mind had joined them.

You have a beautiful wolf there, Adam. Human-Brook said in awe, as all four minds enjoyed being together for the first time.

Yes, he's perfect. Human-Adam replied, wrapping his arms around his wolf-self's neck.

You need to accept the wolf into your mind to fully join, to become two parts of one whole; at which point he will know everything you know, and be able to experience it with you, Human-Brook instructed, *Touch your forehead to his, and share your memories. I have been told, start with when you first saw me, go forward till now, then work backwards. Share everything; don't hold anything back.*

Wolf-Brook stepped back after giving both parts of Adam a lick and an nuzzle, to watch.

Seeming to kneel in front of his wolf, he looked into his brown eyes, murmuring, *I have waited so long for this, I accept you.*

His wolf nuzzled him, **I too have waited a very long time for this. We were selected a long time ago to be two halves of one mind. Just this time, you were born human. I had to wait and see if you could find our mate without me, then for you to decide to be turned. I accept you, too.** His wolf took the step forward, and both tilted their heads down and pressed foreheads together.

The human shared the love and caring of his finding his mate, and of finding the perfect place to belong in the pack, and his plans and ideas for everything, then what his life was before finding his mate, of aching for good friends to curl up with, but mostly finding just a cold bed. What his job was before, where he came from, both moaned at the memories around his father's death at such a young age, and then went on to the loving memories before he died, and the other memories he had of being a child. Some he hadn't remembered in a long time.

The wolf shared the few memories he had of previous incarnations, of running through forests, usually with their mate at their side. Taking down a deer with a pack. The pride of seeing their pups for the first time, and even a couple of ones which felt weighty with age, of helping some humans wearing furs.

Separating, time having no meaning here, it could have been only a moment, or could have been hours, they noticed both Brook's parts had left.

Giving his wolf a last hug and accepting a nuzzle and lick in return, he took a breath to return to the real world.

Opening his eyes, and trying to move, he gave a groan; he was stiff!

Brook was standing over him momentarily, "How'd it go?"

"Well, I think, some of his memories are going to take some time to go through. I thought I saw humans in furs in a couple of them."

Brook looked at him with wide eyes, "You will need to keep those to your self for now. When you have all the memories settled, let me know, as we will need to talk to the elders about it. I have never heard of a wolf sharing memories of previous lives."

Adam gave a nod, not really understanding, but willing to accept it, "How long did it take?"

Brook shrugged, "A few hours. It's early afternoon." She pulled over a covered plate, "I saved you some lunch. I wasn't expecting it to take this long, but I discussed it with the Elders this morning, while not typical, it isn't unusual."

"My wolf mentioned we had been together before, and had been waiting to come back to me, and to find you again."

Brook had a distant look for a moment before blinking a few times, and nearly fell as she sat down on the side of the bed, "What is it?"

This goes no further. Being able to know anything about your previous incarnation is unusual and the fact we have been together before... it is *almost unheard of! We need to talk to the Elders before you say anything to anyone.**

While she had been talking to him, his hands had been at work with the food, and it had vanished into his mouth.

****Run with our Mate**** Adam's wolf begged, wanting to be outside. He had a much better feel of his wolf now.

****Yes! Run with Mate!**** Adam heard fainter, and already could recognise as being Brook's wolf.

Brook smiled, "I heard that! It means we already have a very deep bond. My wolf is now begging for a run too!" It concerned her a little; just one more thing to discuss with the elders.

Adam grinned, having wandered to his desk, to check for messages, and seeing nothing he needed to deal with right away, smiled looking at his mate, "Sure! I heard yours too; the bond must be both ways!" He commented as he pulled on some clothes, before heading out the patio door.

He was surprised to see some wolves out there, Thetas, he could tell from their scent. They were putting in windows on the outside of the patio. He smiled, as he realised it would help keep the building from loosing too much heat and give shelter when they used the door.

The snow was looking beautiful. Although it was looking to already be 15 cm deep. From the business-like way it was coming down, he expected it to get to half a metre before it stopped.

"Here," Brook passed him some metal-framed snowshoes, "I assume you know how to use them?"

Nodding, "Yes, but haven't used them in a couple of years," he commented as he secured them to his feet and pulled on the waterproof jacket. Although they didn't feel the cold, they could still get chills from the snow melting through their clothes.

They ran around slowly, getting used to snowshoes again, falling a couple of times, before they took off for a jog in the fresh snow, their wolves enjoying the brisk weather.

Soon you can come out and play, Adam soothed his wolf, who was pouting in his mind, as he wanted to play in the fresh snow like a pup.

They chased each other for a while, before heading back, leaving the snowshoes hung off hooks with their names on it, which had been put up for them under an awning at the door to the now enclosed patio, which wasn't too far from the door into their room.

After an enjoyable shower to warm up their cold skin, and remove the sweat of exertion, they headed to dinner, Brook reminding Adam to not share the information his wolf shared.

Everyone was wondering where he had been all day and was overjoyed when they found he had been bonding with his wolf. Fondly, he described what he looked like in his mind, while his wolf preened at the compliments passed his way.

There was a discussion about when he was going to shift for a bit, but it quickly shifted back to a discussion about the Solstice in a week's time. To the wolves, Christianity was a new religion, and as such didn't follow it in this pack. There were some members who did privately, but most of the pack celebrated the Solstices, Equinoxes, and the full moons. Brook even told him they even had some who had native ancestry and followed those beliefs, with some who had joined them before the government tried to destroy their culture. The general idea for the pack was religion was personal and each person was able to do their own choice of beliefs, but none could use it to try to force someone to an action or inaction.

There were small sentimental gifts given among friends and family, and there was a bonfire planned for the evening. Brook had already talked to Adam, about it, and they had decided the gifts to their shared friends would be from both.

After dinner, Brook grabbed Adam's hand and pulled him into the Alpha's meeting room, where the elders were sitting. Brook told them what Adam had told her after joining with his wolf, and both were questioned to find out every detail. There was some wary respect in several of the oldest elders' eyes.

Adam's wolf gave him a mental nuzzle of encouragement, **They may be Elders, but they are still just members of the pack. There is no reason to fear them.**

Adam sent back a wordless thanks.

"It sounds like you may be a Chosen Elder before your time. Only time will tell. If you survive, you will know when you enter your fifth century. There hasn't been one in this pack since we left Scotland and split off from our Parent Pack there. We will have to investigate further. As I am sure Brook asked, do not speak of this to anyone. We will notify the Alphas."

Another grinned at Adam, "Thank you for the internet, as it will make it so much easier to communicate with them."

Adam bowed his head in thanks, "I have some projects in the works which will make it even easier and would be fully secure communication. Do you have several packs which you mostly just deal with?"

Getting a nod from several, "Well, once I have this end all set up and tested, we could look at helping them get their own secure connection and make an enhanced secure connection with them. It would allow you to have a secure communication, be it email, phone, or a video chat, and not need to worry about security or someone outside of the packs listening in.

Even the few who grumbled about the changes perked up, "So, even the phone would be a secured line to them?" It meant they didn't need to learn a whole new system to be able to take advantage of the changes; it was something they totally approved of.

Adam nodded, "Yes, but only if I can get the other pack upgraded as well, as it needs to be secured at both sides."

"When would this end be ready to even talk to another pack?"

"I am not sure. I am waiting on the hardware for here, which I'm expecting around just after new years. Once I have the basic network and servers set up and running, which I expect to take a month or two, I will be working to set up the secure system."

"I thought it would take longer, like two or three years." One of the pessimists commented. That had been his complaint, the fact it would be much less disruption and be set up much sooner would not be an issue.

Thinking of another thing to ask them, "I am wanting to set up some sharing of information, almost call it a 'Were-net' as a separate, secured network so only Packs would be able to access, to allow for free sharing, and more friendly communication. I would need to have contact in at least one pack in each continent, but more than one is better. Would I be able to get a list of contacts I could use when I would be contacting others to help get it going? This I know would need to go to Gareth, then other Pack Alphas and Elders before it could be passed on. I would not even be starting this before the spring, at the earliest."

Adam got a nod and was told they would think about it, as he and Brook stood and nodded in respect before leaving the room.

Getting back to their suite, Adam flopped on the couch with a groan, "Please give me a heads up before jumping a meeting with the Alpha or Elders on me!"

Brook sat on his lap and cuddled, "Sorry. I requested it when you first said about it, and it was urgent to speak with them. *I* only got advised to meet with them as we were leaving dinner they had time right then, as the Dinner meeting with the Alphas had ended early."

Giving him a kiss, "I think you did splendidly. I think you even won over a couple of the Elders who were against the changes you are putting in, when they saw how it would help them do their job. Often, they must travel to meet with the other elders, as they lack a secure communication method, or speak in a code, which is often misunderstood."

Smiling, Brook asked "I'm curious how secure this will be?"

Adam smiled, "256-bit Cipher for 'Unsecured', 512 for Secured, and 1024 or higher for Restricted. Not sure exactly how high we have. I may look at getting some young ones building us our own software, to sell rights to the other packs, so the human governments have no backdoors into it. But I want everything else ready and working."

Brook smiled, "Now, no more tech-talk," She just barely understood what he had just said for the specifications. "I know there is something you would rather do instead," as she kissed him. Both him and his wolf enjoyed the time with their mates.

*****

Waking up with a wolf in his arms was something Adam was starting to enjoy as much as finding a human. He loved the feel of her soft fur on his body, and this morning, his wolf was very much enjoying it. Part of it was how her scent relaxed them, another was knowing they were safe and protected together.

He hugged her tight and kissed her nose. She blinked and yawned, before jumping off the bed to stretch before shifting as she padded to the closet. Walking out, she tossed Adam some close-fitted clothes of hers, wearing something similar, as was normal for days they worked out.

His wolf was purring in the back of his mind, as the scent of their mate came off the clothes as they pulled them on, before jogging lightly and as silently as he could behind his mate. Reaching the training room in the first basement, they did their normal early morning warmup workout.

Brook was even slightly warmed up this time, "Good, you are using your wolf to help you train."

Adam was confused, "Shouldn't I be?" he asked.

"Yes, but I have trained others in their turn, and many don't think to use the wolf till after they first shift. Even some born-wolves need to be taught to do so. You are already, on the first day, using your wolf means I can go harder, and you'll withstand it. I may need to have you take the first level testing, soon. That would bring you to the level ten-year old pups are expected to be at." Taking a breath, she gave him some surprising information, "The fastest another I trained this way, was two to three weeks for the improvement you put in each day. It is almost like you were trained, then had a long illness and just needed to get back up to speed."

"Well, they had a head start. They were born-wolf. The fact I am that far already is also partly due to your teaching, too." Adam grinned as Brook blushed, grabbed her hand as they headed for breakfast.

After breakfast, Brook took Adam through more challenging exercises, and if he didn't make them, he was close. When they headed to lunch, Adam was tired. He knew if he was still human, he would be passed out by now. He took his oath as a Pack member seriously, especially since he was a Beta who was highly ranked and was working to get his abilities to the level they needed, as quickly as possible.

Lunch with their friends came and went, with a short break after to check and deal with any work which came and he needed to deal with, and any questions for the tech workers, which wasn't much.

Brook sat him down when he was done, "I was serious this morning about your improvements being astonishingly fast. I am not sure what to make of it. I am going to just refine your current skills the rest of the time before your shift, and make sure you know what you are doing, as I had a short talk with the head trainer while we had lunch, and he thinks your mind is just pulling the skills from mine. If it is the case, we may need to get you another trainer, one who has a different style than I do."

Adam nodded, "I'm not trying to do it, so if slowing down the new stuff will get me better trained, lets do it. I want to be *thoroughly* trained, as not just you and Charlie depend on us, but we have Jess and Joshua, who have probably as much skill as I have right now, and currently, our trio of techs, and it seems the pups who are dealing with the old computer stuff will be future techs too.

Brook smiled at his thoughts, "I'm glad you are taking your pack oath seriously, I know a few who haven't. Two are the current Omegas, and the one they failed was in Medical for a while."

Adam nodded, knowing Omega rank was only used for those who had badly transgressed, and were being given a final chance before either exiled or executed by a Trial by Claw fight with the Alpha; if they for some reason won the fight with the Alpha, they would keep their life, and could try to work their way back up, but it extremely hard to move beyond the Theta for them, as few, if any, would have trust for them. Most chose to leave the pack, and find a new one, where they could try to regain trust in and was willing to ignore the fact they had been ranked Omega by their first pack. Usually, that sort of second chance was only given, if they didn't think the offence warranted being ranked Omega.

*****

The rest of the week followed the routine of the last week, with the Wi-Fi being finished Friday afternoon. He released the techs for the following two weeks for doing any more installs of the new technology, other than setting up a rotation for general support. They would start the heavy work once all the equipment showed up.

On the weekend, he helped the older pups who were dealing with the old surplus computers with some strange issues, and fixed some, but others he showed them a part which had broken, and was the cause of their weird issues, usually the memory. He smiled as they then found several more in the other devices they had put aside for him to look at and had them working before he got to them.

He gave them all a hug and thanked them for their dedication. Giving them the next week to themselves and got a cheer. There was still a large stack of equipment for them to go through, and when they started pulling the old stuff which was still in use, even more work. The Thetas had also started to search the storage rooms as they worked and had cleared the room beside this one of everything else and had started to stack all the computers they found there. It was starting to fill up with even older systems. He had seen some 386's in the pile and even a Tandy! Some he wasn't going to even bother to try to restore, as they were way too old, but likely some who liked old equipment would want to buy it. Some, they would restore for historical purposes, and a few of them they would keep themselves. Many more, newer but 'not working' were also being found. With having the money to just replace, and the need for security, few could take the systems in for service, and these were the ones they were repairing. They would have something to do for several months. By then, he hoped to have more work for them to do.

*****

Monday morning, he woke to getting a tongue bath from his mate, and turning his head away, another from Charlie. Giving an annoyed growl, he sat up, "I'm awake!"

Brook chuckled in his head, nuzzling into his lap, *Don't you want gifts?*

"I prefer to sleep in, and get them later in the morning,"

Well, too late now—Hey, what are you doing?

Adam had scooped her up, as much as he could and laid back on a pile of pillows, with her cuddled on top, on her back, as he pulled the covers up, "Shhh, it's still sleep time."

Noooooo! Brook sent as she squirmed and wiggled until she could lightly nip his chin, which surprised him to release her a bit. At which point she moved to nip at his mate-mark, which had become an instant turn on for him. He could feel the 'no' was not to stop, but because he had gotten the upper hand, and she didn't want him to stop. Otherwise, he would have instantly stopped.

"Now you're in for it!" Adam growled playfully, throwing off the blankets, feeling her enjoyment of their fun. Grabbing the scruff of her neck, he kept her on her back, spinning her on the soft sheet, before nipping at her shoulder where her own mark was. She growled in pleasure, and submitted, staying still on her back as he had his way with her. Presents were forgotten for now...

*****

Late morning, after a shower and getting dressed, they had wandered into the dining room, and exchanged greetings with other members, as they worked their way over to the buffet table which was set up for brunch. It had been set up early, but all morning there was going to be hot food, just a bit less selection.

They slumped down beside a couple of wolves they didn't know and smiled.

Other than knowing they were pack members and Theta, due to their scents, Adam didn't know them, and Brook only knew their faces.

They barely acknowledged they were there and refused to meet their eyes. Adam wrapped an arm around the male, and asked "What's wrong, why so glum?"

After a while the male sighed, "I'm Duncan, and this is my Mate, Keanna. I know you are Adam, and your mate is Brook." After a short silence, he started to lean into Adam, taking comfort from a senior wolf spending time with them; Adam's wolf was whining in his mind, wanting to know what the cause of their distress was.

The names clicked in Brook's mind, *They are one of the lowest pairs in the pack. They only moved into this pack in the spring, and joined the pack at the Summer Solstice, as far as I know, they haven't opened to share details of their life with anyone, not even where they were from.* She shared with Adam; maybe being new, he could help them.

"Since you're new, you didn't know, but we came from another pack. We have not been able to contact anyone in the old pack at all." Duncan replied after a while, not knowing Brook had just briefed him on their history.

Brook moved to sit on the other side of Keanna, wrapping her arm around her, as Adam was around Duncan, "If you tell us your old pack's name, we could arrange a call, if not today, another day?"

Duncan looked from Adam to Brook, they showed genuine concern and care for them, regardless of them being the lowest of the low, "You would do that for us? Today of all days? Today is for spending with family and friends!"

Adam shook his head, "I take my pack oath seriously, including the last part of helping *all* packmates to the best of my ability. If it means spending the morning of the Solstice with some Thetas who don't have anyone and feeling upset, so be it. I may still be turning, and not yet a fighter, but I can give you a shoulder to lean on."

Brook nodded in agreement, "I completely agree with Adam. If I saw you before Adam, I would have led us over myself. Even if we can't talk to them today, we could at least get a short call to them."

Our old pack is Shadowed River. Please don't tell anyone; we left because we didn't like how we were treated. They were going to banish us for fighting back against a delta who was going to rape Keanna. Duncan said silently to both Betas.

Adam had to close his eyes, and calm himself and his wolf, to prevent a forced turn; if the offender was here, he wouldn't have been able to prevent it. The fact they didn't know where the pack was helped.

He did hear the call for the Alpha, but he was trying to calm his wolf down from his near killing rage.

He felt Brook wrap him in her arms and tuck his nose into her neck. He took deep, slow breaths as he worked to calm his wolf. The scent of his mate surrounding him and the murmurs in his ear finally let him calm his wolf down to where he wasn't trying to shift; rage shifts were not the way to go.

Opening his eyes, he saw both Gareth and Maria standing beside him along with Rein and Mikan. Adam smiled, "Sorry for causing a scene; my wolf reacted badly to some upsetting news. I was able to keep control, thanks to Brook," Grabbing a hand, he gave it a squeeze in thanks.

The Alphas smiled, "I see you did. Excellent! Looking at the two Betas and two Theta. I would like to know what happened. Is it something of a sensitive nature?"

Adam and Brook nodded decisively, before Brook confirmed, "Yes. As it was, we were going to want to talk to you." Looking at Maria, "Actually, with both of you."

"Let's go to my office then."

Rein and Mikan returned to what they were doing before; they weren't needed to help subdue a rage-turned wolf, as the others went out to the Alpha's office. Adam closed the door behind them; the room was nearly soundproof. Even listening at the walls, no Were would even be able to make out what was being said.

Adam started, "It started when I noticed Duncan and Keanna sitting alone and looking down. I didn't even know they had recently joined the pack; I just knew I *needed* to try to help them feel better. We were able to get them to open up a bit, just by caring about them.

Looking down, Duncan started talking quietly, "The fact a Beta, let alone a pair, wanted to find out what was wrong, and why we were down, let alone *what* the two said, told us we made the right decision in joining this pack. The fact his wolf was outraged at what I told him, and he didn't even ask details... it very much makes my wolf happy."

Gareth, knelt in front of Duncan so he could see his face, and quietly asked, "Would you repeat for us what you told Adam and Brook, please? Your position in *this* pack is secure. Since you came, you have been diligent and hard workers. You both have impressed your supervisors enough for several to have recommended promotion to Delta. The only mark against you, is you don't interact with the pack; you keep to yourselves and avoid celebrations. I will not hold anything against you from your past before you came here, but to be a Delta, you need to be involved in the pack at a personal level."

Both jerked in surprise, Duncan looked up, "P... p... promotion? We don't have the blood to be a Delta..."

Shaking his head, Gareth corrected, "Although for many, blood gets them a position like their parents, like Brook. But look at Adam, he is not even shifted yet, and he is already doing the duties and showing the skills of a Beta, with almost no training. Or look at Rein; his parents are Thetas. He is another Beta, and basically oversees everything to do with the pack house or domestic. In this pack, my mate and I decided, when we took over, we would go for skills and let the best people for the jobs do them, regardless of who their parents are. Those who are born to higher ranks, but lack the skills and aptitude, and are not interested in working to learn them, are ranked lower, without any sort of penalty or stigma."

Gareth let it sink in for a few minutes. Maria had snuck out and returned with a pitcher of cold water with a few slices of lemon in it, and a stack of cups. She passed filled cups to everyone. Pointedly starting with the two Theta and finishing with herself and her mate.

Duncan quietly said, "We were members from the Shadowed River Pack. We were to be exiled and all our possessions seized for 'assaulting a delta without cause'. What happened was he was drunk and was looking for fun. He caught Keanna just before she came into our room and demanded she 'service him'. I did attack, and push him off her, before retreating to our room with her. The Alpha there took his story without even checking on our side. The Alpha didn't even tell us to our face what the charges were, he just had an enforcer tell us we were to be exiled as rogues the next morning for attacking a Delta. We escaped into the night with some help from an Enforcer." That enforcer hadn't believed the Delta's story but did believe the two when they had spoken to them, then told them what they had been accused of and the Alpha's decision. He had helped them escape.

Gareth and Maria snarled at hearing the story and took a few minutes to calm themselves. Once they were calm, he pulled out a notice from their old pack with their picture on it from a drawer in his desk. It listed them as Rogues and 'Extremely dangerous' before going into details that seemed nearly impossible from what they now knew. It had *Suspect incorrect exaggerated* written across it. "I got this a week after you requested asylum and was granted it. In that week, I had already seen you had been kicked down hard, and no longer tried to get up. I kept an eye on you two till you requested to formally join the pack, at which point I decided you had been grossly misrepresented, and letting you join would start your healing. You *are* valued members of this pack, and I would lay down my life for you, as I know many others here would without hesitation too."

The only secured method for communication between packs for items like this was the couriers. Brook told Adam. *Most are Lone wolves who travel pack to pack and provide a link with other packs. Some have set routes and schedules to visit the various packs. Others had more random travels for their own wishes and took items for the area they were heading to, or along the route. Some Loners are willing to accept calls to take specific packages or letters between packs, as express couriers.*

Packs sometimes had one or two members who were registered as Couriers on behalf of their packs. They could deliver items from their pack or take stuff to their pack, but that was all. Even then, those had to have the Courier status accepted by the other pack they were visiting, so was mostly between friendly packs, while the loners were considered neutral and thus could be used to exchange items between packs who were less than friendly or take copies to many packs as they did their various visits.

Some packs, like theirs, kept a list of the couriers in the area, and any could come in at any point, and they would be treated as Guests. But some packs, like Shadowed River had only a very few who would deal with them. Gareth and Maria had wondered if something like that had happened, as the two they knew Shadowed Valley trusted were males, and any females they asked to carry items to them would refuse to go there.

Both Duncan and Keanna were sobbing, they were so happy. It took a while to calm them and continue.

Gareth asked, "Is there anyone you were close to still in that pack? We do not have good relations with them, so it would need to go through the Elders, but we could pass them a message." Elders sometimes were willing to discuss with other Elders of packs which they had less friendly relations with.

After thinking about it, Duncan shook his head, "No, all our friends had turned their backs on us, and refused to support us against the accusation of a Delta. We have no interest in stirring those feelings up again. Or having word we are safe get back to the senior wolves there. They would come after us."

Nodding, Gareth told them, "Well, I want you to involve yourself in the celebration today. I am not going to order it, as it is not right, just request it. Maybe you can make some friends here." Ripping the notice into little bits before putting them in the recycling box, "What we learned about your past before you joined the pack will be kept confidential and will have no bearing on your future." He and his mate had already agreed to allow them a fresh start, without any stigma of their old pack, and the false statements given and accepted by the Alpha.

Adam had been clinging to Brook after hearing the sad story to keep himself calm, but unwrapped himself, and stood up. His wolf followed his thoughts, and agreed, sent him some encouragement.

"If I may, I am going to introduce them to Jess and Joshua, so they can start making friends." Adam offered before looking at both Duncan and Keanna, "If you two need any help, *day or night*, find me or my mate, and we will help you to the best of our abilities."

Both Duncan and Keanna had tears of happiness falling again, as they nodded in understanding.

Gareth chuckled as he felt the bonds form between the four, "Well, I think they are going to be reassigned tomorrow to your team, so maybe introduce them to the other five who look to you?"

Adam looked shocked, Brook a mix of bemused and resigned, but both nodded.

I'll tell you more later; it's only expected, Brook commented to Adam. His wolf was feeling fairly satisfied now; the two were under his protection. He'd not let anything like it happen here.

Adam nodded as the rest stood up, and Gareth commented, "Well, enough being stuck in an office! It's the Solstice; we should be having fun! Scoot!" as he ushered them out of the room and back to the dining hall where the pack was gathered.

CHAPTER 11

Adam's First Shift

Adam and Brook led Duncan and Keanna and introduced them to Jess and Joshua, and asked them to introduce them to their friends, and hoped they would more fully integrate with the pack.

Brook and Adam headed over to their own friends and quietly advised them the two were now under their protection, which hopefully would let them heal from the treatment at their previous pack. They refused to give any more details, just telling them they had been granted a fresh start by the Alpha.

Their friends nodded and decided to enjoy the day instead of thinking about the bad things. They weren't the first and wouldn't be the last ones the Alphas had wiped their past and given a fresh start when they joined this pack.

Adam and Brook mingled with other pack members, and worked to try to keep things light, and not talk too much about work. Many packmates did compliment them and their team on getting the changes done so fast. Adam just thanked them and said they were just the start, and more changes were to come.

Adam used the time to get to know more members and made sure to speak to many of the Deltas and the Thetas. Talking to Brook, he found out who the two Omegas were, and made sure to have a few words with them as they worked to keep the buffet tables filled. There would be some roasts put out later for dinner, he found out. They may have done something bad and were being punished, but they were still pack members, and if they were respectful, shouldn't be abused for it. They both seemed resigned to the consequences for their action—or inaction, in their case—and were genuinely surprised when he had not just ignored them. He didn't ask about what they did, as it was not any of his business if they didn't volunteer it. They had been tried, convicted, and were serving out their punishment as the lowest of the pack.

Adam enjoyed his day mingling with the pack. Other than a couple 'puritans' who though even the turned wolves were to be treated as beneath them, everyone was very much welcoming towards him. Towards the evening, after everyone had eaten, everyone started to head out to the bonfires. He followed along, an arm around Brook's back. He barely felt the cold, even though his—and everyone else's—breath could be seen, even without a jacket.

Brook had him in some older clothes he didn't care if they became rags, as he was close to shifting and could do it at any point. She was betting on it being this evening at the Solstice Howl.

Reaching the fire, people were continuing the party, *So far it seems there is the main party, then in the evening it migrates to the fire, and goes till all hours?* Adam asked Brook, having seen the similarities to the party introducing him to the pack.

Generally, yes. It allows for the formal part at the beginning, and then for us to bond and just hang out together. It helps us be a cohesive pack and shows the senior wolves, like us, are available for the lower ones. It also allows us to find those like those two, who need some special attention. They usually would barely be around others.

Curling up close to his side, she continued, *As to the looking to us: the fact you not only cared enough to ask them to tell you things nobody else had been able to get them to do, and the fact your wolf was outraged and wanted to attack the one who hurt a packmate. It would have spoken to their wolf, and would make them want to stay with you, since yours is willing and wants to protect them. Not sure if you felt it, but when you offered your protection, and they could ask for help from us, a bond was formed.*

We will know without anyone saying anything if they were in danger or needed our help. I feel it will help ground them and let them heal.

As to where they came from, Brook let out a mental sigh, *Shadowed River Pack is a very aggressive pack. I wouldn't be surprised if they had scouts out looking for them still. Just so they could drag them back, and pass judgment on them, strip them of everything, then kick them out of the pack. If they don't kill them for trying to run. The fact they are here, and part of us now, will also make us a target in their eyes. I bet the Alpha has increased patrols already. They have very few packs who are willing to deal with them, and they are isolationist.*

The clouds cleared, showing a mostly full moon and some shifted, putting up a loud howl. Adam's wolf howled in his head, and he felt some pain start in his back, radiating out as an ache to cover his body. Brook quickly picked him up and moved him back to the edge of the forest, knowing he was going through his first shift, "Clear your mind and let your wolf have control." She told him quietly, "If you don't, the pain will only build. Think of stepping back and letting your wolf go in front of you. This shift will be the worst; everything after it will be easier."

Adam closed his eyes, trying to ignore the pain, and aches, working to think only about giving his wolf control, letting go of control of their body. After a couple of minutes which felt like hours, his wolf opened their eyes; it had worked. They were a wolf! His wolf let out a loud howl to the moon. The other wolves howled back in greeting and welcome, some coming up to greet him. His nose was very busy identifying and memorising the packmates' scents.

Shaking off the rags which had been his clothes, Adam's wolf nuzzled his mate, **Shift and run with us, please?** His wolf gave Brook a sad puppy look as he asked her, begging to run.

Charlie, slowly came forward to sniff him, getting his scent, showed submission, and Wolf-Adam gave him a lick on the cheek, accepting the submission.

Wolf-Brook pounced on her mate as she had shifted while he was distracted with Charlie, before taking off into the trees, **Catch me if *you can!*** she teased, wanting to see what he could do, even being brand new to being a wolf.

Wolf-Adam was totally agreeable and let out a short howl of pleasure, bounded after her. Charlie had to work to keep up with them, followed.

It took him a while, but Adam finally caught up with his mate. Wagging his tail, he rubbed his flank along his mate's side. Wolf-Adam lapped at her mate-mark before moving behind her and sniffing under her tail. Rearing back, he wrapped his paws around her, and with the mating as wolves, finalised the mating. Both gave out a long, loud, joyful howl, as their bonds deepened and strengthened. They heard echoing howls of the rest of the pack sharing in the joyful news.

With the bonds between their wolf-halves now set, they allowed the human-mind control.

All four minds decided to go for a run and explore the territory as wolves. They ran for several more hours, till they were tired. Charlie had given up a while ago, and they found him fast asleep when they padded into their suite as the sky lightened with morning, both panting hard. Adam, having a bit longer legs, could run slightly faster. Charlie woke up as they opened the door, and bounded over to lick their faces in greetings, which they happily returned.

Yawning, Adam climbed up on the bed and decided shifting was too much energy, flopped down on the bed to sleep. Brook wolf-grinned, and snuggled down beside him, draping her head across his shoulders. Charlie sprawled with his back to Adam and soon all which could be heard was three tired canines sleeping.

*****

Brook woke up first and smiled inwardly. Moving slowly and silently, she moved off the bed, leaving Adam and Charlie asleep. After shifting back, she grabbed Adam's Digital SLR camera, which she had him show her how to use. She snapped some nice pictures of him still sleeping as a wolf, and some showing Charlie still sprawled beside him, before putting the camera down on the table, and petting Adam's soft fur to wake him up.

After a bit, he started waking up, and tried to move as a human, and failing it, just lay there blinking as his mind caught up, *Right, I shifted. I'm going to have to get used to this! It feels so strange, but also so good.*

Brook grinned down at him, "We slept all day. It's now almost supper time. Want to stay a wolf, or shift back?"

Adam's wolf whined in his mind, **Stay wolf** he begged.

Wagging his tail, he commented, *It feels so strange having a tail, but again, so right. I'm going to stay wolf, as I need to get used to this body.*

Brook nodded, and pulling a sleeveless robe on, before leading the way for her two boys to the dining room. Although, due to their dual nature, they had no concerns with nudity, by custom they didn't eat naked in the dining hall when human.

Many ran a hand along Adam's fur as they passed them in awe at his colouration, his wolf purring in the back of his mind at all the nice attention. Reaching the room, she grabbed bowls to serve them, as they lacked hands at the moment.

Pulling his wolf forward, he used his knowledge to figure out the best way to eat in this form, which was interesting. Still, when he was done, his muzzle was covered in food, he used his tongue to get it off.

Brook commented, *I'm going to grab Jess and your camera. I want some pictures of us as wolves.*

The idea got Adam's tail wagging; he had to consciously make it stop, *I like that idea. Where do you want to go?*

I'm thinking the thicket behind the house as a backdrop. Nice thick trees, and brush to hide our location. I am thinking those and some human pictures there for your mother and sister.

Sounds good. I want to try one thing, which is going to be tricky to do: double expose to have both human and wolf in the same finished picture Adam sent a mental image of what he wanted it to look like. He had seen art of something like it and wanted to see if it was possible to do it easily.

If you can pull it off, I'd expect you'd be getting almost every member wanting their own! She could see in his sending, what he was wanting to have, and it looked very good.

Once dinner was done, they went back to their room, meeting Jess there, where Brook grabbed a nice outfit for both, a hand mirror, and a hairbrush. Werewolves tended to not wear makeup, as they saw no need for it. Adam made sure the camera gear they'd need was also in the bag which Jess shouldered as Brook shifted to her wolf, and followed Jess out the doors, taking the lead once they were outside, to the spot she had in mind.

Although Jess liked taking pictures, she didn't have anything as nice as his camera. Adam was able to talk her through the setup though. Getting the shots as wolves, playful, curled up, and some with Charlie, and seeming to chase each other first, they then figured out what they planned on doing for the special shot.

After some negotiation and adjusting of the camera, they figured out the poses. First, they took an empty background shot of a spot with no foot or pawprints in the snow, then with their wolves mostly facing each other, to show their head and flank. Once it was done, Jess held her hand where Adam's back had been as he moved off to shift, which was a little painful, but only lasted a couple of minutes, then to get dressed and brushed his hair. Once he was in position holding still, Jess repeated with Brook. Once ready they did that shot then a few nice shots as human with and without Charlie. After packing up, they trudged back. All were looking forward to how they would turn out. After dumping the pictures to his computer, he found the ones Brook took before he woke up, glancing at her startled, "I like them," he replied, "Thanks." Loading photo paper in the tray of his colour laser printer, he sent several unedited, which were good as-is. The outdoor ones, he sent as well. Others he cropped down to make a better shot.

Getting the big finality, he layered in the background, then the wolves, setting a mask to hide the background of that layer, then their humans, also masking the background. With splitting the humans to two layers, he was able to adjust it, and make it look like one shot. He saved then printed the result. Smiling, he grabbed all the copies of the last one: one for each of their friends, and for those who looked to them, and one for the Alphas. He had also made some small ones for his mother and sister. He had some of them just in their human shape for the part of his family who didn't know what he now was.

Adam passed two copies to Jess, "One is for you, one is for your brother."

Jess was grinning ear to ear as she smiled, "Thank you! It looks beautiful! I watched the work you did to make it, and it doesn't seem hard to do!"

Smiling Adam responded, "Well you did help. If you want to use my cameras, let me know, as I might let you use them." As he was caught up in a hug. If the camera was sitting idle, he had no problem with sharing it with someone he trusted not to damage it.

Hiding a smile, *If you catch both Brook and I sleeping as wolves, please take a picture, I want one to match the human one.*

Returning a mental promise, Jess headed out the door to her room she shared with her brother nearby.

Noticing how late it was, but wasn't tired; sleeping all day probable wasn't the best idea, Adam commented, "Let's curl up and watch a movie?"

Brook loved the idea, after sending a selection of the photos to the printer, to give to her parents, putting them in an envelope.

After stepping out to the main entry and dropping the envelopes of pictures into the respective pack member's mail slot and grabbing the little which was for them from theirs, they headed back to curl up on their couch and watch a movie, and open the forgotten presents piled on the coffee table.

Adam even had a gift for her which brought tears to her eyes. It was very sentimental and from the heart. He had ordered it special the week they had stayed in town during a lunch break at his work, and then had it shipped out here.

*****

The next morning, they woke curled up on the couch, about their normal time. Yawning, Adam, cuddled his Brook, not wanting to move, but all too soon she started to wake up too, "Good Morning, Love.

I guess we didn't make it to the bed after all." He gave her a nice kiss as well.

"Morning! Time to go do some training. Let's see what you can do now you've shifted. Just so you know, we will be testing your control over the next couple of days, to see if your control is good enough to travel for Christmas with your family."

Adam nodded and smiled, "OK." Once Brook had got off him, he moved to get his usual outfit for training on and jogged to the stairs heading down. Jumping off the stairs the way he did before, he misjudged how much power he needed, and only his enhanced reflexes saved him from slamming face first into where the roof dropped. Catching it on his arms, it smarted, then he fell and hit the stairs, hearing Brook giggle as she came down, "You're much stronger now. Your muscles are much denser. You will need to watch yourself, as you don't know what you can do now. Try not to get into a fight with a human, but if you do, you will have to pull your punches, or you could kill them."

Doing his normal warmup, he had to push himself much harder to get warmed up. Most of the exercises were very easy now, where before they took much more effort to complete.

As they headed up for breakfast, Adam asked Brook, "I'm feeling a general achiness in my bones. Is that normal?"

Brook nodded, "Sadly it is. It's the fact your frame isn't used to changing. I recommend changing at least every other day, but not changing within two hours each time, till you stop aching. Sadly, it is going to last for six to eight weeks." She had read up on it and had talked with the Healer about it.

Nodding as they walked up to the dining room, "I can handle that." Adam commented; passing pain he could deal with.

Adam stopped suddenly as soon as the door was opened; everything was much stronger in smell, and he could smell individual scents, and at a sniff can tell the ingredients in the food, He turned his nose down a bit, again. He also had to turn his ears down, as it was very loud. He had been getting used to the changes, but now he had shifted, it was to a whole new level.

Moving he joined the rest of their friends, getting some big congratulations to the shifting, "So, who won the betting pool?" he asked, curious. He had ignored it, but knew it was happening.

"Brook did." Came the dejected response, "She *always* wins, if she enters."

"I only enter if I am sure I can win. I hate wasting money." Was Brook's cheeky response, as she was handed the prize for her bet.

Adam grinned, "Good to know: if Brook enters a betting pool, leave while you have the chance."

"So, we got your awesome pictures. It's going up on my wall! How were you able to get both your Human and Wolf in the same shot?" Was asked, with comments of agreeing and wanting to know.

"Magic!" Adam replied, teasing everyone.

"Tell them, don't tease them." Brook admonished her mate.

Just then the Alphas came up fast, "Love the picture! How the heck did you do it? Could you do it for others?"

Adam grinned and motioned them to join them, "I was just about to explain it for our friends, as they asked, too. Brook didn't let me just tell them it was magic." Brook growled at her mate as the rest laughed at the teasing, "So, there are actually three shots in the picture: background scene with the trackless snow, the wolves, and the humans. As the humans have their hand on the wolf, we had to do the wolf first. Then I had Jess put her hand where mine would be when standing there while I shifted and got ready, then moved into place and posed. Then did the same with Brook. The snow on the ground helped, as we knew from the prints where the wolf had been. Once in place the shot was taken. Then came the hard part: I had to mask out all the shots but the wolves and humans, and layer them on top of the scene. There was a little fudging of positions, but as you see, it worked out well."

Answering the Alpha's and the unspoken from the others, "Yes, it is possible to use it with others, although I would want to charge for it, as it is about two hours of work for the one shot. For you, Alpha, consider it a gift. Let me know when and where."

"Today. Ten. First ridge to the Northwest. I want a shot with the mountains behind us." Came the reply. He had been thinking of it with his mate since he received the picture, and they agreed they liked the spot.

Adam looked at Brook, as normally they were training then, and got a nod in reply, "We'll be there. Are you wanting the same, or something similar?"

"I was thinking Wolves just standing in front of the humans; I liked the wolf-poses you two used but have the humans between them." Came Maria's reply as she came up to join them.

Adam was grinning, "That is actually easier to do; the seeming to be touching was the hardest part to get right."

Maria looked at her mate, "Then it's set. Breakfast, then we must get ready." She then glanced at Adam, "Can you do the human part first?"

At his nod, she grinned, "Excellent! Our wolves always look perfect, so I just need to work on our human sides. Can you do bigger?"

Adam shook his head, "I don't have a printer to do it. I was looking at adding a large plotter that could do much bigger, but down the road."

Gareth liked the idea, "See if you can add it to your order, or as a new order. When are you upgrading the PCs?" His PC was annoying him to no end, and the squeal from the monitor was getting on his nerves.

Adam smiled, "Will do. I'm needing to have the network built up and functional first, as the network right now wouldn't be able to handle many more devices. I will look at getting you a laptop for right now. Brook and I will see you later, I'll bring a short-list of laptops for you to choose from; all will be much faster than what your PC can do." As the Alphas left to get their breakfast, he turned back to his own breakfast before it got cold, switching to speaking telepathically, *The rest of you: if you want a Photograph, Talk to me when it's a bit quieter. Maybe next week. Have a pose you want and figure out what you want to give me in compensation.* He was so glad he could still talk while his mouth was occupied with eating, although the food tasted so much better now, he nearly groaned. Looking at Duncan and Keanna, who were sitting with them as they looked a little disappointed when he asked for compensation, as he knew they wouldn't have much in the way of cash. While the pack would cover the necessities, many creature comforts which would be needed to start a new life cost money, even with the pack covering the essentials. It would take them a while to build up a savings, and have only two seasons wouldn't have been enough, *It doesn't need to be cash, it can be an exchange,* Adam told the two. They nodded in agreement; as it would be easier for them.

Finishing a second helping of breakfast before he was full, he stood and gave Brook a kiss, "Well, duty calls; I have some computer specs to research and price out for the alphas, and—" Looking at the clock on the wall, "—I have only an hour to do it in."

Getting back to his suite, Jess and Joshua were changing the sheets on the bed and were startled to see him; he was scheduled to be training at this time. Adam smiled and nodded to them, "Have a priority request from the Alpha. Don't mind me, I'm just going to be on the computer doing some research."

All too soon, *Time to go, Love; you don't want to keep the Alphas waiting.* his mate called, knowing he would have lost track of time.

Already? Just finishing up. Remind me to add more toner for my printer to the order. He grabbed the stack of sheets he printed off. If he got many more requests, he was going to need to get a high-quality photo printer sooner than later. The printer and plotter were on the list of things to get 'once the system was functional', not on the 'need ASAP' list.

*****

The shoot was a success. The Alphas asked for a digital copy, so they could pass it to other packs. He gave a grin, knowing he'd be getting requests for more from other Alphas. Those requests he could mostly push off, or the steps passed to one of their own photographers. He had been tested off and on, and his control was fairly very good for how long he had been able to shift. It annoyed him to no end, but it was part of the point. The most they had gotten was claws at one point, and Adam had been able to pull them back fast. He got approval for Christmas with his family the morning of Christmas eve, although he was not permitted to spend the night away from a pack. The Alpha had got a request from the Longview pack's Alphas as they wanted a photograph too. It was perfect timing, as the Alphas arranged to stay a couple of nights there to take one of them and of each of their Elders on their way back from Christmas with his family. Most of the elders wanted just to have a double headshot, with the forest in the background for theirs, which was easier to do.

He had also seen the way it was going, with several enquiries either for copies, or for other photos of him, themselves, or just random pictures and had ordered the high-end photo plotter, and a smaller printer to do up to 11x17", and plenty of supplies for both; luckily, they should be arriving with everything else, as they were in stock.

The Alpha's laptop was ready, and he had arranged with Tara to pick up it, and the one he was going to be giving her—although she didn't know it—from his old work's office before they closed for Christmas. Surprisingly, Gareth picked the one which was nothing special and was a model he was considering for the rest of the pack.

For the weather, they had signed out a pack vehicle; a large 4-wheel drive SUV with studded winter tires. Although it was not a luxury vehicle, it was equipped with many safety bells and whistles: dynamic cruse control, lane departure warnings, blind-spot detection, backup camera, and a set of cameras which recorded off all four sides continuously— The Alpha ordered it on every vehicle when the one they were trialling it on had another driver ditch his vehicle into a tree, and try to blame it on the wolf, since they had been trying to pass them illegally. It had saved them from a nasty lawsuit and blackmail which had threatened to expose them. It also had a satellite phone and emergency locator beacon, and even a built in GPS navigation system, which had been modified to have all the local packs listed as locations already loaded. There was a tote of emergency supplies: medical kit, fire extinguisher, flare kit, tow strap, visibility vests, emergency blankets, and a section of spare clothes. Adam had smiled when he learned about what tech it had in it; much more than his nearly base vehicle had.

They were in the vehicle at dawn Christmas morning, yawning; they had been up late with the moon party the night before. Knowing they had to be up early to drive in the morning, they quit and went to bed before any of their friends. Adam sighed, as it was the first time as a wolf he got to participate. He'd just have to wait till the next one to really enjoy it.

The drive out was hard in the mountains, as many spots were badly iced. They were glad they had decided to not take Adam's vehicle, as it didn't have studded tires and only All-Wheel Drive. As they were going by the town south of the city where Adam's sister lived at, they had arranged to pick her up as well, and drop her off at the end of the evening, as they went to spend the night at the Longview Pack.

They arrived early afternoon to pick up Tara, and her two cats, to save her from having to take a separate vehicle. She still didn't fully believe Adam could shift, until he had shifted in her living room, and after knocking her down with a careful swipe of his paw, pinned her down and gave her face a tongue bath, as Brook took a few pictures. Wolf-Adam loved Tara, and considered her his sister, and since she was human, had become protective of her.

She finally believed him; it was hard to disbelieve when a wolf sat on your chest and gave your face a tongue bath. She was commenting she was going to get him a collar. Adam wasn't sure if she was joking or not. His wolf was not amused and had him pass on a threat to munch on her vehicle.

Handing her an envelope with copies of the pictures, Tara squealed as they were so cute! Adam was glad they had done so before they left her place, as the squeal made both wolves jump. They had a short chat at her place, as she looked through the photos.

When she hopped in the back seat, she and her cats got a greeting sniff and lick from Charlie. One of the cats thought Charlie made a great bed, and almost immediately curled up and went to sleep. The other didn't know what to do and stayed on Tara's lap the whole way. Charlie didn't really care, but did think of them as family, as he already considered Tara to be, as they had her scent all over them.

Eventually they arrived, and everyone got out. They were the first there, and even though they had called ahead that they were bringing a big dog, Mary was still surprised at his size. Adam put Charlie's collar on him for appearance's sake but didn't bother with a leash, nor his Service Animal vest, leaving them in the vehicle.

Hopefully, the contingency plans they had arranged wouldn't be needed, and Adam's wolf would be able to stand the stress of his human family.

CHAPTER 12

Christmas with the Human Family

Mary gave Tara then Adam and Brook a good hug as they came in the door, "You are looking so much better! So, have you... become a wolf?"

"Yes, I've shifted. First shift was last Monday on the Solstice. It was a bit painful to shift at first, but my body is getting used to it slowly. Eventually I won't feel it. Here, look at these." Adam pulled out an envelope with her name on it, handed it to her, with a smile on his face.

Mary opened it up, and seeing Adam in wolf form, sleeping curled up on a bed first, "Aww, is that you?"

Adam continued to smile as he agreed the picture was really cute, and nodded, "Yes; the first night, Brook and I spent it playing as wolves, so I could get used to the new form, then curled up in our room to sleep the day. She woke up first and took the picture of me."

"Very nice, your wolf looks beautiful," Mary looked at the other shots. Seeing the nice pose of Adam and Brook as human, "I want this for the wedding invites." When she got to the one with both the wolves and humans, "This shot is great! I hope you have passed it around. I love the location."

Adam made a note to which picture she wanted for the invite and promised to get her a digital copy of it. He was going to play with the picture a bit more, to make it even better, play with the colour balance, contrast, and other levels, and make sure there weren't any hidden issues. "Give me a week or two, and I should have it to you."

Brook laughed, "The spot is just a little area right by the pack house; nothing special. We have many more places nearby which look even better. We just wanted one which had thick enough bushes to not be clearly identifiable. Our Alphas complimented us, and then asked to get one of them too! That one made the rounds to some other packs, and Adam already has had a few requests to either come take one for them, or to teach a photographer in the pack on how to do it. We are spending tomorrow with another pack about ninety minutes from here and doing some photos for them."

Mary nodded, as two thoughts connected in her mind, "That is why you declined the offer of spending the night, when you called yesterday."

Brook nodded, "Part of the reason. Another was since Adam has only just shifted, and while he has excellent control, he is still new, and stress can set him off and make him shift. As such, he was given a day pass to be here, but must be back at a secured location, like a pack house, by midnight." Also, wolves sometimes shifted during the night, especially when new or young. Their wolf often felt better able to protect them in wolf-form, so shifted to it. Other times there wasn't a clear reason for the shift, it just happened.

Mary looked concerned, "Should you even have come?"

Brook smiled, "We tested him. He has the control. In case the worst happens, we have an extraction team close, and there is a park with some hidden spots we can take him close enough." The Elders and them had discussed it, and suspected part of it was the fact his wolf was what they had called an 'old soul' and was very steady. Adam's control was already what they expected from someone turned six months prior, and it hadn't even been a week; it wasn't something to be discussed outside of the pack. Doubly for the fact she was just a human.

Mary shook her head, "Making them work on Christmas."

Brook shrugged, "Most of us celebrate on the Solstice, not Christmas, so today is a normal day for us. It is when we share small gifts. With our much longer lifespan, we have some Elders who remember stories of the spread of Christianity from Elders when they were young and talk about being forced to give lip service around humans to not be killed as a heretic. Also, the wolves volunteered for this job." The enforcers who did it got to mostly just sit around in a warm vehicle and wait for something to happen. There were worse things to have to do.

"How much longer?" Mary asked. She had caught onto the longer lifespan and wanted to know.

"Four hundred years is average lifespan. If we get to that, we are considered an Elder. Elders are cherished as holders of wisdom from experience. They are used for inter-pack communications when the two packs are not on friendly terms, and they advise the Alphas." Came the surprising—to Mary and Tara—response.

"That is why you are looking so much younger, Adam." Was Tara's response; he had never answered the question when she asked, seeming to ignore it.

"It's our much stronger immune system, and the fact we heal very fast." Brook responded, since she had more knowledge, and knew exactly how much they could share and with whom, while Adam was still learning the limits. Close family, like these two, there was more they were allowed to share. "It is also why a full turn takes at least ten weeks, but usually about four months."

Smiling, Adam watched as the cats got used to Charlie, who was sprawled near the Christmas Tree, staying out of the way, *Good boy, Charlie* Adam praised, getting a tail-thump in reply. He was listening, just not saying anything; Brook had suggested she answer the questions since she knew what they could and could not answer.

"So, I take it you don't want to have a church wedding?"

Both Adam and Brook shook their heads, before Adam commented, "We would prefer out at Upper Kananaskis Lake, as then we could bring in most of our pack, which is about two hundred who would come. The rest would have to stay, as we can't leave the property empty."

Mary started, "OK. I'll see to it. When?"

"July; Mid-day, so people aren't going to be expected to be spending the night. David and Marilyn can have the Pack Chefs deal with the food and cake, and we can use the back way to get there, and deal with getting the chairs and such. We will have them deal with that side of it."

Mary smiled, "That makes it much easier for me, I'll just have to see what the fees, if any, are for it. Want a photographer?"

Adam smiled, "Already have two. Some of the shots they will be doing, most won't see, as we'll be in wolf shape. I'll be dealing with the printing, in order to control who sees what."

"Minister?"

"You can arrange it," Adam grinned. Hearing a car door slam which he thought he recognised, he noticed his favourite aunt and uncle had arrived, quickly said, "Email me anything else, as Aunt Kylee is here. I am not planning on telling her."

Mary nodded and went to the door as Adam reminded Charlie to not move and be quiet.

Kylee came in the door, commenting about the big and expensive— to her—SUV, and if Adam or Tara had arrived, not seeing either of their vehicles.

Adam called out, "I borrowed it from the group I live with now, and I picked Tara up on my way in, Aunt Kylee."

Kylee just stopped and stared, shocked at Adam, "You are looking good, working out lately, and who's the lovely lady you brought?"

Just smiling at the first question, he answers the second to distract her, as he grabbed one of Brook's hands, "This is Brook; my Fiancée. Brook, this is my Aunt Kylee and Uncle Bill."

Brook smiled, "Hi! Nice to meet you." She stood to give them both a hug.

Brook was wearing the ring Adam had slyly commissioned for her in platinum—partly for strength. It was wolf paw prints lined up claw to heel, without any stones in it, with white gold on every other paw. 'Forever Together' and the date they met engraved inside, which was what had set her crying. Adam had said it was worth every penny—he had arranged with Alpha Gareth a loan for the money, and to take it out of his wages—for the look of happiness on her face when he had pulled it out the day after the solstice, when they opened their gifts. They had decided the one ring being equivalent to both engagement and wedding band, for when they were out in human areas to show they were 'taken'. She had decided to get one which matched for Adam, but it wasn't ready yet and was a surprise for him.

Adam's Aunt and Uncle noticed Charlie laying calmly but watching them, "Wow, is that a wolf?"

Adam shook his head, "Wolf Hybrid," He corrected, not too surprised as he did look like a big wolf, "His name is Charlie" Looking at Charlie, he commanded, "Charlie: friends," Giving the command they were OK, and not to be harmed.

"You should have told us! I would have got something for him, too!" Was the response as they knelt and let him politely sniff their hands.

Adam shook his head, amused, "He's already spoilt and way too smart for his own good, that's why I didn't tell you. We only got him a week ago, but he's well trained. I don't need to walk him or even open doors; we have lever handles, and he knows how to open them. If he needs exercise, he will take himself for a run, and come back. Although usually he will join us on our run, and that gives him a good workout."

Adam pulled out of his bag the envelope of the pictures he had for them. They only got a smaller selection, of only the human shots. They too loved the pictures, and thought they were great.

Adam mentally nudged Brook, *I'm thinking we need to take some nice mountain shots in the background, if they love these ones, they will nearly die over them!*

Brook laughed in his head, *Why not just do the ones with the wedding? I'm thinking we'll be photo'd out following that day!*

Adam gave a slight nod, *That would be perfect!* He started to make a mental list of the shots he would like to do, with his wolf deciding to add his two cents into it as well; with many of his ideas good too, they knew they couldn't do them all.

Turning to his mother, "Who else are we expecting?"

"My Mother and sister."

Adam sighed, *Keep an eye on me when my mom's mother and sister are here. They are the most likely to cause issues and get a rise. I think they like stirring the pot. I think I should be able to handle this, but this is the first time I have even taken a girl home, let alone to meet my grandmother.* He warned Brook, just to be safe. He didn't feel like telling any more of his family, as it was lots of work to do it.

Brook sighed, *There's always one… I believe in you. The team is parked behind the park around the corner, and will be here in under a minute if they are needed*

Have them come up the alley, as it likely would be much easier to take me out that way than out the front. Adam advised, hoping it wasn't needed.

Adam smiled and deflected as many of the questions about stuff he couldn't or just didn't want to answer, saying just he met her while on a trip taking pictures, and he had been offered a position with their group to oversee the technology, and it was just outside of a small town in the mountains. Comments about animals, and he just said, "Predators smell wolves, and stay away. Many of our dogs are like Charlie, and are unlikely to attack, unless provoked." Both his and Brook's wolves were howling in his mind. It was all the truth, just not the whole truth.

Charlie was asleep on his side, in a spot of sun, and both cats were curled up on his sun-warmed fur, also asleep in the sun. Adam quietly got his camera out and took a picture, *If I didn't, nobody would believe us it happened* He commented to Brook, greatly amused at the trio of snoozing animals.

Tara noticed, and aww'd at the cuteness, "I want a copy of that for my wall!" she commented, with a grin on her face.

Adam smiled, "I'll get it for you. How big? I have a couple of photo printers on order."

Tara shrugged, "Dunno, how big can you go?"

Brook shook her head, seeing her sister-in-law walk straight into it, as Adam grinned and replied, "Well, the small one can do up to 11x17 inch paper; the big one is a plotter and uses 100-foot-long rolls, 48-inch wide. I'm not sure it has a maximum size other than a roll of paper."

Tara's eyes bugged out, not having expected that answer, "Ummmm, 11x17 should be fine." She decided, thinking something bigger might not fit.

Adam nodded, still grinning, "OK." He'd have it framed and glass for it before he gave it to her.

They chatted about the changes in Adam's life. Some of the ways he deflected the other questions had Brook chuckling in his mind, while they tried to keep a straight face. They had spent part of the drive working out some ways to deflect or imply something other than the truth, and several they were using.

The presents were waiting for when everyone was there, as was the custom they had decided as a family, when he and his sister were no longer living there with their mother.

Eventually the last two arrived; Mary's mother, Misty and Mary's youngest sister, Angie were quickly introduced to Brook. Their snotty comments of "About time" rankled Adam, as he had been working to integrate himself into the werewolf culture and beliefs; his wolf was helping lots. Her tone was what really annoyed his wolf; talking as if he was stupid in taking over thirty years and without giving any common courtesy. Taking some slow deep breaths, he calmed down. He talked to his wolf about how much trouble they would be in, and shifting here would be disobeying their Alpha, calmed him down. They had said they were having the wedding the next summer, and the three parents were doing the planning, leaving no room for discussion or ways which they could make some of the decisions.

The gifts were quickly distributed. Adam had added Brook's name to many of his gifts, as several he had already purchased them before he met her, and she barely knew them. Most went over quite well. Adam had decided to give from the heart, rather than a certain dollar value. Many were just candy, and although werewolves were not allergic to chocolate, the store-bought ones often caused indigestion from all the other preservative chemicals in it if they ate lots.

Mary was quite surprised at hers being a laptop. Adam had spent the hour on the way up getting as much as he could ready for her, and installing a remote-control software, so he could get into it remotely, and once she had looked at it, handed it over, so he could do more to get it going. Mostly, it was getting several of the programs she used onto it, and he was going to start a file and setting transfer before he left from her old PC.

Seeing the ring not have a big stone on it, Misty made some snide comments, which Adam was expecting and let roll off him and reminding his wolf the only opinion on the ring which mattered was their mate calmed him down this time.

It did riled Brook badly though, who gave a cutting remark, "I like it better without a stone. Adam spent the time and money to have a custom designed ring made, not just buying one from a display case. This makes it worth more to me than a huge diamond, as he was thinking about *me* and giving from the heart." She tamped down on her wolf, but still her rank of Beta was showing, with how commanding her voice was.

It startled everyone, as Brook had been mostly quiet and kind. This showed to Tara and Mary at least, how much the two of them were in love with each other. They traded a grin.

Adam grabbed another envelope of photos and passed them over to distract them. They awed over the pictures, ring seemingly forgotten.

"So," Misty started, "When are you going to have babies?" she asked directly.

Adam shrugged and gave what had become their standard response, "They will come when they come," He commented, not saying anything about them having only one time per year, and Brook had told him having one pregnancy a decade would be considered lots.

"Which church are you wanting to use?" Misty asked, being nosy.

As she took a breath to start offering suggestions, Adam shook his head, "We are not doing it inside. We are doing it in the *cathedral of nature*!" he told her firmly, brooking no dissent. His wolf was as far forward as he could be, without causing his eyes to change, as they stared them down, the dominance showing.

"But I'm too old to walk very far." Misty complained, wordlessly accusing them of trying to exclude her. "You're not taking it into account I won't be able to go far." Not realising she had unwittingly entered a staring contest with a dominant wolf.

Adam had a ready answer for her, "Did you want us to have a vehicle to bring you from your car, or a strapping young man to carry you?" he asked with a straight face, not looking away.

Brook could see Evan pictured in Adam's mind, carrying his grandmother, making her work hard to school her face. Her wolf was on her back in stitches over it, all four paws flopping in the air. The corners of her lips curved, as she tried to prevent a laugh from escaping by biting her tongue.

After taking several minutes blinking to think about it, "How about both? I could decide then." She said, looking away from the staring contest to the satisfaction of his wolf.

"Deal." Adam grinned at how stunned she looked. *I won that round!* he commented to Brook, defusing some of their tension, and trying to get calmed down before her next comment.

Misty's next comments about consummating the marriage on that night and how they should be apart until then really offended his wolf, even though they had discussed it, from the way they had said it. He ended up grabbing the bag he had filled with the gifts, saying he was going to put them away before dinner as an excuse to get out of the room. He stalked out the door, barely keeping it together. His wolf was almost trying to claw out of his skin to get at her. Any werewolf would have heard his quiet growl, although human hearing wasn't that good.

Brook quickly alerted the team to be ready, and out front, where they parked before racing after her mate even as she clamped down on her wolf's anger over it as well, transmuting it into care of their mate. Pulling him into the back seat with the blacked-out windows, she tucked his head into her shoulder, as he was snarling and growling, his hands had grown claws and his fangs had started to show, and his eyes showed his wolf, but nothing else had happened. Only the need to help their mate kept her own wolf from taking over as well, even with her much better control. Slowly, sending love and murmuring they were just human and didn't understand them, and had no control of them eventually calming Adam and his wolf down, and the calmer her mate was, the calmer her own wolf was. Or it may have been: if they didn't calm down, they'd miss the turkey, and his wolf was really looking forward to it, having been smelling it cooking.

*****

Mary, who had been checking on the dinner, stormed back into the room and confronted her mother, waving the wooden spoon around for emphasis, "You are being incredibly insensitive towards the two who are clearly deeply in love. He has found a partner which he wants to spend his life with. Who are you to belittle him for taking thirty-two years to do so! Your comments about the ring were way out of line as well! Not everyone cares about a cheap ring which has a large stone on it to make it valuable. Brook was right, that ring, as simple as it is in design, probably was worth more than a large stone. I agree it looked lovelier than something which is just sparkly from the stones and the ring itself is just a holder for the stones. It also will way outlast a stone ring too."

Mary took a breath, but not giving time for her mother to get a word in before continuing, "Brook is not Christian at all, and Adam has embraced their culture and beliefs. The fact they want to do it out in the mountains is completely fine for me. To me, it shows they want to be fully in God's view and is *their* decision. If you don't want to be involved in their life, then don't bother. If you don't like the location of the wedding, don't bother coming! Don't try to dictate where it will be. They had arranged for help for you before you came."

Looking out the window, Mary didn't see them outside, although their vehicle was still there, "I wouldn't be too surprised if they just leave, with how insensitive, and downright rude you have been to them! This is part of the reason he has not been interested in talking to or visiting with you for the last few years. This was a six-hour drive for them, and they did it just to see family. If you are not nicer, when they have children, all you will see are pictures. You will not see them till they are older. If you say one more nasty or offensive comment to anyone, you will be asked to leave. I am sure Adam and Brook have friends they would like to call in to escort you away." Mary may have pushed it a bit with what she shouldn't be talking about, mentioning they had others to escort them away, but it would probably be missed. Her mother looked overwhelmed, and for once, was speechless. With that, she stormed back into the kitchen, to work on the dinner.

Kylee and Bill almost tried to hide in the couch they were sitting in, trying to ignore the tirade.

Tara had seen the look on her mother's face just before she stormed in. She had whipped out her phone and had started recording it; Adam and Brook probably would enjoy hearing what Mary had to say while they were out calming down. She had noticed her brother had more mood swings, but he was better now than last time they met. When Mary went back into the kitchen, Misty had a look on her face which she had never seen; she was looking like she had a scolding from *her* mother for not being nice, not her eldest daughter.

Tara quickly sent a message to Adam on her phone, letting him know things had been calmed down, and he could come back in.

*****

Eventually, Adam let out a shuddering breath, "I have control again. My wolf finally decided she wasn't worth being caged till I could show I have better control. He *really* didn't want to be in the isolation rooms." He gave her a lopsided grin, "He also doesn't want to miss the turkey." The reminder he had sent his wolf was if they didn't calm down, they would get no turkey was what got them to calm down enough to release the control he had taken.

"It is a good enough reason for me. Let's finish this dinner, then we can relax at the pack house for the night. If we take another day, I don't think anyone will care." Brook soothed. She told the team all was good and could stand down a bit, letting them know it was due to an unreasonable comment by on of the family, but not giving details.

Adam checked his phone which had pinged a new message once he calmed down. He smiled, "My sister just texted me, our grandmother is looking cowed after our mom yelling at them over being insensitive. I think it is safe to go back in. Oh, she also recorded it, and passed me a copy. We can listen to it tomorrow."

Nodding, Brook grabbing each a jerky strip to hold them till dinner, and so they didn't eat everything. Quickly eating it, they straightened their clothes, and stepped out and back to the house. Brook sent a wordless surge of love to him, to help calm him.

*****

Dinner was nice, as usual, Adam had the duty of carving the turkey. His wolf really wanted the turkey. He kept reminding him they weren't the hunter; they were preparing it for the hunter. He begged in his mind for a little morsel, and Adam, took a little piece and ate it so his wolf got a taste of it. It kept him appeased enough to finish carving the turkey, and to wait to be served. He made sure to offer the food to his mate before serving it to himself, which his wolf felt was proper.

Everyone was a little stilted towards Misty, she seemed to be still stunned and still wanted to see their grandkids, she would have to be more accepting of their differences. The rest chatted and had fun time. As they cleared the empty platters, Mary grumbled about there being no leftovers.

Cheekily, Adam just smiled and commented, "I guess we ate like wolves, then,"

Mary had to cover her mouth to prevent the laugh from coming out.

Brook heard and had a hard time hiding it; both could feel both their wolves howling over the jest. She couldn't keep the smile from her face.

Tara was not able to hold it in and had her head on the table laughing.

Misty, Angie, Kylee, and Bill didn't get it, and looked at the four in confusion. None were forthcoming with an explanation.

*****

Misty and Angie left quickly after supper was done, deciding a quick retreat was best.

Kylee and Bill not too much later, the atmosphere of the holiday broken. They did make sure to ask Adam and Brook to tell them when they were next in town, and to come visit.

Adam flopped down on the couch, letting out a sigh, "That was too close. I almost shifted. If I did, it would have been the worst way, and I would have lost control."

Tara sat on the other side of him from Brook, and leaned against him, "Lost control, how?"

"His wolf-self would have acted like a wild wolf which just had its mate attacked. He could have easily killed her." Came Brook's quiet reply, "Among us; trying to separate mates is a major taboo, and those who try, often die before they can carry out their threats by those they threatened, or anyone can prevent it. Even *my* wolf was upset over it but was able to calm her down from needing to help Adam. To us, it would have been considered a direct provocation and would have had no repercussions; but being she was human, a different law would come into effect: protect our secret at all costs. For having first shifted only this week, Adam has *very* good control. But some things will push *anyone* too hard. That is one. I have seen many born wolves which seem to fly and tear apart the one who threatened those who are in their care, regardless of their own safety. It is why some wolves *never* have any contact with humans; they just can't deal with the differences in customs and have no control."

Adam just relaxed, with his eyes closed, enjoying the fullness from eating a nice turkey. His wolf had curled up and gone to sleep as soon as Misty had left. He listened, but just rested. He quietly told them, "It is also part of our Pack Oath, which every adult agrees to: To protect those weaker than our self, even if it means laying our life down to protect them."

Brook looked at how tired he looked, "I think it is time we got going too. Adam commented your birthday is in early February; we should be able to arrange a trip to come in then to see you. Our door is open to you, just give us a heads up, so we can make sure we have a guest room ready for you."

Mary smiled, "Ok. I'll look forward to it. Have a safe trip." She said as she gave each a hug.

All three collected their stuff and animals, heading to the vehicle.

"You look done in; I'm driving." Brook told Adam, who just nodded and went to the passenger door, after making sure Charlie was in. He knew he was in no condition to safely drive and was about to ask her to do it. She also let the team know they were all good, and on their way out, thanking them for their help.

"So, Tara, would you be interested in a pup like Charlie here for your own?" Adam asked, "They are very good at protection; we assign them to people like you who are basically under our protection. Most know what we are, but some don't. They are trained to protect the one they are with to the death and are strong and smart enough to take down a moderately senior wolf." He had already talked to the Alpha and received pre-authorisation for one for her.

"Umm... I'll have to think about it." Tara replied. It was something she hadn't been expecting.

"OK. We do provide a stipend to cover his food, and we cover all vet care." Offered Adam. "Oh, you would need to come pick one out. Often, like Charlie here, they will pick who they want to bond to. If they do, they can feel if they are needed, and are extremely loyal."

"Again! I'll have to think on it." Tara repeated.

Adam just dropped it, smiling. He dozed till they arrived to drop Tara off, and all three laughed as the cats seemed to have become friends with Charlie, and wanted to stay with him, and he whined at them as they were carried inside. He even waved a paw!

"Can I see Adam's wolf again?" She was still having issues wrapping her mind around it all.

"Not tonight," Brook replied before Adam could say a thing, "Due to what happened earlier, our wolves are still riled up, even with the good feeding, shifting here wouldn't be good. At best, they would go for a long run." At worst, they could run back to the city to go after Adam's grandmother, Brook kept to herself. They were close enough still it could be done in a reasonable time.

At Tara's disappointed look, "I could see if you could join us at Longview Pack tomorrow or the next day?" Brook offered. Since she knew of them, and was Adam's sister, it was likely they would let her.

Tara sighed, "I'd rather see yours. I'll come out for a weekend soon!"

"Deal!" Brook said, before they traded their goodbyes and shared hugs. Tara had quickly become the younger sister she had always wanted.

*****

By the time they reached the Longview Pack's house, Brook was the only one awake. The turning the vehicle off the highway onto the gravel access road roused both 'her boys' as she had thought of them, as she stopped at the guardhouse to identify themselves. The guard checked his list of expected visitors for both, checked the vehicle for any stow-aways, and had to add they had a pet wolfdog with them.

Parking in front of the Alpha's place, a wolf met them at the door, "I'm Hank, I'm the second." Seeing Charlie, he sniffed but only smelled werewolf, but not one he knew, "I was told two wolves were coming, not three."

Brook smiled, "Charlie is a wolfdog, not a Were. He's bonded to Adam; he smells like us since he stays with us and has taken a few of our bites in play. We breed them in our pack, mainly for security and protection of the humans we care about, but also to disguise our wolf forms, and the fur we shed."

Hank nodded, "I like the idea! Maybe we can get some from you to do the same. I assume you are wanting to go straight to bed. Any problems?"

Brook nodded, as Adam was nearly asleep on his feet, and the only reason Charlie wasn't too, is it was a strange place, and his person needed him to keep an eye out, as he was trained, "Yes, I need to put my boys to sleep, and I need some too. Only problem was a human who was a stick in the mud for ideas and wanted to keep us separated till we do the marriage in the summer."

Hank turned pale, "She did what?" He asked, thinking he miss-heard.

Brook nodded, "She tried to separate mates. Adam only first shifted recently, and we have a completed mate bond. We had an extraction team ready, and nearly activated them, but he was able to hold on enough we were able to calm his wolf from a nearly killing rage with only claws and fangs showing, with my help. Add a filling turkey dinner... He just needs a good night of rest."

Hank opened the door, pulled the key from the handle, and handed it to her, shaking his head, "It took me two months to learn that sort of control after I shifted, when I was turned, a hundred and fifty some years ago. I know he was an un-mated human when you were last here, six weeks ago, so he can't have shifted more than a week or so ago; so it's remarkable control he has. Since you want to sleep, it is good night to you. I will let the Alphas know you arrived safely and will be up tomorrow to see them. I am on night-watch tonight, so let me know if you need anything before morning."

Brook smiled a thanks, before closing the door, as Hank left; she knew him from previous times she had been there, but never knew he had been turned. At the rate Adam was progressing, she expected he'd nearly be done, if not fully done by the time they went back to see his family. Giving a body shake, she hoped not to see his grandmother until the wedding, and then as little as possible.

Looking around, she noticed Adam and Charlie had already curled up on the bed. She smiled and stripped her clothes off and curled up on Adam's free side, snuggling into him. Breathing deeply, his scent relaxed her and her wolf. Closing her eyes, she was quickly asleep.

CHAPTER 13

Picture Day

Brook woke up first, getting nudged by Charlie to go out. Looking over at Adam, still sleeping deeply from the stress of the day before, she let Charlie out to relieve himself. On the way back in, Louise offered a tray for the two of them, and put a bowl down for Charlie. He sniffed but didn't eat until she gave him the command that she was a friend, and to be obeyed. Brook thanked Louise before heading up to their room to wake Adam, so they could eat.

When the aromas of the food reached Adam, he woke up all on his own. He stretched and blinked before sitting up. Seeing the food, he smiled, "Room service! I like this." Looking around, he noticed Charlie was missing, and looked at Brook.

"Charlie woke me up needing to go out, and on the way back, Alpha Louise had a tray for us and a bowl of food for him. Charlie should be back soon."

Hearing a scratch at the door, as it had only a round knob not a lever he could open, Brook went and opened the door for Charlie. Bounding in the door, he pounced on Adam and nuzzled him, before laying down cuddling him, as Brook passed him some food.

After quickly eating, they got dressed and went to get the alphas and the camera gear which was in the back of the vehicle. They found

Alpha Louise relaxing with a cup of tea in their sitting room, "Good morning," Adam greeted, taking a seat opposite.

"Morning!" Came the cheerful greeting, "I love your pet. Almost thought he was a were. He is very intelligent and acts more like one of us than a dog."

Brook nodded, sitting beside Adam, "They are bred and trained for it. They serve multiple purposes: One, every human mate is given one as soon as they can, to be a loyal companion and guard if needed, when their mate isn't around. Two, they have free rein on our territory, but tend to stay close to our pack house, with many staying in their own area till they bond with someone. This allows us to account for the fur and wolfish canines running around the area to any unsuspecting humans who come across our area. Three, we assign them to humans whom we care about and need to protect, if they are willing, as guards. As you noticed, they at a glance, appear to be a were. This tends to protect the human well, as it keeps rogues or those wanting to attack at bay."

Alpha Grant walked in, and caught what Brook had said, "I like the idea. Know if Gareth and Maria would be conducive to having us get some from you to do the same?" he asked, as he sat beside his mate, "Also, I'm curious how do they bond with someone?"

Brook nodded respectfully in greeting, "To your first question: I'm not sure. You would have to ask them. To your second: they have a very slight telepathic ability we found by accident—by we, I mean the pack; we have been breeding them since our pack moved to that area, and it was found early on. It allows for one like Charlie to find a person they want to be with, and fits with them. If we assign them to someone, without them choosing, they can still bond with the person if they choose, but not all do. If bonded, they can tell where their 'master' is always and can find them. They can also sense their emotions a bit and can tell if they need their assistance. The telepathic ability also allows us to talk to them telepathically; it gives us the ability to show them what we want them to do when training, or when we are in wolf form, to give them commands, and, to hear their thoughts, although they are simple compared to ours."

She knew Adam had been briefed on the abilities she *could* tell them about, "Make sure not to pass any of the details to anyone else, as we try to keep knowledge they are anything more than well trained wolfdogs quiet. If Alpha Gareth approves, you can let your pack know." Brook got a nod from both the Alphas, knowing they had been let into a pack secret, not knowing Alpha Gareth had approved Brook telling it, "One other thing, if you use lever handles, they do know how to open the doors, and if the doors are counter weighted, they will close behind. We have all the doors in our place that way, except a few like the pantry. It means if they need to relieve themselves, or feel they need exercise, they will just go do it and come back. All without any commands, once trained."

Brook knew other skills they had been taught, but those were pack secrets. Many, Adam hadn't been taught, as it had been a very busy week since he turned, but it was expected with him turning at the Solstice. If next week was quiet, he would be given some of the pack secrets. Others he would learn over time, as he interacted with stuff involving them.

After thinking about it for a bit, Grant nodded, "Well, I'll talk to Gareth about it."

Seeing their pack photographer arrive, he stood up, and introduced Lucas to Adam and Brook, before heading to the door.

Adam nodded in greeting, getting up and throwing his camera bag on his back to follow the Alpha. One thing he noticed since turning, his camera bag felt much lighter, even though it was over ten kilos, if not more. He just had to find a way for his wolf to carry it, so they could reach areas which needed their four-paw power to reach, instead of the two-feet he had as a human.

He smiled as the Alphas lead them around the house and down a short trail to a beautiful lookout point. Adam had the Alphas stand with Charlie, so he could figure out how best to set his camera up, and once ready, took a couple test shots. He also explained to Lucas how he set up to take the shot.

With the approval of how he wanted to take the shot, he called Charlie over, and found him an out of the way spot for him to stay while he did the pictures. They had chosen to do a very similar shot to what his own Alphas had used. Once he had all three parts—background, human, and wolf—he was going to use the one scenic shot as the background and do the rest inside, since they were just heads, he could have Brook work on his high-end laptop to edit and generate the finished photos fast. Lucas helped with arranging for the Elders to come in, so they weren't standing around waiting.

He had a plain green sheet hung along the wall and set up the shot in the small meeting room they had been assigned. Setting up the camera and cables took a bit more work, as he was tethering the camera to the laptop, and a cord instead of the battery for the camera. He took a head shot of Brook and Charlie for test to show Brook how to turn the green background quickly and precisely into a transparent part of the photo, and to layer them on top of the sample background.

After a couple of tries, he smiled, "I'll make a photographer's assistant out of you yet." He teased, nodding to Lucas to call for the first elder. Nodding in respect to each in greeting, he quickly took the human shots and once they shifted, took the wolf ones. Then Lucas helped them choose which shots to use, and Brook was able to quickly edit them to make the finished pictures, while the Elder watched.

A couple of the elders looked in disbelief, and commented it was almost like magic how fast they could turn them out. Finishing taking the pictures mid-afternoon, the printing of all the copies requested would take a few more hours. Packing up the camera and the accessories, and returning the sheet, they were just organising the envelopes for each of the elders.

Adam had borrowed Lucas' photo printer, and it had been working hard since they started. A bag full of empty ink cartridges and several packs of photo paper later, they had finished the prints. They were able to hand the pictures to the Alphas ands each of the elders as they joined the pack for a dinner. He had also left Lucas with a thumb-drive of the finished photos, to pass the individual ones to each person and so they could make more if they wanted. He also passed him a second thumb drive of the raw shots, so he could deal with hanging onto the other shots, for if they decided they wanted one of the others. The printer, ink, and paper had been supplied for him, so realistically the only cost was their time and effort.

Brook and Adam both felt their time and effort had been a reasonable exchange for the couple night's stay and the food.

"If you can do them this fast, you should be able to do the entire pack in a week or so," Alpha Grant commented, as they lingered over dessert. Many of the pack had approached him asking if they could have a similar picture too.

Adam looked at Lucas, with a feral grin, "Now I've shown you how, that is your job!"

Lucas looked a little pale, from the amount of work it would be, looked to his alpha, "If you want it, I will need three helpers, and to get some different camera gear, and a better computer." He decided, answering firmly.

The Alpha smiled, as if Lucas gave him a gift, "You can do them? Excellent! Submit your list of equipment for approval. I assume you have some in mind to be your helpers?" At the nod, Grant smiled, "Send their names, and I will have them reassigned. This is now your job. You are excused from all patrols and other duties for the time being. If they turn out well, you will be promoted to Beta, and oversee taking more pictures of and for the pack."

Lucas just sat there blinking for a bit, stunned. When he caught up with his wits, he grinned and nodded, "Yes Alpha." Turning to Adam, he grinned, "If I have any questions, can I call you? If this works out, you will have a friend for life for helping me see this opportunity."

Adam nodded, "Of course, I'll help you all I can. You have my card, so you can contact me."

Brook commented, *Already making friends in other packs?* She teased, *Good for you! I'm impressed!* she praised, where as a human, he had very few local friends, and none he saw on a regular basis.

Adam ignored the affectionate teasing from his mate, turned to the Alpha, "My mother's birthday is in February; would it be possible to borrow a room for the night? Personally, twelve hours of driving in one day with a stop is more than I'd prefer."

Alpha Grant nodded, "Not a problem. Let me know the date, and we'll make sure you two and your dog are welcome for the night here. The work and skills you have are excellent."

Leaning back in his chair, "Now, I have heard something about some sort of secure communications between packs which seems to be the discussion of the elders? From what I know of your background, I suspect you are at the bottom of it, Adam. Am I right?"

Blinking in surprise, he didn't realise it was already being discussed beyond his pack, or his skills were known beyond the pack; Adam had yet to learn how much werewolves gossiped. "Yes, it started with me. My Alpha and elders were only discussing it, as far as I knew. Didn't realise it had gone beyond them to other packs yet. I wanted to get our network upgraded completely and stable before I start working on inter-pack networks."

Alpha Grant smiled, "It was mentioned during an Alpha conference call last week. Most packs are interested in the concept but want to know what they need to do it, and how much they would need to pay to do it."

Adam nodded, "Well, at this point: I don't know. I need to research it. I may discuss it with you to be a test link if you are interested? If you upgrade your phones to a network-based one, the servers can be configured to use the secure link where possible. To the person calling, it would be no different than them doing it now but would be a secure and encrypted connection. The earliest I could start anything would be the spring. Probably towards summer, due to the amount of research I need to do. Your pack, due to its proximity and being on such friendly terms, would probably be the first one used to test the link."

"Excellent! I assume you will need network administrators in each of the packs, to manage their own pack stuff?"

"Yes. I don't want to be responsible for more than my own pack's stuff. It is more than I ever expected to manage. I could help design but would want help doing it."

Brook nudged Adam, "Time for bed. We want to get a good night's sleep before the long hours of driving." If he got into it, they could be chatting all night, and she wanted some cuddle time.

Adam smiled, and exchanged goodnight with the Alphas, ignoring their knowing look, and those who had come to hear what he was talking about. Lucas pulled Adam in for a good hug before he left as well. He grabbed Brook's hand and headed off for their room. Closing the door behind them and Charlie, who as the faithful dog he was, had followed him closely, he gave Brook a deep kiss and smiled, "We'll sleep, eventually. I want some time with my Mate. Haven't had any in the last couple of days!" Brook just pulled him close in wordless agreement. They spent the evening quite enjoyably.

*****

The next morning, Adam woke as a wolf, and gave Brook's wolf-muzzle a good wolf-kiss. She woke and stretched, laying on her side, curling into him, before tucking her head under his chin, *Don't wanna get up.* she complained.

Sadly, you must get up, Love. We need to get some breakfast, and head out, to get to our pack before sunset. I prefer to see the ice before I slip, if possible. Adam replied, *We can go wolf, and spend the night up at our private corner tonight, and sleep in as late as we want.*

Adam stood up and did his own stretch, before nudging Charlie on his other side, to wake him up, before turning back to his mate. She was laying flat on her belly, with a paw over her eyes, *I guess I must take more drastic measures...* He grumbled at her, before he grabbed her scruff and dragged her off the bed, getting a slight "oof" from her, across the bedroom, into the bathroom, then into the shower. With a hind paw, he closed the door, as he lay her down. She decided she was playing dead, as she was still tired, and had just let him drag her. Giving a snort, he stood up, paws braced on the wall and turned the shower on... ice cold. Sadly, he couldn't escape, and he got the cold water too. He just could brace for it.

It did have the desired affect, though: Brook yelped as if he stabbed her with a knife, and stood up, "OK! I'm awake! I'm awake!" she said, once she shifted to human and turned the shower hot to warm up. Adam just gave a wolf-grin and wagged his wet tail, before using the opportunity to slip his muzzle between her thighs and lick, causing another loud yelp before he let her push him away. He was quite happy the room was soundproofed to werewolf standards.

"You are a very dirty wolf, Adam! Didn't you get enough of that last night? Shift back, and we can continue when we are back at the pack."

Adam wolf-grinned before shifting back and helping wash her hair and back. She grumbled but helped him with his when asked.

Today, sadly; they both wanted to be home, so were helping the other get ready. Once washed, they headed out and Brook went to the pack of their clothes. With a grin she pulled out some clothes and tossed them at Adam. Opening the bundle, he blushed slightly: a thong and matching padded sport bra, thigh-high socks and a skirt the fell to just above the knee. There was a stretchy tank and a long sleeve short shirt in a different colour which would show the belly of the tank, and both tops were close fitting. "You want me to wear this out of *here*?" Normally he enjoyed wearing whatever she decided, but this was beyond what was usual, and much more of a girly look.

"Call it payback for the ice-cold shower to wake me up!" She mock-glared at him, "Put it on." She then grinned, "I want to see how cute it looks on you!"

Adam shook his head and pulled the outfit on. It was surprisingly comfy, and the scent of their mate wrapped around them made his wolf purr in contentment.

It didn't distract him from the fact she had decided to pull on his clothes from the day before as he dressed how she wanted him. She glanced at him, with an innocent look on her face, "What?"

"Your wolf purring too in enjoyment of being wrapped in my scent?"

Brook blushed, but nodded, "Yes. I love the feeling of her enjoyment too. I should have had you wear something of mine when we were at your mom's; might have helped our wolves stay calm."

Adam shrugged, "Well, maybe next time we have a time she is around." He planned to see her as little as possible, as he didn't really care to see her at all.

Once they had everything collected, they grabbed the laptop and camera bag, and took them out to their vehicle. As usual Louise was up making breakfast. She had to stop and stare at the two, before shaking her head and didn't comment on it. Most wolves had something others thought was strange which made them happy. Wearing their mate's clothes was one thing even she had done occasionally. But it usually was when he wasn't around.

Once they were packed up, they returned to the kitchen and joined the Alphas for breakfast. Grant didn't even visibly show what they were doing was anything out of the ordinary. He knew three couples in his own pack who did it regularly too. One even played a service animal for a couple of years, to protect his mate while she did her job.
*****

After a good breakfast and given some food which would keep for the long drive, they were given a good hug each and wished a safe trip. Even Charlie got hugs from the Alphas. They had flipped a coin, and Adam was driving for the first half, so he got in the driver's seat. Brook sat in the passenger, and Charlie flopped across the back seat and went straight to sleep. At the gate, they were checked out, and a little staring, which a growl got the correct deference for their rank and guest status. They were quickly on their way and heading home.
*****

The only eventful thing which happened as they drove home, was during the stop for a stretch while they filled it with gas. Adam got some comments, till they noticed he had Brook with him; after that they just chuckled, commenting he must have lost a bet or something. Once they drove off, they had a good laugh at what they commented supposedly out of their earshot.

Brook had given Adam a few of the secrets she was now able to, about the wolfdogs: some of the original ones had been injected with werewolf blood, and others bitten, to see if they could be made to turn, as there had been very few werewolves at that point. Both failed to turn, but they did get much smarter, and their scent changed a bit to resemble a werewolf. Their pups had also grown much bigger too.

Another was due to their smarts, they had some doing limited patrols; three or four wolfdogs and a single werewolf, to organise and direct the dogs. It made it seem like their pack was twice as big, and able to have more patrols. Still, they did have large gaps in the monitoring due to the ruggedness of the territory. They occasionally even had humans get deep into parts of the territory before they were detected and monitored. Seeing a thoughtful look on Adam's face; she knew he'd figure out something to boost their security, and once it was in place, there'd be no way someone would get in undetected.

Due to the werewolf DNA fused into them, their wolfdogs had the werewolf healing and longevity, and it was where the partial telepathy they had came from. They had been smart before, and over time, the werewolf DNA and the breeding had brought them to the point they can take complex commands and learn complex skills.

Some of what they discussed during the drive, was customs and beliefs of the wolves, as Adam was working to at least be aware of them. Many of them his wolf was sitting in the front of his mind and interested as well; to both, many of the beliefs made sense, much more than some of the ones he had been raised with, since he had never been given a reason why they did it.

*****

Arriving back at the pack, they parked the vehicle in its spot in the hidden garage, built into the side of a little ridge beside the road. It was basically a nice underground parkade, with a hidden and camouflaged entrance and exit. It was heated to keep the temperature above freezing, but not much more. It did mean they didn't need to worry about the vehicles freezing or being hard to start. There was also a mandatory wash down when vehicles entered, so they all gleamed. It took a while, but Adam now had a spot assigned for his vehicle in there too, and no longer needed to use the visitor parking, which was less secure and didn't have the wash bay.

Since he had left his keys with Joshua and Jess, he hoped they moved it while they were away.

They cleared all their stuff out of the vehicle, both with a pack, and a bag. Brook guided them to a tunnel, "This tunnel was bored about eighty years ago, then lined with concrete. It leads right to the pack house." About every 500 metres, they had to swipe ID cards to unlock the steel rollup door. It closed behind them and locked before they got to the next one. Passing by a latched steel door between every other section, Brook commented, "Those are escape tunnels. There is a ladder which goes to the surface, and a hidden hatch, usually disguised by a rock. They are locked from the inside, so you can get out, but not back in. They also set off an alarm in the security office if the doors are opened."

Seeing the basic switch which was easy to bypass, he nodded to himself *One more thing to enhance the security on* he thought.

By the time they hit the last one, with a keypad as well, he thought they had walked forever. Brook tapped her access code and swiped the ID to unlock it. Entering, he realised it was right by the stairs and the entry to the gym. He had seen another doorway which led into the tunnel. He wondered what was behind the secured door, but not enough to investigate it now, it would be one for the future.

Heading upstairs, they grabbed the mail. Reaching their room, they dropped the bags on the floor, as Charlie raced for the outside door and went out.

Opening the important looking one addressed just to him, he noticed it had his permanent pack ID and security swipe, "Nice! My own Photo ID!"

Brook grinned, "Yea, they had to wait till you shifted, then the holidays caused them to be slow on getting it made."

Brook had grabbed the other one which was addressed to them both. It was a quick note from the Alpha, "Gareth wants to meet with us at nine tomorrow, after breakfast. Says he wants to make it a regular meeting, since we are becoming so essential to the pack."

Adam sighed, "There goes our plan!" Looking at the clock, "Well, we can go say hi to our friends and get a good hot lunch, come on!" He grabbed Brook's hand and pulled her out to the dining room, to have some nice hot food.

Dropping into the seat beside Joshua, who was having his lunch, Adam greeted him warmly, "How was the two—well, day and half—without us to hound you?" He had decided they didn't have to be silent shadows during the solstice and did want to get to know both well. Having lunch with them would be a start.

Joshua grinned as Jess, who was on his other side, laughed, "It was good. We got some heavier cleaning done in your room; looks like it wasn't well cleaned before you moved in. I moved your vehicle. The key is on your desk. Your spot is on the middle level, about halfway down. I gave the outside a good wash and vacuumed the inside for you."

Adam nodded, "Thanks. I do want you to take it easy this week; I want you to relax a bit."

Joshua nodded, "If you say so; it is not like you two are at all demanding. I am very glad we got assigned to take care of you. Let us know if you need anything."

Adam gave him a side hug, "I'm glad we got you too! I want to get to know you—and your sister—as I grew up having to take care of myself, so I don't want to make it any harder for you than it must be."

Both Jess and Joshua had bright eyes for unshed tears of joy, "You want to get to know us as people, as friends? Not just as your Thetas? We would love to!" They answered together, which just amused Adam.

Adam smiled, and this time he *did* feel the bonds forming between the two and him, and he suspected Brook did as well. Reaching past Joshua, he patted Jess's shoulder, and gave Joshua another hug before digging into his food, **Just because you are a Theta, doesn't mean you two are not important. If you were to disappear, I would not have the time to get all my work done, and take care of my suite, laundry, and such. I take my pack oath very seriously, and the way I take it, as a senior wolf, I need to take care of the lower wolves which I deal with. I may need to discipline rule breaking, but not make your life hard or depressing. I do hope if you* *have concerns you will bring them to us to deal with before they become a problem! I know your job is to help and support the pack. I take my job as being not only to help and support the pack, in a slightly different method, but also to protect the pack, and be there to help any other wolf who needs help. Even if it is just simply being kind or being there when they are feeling down.**

Both sat there stunned one of the highest-ranking Betas would take the time to befriend *them*. Adam sighed, **I take it, being friendly and kind to the Theta is unusual?** he asked Brook, privately.

CHAPTER 14

Finally Settling In

Adam sighed, *I take it, being friendly and kind to the Theta is un-usual?* he asked Brook, privately.

Brook sighed and nodded slightly, *Yes, the pack has become very strat-ified, and especially the lower wolves, have started to feel they no longer work* with *but* for *the higher ranked wolves. They have been pushed down enough many are not happy. Just be careful; I don't think the Alpha would be happy if you collect all the Thetas under your watch,* The last was said as a bit of a tease, *I have been trying to train it into people, but it doesn't seem to stick well. I have been trying to do what you seem to be doing almost instinctively. I'm a little jealous, but you like to share and have me help too, so I just watch you to find the ones we need to help. I can already see you're starting to help the pack run a little smoother; even the Omegas seem a bit happier.* she sent a wave of approval, and love to her mate.

As Adam stood up to get a second helping, he smiled as he saw Charlie pad into the room, clearly trying to track him down, "Here, Charlie! Let's get you some food." He called, and Charlie immediately trotted over to him. Placing the food down on the ground, Charlie gave him an affectionate nuzzle before nearly pouncing on the bowl of meat as Adam grabbed his refilled plate and headed back to the table, "So what is everyone's plans for this afternoon?" he asked.

Jess and Joshua said they were going to deal with the dirty clothes, now they were back, but had nothing else; the cleaning had been done early in the morning. Erin, Aurora, and Nikki had nothing scheduled, as Adam had given them the week off, other than supporting any issues which came up—Other than a couple of user-errors, it had been rock solid. Most of the others had the day off as well and were relaxing.

Adam decided the clothes could wait for the next day. He looked at his two helpers, "The clothes can wait till tomorrow, it's not like they need to be finished today." Sharing the thought with Brook, she thought it was a great one, his wolf was also eager for it. Looking around, he noticed everyone was done eating.

"In that case, lets go for a run!" Adam suggested, and made sure Jess and Joshua knew it included them as well. All were quite happy for it, too. On their way out, they had a couple of older pups quietly mention they overheard and asked shyly if they could join the run.

Let them. The pups always need the exercise, and the rules are they need to have an adult with them if they go for a long run, as they could get lost, or into trouble. Brook encouraged. These two she knew, and had good hopes for them, if they applied themselves.

Smiling, Adam welcomed them, and lead them out the door. As soon as they got outside, Adam stripped and shifted to his wolf, who was happy to be getting a group run. His shift was slower than all but the pups, but every time was a little less time. *It will speed up with each of your shifts, as your body remembers how to shift, and gets used to the changes. It will just take time.* Brook had said when he grumbled about taking much longer than she did. The pups looked like long-legged yearlings. Wolf-Adam padded up to them and gave each a good sniff to learn their scent and a friendly shoulder bump, before giving a short howl which everyone else echoed, before starting to run.

Adam let Brook guide him, as he didn't know the territory, yet. They did have to keep the pace down, as to not leave the pups and Thetas in their dust. Charlie was bounding around the group, enjoying the leisurely pace. Wolf-Adam growled slightly, to get him to behave when

Charlie bumped him a little hard. Charlie whined in apology and then just paced behind him, deciding to be good.

After a good couple hours of running, they stopped for a drink at a stream and then moved to a nearby meadow, to rest. Charlie, who was getting used to Adam and Brook's training pace, wasn't tired, and decided to pounce on Jess, who's smaller wolf was not much bigger than him, wanting to play.

Jess turned and growled playfully, and they started to wrestle. Soon all of them, but the pups were playing. *Come on, you two can join in. Brook and I will keep an eye out and make sure everyone isn't too rough* He encouraged, pouncing gently on them.

*****

It was getting towards supper when they arrived back at the pack house, everyone was tired, but it had been an enjoyable afternoon to let their wolves out and play.

After dinner, Adam and Brook were heading back to their suite, and passing the entryway, they heard some whimpering. One of the two pups who had been on the run with them was surrounded by larger pups. As soon as they saw it, Adam's wolf wanted out to bite them and was growling in his mind. He got his wolf to agree to let him handle it. He gave Brook a look, and both nodded to each other, before moving silently behind the bullies, *Two each, I see,* He commented grimly to Brook.

They both placed a hand on each of the bully's shoulder, to keep them from running. The bullies jumped, not having heard the two come up to them, and cringed when they realised it was Betas, "Now, why are the four of you picking on this boy?" Adam asked them, an undertone of a growl could be heard. *Brook, call Jess to take care of... this pup, I don't remember his name, please,* Adam asked, turning his attention to the bullies.

Toby came Brook's prompt reply.

The biggest tried to shake Adam's hand off him but stopped when he just dug it in deeper, tightening his grip, "He's just the pup of a lowly Theta. Why shouldn't we have him work for us? Our parents are Deltas." Thetas were there to care for the senior wolves. He wanted someone to do the chores, so he had more time to play with his friends.

For some reason, it really pissed Adam's wolf off; it was what he said not just he was very disrespectful. The snarl which came from his lips made all four pups cringe. Jess had Toby in her arms and had pulled him to the side. Deciding a lecture now, *then* hand them to their parents was in order, asked Brook to call their parents to pick them up when they were done with them, as he lined the four up against the wall, and left them under Brook's and Charlie's gaze for the moment.

Crouching down beside Toby, Adam got his side, "They often bugged me. They expected me, and other Thetas to do what they wanted. Tonight, they were asking why I was sucking up about going on the run." Toby told the older wolf.

Nodding, Adam let him go, "Let Jess know if these four bugged you again?" He asked, as he knew he would speak to their helper more than himself.

I have the perfect idea but would need to run it by the Alpha and Rein first... He went on to explain to her he wanted the four of them to serve a punishment under Rein, who had grown up being a child of Theta, like Toby, but is now one of the Betas in the pack through his hard work. *I think this pack needs a shakeup and to stop letting the lows be bullied. They are as important as the higher ranked ones.*

Brook was impressed, and wordlessly gave her agreement, as the parents showed up, *Give them the lecture now, and let them know you will be discussing their punishment with the Alpha, but don't tell them more, and let them stew in their thoughts for the night. I'll talk to Rein right now, as I'm sure he can figure out what to have them do for their punishment.* She also was very upset with the pups and was happy he wasn't letting them go easily. She hoped this would help the pack start caring about the lows. Both her and her wolf had very loving feelings about how caring their mate was for the pack. She glared at the parents, when one tried to just take their pup, and shook her head.

Turning to the four, they paled at the hard look on Adam's face as he moved to them, "I am very disappointed I need to be involved with this. You should know better. I know Brook had been one of your instructors and has taught this sort of behaviour is unacceptable. You may have parents who rank higher than Toby's, but it does not mean you will outrank him." Adam stopped for a moment for it to sink in, and he could almost see them thinking he was going to make them Omegas; he did have the power, although it would need to be confirmed by the Alphas. He had decided he was only going to do it in very extreme cases, and this was only a squabble; not worthy of being made Omega, as being made an Omega would make their entire lives difficult and would limit what they could do.

I have confirmation from Rein. He, and I quote, 'Would love to teach those bully pups right from wrong in a painful way, so the lesson sticks'. I think he's going to be having them hauling and doing the most labour-intensive tasks, so their muscles will be screaming at them by the time they are done. Brook commented, with an undertone of satisfaction and grim pleasure. By now, there were other wolves, not just their parents watching this after dinner show. Adam and Brook thought they could do with hearing this as well; it may reduce some of the issues they had found.

Excellent. I'll leave the details in his capable paws. Adam replied, with the same feelings, *Now to scare the pups a bit.*

"The fact Toby and his friend had the *courage* to ask to come on a run with me and my friends shows he is not likely to stay a low Theta. He may become your boss." Again, he paused, smiling at the paleness, as they would be scared Toby would do to them what they did to him. They may get undesirable jobs, or the worst shifts, but he doubted Toby would stoop to outright harassment but would make sure he understood what they were doing to him was wrong, and would not be good to retaliate with the same.

"I do not think making others do your duties for you is right. I will be keeping an eye on you four, as will others. Without the Theta wolves, there would be no pack, we would all be lone wolves, and be very lonely for company. Your duties as seniors are to *protect* and help the Thetas. The Alpha cannot be the only one to go to for protection. We *all* share in it. The Thetas should not need protection from the senior wolves in their pack, *ever*. I already have a meeting in the morning with the Alpha, and I will be commenting on you four to him. If I hear about you four abusing the abilities again, the punishment we will be coming up with will seem light."

Adam nodded at Brook, who called their parents forward, and had them taken home to their family suites, to be lectured at by the parents, he hoped. His wolf was satisfied the punishments suited the crime, and both thought they would be dreading what they would be getting.

Turning to the crowd, both he and his mate hoped they wouldn't need to do this again, but the pack needed a wakeup call. Adam spoke to them, letting his eyes roam over them, "I may be new to the pack, but I *will* be using my powers to help and strengthen the pack. That includes helping the Thetas and the senior ranks act better together. Pass it around. I *will* be punishing those responsible for putting themselves before the pack. This pack is only as strong as the weakest member. The Thetas are the foundation of the pack. This doesn't mean they are there to be trod upon, but they support the rest of the pack. If, like this building, the foundation fails, the whole building will fail. They need to be treated with respect and care. They may not have the skills to fight, but it means those of us who can, should be willing to honour our pack oath and be willing to not only give our lives to protect them during a fight with another pack, but to help support them with their duties, even if it means we go beside them and help them scrub a toilet, just because we have the time to help." Taking a breath, he continued to show even he was working on it, "I am spending as much time as I can to be trained fully and as soon as I can, to give all I can if this pack was to be attacked. If any Thetas were to ask me to help them with their duties, I would help them as I was able." He stopped there, as he saw he was losing some, "That is all for tonight. Sleep on what I said, and discuss it with your wolves, your mate, your friends, and with the Theta members. A pack is the strongest when we all work together, and *all* are happy."

*****

Brook was impressed. She could tell he was speaking from the heart, and just saying what came to him, not a rehearsed speech. Wordlessly, she wrapped an arm around her mate and led him to their suite. Once the door closed behind them, Adam let out a big sigh. Brook pulled him to her and nuzzled his neck, "I am very proud of you; it took lots of guts to go out and tell everyone how they were behaving was wrong and you were going to try to change it. I think you need a reward." Brook slid her hands under his top and gave him a good kiss. The rest of their evening was very pleasurable for both.

*****

The next morning, as they walked into Alpha's wing, they could see the Alpha's office door was standing open. Knocking on the frame as they paused for a moment, they walked in and had a seat as he finished a phone call.

Leaning back, Gareth started, "Good Morning you two. I happened to catch most of what you did with the four pups, last night. You handled it very well. I loved how you turned it into a lesson for the pack. I have been trying to prevent the pack from stratifying, but my duties prevent me from doing too much. What are your ideas for the punishment?"

Adam grinned, "Well, as I was dealing with them, I had Brook link to Rein and ask if he would be interested in handling their punishment, with your approval, of course."

The alpha sat there stunned for a moment, then nearly fell out of his seat laughing, "I couldn't see any better idea for a punishment! The Theta who became one of my most trusted Betas? He'd know just the right punishment and give them an earful while he was at it!" He got a distant look for a moment, "Well, passed it on, and it's approved. Rein can determine the length of the punishment too."

Once they calmed down, Gareth continued, "Well onto the next part. For these sorts of punishments, if both of you agree, and your wolves agree, you don't need to bring them to me for approval. Just drop me a note of what the offence was and what the punishment is.

You seem to have a level head for making the punishment fit the crime and include the rank and skills of the offender."

Adam was surprised and could feel Brook was just surprised they were being trusted so fast. She knew it often it took years or decades to be trusted this much. They both nodded in agreement.

"Now, how was the trip? I got one report of you linking the team to prepare, but it was then stood down."

Adam nodded at Brook to tell it, "Well it was fine till Adam's grandmother arrived. Adam had already given me a heads-up they liked to stir the pot. It started from the first things they said. Then it was the belittling of the gift of the ring Adam gave me," She had hung it on a short chain which would become a thin collar nestled in her fur if she shifted, which she pulled out to show the Alpha.

"Beautiful; simple but elegant. Custom?" Commented Gareth, leaning forward to look at it. It was a beautiful piece of workmanship. Well worth the money he had loaned Adam.

Brook nodded and continued, "That really rankled my wolf. Then they commented about what *church* we were doing it in and belittled our decision to have it outside. We did get them good by offering to have someone carry his grandmother in answer to her comment of not being able to walk far."

The Alpha laughed, shaking his head, before motioning for her to continue.

Brook took a deep breath, "The one who was the problem was her expectation of not consummating the marriage till that night, and we shouldn't be living together till then either."

The Alpha let out a snarl, as Brook continued, having expected an outburst, "Adam was able to get himself out of there and to the vehicle with an excuse before anything happened. I linked the team to stand-by and ran to help him. I was able to control my wolf by needing to help him get control of his. It took a while, but both of us were able to contain it and calm down. Adam only had claws and fangs at the most." Brook smiled, "Adam's mom gave a very good scolding to her own mother while we were out calming down, and the rest of the evening went without issue. His sister gave us a recording of it—it was quite funny after the fact. We spent the two nights at Longview, and they loved the pictures. We worked out an easier way of using one background picture and then a green sheet to simplify the removal for the other shots. With the help of Lucas, we were able to do them all over the course of the afternoon. Yesterday morning, we drove and got back here just in time for lunch. Afternoon, we had a good group run and play time. Toby and his friend had asked to join us, and we agreed. It may have been what set off the bullies, as we got back just before dinner."

Gareth nodded, "Sounds like you handled yourselves extremely well. Adam, you especially. Did you know your grandmother would be there?"

Adam relaxed at the praise, and shook his head, "No. I didn't think to ask until we were there. I rarely see her, even on the holidays. If she says anything derogatory, she won't be seeing me until our pups have complete control and I have a written apology." He suspected it was unlikely to get to that point, and more likely she would pass first. His wolf was all for that idea.

Gareth nodded, "Good. I'm curious, did you still have the recording?"

Adam grinned, "Thought you might want to see it, so I brought it with me." He pulled it up on his tablet, since it was easier to see it there than on his cell phone, turning it to Gareth.

They all had a good laugh at the recording.

"If your sister or mother visit," Gareth said with a grin, "I want to have you introduce them to me." They sounded like they cared a fair bit for Adam, and now Brook.

Adam smiled, "I'm not sure about my mother, as she doesn't like driving, so more likely to be visiting her. As for my sister, I am trying to get her to come for a weekend she's free."

Gareth poured some glasses of water, and offered it to the other two, "So, I want to have these meetings weekly, as you are integrating well into the pack, and it will let you bring up anything over the week you find you need to have brought up, or I need you to deal with. This week you are just waiting for the major load of gear?"

Adam nodded, "Yes. I gave my techs the week off except for any support issues. The few have been the usual issues with connecting, which rebooting the device fixes. I do need to look at the location of the data centre to figure out if I need anything else before we start work on it. I had been told the location was secured, and I had to wait till I shifted."

Gareth nodded, "You got your ID, right?" At the nod, "It clears you to the areas and gives you full access to them. Make sure you try not to lose it." He had been needed to approve their access to the areas. Turning to Brook, "Show him the security office and the data centres when we are done here."

Brook nodded in agreement, "That's what I had already planned."

Gareth smiled rubbing his hands together, "Now, the last thing: My new laptop!"

Both Adam and Brook laughed, as Adam pulled the laptop up and onto the table, he turned it on, "I have set it up with a basic, current Windows and Office. I haven't set much up, as some of it will need to be reconfigured once I get the core servers online, like e-mail. Since you are jumping from Windows 98 to Windows 10, this is how it works..." Adam went on to give him a couple hour tutorial of how the new laptop worked. At the first complaint of the trackpad, he had grinned and pulled out the Bluetooth mouse and turned it on, setting it down for him and continuing with the tutorial. "For right now, it should be secure enough for us, but..." he shrugged, "It's something for the future."

What's the time? You win this bet? He asked Brook, they had betted how long he would last on the trackpad before he complained, and they pulled out the mouse. "Make sure you don't forget the mouse behind. I have done it a few times myself. I have more in the order of the hardware, but as we agreed, any lost will be billed to whoever lost them." He wasn't even going to make an exception for the Alpha, so nobody was excluded. Gareth smiled, seeing what Adam left unsaid, not commenting further on it as he agreed with the idea to treat everyone equally.

No, came the grumbled response, *You did; I thought he'd last longer!*

Adam chuckled in her head, *It is just experience, and knowing how users react*

They walked out of the Alpha's wing, and their stomachs growled, as their nose picked up the smell of lunch. Adam looked at the clock, startled, "I guess time got away from us! It's already lunchtime! I'm hungry!" He grabbed Brook's hand and made a beeline for the food line, which was short.

*****

After lunch was over, Brook lead Adam down the stairs, as he sighed, "I'm glad that is over; having all the Thetas come over to give me hugs and thank me for what I said yesterday was getting tiring. It was making it hard to eat! I like making a difference, but it was a bit much."

They went past the door to the tunnel, and up to a very heavy-looking steel door, "Swipe your ID, and go through the door with Charlie. Once you're through, I'll step in; only two bodies can go through at a time."

Adam nodded and did as he was asked. Stepping in, he waited for Brook to step through. He grinned at Martin, as he sat in front of a tiny screen which flicked grainy pic to grainy pic, "So this is where you work."

When Brook stepped through, "Hi Martin. Showing Adam the security office and data centre." She greeted. He stood up, and smiled at Adam, "Martin is the Beta in charge of Security."

"Fine with me, I rarely get visitors." Martin commented as he gave each a hug.

Martin gave Brook a pointed look, who nodded, "He has had top Beta clearance, as of his shift at the Solstice. He is slowly being briefed on stuff; we just don't have the time with our duties to do it all at once."

Martin nodded, looking at Adam, "What I do in here is Classified, and cannot be discussed elsewhere." Getting a nod of agreement from

Adam, he asked the question he had been dying to ask since he found out he was a tech wiz, "I'm wondering if you had any way to upgrade this?" he waved at the screen.

Adam laughed, "Want a wall of large screens, where you can zoom in and read the cover of a book at a hundred metres? *And* have it all recorded to review later if needed? Or pan and tilt to the view you want?"

Martin looked shocked, "It's possible?" Even Brook looked surprised.

Adam nodded, "I saw that sort of system where I last worked. They said it took millions though. I have no idea how much money we have, but *technically* we could do it." Pausing for a moment, he thought, "Any other security concerns you have? I might be able to do something."

Martin nodded, "We have cameras only at the entrances to this building. We should have them in all the common areas, and around the parking areas and tunnels. My wish list: sensors around the property to be able to track the property when there isn't a patrol in the area. We have no way of monitoring it all, even if every wolf and dog patrolled around the clock; we'd still have gaps."

Adam nodded decisively, "All of those I had considered, as I can think of five or six sensors which would work for us. Cameras: definitely. With the network I'm designing, we'd have the capacity to have all the cameras we want. Depending on cost, we might be able to set up some rings of night-vision cameras hidden in the trees."

Both Brook and Martin shook their heads in awe, before Martin answered, "What will be the next change?"

Adam did some thinking out loud, "I'm also thinking we could look at the cost of implanted RFID tags, just above the wrist, and use them instead of the ID cards, which can be lost or stolen, and are very hard to take with you as a wolf. Something like the tags people can implant in their pets. I'd have to talk to the Alpha about too."

Martin nodded, "I'd get one. No more needing to hang onto a card. Maybe offer a RFID in a card, or a tag, if they didn't want to have it embedded."

Adam grinned, "I like it! I do know off-the-shelf gear which can be used to keep the costs down. Have it at all doors, and we could even teach Charlie to do it too. It would also be able to log when people come and go, and have it set to flag to here if used at an unusual location, out of a normal time, or just denied." He smiled, "Would give you more work to do, but with more screens, and them being clear, would be less monitoring."

Martin shrugged, "Fine by me. I'd be able to do my job of keeping the Pack and Territory secure. May need to recruit some more staff, though. Would give work for any who are recovering or unable to do patrols. Heck, even Thetas could help with the monitoring." He'd still want one more senior to be there.

Adam nodded, "The upgrades will be not too hard for you here, as I can tell it's a raised floor under the carpet. We'd need to open some of the tiles for running the wiring."

Martin grinned, "I expected you'd not need to be told that! By the way, I want all the information backing up to the secondary data centre too."

Adam was confused, "There are *two* data centres?"

Martin and Brook nodded, before Brook took over, "Secondary is attached to the vehicle garage. Used to be an old safe room, way back when the pack settled here, as a location for those outside of the pack house who couldn't reach it when there was an attack. It was before they had the tunnel, even."

Adam nodded, "Since there are two already, I don't have to ask for a second one. With that, I need to see what I have to work with here." There was also the one in town, which he could also use.

CHAPTER 15

Pleasant Surprises

Brook guided him through another set of locked doors. Once she did, a look of rapture was on Adam's face. The room was huge. There were two HVAC units, with space for many more, which weren't needed till the room was more in use. Overhead rails for the racks to plug into for power, and a foot above it, a frame grid to support the data cables, and above that, plenty of space for the ducts to remove the hot exhaust air from the servers.

Seeing the size of the equipment for the power system, he'd have plenty of power available to do whatever he wanted.

There were two racks sitting dejected in one corner of the room, each with almost nothing in it; one had some of the gear he had purchased to get what they had connected now, and all the network cables coming to it, he assumed it handled the floor, and the riser lines to the floor switch rooms. On the wall, there were bundles and bundles of dust covered wires, passing through a punch-down splitter, which was what he expected for the existing analog phone system.

"I guess Christmas came late." Adam commented, amused, "This is a wonderful surprise. When was this made?"

"We've had the room for a long time. Thanks for making me an alternate contact, by the way as it made it easy to surprise you with it. The floor I ordered after we did the warehouse, while you were in the first stage of the Turning, and the power connectors are new too, I talked to a wolf who is an electrician and had this installed. Your techs and some others of Rein's got the floor installed, after we moved all the junk out and cleaned it up. There was an old, raised floor of wooden slats and plates. From what I learned, it had been built when the floor was renovated about thirty years ago, and the camera system was installed.

Walking to the racks, he noticed about a third of the rack had TV cables going to a box and one running along the roof to near the door they went through. "Getting rid of the old system is going to be easy!" Spying a loose connection, he turned it slightly to secure it. Moments later, Martin walked through the door, "What did you do; the screen is much clearer!"

Adam shrugged and grinned, "Often I'd just say 'magic' and leave you wondering. For you, I tightened the video cable which runs to your screen. The ground shield was loose."

Martin shook his head, "It has been that way since it was installed. I had been told that was the best they could do." Walking back to his desk, Martin muttered under his breath, "I've had headaches for years because of a loose wire..."

Spying a roll up door on one side, "Into the tunnel?" he asked Brook.

"No, to the side of the medical centre's access ramp. It is on the other side of the security centre." Pointing to another on the other side, "That one goes into the tunnel." There were two three-inch conduits which started above the door, "There is a half-metre space in the roof for the utility links. Rein was kind enough to run the conduits for connecting stuff between the two data centres. Both of those doors can only be opened from in here and set off an alarm in the security office when they are opened. The other room is half this, but it was set up the same. It has the same security as in here, as it had been set up as a second safe area. While you were working on the little room in the warehouse, I picked your mind, and worked on these, and while you were in the first part of your Turn, we ordered it. I had them do it on the sly, so we could surprise you with it." She didn't think he'd mind she dug deeper into his mind, as he kept worrying about having the space to do everything and about not having enough time.

Adam pulled Brook in for a good kiss in thanks, "You are awesome! This is basically my dream, not what I was expecting to have. I am glad we make a good team, and we'll be ready for all the gear when it comes." Thinking of one thing he hadn't thought about yet, "Did you order more racks and HVAC units?"

Brook grinned as she nodded, "There is more HVAC on order, this was what they could give us immediately. More should be here next week, and the remainder the week after. The racks on order. I didn't know how you wanted to lay them out. I knew you would want a system for them." She knew within the year they would need to fill it up, so it was easier to do the full order now, than spread it out, since the pack had the funds. It also got them at a very good deal, especially when she said she was open to having them send them in multiple shipments, not needing them all at once. She had paid up front for the first shipment, and then for each as they shipped, not expecting to be billed, and pay months later, which she felt was likely why they got such a good deal.

Adam smiled, "You and I will be busy with it between training this week."

Brook nodded, "I expected it! Now, we need to go see the Pack Healer, for your physical; to make sure your changes are going fine."

Adam sighed, "Fine, Lead the way!" he said slightly reluctantly. He had never liked seeing a doctor, but most of it was the long waits and the costs which seemed to pop up. He liked it here, where you generally didn't have waits, as they didn't need to cram as many patients in as possible to make ends meet, so they had the time to talk.

*****

Brook led him back out of the server room, hitting the control to turn the lights out. Once they were into the security office, they headed down a short hall and out another heavy door, and straight out into the medical area. Adam hadn't been down here, as the other check was in their room before they let him out.

Spotting a Wolf in a nurse's uniform, "Beta Adam is scheduled for a physical, to make sure his Turn is progressing normally." Brook told him.

"Yes." He replied, with a smile, "Right here, and I will notify the Healer." He was quickly ushered into a room.

Adam smiled, here it looked modern, although the machines were set in heavy cabinets attached to the walls and had thick Lexan panels covering them. Currently, the panels were open, probably so they could set them up if they were needed.

Brook nodded, "They are secured when there is a person in here, so if they wake up in a rage, they won't damage the very expensive instruments. The leads are cheap compared to the machine."

"Hello, Adam, Brook." Said a male, who looked to be in the peak of his life. "I see your trip went off without much of an issue." He had been a little reserved about letting him out so soon after being Turned. The safeguards, and the fact it would have brought *more* notice if he hadn't attended, was what let him sign off on it anyways.

"Hi Len." Brook greeted, "We had a slight issue, but both packs felt how he responded was as good as one born, for control." She said it with pardonable pride, as her mate was turning out to be a good match. The pack had four full healers, and several who didn't have the healing gift, but worked in medical, generally as nurses. She had always preferred Len as her healer, so had requested him for Adam, even if he wasn't the most senior of the healers.

The healer smiled, "Now, let me check..." he replied, putting his hands onto Adam's shoulders, and staring into his eyes.

Adam felt time almost seem to fade to nothing, and when he blinked the healer had backed off.

"Well, it seems to be progressing well." He told them both, but speaking to Adam, "No issues, and you've already proven your control is good." They chatted for a few minutes, but the healer had other work to deal with, and left soon after.

*****

Coming out of Medical and back to the data centre, Brook commented, "See, that wasn't too hard!"

Adam smiled, "Still wondering why you had a data centre, and some tech, but basically nothing new. It has confused me."

Brook shrugged, "From what I can gather, we had someone, but they found their mate in another pack, and she didn't want to leave, so they moved to their mate's pack, nobody bothered doing any changes or updating it. It was about three or four decades ago. If he had vision, the pack lost it after they left. Now you are here, even I've been motivated. I'm still trying to catch up to you, though. Now you're into upgrading security as well! I hope you are not going to take over other stuff, too! My head may explode."

Adam shuddered, "No; I'm not planning on doing anything in the kitchen, unless asked. I don't want to be beaten with a frying pan!" He already had a healthy respect for the head chef, and the two other Chefs and how territorial they were. If they asked, he'd do what he could. "Medical, they look like they know what they are doing. Rein and the maintenance: most isn't going to be touched, although will offer a way for people to report problems, and a way for him to track the work. I'd rather keep him happy, so he'll help with the changes. Housekeeping: not much I can do right now. Going to leave it and let them decide. Other than the network, phones, and eventually cameras, the rest is going to be in the data centres. Once it is set up, the maintenance should be easier, compared to my previous job. I am going to look at the cost of running a fibre link from the warehouse to here. It is much harder to disrupt or follow than the Wi-Fi."

"Why are you worried about attack?" Brook asked.

"It's better to design to mitigate any opportunities to attack before they attack, rather than to be just reactive and let the attacker have the element of surprise. For the territory, I like the idea of passive sensors, so if we have an attack, we can stage the defence where and when we want it, rather than just reacting to when we encounter them. It allows for better protection of those who can't fight too, as we have more time to prepare."

Brook smiled at his response, "I take it you have put lots of thought into it."

"More thoughts into an overall strategy than actual planning and specific tactics and building in redundancies. It's due to time and effort, and the fact of technology changing. Although now I have near limitless resources, I can take my skills from my schooling to make proposals to show what it can do. First is to figure out what I need for the data centre here, and work to get it organised, so we know where everything goes which is arriving in about a week. Within two weeks, I want the basic servers functional. Then I can look at enhancements, like the security systems, which will take a bunch of room here and more at the other data centre. Or the research for the inter-pack networking."

Grabbing a sheet of paper, Adam quickly sketched the room, and where stuff was currently, muttering to himself while Brook looked on, amused.

Finishing quickly, he hugged her, "It does mean lots to me you are into it as well and are willing to slide in quickly to take over for me when needed. Once the servers start going on, I am going to need to have you do some work with managing our techs. I'll be busy configuring them."

Brook nodded, "We'll work together." She liked how he wasn't expecting her to just support what he did, but would share his workload, and treat her as his partner.

Heading back to their room Adam's mind was abuzz with the thoughts he had done for a number of servers. Sitting down, he started mapping out how he wanted the network laid out, leaving lots of room in the data centre for future expansion. He would need to re-assign and reconfigure the setup of the Wi-Fi a bit, but it was not too hard, as he could do it from his desk once the servers were installed.

Pulling up knowledgebases, he started researching on one screen, taking notes of what he needed to do, and making any decisions on what settings to use for the servers, and what information he needed to collect. He had already registered the .ca (For Canada), .com, and .net of the pack's name. He was going to set it up so all three would work for external sites. He had also set up a much easier name for internal use and would not be used for external.

"I'm glad I can set it up from scratch, no need for any legacy to work with older devices, and definitely no old servers! This makes it much easier and allows me to make sure I do the best-practices for it," Adam commented, as he continued to review the documents, "Some parts I don't understand well, but will understand when I actually set up the first one."

*****

By dinner time, he had it planned out as much as he could, including laying out the servers, and deciding which he wanted as physical, and which were virtual. It was going to have to be a learning on the job, as he knew the theory behind running servers, but physically in charge of the domain network? Other than some devices he played around with at home a few years before, he hadn't. He did know where to find assistance, so he'd be able to get some help.

Again, the Thetas wanted to come have a word or two with him, but some just gave a faint sniff and a hand brush passed, across his back. That he could handle much better, as it didn't interrupt his meal. Brook had suggested he make himself available, so he decided having a firepit gathering would be best. He had Jess and Joshua let the Thetas know they were welcome to join him at the fire.

Heading out to the fire after finishing, some of the senior wolves got curious as well. Rein and his mate Mikan came and stayed; most of the Thetas liked him, as he had several as his friends growing up. Sitting by the fire, Adam relaxed and cuddled to Brook. At first it was just the two of them, and he found out what the four miscreant pups had been up to for the day, and he was going to keep them very busy for a few days. Soon some of the Theta came to the fire, and went to the two Beta pairs, and got some friendly hugs.

Some of them asked questions of Adam, most were curious about what he did as a human, and his view of being a wolf. Most were surprised his job hadn't included any management duties, and while he wasn't doing it for another, he had been doing the cleaning and cooking for himself. His views were a bit different, but most felt it was a nice fresh view, and they enjoyed being able to speak frankly, and without a care about ranks.

Late in the evening, Adam caught himself yawning, and decided it was time to go to sleep, several went with them. He had heard more people standing around in the shadows, listening, but not participating. He was sure it was the shyer Thetas, who weren't sure about coming to him, yet. A few stayed with the fire, so he didn't need to worry about making sure the pit was out.

After they walked into their suite, and the door closed, "I think this evening was a success. Allowed me to be friendly with many of the Theta, in a safe method which doesn't create the bonds directly with us. I am not sure I am ready yet for more than the seven we have who look to us now. I did notice Duncan and Keanna both looked much happier tonight when they said hi." Adam commented to Brook, as they got ready for bed.

Brook giggled, "I'm glad they are working out well helping our three techs do their support and taking care of them. Well, it was a fun evening to hang out with everyone, I did like your approach, as it allowed for the lower wolves to see you were approachable, and willing to listen. I think it was drawing them to you. We should do the fire pit thing again. Maybe invite the others of ours to come? I do expect we will get more; probably your tinkerer-pups working on the old equipment among some others. We will need more staff to handle the servers, and to support the pack when you start rolling out the equipment." Brook snuggled against her mate, "Now sleep. You have training to get back into tomorrow!"

Adam just kissed her hair, and with her scent wrapped around him, it lulled him to sleep fast.

*****

The next morning Brook poked Adam, and he just groaned. Smiling, she teased, "Time to get up, or else..." Getting him just burying his head under the pillow, she pulled the blankets off him, and still got nothing. "Fine, turnabout is fair play, then!" Picking him up, she took him into the shower, and then holding him up, Adam grumbling and wanting to sleep more. She turned it to ice cold and he yelped loudly, suddenly awake.

Adam quickly reached up and warmed the shower up, sighing. "It was not nice," he pouted.

"You did it to me when you wanted to leave Longview. At least I carried you!" Brook retorted. Adam had just dragged her by her scruff.

Adam just leaned in, sighing, "You're right. I love you." He commented before kissing her sweetly.

Adam quickly reached around and grabbed some shampoo and started washing her hair, even as they were kissing softly. Brook had started on his too. They had to break the kiss to rinse the soap out, but kissed again as they worked conditioner in.

"We have to stop," Adam said breathlessly, "Or we won't make it to breakfast, as it is, we missed the early training."

Brook's stomach growled, and both laughed. "I guess my stomach answered, I'll be good."

Shortly after, both finished washing, and they climbed out of the shower. Throwing on their training clothes, they went out to the dining room to have breakfast, before training. Chatting with their friends, soundlessly as was most people, for good manners, other than occasional laughs, it was a normal breakfast.

After a relaxing breakfast, they headed down and started their warmup. They moved seamlessly into their training, and worked hard to get Adam up to speed, now that Brook didn't have to hold back, since he had the basics down and his speed was getting up to near the normal for a Wolf.

Late afternoon, Adam painfully climbed the stairs, as Brook was amused, but helped him, "A hot bath before dinner would be good to ease the pain from the bruises. They will be gone before morning."

Adam just nodded, not having the energy to do anything more, as they finished up the stairs, and led him to their room.

Joshua was already filling the tub with hot water for them, smiled and commented, "You look like I did when I was doing my mandatory training with *her*," as he pointed at Brook, "But it was good, in the end; I was able to fend off the bullies till help came."

Adam laughed, as he settled in the tub, "Well, I did want to be fully trained, so getting bruises when I fail to do something comes with it. They will pass. Glad it is much faster than with humans, though. If I was still human, I'd not be able to move from the tub without help. This week, I will be doing as much training as I can, as next week probably will be busy!"

Thinking one thing, "Joshua? What are the Theta wolves' thoughts about what I did last night, with hanging out at the fire to let them come and just talk and be together?"

Joshua stopped, and thought for a bit, "Most didn't know what to think at first, thinking you were just trying to show nice. When you started opening up and sharing your life as a human, and how you were almost like us, I think it made more come out and listen. You were treating us as equals, and as valued packmates. Many valued it as much or more than the hugs you gave freely. Many wondered if you plan on doing more."

Adam nodded, pleased with the comments, looked over at Brook, "Well, what do you think, Love? How often should we share our evening with the Thetas?"

Brook thought for a moment, "I'm thinking weekly, starting next week, on Monday nights. Although I think we should have another tomorrow night."

Turning to Joshua, "I agree with Brook. Weekly on Monday evenings, but not as late. We'll also have a special one tomorrow night. Will you have word spread around for us? I won't exclude anyone, but ranks are to be left at home; all will be considered equal packmates at the fire."

Joshua nodded and grinned, "You are going to piss off some wolves with that."

Adam shrugged, "Like I care if I piss them off. If they don't like it, they can stay away. They will not be required to attend. This idea is more for the lower ranked to get to know the upper ones." As Joshua turned to leave, "Oh, one last thing: invite the Omegas. I want to show

I still consider them pack members' worthy of some dignity, even if they are being punished. They already have a hard life from their decisions, hopefully they learned from them. If their supervisor needs me to do something for them to attend, have them let me know."

Joshua nodded again and stepped out to pass around the word; many of the Thetas didn't believe they would have more, and some were disappointed they missed out. Either they didn't hear it in time, were busy, or were too shy. In Beta Adam's name, he even marked it for the fire pit's booking calendar, as he wasn't sure anyone had told him the pit had a schedule.

Thinking about it, maybe Brook had noticed Monday was the one night which rarely was booked. They only had the next 3 months up, so he got it done. Next, he went to the kitchen, as it was one of the main places Theta went for news. Once he passed it on there, he went to the laundry, and the living room they tended to gather in. In each place, he asked to let the rest of the pack know.

Joshua went to the later dinner, with a warm feeling in his heart; it was nice they were wanted and cared for by the two pairs of the highest-ranking Betas. Everyone thought Rein was a fluke, but getting to know Adam, realised he would have, at most, been a Delta when he was human, even so he had to do without anyone helping him with laundry or meals, or even dishes. He knew what it was like not to have those who took care of them and made sure to let them know they were valued for their services.

He thought to the picture he had been given fondly and smiled; the little things he liked the most. Notes with bits of cash, or a treat attached. It seems Adam had found out often things were bartered and had been making sure to pass on some of the fruits of his labour to those in his care.

*****

Adam woke still as a wolf and stretched the next morning. He had gathered all the pups who had helped him, and a few of his friends, and a few other pups which didn't want to be left behind and went for a long enjoyable run as wolves and some play time in the meadows the previous evening. The Alphas even joined them for a bit, playing with some of the youngest pups. He had spent about half his time being pounced on by several pups, painfully, which annoyed his wolf a little, but both were indulgent to them and didn't retaliate, as they still had fun.

The way back, both him, Brook, and some of the oldest pups carried the younger ones, all tuckered out from the romp. Their parents were quite happy with the fact they were already nearly asleep and could just be tucked into bed.

Leaning over he nipped Brook's ear lightly, *Time to get up, so we can do our early warmup* he told her.

The nip earned him an annoyed growl, *Pesky mate; ruining a nice dream,* she complained, mock-annoyed as she woke up, *But the reality of having a mate is nicer.*

Getting up off the bed, Brook stood and stretched her wolf body, *Today, we are going to start you on how to fight as a wolf. It is one skill you need.*

Wolf-Adam took control and was nearly bouncing he was so happy, **Yay! Learning to fight!** he commented, as he wagged their tail.

Brook just snorted her laughter, *Sometimes, you are such a pup!* she teased as they got up.

They wandered out, with Charlie following them sleepily. Reaching the area which they used to train the wolves, they directed for Charlie to stay over to the side, which he was happy to do; there was a nice hollow at the base of a pine tree which was free of snow and had a soft layer of pine needles. For now, he wanted to nap.

As with the human fighting skills, both halves of Adam picked up the wolf fighting skills extremely fast. As they were needing to still learn their body, it was a bit slow at first, but by the end of the morning, Brook was considering turning his wolf training over to the Alpha soon. He needed someone above his skills to teach him, not one who was at their level and could do with a challenge too. She had noticed her own wolf-fighting skills were not as sharp as they should be, and some movements of her body felt sluggish. She made a mental note to bring it up to the Alpha at their next meeting.

They had broken for a quick lunch Jess had brought out to them, some raw steaks and spring water from a local natural spring. Being wolves, they enjoyed the meal. Adam had noticed since he had his wolf awake in his mind, he had started to like his meat less well cooked as a human. Part of it was the urging of his wolf but was also his own changing tastes.

After lunch, they went back at it. Brook was being ruthless in her training. She knew he wanted to get up to speed as soon as he could, so he could take his place as one of the pack's fighters. If a human saw them, they would think they were fighting to the death for all the snarling and growling, and yelps.

A bit before supper they went back to get cleaned up. Just outside the door, they shook the snow off, and used the thick bristle rug in the enclosed patio to get the caked snow from between the toes of their paws.

Both padded into the shower and shifted back to be refreshed. Brook checked Adam for any major injuries but found just minor ones which were already sealed. She swatted his hand away, "No scratching! I'll get you some anti-itch stuff."

Adam noticed Brook had only a couple of scrapes, which would be mostly gone by morning.

Getting out, after applying some cream to Adam's healing wounds, to stop them from itching, they dressed in some soft, loose clothes to help them heal faster, and went out to dinner.

Sitting down, Brook got some ribbing about the injuries, as they were very surprised she got any, "Adam's learning so fast, I can barely keep up with him!" She complained, "His wolf seems to be an instinctive fighter, and it is carrying over!" Realising they were dangerously close to revealing details they couldn't, she dug into her food and refused to say anything more on the topic, no matter how much her friends ribbed them.

Dinner finished; they headed out to have another firepit gathering.

CHAPTER 16

It arrives!

The evening fire gathering was even more of a success. The two Omegas stopped in and stayed for a while, but barely spoke to anyone, after thanking Adam for the invite and getting a hug but did join in on the songs. Many of the Thetas chatted about how the fact it felt like there was now interest from the top on their well being.

Adam did tell them, if they had concerns which they wanted them to let the Alphas know about, they would be willing to do so. They passed on a couple small requests and comments. Adam had brought some paper to write them down, so he'd not forget to ask them the next week, and so they could see they weren't just giving lip service to the idea.

Other than that, he welcomed the warm cuddles he got. A couple who were having a bad day curled up beside Brook and himself, leaning against them. Brook and Adam left at a reasonable hour, Rein sticking around, as he was just able to get there not much before Adam and Brook left, as they were up early to do training, giving them another touchstone with the senior part of the pack and for the gathering to go on later.

*****

Adam and Brook took a bit of a walk and enjoyed the cold night and some time just being together. They still curled up together for sleep at a reasonable hour.

Brook woke up first, with Adam laying on his back, an arm around her, and she was laying half on top of him, her ear right over his slowly thumping heart. Smirking, she moved to wake him with a kiss. He took a deep breath and before she could move away, wrapped her tightly in his arms and deepened the kiss.

After a while, Adam let Brook go, "Now that was a very nice way to be woken up." Adam commented, before giving her a hug, and climbing out of the bed, getting ready for another hard day of training; just glad to be starting out the morning with unmarked—or nearly—skin was nice.

*****

Friday and Saturday came and went. Both days whoever woke up first tried to find a new way to wake the other up before spending the day training, then relaxing with their friends or alone in the evening.

Adam was as ready as he could be for all the equipment arriving the next week; he had got confirmation it would all be there Monday afternoon, as it was a full semi truck load between the disassembled racks, UPS, servers, networking gear, and even a spool of fibre optic cable and the equipment and supplies to terminate the ends. The gear was going to be taken into the garage, then up the tunnel to the main data centre. It was slower than the road, but with the amount of snow, it would be hard for them to use it, and it was more of an emergency route. He could get permission from the Alpha to be able to use it, they decided it would be easier, and less chance of damage. He didn't expect to ever order such a large load again, unless they built the entire Inter-Pack-Net all at once, and as it would be a huge undertaking he wasn't interested; they would build pieces then expand the resources in the number of servers available for each function as the network grew.

Sunday, they took for themselves, as they had decided whenever possible, to take one day a week to rest and relax and play. Many of the pups had asked to go for another run, including Toby, and the number of pleading eyes was too much for Adam and Brook, and they agreed. Spending most of the day with the pups was quite enjoyable. By the time they got back in the evening, they were ready to collapse in their bed. Charlie had abandoned them several hours before, and they found him curled up on the bed, blinking tiredly as they padded in as wolves. Both just hopped up on the bed and curled up into a single ball of fur and fell asleep. Charlie just put his head back down and went back to sleep too.

*****

The next morning Brook and Adam were awoken by the clicking of a camera. Looking around Jess was smiling as she held Adam's digital SLR and took a couple more pictures.

Getting up, Adam stretched then shifted, "Let me see!" he demanded playfully.

Jess laughed and handed over the camera. Adam aww'd at the very cute picture of them curled up in a ball together, heads resting the other's back. Adam showed the picture on the camera to Brook after she had hopped off the bed and shifted.

"That's another for the wall!" She commented, giving Jess a good hug.

Adam nodded and tossed some clothes at Brook as he pulled some on. They'd do some training after the meeting with the Alpha, if there was time, then be down at the warehouse after lunch.

*****

Adam passed on the notes from the Thetas as the first thing in their meeting with the Alpha. The Alpha smiled and commented, "Keep them coming. I know some are too intimidated, just by my being *Alpha,* to talk to me directly, unless they really needed something. However, they come, I will deal with them as best I can."

Adam smiled, "That's what I thought. On to other things, how's your laptop?"

Gareth grumbled, "It's different." He said before sighing, "Eventually, I'll get used to it. Other than that, I am quite liking it. Almost done transferring all the data off this old beast." He added, meaning his ancient pc. It was aggravating how slow it was compared to the new one.

Adam and Brook laughed, "Once we have the network storage up and running, anything you put there will be able to be accessed securely on any device you logged onto the network," Adam commented.

He also passed on the suggestion of enhancing the security, following the chat with Martin.

"Hmmm..." Gareth said, "I'm going to need to talk around with the pack. It would enhance the protection, but also could be seen as a reduction of their privacy, even if only a few could access it. We'll have to follow up later."

Adam and Brook nodded. He had thought it would be his answer for it. They worked out approval to do a little research on what they could do, and how it would work at a general level. Beyond that, it would require pack approval.

*****

After lunch, Adam and Brook were hanging out at the warehouse, waiting for the equipment, which was scheduled to be there shortly. Adam whooped in joy when he saw the large semi back up to the dock. Meeting them at the door, as Shana organized the three warehouse helpers. They quickly were able to get everything unloaded and checked all the boxes for any physical damage. Adam smiled as the only damage was to a couple of boxes, and upon inspection, the items inside were not harmed. He still made note of it as he signed off on the shipment and took many pictures to back up the cameras on the dock. With the amount everything was worth, he wasn't taking any chances of damaged parts being counted as damaged by the pack.

After the truck left, Adam pulled aside the items which were staying here; a fibre-channel switch, and a gateway firewall, and a couple of backup servers, along with all the printers and supplies. The rest he organized, sending the items he needed first, racks and the UPS equipment, in the trucks to be taken to the main and secondary data centres. There were others waiting to help get everything assembled and installed at the areas, with some of their techies. Splitting the servers up by data centre, he smiled as everything so far had arrived safe and sound. Once done, there were only a few boxes of miscellaneous stuff left.

Throwing them in his vehicle, he followed the last load to the garage and the secondary data centre.

Unloading it and a small cart, he poked his head in and smiled. He got one person ready to get the fibre and headed to the main data centre. Reaching the door, the rollup door was wide open, to allow easy access, while they were setting up.

Quickly, he found the large spool of fibre, and set it up to unroll the cable as he hooked up the end to a pull line and ran the first link. They ended up running eight lines between the two rooms, leaving plenty of slack at each end to connect the equipment.

Adam checked against his layout design for the racks, and approved where they were all being placed, having them bolt them down to the panels and cross-members using special brackets, so there was no way the racks would move. Which they tested by lightly body-checking the rack, and it didn't move at all.

He arranged the next morning to run a couple of fibre lines up to the cave, to increase the quality of the link, and allow for future expansion.

After a silent discussion, Brook was keeping an eye on the secondary data centre, while he managed the main one.

*****

By the end of the day, they had all the racks in place and secured, the UPS at the bottom of each rack was starting to charge—he expected it to take till morning—and the main core servers were mounted. Looking around, all the Blade Server chassis units were mounted, too. They were figuring out which blades were which and which chassis they would slide into.

Adam had left plenty of room for expansion, as he didn't know how much he would need. Adam got his gear set up on a cart beside the core server rack and would be doing the first OS loads in the morning. He was expecting to take all week to spin everything up and then a month to have it all configured. By then, he should be able to start ordering all the computers for the pack. Most were just wanting the laptops, so he was planning on a basic build with their site-license of Microsoft Windows and Office, and some management tools, and go from there.

Letting out a howl, everyone stopped, "One hour till dinner! We are done for the day! I'll see you all after breakfast and we'll get all the rest of the hardware finished!" He called, dismissing everyone as they cheered. They had worked hard, and with how much moving and lifting they had done, they would want to clean up before dinner.

I just let everyone go here, to have time to get cleaned up if they want for dinner. Meet me at the end of the tunnel, Love? He called to Brook.

Nice plan; I'll let everyone go for the day, Brook called back, *We are almost done with the hardware here.*

Same here. It should be all installed by end of the day tomorrow, then starts the building of the operating systems and getting it all ready.

Smiling he secured the room, started the hardware testing on the first few machines he needed to get started on first, and locked up all the cargo doors for the night. Adam and Charlie walked out the door, passing through the security room. He nodded at the wolf covering the cameras, "All done for today! Have a good evening." He called. "We'll be back tomorrow after breakfast."

The wolf nodded back, "Good, now I can have my nap without anyone knowing," he joked; the walls around the data centre were well insulated, so it wasn't noise, but with all the people, he felt watched. Tomorrow, before they started anything powering on, he was going to be handing out earplugs to his workers, as it was going to get loud in the room.

They waited at the end of the tunnel, and Brook came through chatting with the last few, "All secure?" he checked, getting a smile and a nod, "Make sure to grab a bag of earplugs from me, as once we start powering everything on, it is going to get very loud." He warned, having found the packages in his boxes. Once they had the first couple of servers running, he could start using the remote tools, and showing Brook how to get them going enough for him to get into them.

Adam wrapped an arm around Brook's waist, as they walked back to their suite, and a quick shower.

*****

Dinner was a bit loud, and many wanted to know when the new computers would be coming in. "Once the network and servers are up and running," He told those who asked, "And No, they were not in the delivery." Everyone had seen the vehicles piled up with computer gear, and many had been hoping for the new laptops.

After dinner was the weekly fire which some had dubbed the 'rank-free gathering' he was starting to get some of the other mid-ranked wolves, and if they were civil, they were welcome. Sadly, the first to have to be asked to leave were a couple of Thetas, who couldn't get the concept of 'if they are civil, all are welcome' and instead thought it was for betas and the Theta alone. A couple of deltas were ejected after them, as they were making rude comments about the ones kicked out. After having to be firm with them, Adam and Brook got to relax and enjoy the evening camaraderie of being Pack together with everyone. "Spend the week thinking about it. If you are better mannered, you can come next week." He told the wolves who he made leave, firmly.

*****

The next morning, Adam, with some help from Brook, used the time before breakfast to plan out how they wanted to go with everything. As they got the chassis turned on and the hardware tested on everything, Adam was going to get the Windows Server operating system loaded on the ones he tested and get the essential core up and running. He wrote down the key domain admin password which would be secured in the security office.

"Nobody should need this password, as it is for the key encryption." Adam told his mate. "Everyone, including us, will just have a second user with the admin permissions for when they needed it." Brook just nodded; sure she would never need that password.

He planned on having the local admin passwords on the computers set by an admin software, so it would change once a month, and each one would have a unique one. They needed to get the infrastructure up and running before they could configure something like that. The fewer who knew the default system administrator password before they did it, the better.

After a quick breakfast, as both were really wanting to get going, they headed back down to the basement. First, Adam got the automated install started, then they worked together to get the key network fibre links between the two data centres terminated and tested. Once it was done, the two rooms would be able to share data at a very high rate. He looked forward to testing and expected to be able to transfer a Blu-ray movie in only a couple seconds.

As they were finishing up at the first end, their helpers started to arrive, so they opened the big doors, and when done, headed to do the other end. When Evan and Kuri came to see him for the work at the cave, he showed them how to unwrap the end of the terminated cable, and how to handle it while connecting it up. They had all morning to get the fibre lines up, as they had scheduled a noon outage, while lunch was being served, to switch from the network cable to the fibre lines.

Notes had been placed around on the notice boards, and Adam himself had put one right beside each of the machines which the pups were gaming on. He had made a bet with Brook they would 'forget' about it and complain about the network going down on their game.

After passing them all the gear they would need at the top, he went back to the servers while he waited for them to get up there. All to soon for his liking, they let him know they were up in the cave, he had them pull on the fibreglass rope they had put in while running the network cable and pull up the first strand of the fibre optic cable. The pipes were run in such a way it was a nice smooth run and didn't need anyone in the middle. They were quickly finished pulling the first one and waited while Adam cut the cable to length and terminated the end for them to pull up the next one. As Kuri and Evan were pulling the second strand, Adam terminated the server room side of the first.

They ended up running a couple of extra pairs, as they had the parts and extra cable. The spares Adam had taken extra effort in protecting, as they wouldn't be connected to anything, as he didn't have the ports for it, and had purchased dust caps for them specifically for this purpose, and each of the spares had been labelled, so they would not be confused. Testing went flawlessly and they were ready to go over an hour early.

Adam gave the two on the cliff leave to have fun and to take a break, knowing they would enjoy some climbing around the cave.

Adam was ready for the switchover, as he could connect his end all up, they just couldn't cut over the other till their window started, or they would have snarly packmates. Grinning, he watched the traffic die down, but not all out; there appeared to be an Xbox game still going, as the time for the lunch came, and their window started.

The game's data usage didn't stop, and Adam grinned at his pouting mate. She knew he had won the bet. "We'll give them five minutes." He told his mate and watched the clock.

Once they were five minutes after the scheduled time, he grinned, *Just disconnect it.* he told the two on the cliff, *Whoever is gaming, must learn when I post outage at noon, they will lose connection at noon.* He grinned at his mate, trying to think of what he should tell them if they complain.

Even though they had scheduled an hour to be down, they were switched over, and the new gear in use in under five minutes, as they only needed to unplug the radio network cord and plug it into the small fibre-fed switch, and to have it initialize on the new connection. It even had a couple of regular LAN ports, for failover, so they wired up the network cables which they had been using, as a second backup.

Adam grinned and liked the switch time. Brook, who had been looking over his shoulder, was astonished it took so little time, "The rest of the time was for *if* it didn't go smoothly." He commented to the surprise he could feel through the bonds, "I may have needed to get to the cave, which would take over half of the time. Also included a back-out time to restore the original system."

Brook nodded, "Makes sense now. Plan in time for dealing with the issues, and when you finish early, everyone is happy."

They next did some testing on the upgraded link, as they waited for Kuri and Evan to get down, and the numbers were right where Adam had thought they would be. They had taken the slowest section out, which was due to the length being a bit beyond what the technical limit for length of a cable, so saw a bump in their speed available. So no one person could hog the connection, or especially the pups while gaming, he did put in some systems to manage the priority of all the traffic. The gaming got the lowest priority. To make sure they couldn't get around it, he had collected the MAC — Machine Access Control — addresses, and set it for the network switch ports.

Once people started trickling in and he cleaned up the scraps from his wiring work, the two of them headed up to their suite, to meet with Evan and Kuri, leaving the rest of their helpers in Erin's paws. Her feral grin made him laugh, but also a little nervous.

Adam had arranged with Jess and Joshua to have some nice Bison steaks for the six of them, out of his own pocket. He hoped word would spread for if someone was asked to help over a meal or some other unusual duty, they got something special in exchange for it. He planned on using it for any overnight work too; either arrange for a nice late meal before, or a good breakfast in the morning.

As the six sat down for their meal, Kuri commented, *So, who's bet was the closest?* she asked Brook, expecting her to have won.

Brook gave a low, annoyed growl, *Adam did, again. I'm not betting against him again! I'm just glad he only bet a lunch in town instead of paying for this meal; I saw the bill he paid for it: it was not cheap, and he went straight to a butcher!*

Everyone laughed, and Brook growled again, as she bit into her steak, the growl turned to a moan of pleasure as the taste danced around her mouth making her annoyance melt away in the pleasure of the good meal. *OK,* she conceded, *The price was well worth this.*

Adam smiled at all the sounds the very happy wolves made; it alone made the food costs well worth it, *Feel free to tell others how well I treated those who had to miss the normal lunch. No cold leftover scraps for them. I plan on using the same reward for any time I ask for unusual times. Although, it may be different meals.*

Privately, Jess commented to Adam, *Thank you for having us join in.*

*It was the least I could do for making you spend your morning getting the food, then preparing it so excellently. If you have ideas for other good *food, especially stuff we normally don't get, let me know. I plan on having one or both of you helping me prepare, in the occasional times it is needed.* Adam replied to both Jess and Joshua, *It would be mean to not let you have some when you worked so hard to make them good. Think of it as an occasional thank you for your hard work taking care of us.* Jess had asked to deal with the meat, as she did occasionally like to make food, she just very much didn't want to be doing it often.

Both looked very pleased.

Adam stretched after the meal was done. Charlie had begged for some, even after having got some scraps of the meat as his lunch till Adam glared and growled at him. He quickly stopped and lay down, but keeping his eyes on the wolves, hoping they would share more. He did place his plate down for Charlie to lick the sauce from the plate. The others did as well, and Joshua even commented laughing, the plates barely needed to be washed now, as they looked like there hadn't been lunch on them!

Smiling, they broke up, Adam and Brook went back down to see how the hardware testing was going; they had been tested before shipped out, but they bounced over many highways and may have caused a problem or two.

*****

Turned out only one blade had anything dislodge and reseating the memory module fixed the issue.

By the end of the day, Adam had the core devices up and running, and he showed them how to have the other servers pull the operating system down. Brook then went off and showed those in the secondary data centre, so they could have the servers up to basic as soon as possible.

Putting in some systems to turn on the remote settings automatically, so he could get in as soon as they went live was easy. He would be able to do it while he had them start preparing the equipment for the pre-production and test racks.

Closing for the evening, he was again quite happy with the amount of work which was being done. He sighed as he left the data centre, and closed the door behind him, pulled the earplugs out and tossed them in the garbage. He waved as he passed the security guard and headed to meet Brook and go to dinner.

*****

The next day, most of the servers were ready. Turning to his laptop, one after another he got them initialized and starting to work. Now he had the core network up and running, he started reassigning the Wi-Fi to the managed system, and enabled a virtual guest network, which was isolated to only have internet access, and the network port which he was going to install a network printer on, in the hallway of the guest wing. The guest wing's Ethernet ports (one in each guest room) were also ready, as a test.

Another day and Adam had most of the servers up and running, and all the physical gear was up. Checked his own PC was correctly on the network, as he could do the rest without visiting the data centre in person. He shooed the last few out with the last of the packaging and closed it up.

Seeing Martin was back on duty, Adam sighed, "Well, we are all done, I hope; two days of earplugs all day is annoying. Three days to get the servers all installed and operating systems loaded. All the rest of the work, I believe can be dealt with remotely. I should not need to be down till we start upgrading your stuff. I'm going to start researching it for the Alpha as soon as the network and servers are all fully working. As soon as I can do it, I will."

Martin smiled, "Excellent! I can't wait for your upgrades."

Adam smiled in reply, "Well, beyond that, I would like you to keep a log of anyone accessing the data centres; includes authorized access. Also, the only ones who should be going in there are Me, Brook, Erin, Aurora, Nikki, or someone with one of us. For cleaning, I have Duncan and Keanna tasked with it. I'm going to show them what to do after breakfast, tomorrow. Generally, they will be in once a week. I did ask them to do it randomly, as they will also be doing a physical and tamper audit inspection for me." They had put serialized seal-tags on the server racks, and they would be making sure they had not been opened. The authorized people would have access to the logbooks, both physical and electronic, and would have to note the broken seal and the new one on both places if there was anything done.

Martin nodded, making a note to pass on the requests to the rest of the wolves who manned the room, "That's totally understandable. I'll pass it on." Since they were putting a fair amount of hardware in the server rooms now, it was fair to restrict who can access it, and have the access monitored.

They exchanged a little small talk, but soon he got the mental message from Brook she was waiting, and he quickly excused himself and joined her for dinner. After dinner, Brook and Adam headed out to enjoy the weather and to let their wolves out, as it had been a very busy few days, and they were getting restless. Charlie bounced around them, ecstatic. They had spent the last few days inside working on the tech.

I think we need to take more time outside, and a bit less on the tech inside. Maybe some training? My wolf is not *happy about all the tech all day*Adam commented.

Brook nibbled his ear, *I know how you feel, but since you can do it from up in our suite, I think our wolves will be much happier. How long till we start loading names for accounts?*

Adam nibbled back playfully, wagging his tail, *Well, if you want to get the names loaded into a table, I can generate a script to load them into the system to generate the names; race you tomorrow?*

Brook growled, as she nipped his flank, *No. You would win. My winning streak has been broken by you! I have yet to win against you! I'm starting to think you cheat,*The last part was in a teasing tone.

Adam just gave her a wolf grin, *I just know how to make something which looks to be a very complex task take a short time!*As they bickered and teased each other, they let their wolves have control of their bodies, and they had a romp through the snow, as it was just reaching their bellies. It was a bit higher on Charlie, but all three had nice thick double fur coats, made for this climate, so they were nice and warm, and their wide thick-furred paws worked like snowshoes, so they were mostly above the snow.

Eventually, they headed back to their place. Entering their suite, all smelling of damp fur, they noticed a large heavy pad with a waterproof cover had been laid down in front of the warm fire which had been lit. Sniffing the pad, Adam could smell Jess and Joshua; he wagged his tail at their thoughtfulness. All three flopped down in front of the warm fire and went to sleep.

CHAPTER 17

First Hunt

The next morning Adam woke with a yawn, standing up and stepping off the pad, and over his mate, he then gave a good stretch and shake of his fur to settle it. He had come to enjoy waking up as a wolf; no need to unwrap from a warm bed and get a blast of cooler air on the skin; the fur came with him.

Why not sleep more as a wolf then Commented his wolf, having followed his thoughts.

Why not? Maybe we can get Jess to bring us some breakfast, so we can stay here? Adam commented. The room's door opened, and instinctively Adam jumped in front of his sleeping mate, ready to attack, but it was just Joshua, bringing a tray with three large bowls on it, full of meat from the smell. Standing down his guard, he wagged his tail in thanks and nudged Brook awake. *Breakfast is here, beautiful*

As she woke up, yawning and showing of her set of gleaming white teeth, he went to one bowl and started eating. When he was done, Brook snickered in his mind, as his muzzle was covered, as he tried to clean it off.

You need to practice eating more as a wolf, Brook commented, amused. She had finished hers, and still had a clean muzzle.

Of course I do! I think this is only my third meal as one! You also need to teach me to hunt! Adam begged Brook. His wolf had perked his ears and was interested too. He had a couple memories of hunting, but not enough to know how to do it, let alone well enough to catch something.

You want to hunt instead of working on the computers this morning? Brook asked.

Yes, yes, yes! Both parts of Adam were very much wanting to know how to hunt. They bounced around like a puppy, excited.

Brook laughed in their head, *Ok, ok. But you must be calm, and silent if you want a successful hunt.* She admonished, as she pawed the patio door open.

Adam followed, and Charlie had been told to stay, while they went for hunt-training, as he could be in the way. He whined but he listened, putting his head down on his forepaws, and his ears back, looking miserable.

Once they got past the Winter Patio doors, Adam calmed down, and tried to be as stealthy as he could. He was glad the snow would keep most of the sound down, and the twigs were hidden deep under the snow.

Brook guided him through the tracking and finding of some rabbits.

Seeing the white fur on the white snow was hard, till it moved; he could smell it, and if he listened hard, even hear its heartbeat. Adam tried to get in close, but it being late morning, his dark fur, he stood out a bit. Trying to follow Brook's instructions to stay hidden behind bushes, he was able to get closer, closer, closer... but missed when he tried to pounce!

He ended up just getting a face full of snow and Brook taking down the rabbit. Happily, she was willing to share the spoils with him.

They tried a couple more times with similar results. The last one, he ended up getting a mouthful of fur, as his teeth groomed the rabbit's tail, but having the rabbit escape as it successfully dodged.

Heading back in, Adam was feeling very discouraged, even though he was full of the portions of the three rabbits he got to eat. His wolf was satisfied, and just wanted to go have a nap, which would be fine while he worked on getting the email server up and running. Once it was up, he could get the virtual fax, phone, and the corporate IM system up and running. Once it was all done, which should take him the rest of the week, they could have fun getting the plotter and the photo printer going. Both were sitting in his section of the warehouse, waiting to be sent up to the pack.

Brook had smiled at his disappointment of not catching any of the bunnies but soothed him as the last one he almost had, and soon he would be able to even take down a deer on his own. She did share her own memories of learning to hunt, and how it had taken her weeks to even get the fur.

Brook worked at typing up all the names and other details in a spreadsheet, along with information they were adding into the systems. Currently, the records were only in paper form.

Adam had the email up and tested, although some external tests would take a while, up to 24-hours for the information to travel and get out to the servers it needed to so people could respond. He started on the communication servers, settling on a virtual phone software, and using it to talk to phones, which looked like normal phones, but talk over the network, instead of phone lines, as they could use the e-mail address book for the internal contacts. Ordering the software, enough bases to put one in each room, and a few Wi-Fi-based wireless ones to try out, which could be used anywhere within the range of their wireless network.

While they were waiting for the e-mail confirmation with the licence key to turn the trial program into the full version, Brook finally finished typing all the info into the sheet.

Seeing the reams of information, Adam commented, "Entering all the data would be a good job for those who want to learn how to type, especially the pups. If the data isn't confidential."

Passing the file to the brand-new file server he had just set up, so he could take the data and upload it into the system to create the user accounts, she shook her head, "All the confidential records are in the Alpha's office. I do like the idea of putting them to work doing it."

Taking about thirty minutes to create the custom script to take the data and use it to create the accounts and populate the address book information, with all the accounts set to need a new password at first logon, and using the same initial password, to make their lives easy: 'OurPack123!'.

He enabled some configurations, where the passwords expired every 90 days, couldn't be any of the last ten passwords, and they could only change the password once a day. He even turned on the nemesis for many: complexity. For basic, it had to be minimum eight characters long, but for anyone with Local Admin on one machine, it had to be twelve, and for those who were the techs, and had admin everywhere, had a minimum length of fifteen! He knew the techs would hate him, but it was just one more thing to help with security.

Once done, they headed to the computer lab, which was looking much better now they had shipped out all the tested and rebuilt computers to several local charities who had been ecstatic about getting the donation. He had refused the tax receipt as they had the money to pay their tax bill and didn't bother hiding it. He had been told they were quite happy to pay the bills, as it kept the money moving out to those who needed it.

Adam had a few test machines he had the pups set up, but not turn on, as he was going to capture their factory images, so they could reload the factory default onto them when they were going to get rid of them instead of manually installing the system and drivers. They would make a corporate "core" image which all the machines would get, which included the OS, drivers, and other basic applications everyone would get. They had a few each of several different models to decide which they were going to use for the main order.

While he waited for the images to back up to thumb drives, and then while imaged them over the network, he worked on his laptop to configure more of the servers. By the time for dinner rolled around, most of the pups were in awe he could do it without any disks!

He had the phone server set up, and right now just sent a generic 'sorry can't answer the phone' message and not take any messages. He had decided to have one phone number and then to set up an internal extension set; he would have to set up the extensions, but there was an import function. He was going to use '1' to access key roles like the Security, Management, Tech Support, etc., '2' then three digits for the base stations, '3' to call a person by name, using voice recognition, and '4' with a random 4-digit code, which would route to ring on their IM system, and any phone they had set up—each pack member would be able to customize their own configuration. '0' would send them to the security desk to manually route the call, although there eventually may be a receptionist to do it, another good job for responsible pups. The Fax module had been activated, and he had made a network fax printer available, to send faxes, they just hit print and it would gather the phone number or numbers, and then send them out, and e-mail them with the success/fail report. Incoming faxes came in with extension 5 and then their 4-digit code and got turned into PDF and then e-mailed to the user, to save the paper for those who just needed to be filed. Those who had video, could answer the call with video as well, not just audio.

The first non-test call was amusing. Adam was surprised when his cellphone went off, as it was to the new system, and wasn't a number he recognised. "Adam speaking." He answered it politely, but not giving anything away.

"This is Gabriel from Barker Communications. I have just seen the large order for your equipment and wanted to confirm it."

"Yes," Adam said, grinning his mate. They sounded skeptical to him. "I did do a large order, as I am rebuilding a company's office." Brook was listening in and grinning back at him.

"OK." Gabriel replied, sounding relieved. "That was two *hundred* of our PML-304 multi-line desk phones, twenty PMLW-206 Wi-Fi hand-set, twenty WH-6 wireless headsets. I also see server licensing for our PBX system, with Exchange and IM integration license, with four hundred user license, four hundred Voicemail license, global Fax-to-Email license, smart call directing, and the global Military-Grade Encryption add in. Is that correct?"

Adam grinned, "It sounds right." He wasn't certain on the model numbers, but the number of units was what he had ordered.

"Since I have you on the line, the shipping address is..." Gabriel read off her screen, checking the other details with them. This would be a very good payday for the company, as it seemed not many were buying their hardware, as they were a new company, and here looked like a whole new setup.

Adam quickly confirmed the information. For the server, he was glad they had it set to deal with multiple plugins, as there were a few others which he didn't want, and that they could set how many users they wanted, and then buy additional later. The encryption add-on was as much as everything else combined but was needed, and the company was one of the few who offered end-to-end encryption.

The trial alone was nice. It gave him 30-days with a 10-user license. 10-user Exchange/IM integration, no voicemail although it had let them record a message to be given, fax-to-email had "demo" across each page as a watermark, and no encryption. It also only had 0 to 9 as options for directing calls, no two-stage like he wanted to do. The 90-day money back guarantee for the server licenses and the hardware sold him.

"Well, I have good news and bad news." Gabriel said after putting them on hold for a bit, after confirming they didn't need to have their technicians do the server configuration for him. "I have the server licenses going out shortly and will be to you shortly by e-mail. With them will be our premium support contact number. That is me, during the weekday, and we have others who rotate to do after hours and weekend support." She was glad it was usually the engineers who she would contact who took it, so they had some experience supporting it. It also meant the bugs were dealt with fast, as if one had issues, likely others would too, and nobody liked being woken up at night.

She took a breath, "We are also upgrading your shipping from ground to express courier at no charge. But we don't have enough on-hand to ship right away. It will be two or three shipments. Is that alright?"

Adam wanted to laugh; He hadn't bought the premium support as it was pricey, same with the express shipping. If they wanted to give it to him for free; fine with him. "It is perfectly fine. We are building the network as well, so all of them weren't going to be installed all at once, anyways."

"Then, I will send you the invoice for the first shipments and estimated delivery for the rest. You won't be billed until the equipment ships. The first order should be there within three days and will include physical copies of the licenses and software as well. Thank you for considering Barker Communications and let us know if you need any assistance getting anything up and running." Gabriel finished.

"We will." Adam replied, "Have a nice day."

Adam was just able to hold off his laughter, till he had hung up, over their luck. The premium support also included configuration help, and details on how to set it up. He had wanted it, but it was outside of what he wanted to pay. They also had a cash referral system; ten percent of any referrals they got back as cash. If it worked, Barker Communications might be posed to have serious expansion in their future, as their name became known to the other packs as their recommendation. Again, he snickered at the name of the company.

Tying in the IM was a bit of work, but since it was designed to integrate, he just needed to set the configurations for it; not only did it now use the address book from the email server, but it could also be used as a phone to make outgoing calls using the phone system, to call directly and securely other packs once they had a similar setup, could even connect to other IM, or even the regular free public IM service! Incoming calls could also be picked up on it instead of handsets since they had purchased which integration add-on. The e-mail with the licenses, and the login for their premium forums and documentation was there within minutes, and he signed in to get the details on getting the IM integration done, after inserting the keys and restarting the services to activate it.

Once the workstations were ready, there was enough time for a few pups to get signed in and Adam could make sure the right permissions and security were being applied. Doing that, he let them play with it, but had Duncan and Keanna keep an eye on the computers while the pups were on them, more than to keep them safe, more than to prevent the computers from catching a virus; to keep the secret of being werewolves. They had not been allowed to post anything anywhere, nor join sites, but that they could even look around was a novel thing for them.

All seemed to be going well. When the dinner time came, he had to growl at a few to get them to sign off the computers and head for the meal. He smiled and pulled Brook with him to the dinner. The computer lab he suspected was going to be full around the clock. Duncan and Keanna seemed to have the room in hand and had some budding friendships with several others to set up a shift rotation for coverage of the computers, and to set up the schedule for use of the machines. He would figure out which computers were the best fit for what the pack wants to do with them in a week or so.

Telling their friends, they had brought several of the computers fully online in the lab nearly had everyone wanting to go get on them. He let them know they would still need to watch what they said online. He did assure them their accounts had been created, and they could log in.

I'm wondering if we need to have a class for how to be online safely. Adam commented to his mate and she gave him a mental nod as well, as she was describing the call from the phone company to their friends.

Adam gave his trio of techs their orders: they were to start scheduling to install the network ports in the pack rooms. Each room was getting one for each person plus one for the phone, so for the more senior spots, it would be 3 ports per room. He wasn't sure how easy it was going to be to retrofit the network in, so he didn't set any targets, yet. He left it in Erin's hands, smiling at her frown.

"I do expect it to go slowly at first. Run the wires to the wiring rooms on each floor, which we ran fibre to, as there are switches designed to handle them there. Just run a plain line for now to security, as I need to finish with the servers, then start looking at the tech for upgrading security before we start working on them, and unless medical asks for some, we are doing them later."

Adam got a nod of understanding, "I'm thinking start here on the first floor, and upgrade everything in the common areas first. Then offer it by seniority?" Erin asked.

Adam nodded, "You got it! Doing the common areas first would give people an idea of what they will get installed. If people have desk phones, let me know, and I will have their numbers integrated into the new system, so they can keep them for a while, if they want. If they don't want the old number, I'll show you how to program the new phones when they come in. I'll be assigning one of the wireless handsets to each of you three, so we can test how they work around here."

All three smiled; they all liked new tech, and being the techs, they were going to be his field testers for any of the equipment before anyone else would be permitted to test it further. It was one thing he hated the most at his last job; at times, the first they heard of a piece of equipment was when they had a service call of something was broken, and then had to figure out even the specs of what it had and how it should work.

After dinner, Adam and Brook shifted and decided to go see their little hidden spring. The trip was much faster now as wolves, and the climb of the rocks was easy, even with the thick snow. They arrived, and Adam found the cold spring was iced over, but putting a paw on the ice, it punched through to water which felt barely above ice itself, letting out a startled yelp, before shaking it off and licking it. He decided to just jump it and landed cleanly on the other side and trotted to find the right temperature hot pool, not feeling like shifting back to human.

Adam slipped into a warm hot spring and found a spot he could lay and be fully in the water, but with his head resting comfortably on a moss pillow on the shore, and sighed, *This feels soooo good!*

Brook chuckled and found her own spot near him, *I know. Before I met you, I'd come up here whenever I had a chance, and wanted some privacy. I sometimes thought about sharing the place with some others, but the increased traffic could damage it.*

Adam sent a wordless agreement to it and enjoyed the evening to relax. They talked idly about the plans, and about parts of their life they hadn't shared yet; both knew they shouldn't keep secrets from the other and agreed to try to be as open and honest with each other as possible, although they agreed fun surprises were nice.

Adam found out Brook's grandparents had been killed in an inter-pack skirmish when she was fifteen, and she found out he had never known his grandfathers, his father's side died before his parents were married, but it seemed he was very similar in interests and skills. His mother's father although passed away in the last decade, his mother never saw since she was a teen, and he never knew him. His father's mother he loved, but she passed after a lengthy illness when he was a teen.

Brook still wondered if he had some Wolf in his ancestry, as he had shifted and taken to this life very easily.

That it could. Part of it, is I didn't feel my human life was right for me; it always felt like a part of me was missing, and I never could find it. Finding the furry community did make it easier as it felt close. Always felt wolfish and always enjoyed spending time with wolves. This life especially with the wolf in my mind, and you by my side, feels right. I want to enjoy it. Some of the ideas I was raised with by my mother was a bit sexist— Whatever she didn't like doing was 'Man's work', like barbequing, doing the lawn. While she was firm in how women could do anything a man could and would get mad if something was called 'Woman's work'. *—But she did try to teach us to not be prejudiced but had some strong beliefs which me and my sister have worked to change. I think this change pushed her much farther than we expected.* His wolf gave him a mental nuzzle and whine in caring.

Brook sent him wordless love, *Well, for whatever reason, you are doing well, and have many friends here who care for you. It's sad your human life was so lonely for those who could understand you.* Standing up, and shaking the water from her fur, *Well, I think it is time to wake Charlie up, and to head back*

Adam stood and shook his fur out and looked over at Charlie: asleep on the moss. Since this little pocket was warm from the hot springs, the moss was still snow-free. He padded over and nudge him with a paw and motioned to follow with his head when he woke.

The three of them headed back down the mountain, and headed into the safety of the pack house, and again curling up as wolves in front of the fire. Adam commented he was very much enjoying his wolf shape, and he needed some training in wolf-fighting; Brook agreed but was going to soon need the Alpha's attention for the advanced training, as he may surpass her current training. Her wolf was looking forward to it, as they themselves could hone and learn more fighting skills.

*****

In the morning Jess woke the trio up, and Wolf-Adam jumped up and over Brook with a snarl, before realising who it was. He stopped and whined an apology to Jess.

Jess had stopped just inside the doorway, and waited for him to realise who had entered, with how fast he realised it she smiled, "I guess you are already very protective of your mate when she's sleeping? It's normal for us. I'm surprised you could tell it was me from that distance."

Adam wagged his tail, *I still feel bad snarling at you. You and your brother have done everything in your power to make both of our lives easy and comfortable.*

Jess smiled as she placed breakfast meat down on the ground, as Adam turned and nudged his mate and Charlie gently, "Well, from my side: I get a single pair to serve for life, rather than needing to learn new people constantly. I get two very strong and smart wolves who care about those under their protection. The fact even your wolf-mind does care about us as much does help."

Wolf-Adam had been hungry and had eaten the food while they were talking, and still ended up with a dirty muzzle, as he was new and although full adult-sized, was still learning some things like a pup.

Jess smiled and pulled out a damp cloth and helped clean his muzzle, "Brook let me know you two are going for some more wolf-training and will be back for lunch. I'll get some from the kitchen and have it ready here for you to eat as a wolf, so you can learn more."

By then both Brook and Charlie had finished their breakfasts too and were ready to go for some wolf training.

Same clearing as last time. How's your memory for the way there? Brook told Adam.

Discussing it with his wolf, *We think we remember the way.* Adam commented.

Well, lead the way, then. Came her response. *Path finding and remembering the way is a skill you need to learn.*

Adam pawed the doors open and headed outside into the fresh snow. Brook and Charlie bounded less than a body length behind him. Eventually they reached the meadow, with only one wrong turn due to the snow.

They trained hard for the entire morning, and this time Brook received almost as many hits.

Adam was limping from a hit to a forepaw, which had turned out to just be a deep scratch when it was checked, as they headed up from the medical area after having it checked out. Needing a medical check after doing wolf-training at their level was normal and the fact they were already there surprised the healer who checked them out. It usually took half to a full year of full-time training at minimum before one was at the level to need to be checked, after being turned.

They reached their suite, and they found a large meal set out for them and they dived in. This time Adam barely had anything on his muzzle, and it was quickly licked up.

After turning back human so they had hands to work on the computers, they pulled on some clothes, so they wouldn't stick to the chairs.

Brook smiled at the parcel sitting on the coffee table, and pulled Adam over, "Here is a little something I got for you, Love."

Deciding to open the large one first, it was a stuffed wolf which looked exactly like Brook did in her wolf form. Adam smiled and loved it.

"I had to get one for your stuffed wolf pack, and for you to cuddle if I'm not around." She commented. Adam didn't know what to say, so he just sent her a wordless surge of love over their mental bonds, and what he thought of the gift.

Opening the smaller package, it turned out to be a ring box. Opening it he gasped: it was a ring which matched the one he gave Brook but was slightly wider in the paws and was yellow gold. It also said, 'Forever Together' on the inside. Adam could barely see, as tears of joy were running down his face, showing how much it moved him.

Lifting the tray of the box, she opened the bottom, showing a chain there, "I had the chain sized to be like mine: to be somewhat like a collar when in your wolf, so you don't loose it.

Adam nodded, getting himself under control, "I'd prefer it that way. Put it on me, please?"

Brook smiled and nodded, as she pulled the chain out and threaded the ring on it before she secured it around his neck. She smiled, knowing he wasn't much for rings, and jewellery but knew this would mean much to him. They had a short but passionate kiss together, as they opened their minds fully to each other, and shared how much the other meant to them.

Adam sighed after a bit, "Well, I want to get everything I can do for the servers first, as then we will be able to work on the other project I want, to get the security upgraded."

Brook smiled, as she started playing with the systems he had configured, to make sure there weren't any bugs while Adam finished spinning up the servers, "I think a couple of the pups in the lab are interested in web development," She commented, seeing him set up just a basic coming-soon page.

"Good, I'll happily have them deal with that! I don't want to do it." He sighed, "I learned how to do basic websites when they were mainly text. Trying to make one which is mostly graphics is much harder, and something I don't have much interest in doing."

Just before dinner, Adam smiled, "Well the basic servers are now all up and running. I think we'll leave them for now."

Getting a knock at their door, "Looks like your phones are in," Brook commented, as she let Shana in with a cart load.

Adam grinned, "Excellent!" Since he had already put the registration codes into the server, the functionality was already there. The encryption module had a separate install and had required a fair amount of configuration. He hoped he had it all configured right, as he had followed the documentation.

Shana commented, "They came in just as I was closing up and decided to bring them here. I did take out two, and left them there, as you commented a couple were staying there."

Adam nodded, and pulled out one, and plugged it into a network cable, "The network is all configured for them, so this is how you program it..." And went on to show Shana how to get them ready so they could have the upgraded phones right away. She pocketed the copy of the configuration cheat-sheet, and the note containing the specific configurations, since he had left it enabled so they could program them from the handsets, not just remotely. Once the code was entered the first time, the server would lock the handset for the location. Eventually, he would turn it off, and just pre-configure them if they needed to swap them out. Shana was relieved they still looked like a normal phone, even if they used a network instead of a phone line. They were even generally powered from the network cable, although he had brought in a few adaptors for if it was not possible, or they needed to test something. He didn't plan on using it, but they also had a second network port for something to use.

As they walked to have dinner, Adam asked for the printers and plotter to be sent up first thing in the morning and put in the tech lab. They were finally ready for them to be installed.

After dinner Adam showed Erin how to set up the phones, so they could get them out in the public areas right away and passed them the programmed Wi-Fi handsets and bases to charge the battery pack in them. They looked like a standard cordless phone handset, with a larger screen. He would need help with the plotter and printers when they arrived after breakfast, as they'd need to roll them down the tunnel from the parkade.

The rest of the phones would be brought in as needed, and deployed with all the wired networking, so they could get them all done at once. "While you're here, I'll show you how to migrate the old phone number into the new system…" Adam commented, showing the interface to the phone system, so they could program in the second number for a base if they needed for the few who had existing numbers.

*****

The next morning Adam kissed his human-shaped mate and started the new day. Adam was excited, "Get to play with a plotter!" he exclaimed, "Been looking forward to this!"

Brook laughed and pushed him out the door once they were dressed, heading to the dining room for some breakfast.

"Well, look who decided to join us for breakfast today!" Kuri teased.

Adam and Brook joined in on the laughter, "Well, we didn't sleep as wolves, so we didn't ask Jess and Joshua to grab us a bowl of food!" Adam commented, "Waking as a wolf feels so *right* to me."

Knowing smiles and nods were shared, as they dug in, switching to mind-speech. They all knew the feeling and were glad Adam was enjoying it. Some who were turned took decades to get comfortable being a wolf, and there were stories of some who never did.

What's on the plans for today?　Kuri commented silently as she munched on her food, *You two seem to have a busy schedule,*

Plotter and printers. Should be at the garage soon. The stand and output rack come disassembled, so will have to assemble them then put the plotter on it. Want to help?　Adam replied.

Sure. I have today off from doing patrols.　Kuri commented, *I love getting to see new equipment.*

In that case, we are finalizing the selection of PCs and laptops we are going to offer. Could we get ideas on which you feel would be best?　Adam asked generally of everyone. By the time breakfast was done, the selection was ready. He would finalise it and generate the report before their meeting on Monday with the Alpha, for signoff for what and how many.

Once breakfast was over, Adam nearly ran out the door to wait for the truck with all their stuff. He grabbed a flatbed cart from the storage room in the basement and nearly ran down the tunnel with it. Brook chuckled at his eagerness. A few of their friends with the morning free came to help, when they heard how much they had to move.

Luckily for Adam, by the time the rest had made their way there with a second cart, the truck was there for them to unload the double-length pallet of plotter, the pallet of the stand and output rack, the three colour photocopiers—which worked also as network scanners, fax machines, and printers, the large box of the photo printer, and the wrapped stack of supplies; ink, toner, and cases of paper of various sizes and types— regular, photo in both glossy and matte.

They took the photocopiers off the skid, so they could roll them along the tunnel's smooth floor, they stacked the paper on the carts, and the photo printer on top of one with the larger cases of the paper.

They decided to unpack them in the first section of the tunnel, as it had good lighting, as they had recently replaced the lights in the tunnel with nice white LEDs, instead of florescent tubes which always seemed to be buzzing annoyingly or being burnt out. Also, the dumpster was nearby. The wooden pallets were stacked outside, to be picked up later and cut down for the fire pit.

Adam had claimed the Plotter setup, much to the amusement of the rest. While they pulled out all the shipping tape and retaining clips, and loaded the initial supplies, Adam screwed together all the pieces for the plotter stand and output rack. Once it was ready, and attached to the bottom of the plotter, he called everyone over to help him flip the plotter onto its wheels. With the four wolves working together, it was easy to do the lift. The rest of the plotter setup they would deal with when they were in the tech lab, along with the smaller photo printer.

By the end, they had a football sized lump of tape, and a box full of other bits, most of which was recyclable plastic or cardboard. They separated them as they dumped them in the big bins outside the parkade, which the pack took in when the bins were full. Sadly, they didn't have anywhere nearby to recycle the big stack of Styrofoam panels. Since they had a pallet full, they decided to ship them to the manufacturer, with a note to recycle or reuse them, and to next time use recyclable packing materials instead of something which usually is just landfilled.

They had it in the agreement to not have used them, so Adam was not happy to see them. They also noted the cost to ship them back was going to passed to them to be a refund, referring to their addition to the standard agreement, or they would take their business, and any referrals, elsewhere in the future.

They worked to push and pull the two carts, three photocopiers, plotter, and plotter's output rack down the tunnel when Jess and Joshua and a couple more came to help. They quickly made it to the large cargo elevator, and Adam called it as most was too big to move up the stairs.

Most of them had never ridden in the elevator, so they smiled as they quickly went up the floor. The photocopiers were quickly placed: one in the Alpha's wing, between his office and the boardroom, another in the guest wing, and the last in the tech area. Erin quickly rounded up her techs and got the photocopier in the guest wing and tech area on-line, and the test prints Adam had sent to the print queues quickly came out. The one in the Alpha's wing was waiting for them to network, which they were starting after lunch.

Adam growled slightly as everyone crowded around the plotter. Assigning tasks, he had some pups putting away the three rolls of paper he didn't need for the plotter, or the several cases of paper for the other printer. Turning on the printer, he followed the directions and had it printing out the first alignment page within the hour. Smiling, he told them the print queue was monitored, and few had access to it, as to not waste supplies.

Everyone but Adam was surprised when Adam loaded three rolls of different types of paper into the plotter; one which looked like normal paper, one of glossy photo paper, and one of a matte photo paper, with each roll being 42-inches long and having an eight-inch diameter cylinder. He also had to put in eight ink cartridges, each the size of a hard cover book.

When it finished the initial alignment, some of the pups jumped, as the plotter cut the paper and it slipped out and landed in the output rack. He didn't think they would be using it enough, so he hadn't ordered the motorized sorting output tray, using just the basic one which came standard with the machine.

He spent the last hour of the morning setting up the other photo printer beside the plotter and smiled as it sent out the test shot of him and Brook curled up together as wolves. It just looked like a large normal printer, even if it had three trays and could handle 11x17 paper in each. It too had quite a few ink cartridges in it as well. Many of the pups aww'd or commented how cute they looked as they looked at the picture. He shooed them out the door ahead of him playfully as they went off to lunch.

CHAPTER 18

New Trainer

At lunch there were many comments about the pictures Adam had printed out. He smiled and wrapped an arm around Brook, feeling his wolf preen at the complements. "We can now print out photos like that." Adam told them, making many happy, although they knew they would have to pay for them. The prices he quoted were to many very cheap.

Adam had set up a system to generate costs when people printed, so they could be billed monthly. It would just come out of the stipend the pack gives to all members, and the pack would pay for the supplies, although he would be responsible to submit the costs, and maintain the supplies. The machine in the guest wing was monitored more, and sent him daily reports of usage, but reasonable use was going to be covered by the pack. Reasonable use of the photocopiers was also going to be covered by the pack, with a quota of print outs covered, and to be kind, the unused portion would be rolled into the next month, which meant if someone wanted to print out a novel, they would be able to do so about once or twice a year. If it got used up, they would have to pay for it as well.

All he had to work out was the cost per page on each machine. Now with them installed, he could do it, using the estimated pages per supply for toner or ink to generate costs.

After an enjoyable lunch with their friends, Adam spent an hour with a spreadsheet to work out the per-page costs and entered it into the printing system. Happily, the machines were efficient. Once he was done, Adam and Brook took the rest of the afternoon to work on his training in human form. He was starting to get near Brook's level, so he started to get through her guard. Normally it took six months of training daily, not the broken training schedule they had. It was almost as if he had been taught but was just having to re-learn it now.

Mid afternoon Martin poked his head in the training room and saw them sparring. Brook smiled, and called him over, panting, "It's been only a month since we started, but he is almost at my level. I want to see if he is just anticipating *my* moves, or if he's learning the skills at an astonishing rate."

Martin grinned "Let me get changed and I would love to." He told them before he headed to the change room at the back, to put something on which was easier to fight in. He rarely got to spar with the top level of the pack, as there were few who could match him. Most were very busy. Brook was one of the few which he didn't need to pull his moves when they spared. If Adam was up there with her, it would be good for the pack.

Adam waited and caught his breath smiling. He was certain he could hold his own.

Martin came out of the change room wearing just some plain shorts and smiled as he walked over to where they were sparring, nodding at Adam, he smiled and moved to attack. Both fought well, and the sparring stretched on; Adam was taking most of the hits, but mostly was able to hold his own.

Eventually Martin was able to win, but he was grinning, "Excellent! If you have been working out since you came down here today, he is fighting well and is getting good endurance. If you want, I can meet you two down here to help train." Looking over at Brook, "You could always do with some refresher too."

Brook nodded, "It is always better to not fight the same opponent all the time. We will let Gareth know at the meeting on Monday how well he is able to fight. He will need to be involved at some point."

They discussed a schedule to have time to train. Martin also wanted Brook to start Adam on some weapons. Bow and staff to start with, then sword. When they were wolves, quite often they didn't carry weapons with them, but with a staff, it could be just a branch they picked up. Bows were used as the arrows could be readily made without outside intervention and were silent. They rarely carried guns as they were much harder to get and had much more oversight by the government. Not to mention they needed to maintain a supply of bullets. For the fact few were licensed and trained on them, and most were considered "Estate Security" by the government. Brook knew eventually he would be trained, but couldn't start till the human licensing was complete, which took many months.

By the time they were done, it was almost dinner time. All three went to their rooms for a good scrub before dinner.

Adam had a good bounce in his step, since it showed his body just was learning the fighting at a very fast rate, not he was learning how Brook fought, which in a real fight would be disastrous.

*****

At supper, Martin was questioned about his black eye, he just called it a training hit. Adam had a lucky strike and had got him good. It would take a day at most for it to heal. The rest of their group just gave him a ribbing, and it took them a while before they would give the name of the person who gave it to him.

They were startled to say the least when Adam's name was given. They stared at the two of them with wide eyes for a long moment, before ribbing Martin more; he had let one who had just started his training get through. He was one of the elites in the pack and was part of the reason he was the one in charge of pack security under the Alpha.

Both Adam and Martin grinned and were looking forward to more training. Martin got someone who would be up at least at his level, if not closer to the top of the pack, so could get a good workout to hone his skills. Adam was glad to be able to have someone else to train with; he enjoyed a challenge and had found the training fun. Brook had commented he would need the Alpha's attention for training all too soon.

Something did bother Martin; something about the way Adam fought, he just couldn't pin it down. Something seemed similar... He put it from his mind, as he'd remember it another time when he least expected it. He was certain about one thing; it wasn't something bad.

With anyone else, he'd be worried about his job, but Adam had his own responsibilities, and even he was making sure to get his opinions for what security for the network he needs to put in and gave him much in the way of learning to help him give more informed feedback, from a security point of view. They were both looking for someone who was very good with security *and* technology to oversee the security side. Adam was going to have them reporting to Martin, as he would be security, but working with the IT group to make sure they followed the security policies which were in place. Martin had been surprised at the thoughtfulness, and the fact he didn't want to step on his toes. It made it all much more satisfying where Martin had more knowledge, Adam was deferring to him. He did like the idea of not only having the technology standards but having someone who's main job was to make sure they were followed, didn't take any shortcuts, and then had the authority to enforce changes on any issues found. Adam's thought of having them outside the IT chain of command, and instead have them in the security one made sense too, as it would prevent orders to ignore issues or for complacency.

Being the Alphas, Adam knew Gareth and Maria were going to be the strongest warriors the pack had; he was needing the attention for training as a wolf, this pleased his wolf to no end; it showed they had the ability to help protect the pack. As a human, Adam was surprised he was progressing to that level at all, let alone already, since he had not even taken a self defence course or been trained as a warrior.

*****

Sunday was their normal day to relax, but Adam and Brook spent the morning training, and then relaxing in the pools in the greenhouse, as a bitter wind and snow had come down from the arctic, and any who didn't have to be outside was enjoying the warmth. Adam was using the time to get to know many of the Gamma fighters, and Deltas, as they didn't bother coming to his fire gathering, either having to work or wanting to just relax in their rooms.

Many of them were the ones who had jobs outside of the pack, some as security or the ones who did the patrols, so were not around the pack house as often. He learned how much work they had to do to make sure the territory was secure, which was near constant patrols. Many of the patrols also used the wolf dogs as backup or to watch their backs.

Adam hoped the Alpha would let him make the changes to help those securing the pack.

Many commented on their rings, which both Adam and Brook had decided they would wear them on the necklaces, generally. They liked the idea of wearing them and when they explained it would nestle into their fur when they shifted, so they didn't need to worry about removing them before shifting, many liked, and considered something similar, or a pendant on a necklace. The couples liked the idea of custom ones they designed from the heart, over something generic.

That evening, after dinner, Adam and Brook decided to just watch some movies, and cuddle over doing anything else.

*****

The next morning Adam woke early, but just snuggled down against Brook and dozed. He had almost fallen back asleep when she woke up. Trying to get up, she found her mate grinning as he pretended to sleep, as he tightened his arms, holding her in place. It took a growl and plenty of squirming for him to release her.

Once he released her, Adam acted like he had just woke up, "Morning!" as he smiled at her.

Brook glared, "I know you were awake, so drop the act!"

"But I wanted to cuddle!" Adam pouted.

"Not today. We have breakfast and then the meeting with the Alpha." She reminded him.

"Fine." Adam called, as he stretched.

Brook grinned and decided to dress Adam fairly girly today in revenge. She picked out a lacy thong, and matching padded bra, then a short skirt and a stretchy shirt. Tossing them at him, as she glared, daring him to comment.

Adam just grinned and pulled the clothes on. His only comment was, "I hope you have something similar to wear too!"

She smiled and decided she would accept the request. Only difference they had was she was wearing a short shirt which showed off her flat belly.

Brook decided to braid Adam's hair, as it was now long enough, in a French braid. Adam just sat still and let her. Once she was done with his, he helped her get her nice long hair into a similar braid.

Neither bothered with socks or shoes, same as many of the pack, unless they had to go into an area with humans, as they preferred to feel the ground beneath their feet. Adam had agreed and was working to toughen his feet to do so, too. Dressed, they headed off to the dining room for breakfast.

Other than some knowing grins from some of their friends as to their outfits, the few comments which were said were deflected with witty replies, which had everyone laughing. Adam liked the outfit, and had caught his reflection in a mirror, and thought it looked nice. He didn't say a thing, though, as Brook had meant it as a punishment.

Once done, they grabbed the papers they needed for the meeting and went off to the Alpha's office. He laughed when he saw the two dressed similarly, shaking his head, "You two have just way too much fun playing 'dress up' it seems."

Both just grinned and sat down as Brook commented, "Well, why not? We aren't going to be heading anywhere we could be seen, and if we were, we can change." Brook just thought her mate looked really cute in the outfit. She was thinking he would need to wear some of her more girly stuff occasionally. She still planned on him wearing a dress at some point.

With that, they bent their heads over the final choices Adam had made for the PCs and laptops to order, and how many. Most were wanting laptops, but a few were wanting a PC. He had decided on mostly moderate powered laptops, but there were a few higher end ones. There was a standard PC, and if someone wanted something different, they would need to pay for it. Several of the pups pouted about the decision as they had requested high-end gaming systems, and the fact their parents were limiting what they could do on the systems, and Adam had shown them how to enforce the parental controls. When asked, he refused to help them find ways around it, and threatened punishments if they tried. Repeated punishments would be brought before the Alpha, this went without being said.

Gareth agreed with Adam and Brook's decision that unless a person wanted a PC, they were getting a laptop, for the mobility and for the most part, there wasn't a noticeable difference in performance. They also used less power and was one more way they could reduce their energy usage. With the decision made, Adam worked out the costs, and gave the rough number which was approved. For the few who wanted both, or were undecided, they got a laptop and a docking station to connect the external hardware.

The next topic was about the security, and all three sat up straighter, and Gareth even had Maria join them for it.

The Alpha started, "First, there are privacy concerns with the video cameras. Many are not wanting them. At this point, we are not doing them. You can upgrade and replace the existing cameras with new equipment, but not add a blanket of them."

Adam nodded in understanding, hoping not all his ideas were shot down. They could review the decision and bring it back up another time.

"Second, the idea of needing the ID all the time and securing all the doors was one the elders and many seniors didn't want either. Some it was just cost, so maybe get a good pricing for it, and the discussion will continue."

Adam nodded and made a mental note.

"Third, sensors in the forest was an idea they liked, as it can cover some of the holes the patrols leave. The infrared motion and thermal camera were approved. They worried about ultrasonic harming hearing, if not us, the animals in the area. The vibration they didn't think it was worth it, but from what you said, I was able to get agreement for the outer ring of the property. The laser trip lines were not approved. Let's see how those three do, and we can go from there."

At least we got some, Adam commented to Brook, slightly disappointed.

"Sadly, I could only get agreement for one ring, not a nested setup of what I too was wanting. Too many didn't want it. This decision may be revised in the future." Like once they had the first ring and could show how it didn't affect privacy but did increase their security, he planned on permitting the full deploy.

Adam nodded, not liking it, but it could always be expanded.

They went through the other minor topics, which didn't take too long. Once done, Adam and Brook went to find Martin to tell him the mixed news, and to figure out how they wanted the sensors and how to connect them.

They ended up looking at the large map in the security office. It was more of a cross between a satellite photo map, a topographical map showing the changes in elevation, and a 3D model. It was almost like a toy story board. Looking over it, and spec'ing out items online on Adam's laptop, they were able to determine where the sensors would be installed. They were placing them in the highest risk areas first: north and south, and a couple of mountain passes to the east. Next, they planned on getting them in the hardest places, along the ridgetop borders, then fill them in the rest of the way.

Looking at what the map was made of, he started to grin, "I can add lights to the map to show were the alarm triggering is, so you can see at a glance where the issues are."

Martin liked the idea, "Do it." He commanded.

Adam and Brook spent the rest of the morning in their room deciding what equipment to get, and how to connect it. Due to the size of the territory, they had to run some wired, then could use wireless networks. They settled on some Wi-Fi standard gear, and sensors which would use them. Once they knew what they were getting, they ordered them, just enough for the first phase, as if they did everything at once, it would cause a flag with the government, and they would wonder what they had to protect.

*****

After dinner, they changed into some warm fleece, as although the wind and snow had mostly stopped, it had dropped to -20 C already, and was expected to be -30 by morning. They expected many to come as wolves, and for it to be a short fire.

Heading over to the fire along the beaten down paths, they eventually reached the fire. Both were surprised at the large roaring fire, and the number already there.

Jess walked up to them and commented, "I thought we could get your fire started early and have a nice warm space for everyone to come." She handed each a hot drink.

Adam smiled and settled to just give her a good hug in thanks. Linking his mate, she gave him a mental nod of agreement, and they pulled Jess onto the bench between them. For the night, all three were treated to a near lineup of hugs and they didn't get cold, because they constantly had someone curled up against them, and a warm wolf against their backs.

The fire was fairly short, with most heading back to the pack house early, as even if they could handle the cold, they didn't have to stay out in it. Brook and Adam decided to snuggle down in front of the fireplace in their room and invited Jess and Joshua to join them. The two young Theta wolves were startled to be sure but were very pleased. Brook and Adam pulled them both between them and curled up in front of the fire and watched a newly released movie which he had just got, and none had seen before.

At the end of the movie Jess quietly thanked them for the time and attention. Pulling her in for another hug, it slipped out they hadn't had anything like this since their parents died when they were fifteen in a rockslide. Adam just tightened his hug, as his wolf was feeling upset for them. Looking over, Brook had done the same to a crying Joshua.

Adam could feel Brook's wolf was just as worked up, and he could feel an almost maternal instinct from her, caught her eye and nodded, "You two are staying the night with us. Both our wolves are feeling fairly worked up over this. In the morning, we can work out the changes, when you are in a better mind." No words needed to be spoken; they both cared a great deal about their two helpers.

Sending a quick mental command to Charlie, who could also feel the pain and was whining, wanting to help, to pull the blanket from the bed, brought it over to them. The pad was as big as a king-sized bed and had plenty of room for them to curl up together on.

Brook and Adam pulled the two down between them on the pad, curling up against their backs, with Charlie curling up beside Adam. Brook and Adam worked to pull the blanket over the four of them and enjoy a comfortable night providing comfort and security.

*****

The next morning Adam awoke slowly, till he realised he had a female in his arms, and it wasn't Brook. He was suddenly awake, but didn't move, as his wolf was able to realise Jess was still curled up against him. He could smell Joshua and Brook were still here, so he probably was the first to awaken.

He just lay there holding Jess close, and decided to have a chat with his wolf, he looked inward at his wolf.

What should we do with the two of them? he asked his wolf.

Comfort and protect them. It seems they have been missing the comfort part for a while, so they need extra comfort and caring. He whined, not liking the idea of pups not having much comfort.

I knew that, but anything more than just doing comfort like this? What else should we do? He nearly begged his wolf, feeling a pull from them which he didn't understand.

Adam felt Brook wake and turn inwards. Both her and her wolf seemed to pad out of the darkness and up to them, *I caught what you were talking about as I awoke... I am not sure either of what to do for them, other than provide them care and attention. I remember that slide. We lost several wolves that day. I didn't realise there were children orphaned by it which weren't snapped up by another, and everyone was affected. I thought Jess and Joshua were fine and had someone they were close to; I guess nobody noticed, and they seemed to be doing fine. The fact you care deeply for all pack members not just those in your sight or direct control is an Alpha trait. Many elders must learn it, but some are more successful than others. You are opening my eyes, and helping me be a better wolf, thank you.* Human-Brook told him.

Wolf-Brook had been trying to push her human half, but until Adam joined them, wasn't getting much traction to show where they could go and be, **Ask them what they want. They are old enough they should know.** she advised, **They may just want care like this occasionally or may want someone to look to and be their surrogate parents. They may not want to change anything from what it is now.**

They felt the others start to stir, and without a word, broke their conference to return to the real world. Opening their eyes, they greeted the twins, who were sandwiched between them; Jess was curled up and holding him tightly, and he still had an arm wrapped around her. Her brother also had an arm around her and was spooned against her back, and Brook was cuddled up just as tight against Joshua's back.

From the light, they had slept late, and probably missed the breakfast meal, but as there was always the snack buffet, or they could hunt a rabbit. Adam's wolf begged to do the last, but reminded him he still needed to practice, and didn't have time unless they wanted to leave those in their care alone got him to settle down; these two young wolves needed them much more than they needed a bunny. He smiled as Jess opened her eyes and blushed. Adam just gave her nose a chaste kiss, and a soft "good morning" which made her blush deepen. Neither tried to move though, being very comfortable as they were.

Joshua woke with a start, panting. Looking around he started crying again, which set Jess off. Looking over them, Adam commented to Brook, *Do we have anything scheduled today?*

Ummm... Brook thought, *Other than your training, checking up on our techie-pups, and dealing with any major issues; no; nothing I can remember which can't really be put off.*

Adam smiled, and linked Erin to hold anything not critical and to pop her head in on the pups in the lab when she had a minute. Once done with it, he turned his attention to Brook, *I think these two need our attention for today. Erin can hold anything which isn't a big major issue for another day.* His training, while important, was less important than providing care and comfort to a couple of wolves who seemed to not have gotten much.

I agree. They need us.

Adam and Brook sent them wordless love and caring over their bonds, trying to sooth them, but just letting them cry all they needed. Sitting up against the base of a couch, he sat Jess up gently, and pull her into his lap. Brook quickly followed, pulling Joshua into hers, and tightly wrapping him in her arms. Both took a while to cry themselves out. Adam had a thought, *I don't think they have had a chance to really grieve. I don't think they had anyone close enough they felt safe enough to break down and cry with.*

Brook nodded slightly, *From what I remember seeing, they were basically treated as adults after that. I know they never came to me, and I'm thinking they didn't come to anyone else, either.* They both helped by being strong, silent, caring people for them. *I let Gareth know we are indisposed, caring for our two, and to only disturb us if essential. His comment was 'take all the time you need' and if we need someone to bring meals to let the kitchen know.*

I am certain we should ask for lunch at least. Have Toby, or his friend... Adam had to think for a moment, *Robin bring the food. They would disturb us the least.* Adam liked both pups and was keeping an eye on them. He had noticed they hadn't joined in with the ones having fun with the old equipment, but had been hanging in the shadows, watching. He was thinking they may be shy or had been something else. If they did have the aptitude for technology, he was planning on folding them into his group, as both he and his wolf felt they could become more than just Thetas, if they applied themselves.

Jess and Joshua ended up taking nearly to lunchtime to calm down and stop crying. Both were dozing in their arms when they were startled awake by the quiet knock at the door.

Adam smiled and had Charlie go open the door, and he happily went to do so. As soon as he did, they could smell some excellent stew and soups. Adam smiled at Robin, who stepped in, "On the table over here, please. You can put Charlie's on the ground for him." Charlie was well behaved enough to not try to take the food from the pup, but was very much wanting some, and followed them closely but knowing to not be too close or get in front of them.

Robin nodded and placed the large tray down and the cooler one for Charlie on the tile floor before stepping over and giving both Jess and Joshua a hug silently and heading out; he knew how they felt, as he had lost his parents too, and he was now staying with his cousin, Toby.

Adam smiled as he watched Robin give the two a hug before departing, and feeling he had a similar feeling sore point. Making a mental note on having a talk to him, as he was uniquely suited to help, having lost his own parent when he was young. He gave a mental sigh, and started considering taking a counselling course or two, as it seems he might need the skills.

Adam and Brook coaxed the twins to eat and since their stomachs could be heard demanding food, they quickly ate. Adam and Brook stayed close and once they were all done, pulled them back close, this time Joshua went to Adam, and Jess to Brook. Quietly, Adam told his life story to them, showing he could understand the sudden loss of a parent, but he knew it was much worse for them, since they lost both. The pack was what kept them mostly there, but still didn't give them much time to grieve properly.

They talked all the afternoon, and towards dinner were asked if they wanted it here, or with the pack, they decided to join the pack.

As they walked together out of the suite, Adam commented, "If you two need to come to us for support, let us know. If we are asleep, come join us. We are always there for you."

They both nodded. "I think we'll just go to our room after dinner and sleep," Jess commented, "Just having you both care makes me feel so much better."

*****

Everyone in their group was concerned at the way Jess and Joshua looked, but seeing them flanked by the Betas, realised they were in good hands and were being cared for. Most realised all four must have spent the day together. Quite a few gave them gentle touches or soft words of support on their way to their seats.

At the glare Brook gave, they lowered their eyes, and didn't say a thing about it, but continued their conversations from before they entered. Erin had stepped away as they arrived at the table and came back with four laden plates for them. Adam smiled his thanks, but didn't say anything, almost as drained, and ready for a nice sleep. He hoped the twins would get a good sleep.

Getting back to their suite after dinner, Adam checked his messages for the day, and other than the status updates, a few newsletters, all he had was a message from his sister; Tara was looking at spending the weekend with them. She also said she was willing to accept one of their wolfdogs.

He quickly sent his thoughts to the Alpha and got the approvals for her staying. Since it was January and she was staying three nights, he got her a spot in the heated parkade, although it was down at the bottom; he also updated the approval for the wolfdog.

Once it was done, he replied to her, saying he'd meet her at the warehouse Friday evening, so he could direct her to the secure parking. He told her to pack some warm outdoor clothes, and her swimwear. He doubted she would join them without anything on.

He then gave a heads up his favourite Chef and let her know his sister would be there Friday night for dinner and would be staying till Monday morning breakfast, so they could have time to prepare her meals, remembering she had some food allergies which would need to be dealt with.

Lupita grumbled about not much notice, but didn't say much else, other than there would be food for his sister.

Brook had been leaning against his back with her arms over his shoulders, watching the screen, as he sat at the computer, just as worn out. She smiled, "So, what's planned for the weekend?"

Adam smiled, "Hoping to show her some of the beauty around here, and have her spend the time with the dog, which we should do right after breakfast on Saturday, so we can see how they get along. The rest of the time, I'm not sure."

Brook stretched high, "Well, I think we need a shower, then a bed. Soothing the twins took a lot out of me, even if they are totally worth it."

Standing, he turned off the monitors, "I agree! Do we celebrate birthdays? I think we should get them something. I found out they were March twenty-fifth."

Brook stopped and turned as they were heading for a shower giving him a startled look, "Not celebrate a birthday? Are you crazy?" Then she smiled sweetly, "I got yours and your sister's too. Not sure if we'll do much for your sister, unless we can get her here for it, but yours: I think the twins and I can think of something."

Adam sighed theatrically, "If you wish. Now you were saying shower?"

That night they just made their bed and crawled into it and were asleep moments after curling up together, for their own healing sleep. Neither noticed Charlie climbing up and curling up against Adam's back, when he got back from his run later in the evening.

CHAPTER 19

Surprises

The next morning, Brook and Adam woke up in time for breakfast. Without saying anything, they dressed for training after breakfast. After eating a light breakfast, they met Martin and started their warmups. Martin started with some more advanced moves with both, as Brook hadn't even been taught them. Martin knew they had been dealing with pack members the day before and hadn't been out till suppertime. Since Brook was now senior on par with him, rather than mostly just training the pups, she needed the more advanced skills she hadn't bothered learning.

Grinning, he had noticed both were progressing well with this new skill. Adam was only going at what he thought was his normal rate, not what Brook had told him was the rate till this point, which showed; it didn't matter. Showing Adam the basics for the staff late in the morning, Martin advised Brook to make sure to brush up on hers, too. Now that she was a high-ranked Beta, she was expected to be proficient at it, and she admitted, a bit sheepishly, she rarely worked at it beyond what she needed to teach the pups. He smiled and told them he'd see them next Wednesday, but to work on the skills they had started that day, and to work at the archery.

Following their well-needed lunch break, they checked on the pups doing the computers, and on the status of the wiring. Just as they finished, Shana linked them, *You have a delivery of several pallets of stuff... looks like laptops for the most part.*

Brook grinned, "I know what you want to be doing for the afternoon!" she teased.

Adam just grinned back, as he replied to Shana, *Thanks. I'll be down with the truck shortly to pick them up.* before turning to her, "You coming with me, or staying here?" he asked his mate, holding out his hand.

Taking his hand, "Did you even need to ask; I'm going with you!"

Walking into the kitchen, they signed out the cube truck, before arranging with the pups and Duncan they would be needing them with the carts and some straps to grab the pile of computers in from the garage.

*****

Other than some slippery spots, the pickup of the equipment went without a hitch. Parking the truck back in its spot on the tall first level of the parkade, , they started unwrapping the pallets while they waited for the pups.

Not too much later, they had the chatting pups arrive and had them load up the carts with the computer boxes. Using straps, they piled them high, and with the number of carts, they still needed to make two trips. Adam went with them, to operate the elevator, which they were all excited to be able to try out. Most for the first time.

Once the stuff was stacked in the computer lab, he took them all back down the elevator and back to Brook, who had stayed with the truck. They quickly unloaded the rest of the equipment and locked the truck up.

Once they had everything back in the lab, he had the pups unpack two of each of the models, one to capture the factory image, and the other to load a bare-bones image from the server. Once the barebones was installed, Adam started the installers for the software they were using and made sure all the drivers were up to date and installing all the updates to that point, teaching the others what to look for. Once done, he prepped the machines to be a source image, then captured the image to fast image the other computers.

When it was ready, he loaded them to the server, and let the pups' image the 300 laptops. Adam and Brook watched for a bit, but seeing they didn't need to help, left them to it, showing they trusted the pups to get the work done. He did tell them he'd rather it be correct instead of fast, and if there were any issues, they could just start over the imaging on the machine.

"Well," Adam commented as they walked out of the lab, "Since we still have a few hours, lets go do some work with the staffs."

Brook grinned, "Sounds like an idea." She was still embarrassed on how her skill with the advanced moves had slipped.

*****

Brook guided Adam through the first basic movements when it happened...

A surge of fear from Duncan and Keanna was felt by both Adam and Brook, then a call for help from them as Adam shifted fast to his wolf, shredding the clothes, "He's in our room!" he was able to make out. Brook was startled for only a moment and was already on Adam's heels as he dashed for the third floor, having shifted faster.

Arriving at their room, they saw a broken window, and heard the glass fall, showing it had just happened, and the two sobbing, with Adam trying to get anything out of them. They were able to make out "Scout" and "Shadowed River", which had Adam leaping down the stairs, going full out trying to catch the intruder. Brook stayed with the two, calling Erin for help, and alerting the Alphas and Martin to the intruder. Charlie arrived panting; he had been caught napping, literally. Brook ordered him to stay with the two as she ran in pursuit of her mate, knowing Charlie, while fast, would not be able to keep up with them going full out.

Moments later the pack house looked like a disturbed beehive. Brook passed Erin at the top of the stairs as she ran to protect and care for the two, and Brook continued to run to catch up with her mate. He was likely to need help, as he hadn't had much training in wolf-shape.

She passed the guards on the stairs guarding the upper floors with the Thetas. She burst out the front door, following Adam's scent, and the Alphas joined her. She quickly updated them on what she had found out. All three ran flat out to catch up with Adam, but he was such fleet-footed wolf now, they didn't make much headway and had Marten redirect a nearby patrol to support Adam.

A couple hours later they caught up to Adam and the patrol. Adam was snarling and tearing his claws in the ground that the wolf got away. The patrol was just staying back, not wanting to have the anger redirected to them. They were quite a bit outside of the pack territory.

Brook went to her mate and started working to calm Adam down, as she knew he wouldn't attack her. Slowly, he calmed under her ministration.

I caught sight of him: Male. Solid white fur. Not our pack, from the scent. Lost the trail about here. The patrol was not able to pick it up either. Adam continued to growl, *Alpha, I want to find out how they were not only able to get into the territory, but all the way into the pack house, and up to the third floor and harass a pair of Thetas without being caught!*

Gareth growled and had no luck finding the trail either. *Let's get back and see what we can do about it. I am overruling the decision and approving getting all the cameras and sensors you requested. I want the full plan implemented as soon as you can secure the hardware. Don't worry about the cost, just get it done.* Those which had been opposed to the work for any reason would now have to deal with the fact two Theta wolves had been attacked, in the pack house, in their room, and what would have prevented it was what they had refused to support, regardless of the fact they wouldn't have been installed yet.

Adam growled under his breath, not happy he had *his* wolves attacked, to get what would at least have given them notice of the penetration in time to prevent them from getting in the pack house. Adam and Brook ran right behind the Alphas. On their way back, they picked up many others who hadn't made it all the way before they turned back.

Getting back to the pack house took more hours, and although at a slower pace, all were feeling it. The alphas called the elders and all the senior betas to a meeting in an hour. Adam and Brook ran to the security office, where Erin had secured Duncan and Keanna, who had been too scared to stay in their rooms.

Now they were calmed down a bit, Duncan told them what he knew, "He's a scout from the Shadowed River pack. They had wanted to drag us back as deserters," He told the Alphas, who snarled in reply, "We were to be given the maximum punishment for the 'unprovoked attack of the delta' and being considered guilty for running." His voice dropped to nearly a whisper, "The punishment he said was a painful death."

Keanna added the last part, "When he realised he couldn't make it out with us before help arrived, he had bolted out the window and away." Before sobbing more.

They both refused to budge from the security office, even to go stay with Adam and Brook. After trying for a bit to even have them stay with him, and being refused, Martin reluctantly agreed to have them stay for now and showed them to a side room which had a pad for them to sleep on and a bathroom off the side of it.

Charlie stuck to Adam's side, glad to be back with him, as the Alphas, Brook, Adam, and Martin headed up to a hasty meeting with the elders and other senior members of the pack.

*****

Reaching the room, the three were the last ones there, "Now that everyone is here," Gareth stated, pointing Adam and Brook to seats which had been reserved for them at the front. "I am calling this emergency meeting to order."

William and Joan, the pack's Seconds were on the other side of the Alphas, in their normal spot. They were old enough to be Elders, but as there currently wasn't anyone to take over, they had stayed on. Soon, the Alpha's children, John and Bri, would be back from their training, and one was expected to be the Heir, and the other taking the Second, if nobody else was around to take over their role. Mostly, they did the day-to-day paperwork for the Alpha, letting the younger wolf do the more active duties.

"I'm going to have Adam tell me what happened today, so everyone is up to speed first." Gareth nodded, as he sat down.

Adam hadn't even bothered sitting, "I'm going to say what happened, not the order we found out," he started, "Apparently a Scout from the Shadowed River Pack tracked down Duncan and Keanna. I am *not* going to go into what happened there, as it is very personal. The Alphas, myself, and Brook know what happened, and they have been given a fresh start. All I'm going to say is they were from there but fled before they could be tossed out with nothing. They decided to call them 'dangerous rogues' and ordered to be killed on sight." Adam had to stop, as there was an outbreak of growls; the two in question were considered shy and they knew there was no way they were dangerous to another wolf, unless provoked; which was basically all Thetas. Since Adam had taken them under his protection they had started to open up and make some friends.

Adam raised a hand, to stop the growl, "They had requested and been given asylum here before the notice was received by the pack. It seems Shadowed River wasn't willing to leave them be, and had scouts out looking for them, to 'retrieve' them for sentencing. Apparently, they picked up their scent here, and had been in the territory for a while. Martin passed on some reports of glimpses of a white wolf, but they disappeared before they could be found."

It caused some more growls for the invasion of the pack's territory. It took Gareth to stop those growls.

Once it died down, Adam continued, "We are not sure how, but they somehow were able to get inside the pack house this afternoon and go up to the third floor and enter Duncan and Keanna's room. They instantly recognised the pack scent and called out to me. In the minute they had before I nearly knocked the door off the hinges, they were able to break the window, and jump out it. By the time I had made it out the door, they were already half a kilometre away, and I gave chase. I chased them for over two hours. I may be fast, but he was much faster, and somehow was able to mask his track and scent. I know I am young as a wolf, but by that point, there was a patrol with me, as were Brook and

Alpha Gareth. None of us could find a trace. We came back and got the information from the two." Adam nodded to the Alpha, and sat down, drinking the glass of water in front of him, before refilling it and doing the same. The third glass, he started to sip.

Gareth stood up, as he had also been gulping water while Adam had been talking, "Beta Adam had come to me previously about adding some security. I consulted you and other pack members about them," Many nodded, remembering the questions, "From many of you, you didn't want to have any sensors, and many didn't want any close in, as you felt they would give less privacy. At the time, I gave in, against my judgment, and we just had the example of how we *need* them. From what little I know, he would not have been able to skulk around the territory unchallenged, and definitely would not have been able to penetrate the pack house without setting something off."

Gareth took a breath, letting the information sink in, "As Alpha, I have now ordered we will be doing not only sensors at the edge of the territory but will be doing them throughout. Cameras will also be scattered. All the sensors will only be able to be controlled or viewed from the security office. As planned, there will not be cameras in the rooms, they will only be on the hallways and common areas, or outside. The sensors will be throughout the territory, in a method which will only be known to Martin, Adam, Brook, Maria, and myself. Other than the cameras, the rest will detect creatures. The thermal signatures can detect if it is a Were, and then the cameras will be used for ID. Adam had considered electronic locks, like what we have for the tunnel and the safe areas. Or even using implanted ID tags, but I would prefer not to do it, at this point."

Gareth looked over everyone, and saw mostly reluctant agreement, and even shame on the most opposed. Taking a deep breath, "I am releasing the Alert Four, and reducing to Caution Two until this issue with Shadowed River Pack is resolved, or until all the sensors are installed and operational. They had started laying the connecting cables yesterday for the infrastructure for dealing with the sensors. Adam is dealing with the procuring of the technology including the sensors right now, and we will be changing the order."

Looking up at the clock at the back of the room reading 01:26, he blinked and realised how late it was, "In the morning, I have instructed Adam to get all the details finalised and equipment ordered. As it is very late, those who missed dinner, the kitchen has informed me, they have kept warm trays for you take to your rooms, to have before bed."

Heading out the door, Martin stopped Adam, and passed him his ID, "You left this in the gym, along with what was left of your clothes."

Adam looked down, and blushed; he didn't even realise he wasn't wearing anything. Looking around, there were quite a few less than dressed wandering around, including his mate and the Alphas. "Thanks," he commented and headed towards the kitchen. He met Brook on the way with dinners for them both, and they nodded to the wolf guarding their wing. Opening their door, Adam flopped on the couch.

Looking at the thick pad, Jess and Joshua were laying there blinking. "We felt safer here. Can we stay for the night?" Jess asked quietly.

Adam and Brook shared a nod, before Brook answered, "Yes; there's no problem, we're heading to bed as soon as we eat."

Just as they finished, there was a knock at the door. Curious, Adam answered it. Robin threw himself at Adam, as soon as the door opened. The fact they recognised his scent just as the door opened saved him from a counterattack from Adam's worked up wolf.

"Can I stay with you tonight?" Came the muffled reply, he was dressed some soft clothes, seemingly for bed.

Adam held him as best as he could, "Of course. Brook and I were just heading to bed ourselves." Brook was already in the bed waiting. Adam turned the lights off, before directing Robin to climb into the bed, and following him. Robin curled up hesitantly, till Brook slid over and pressed her stomach to his back and held him close. Adam smiled and slid in on the other side of Robin and held him, Charlie climbed into his usual spot at Adam's back, and all went to sleep.

*****

The next morning Adam was woken up way too early by Martin. *Sorry to bother you, but Robin was reported missing this morning, and his scent lingered near your door.*

Yes, he seemed very scared and asked to stay with us. Brook and I have him asleep between us.

OK, I will let his aunt know.

Adam snuggled back down, with his arm wrapped protectively around the pup. His wolf was awake and keeping watch while his human slept, with the excitement from the evening before, he was still riled up and wanted to rend the white wolf apart. He approved of the sensors his human planned; it would make sure they knew when the intruder came back, in time to catch them. The electronic eyes, ears, and noses would make sure they caught the intruders before they could scare those under their care.

Waking up in time for breakfast Brook smiled as Adam had Robin snuggled close to him, still asleep. She knew he would be as good with any pups of their own. She nudged both, before heading into the closet to get some clothes. She pulled out some comfy ones, as they would be sitting at the computer to get the new cameras and sensors as soon as possible.

Coming out, Brook tossed the clothes at Adam. Robin was doing some stretches as he got up, looking more settled, and came over to give her a good hug, "Thanks for letting me spend the night. My aunt doesn't like us sleeping with them, she thinks we need to sleep in our own beds, but I was too scared."

Kneeling, so she could look him in the eyes, "You are welcome to join us any night. We will make room. Tell Toby too." Seeing Adam dressed, she stood and smiled, "Come to breakfast with us?"

Robin smiled brightly and nodded his head enthusiastically. Grabbing his hand, they headed to the door Adam held for them, smiling.

As they were sitting down, Toby joined them, and silently, Adam sat him down beside his friend, with both pups bracketed by the Betas. Toby looked like he hadn't slept well, if at all. *Next time you have a bad *night, instead of shivering scared in your bed, you are welcome to do what Robin did and join us. We'll keep you safe**

Toby leaned against Adam, getting some comfort, as he ate his breakfast slowly. He hadn't gotten any sleep, but wrapped in the beta's scent, he felt safe. Once it was done, he just sat there dozing, leaning against the Beta. Robin chatted with Erin about what the other pups were up to, not noticing his cousin was nearly falling asleep beside him.

Adam noticed Robin's enthusiasm, and had Erin show him what they were doing and got him involved. As they stood up, Toby nearly fell over, asleep. Adam quickly scooped him up, and smiled at Brook, "I'm going to put him in our bed to sleep while we work on the computers, so we can protect him.

Brook nodded and led the way. Toby just cuddled into Adam as he carried him. Charlie padded behind them back to the room. Placing Toby down on the bed, Charlie jumped up and sprawled against him, knowing to protect the pups.

"Hopefully, he gets a good sleep this morning while we work, not sure he slept at all overnight." Adam commented, as they started with the cameras, and the supporting hardware.

Brook and Adam bent their heads over some blueprints of the pack house and laid out where the cameras would go with a dot. They laid them out to minimize blind spots, but to be economical for the numbers of cameras. Then they worked out how they were running the cables; the nice thing was they were digital and worked off the network. They just needed more PoE or Power over Ethernet switches, so the network cable would not only get the signal, but also provide power. They worked out the calculations to make sure there was enough power for all the devices.

Writing down the number of cameras, and how much more cable they estimated, Brook ran off with the blueprints and how big of holes they needed, she met Rein and Erin at Rein's office and handed them the details. They knew this was priority.

"Do we have enough network cable?" Erin asked. Once Rein had the holes made, it would be up to her to get the network run.

"No. We are ordering more today. Use what we have right now, as it will be the same cables. A separate switch for each wiring cabinet is also needed and Adam's ordering those right now, too. When done with the plans, pass them to Martin, so he has a layout of the cameras. We can be ready to just install the cameras as soon as they come in; we will be express shipping them."

Both nodded, and quickly worked out a plan to do the work efficiently, as Brook headed back.

Adam had brought in Martin to figure out where to lay out the cameras and sensors over the whole territory. They figured out what they wanted for the cameras—all with night vision—and how they would cover areas. By lunchtime, the three of them had worked out the layout of the cameras, the infrared motion detectors, and thermal cameras, and would do the Seismic vibration sensors and laser trip lines, and even a new one he just learned about: EM motion detection which detected the changes in electromagnetic fields for movement. They would also need to find out how they wanted to wire everything.

Jess and Joshua, came in with a cart of food, "I know this is very important, so we brought you some of the selection which was out for today."

Adam looked up and smiled, "Thanks! We were thinking we'd have to go to the dining room for food!"

The smell of the food brought Toby over, looking much better, but still sleepy. Adam pulled out a plate, handing it to him; pups and pregnant females got first choice of the food. All the adults waited while he made his choices.

Jess smiles and had put down Charlie's bowl of food for him.

Once Toby made his choices, he was directed to sit on the couch, while the adults made theirs; Jess and Joshua, smiled and joined Toby on the couch, while the rest took a working lunch, to get as much done as possible. After Toby finished his lunch, Adam sent him to join the pups working in the lab, saying he was expecting him and Robin to join them for dinner.

Shortly after lunch, they started finding vendors for the equipment. They had also ordered another spool of fibre optic cable, more ends, and even a second splicing tool, as they needed much more. Many of the items were also going to be wireless; luckily, the network was already there for them to get the equipment going outside easily, they hoped. To power some of the remote equipment, due to the distance, they were using small solar panels and batteries, and luckily there were off-the-shelf items. The number they needed was going to drain several companies, too.

They passed on where the cabling was going, and which order they needed to be done. Rein was delegating the work out to get the cables into place and the holes which needed to be drilled ready.

Once it was done, they moved to getting the security office upgraded for the new equipment. One company they were looking at was willing to do what they wanted but would not allow them to install it; they wanted to do it for them, and since they refused to budge, even when told they couldn't get them clearance for the facility access in time, they kept pressing. Finally, Adam hung up on them with a, "We'll get back to you with a decision, if we decide to order with you."

Doing some further searching on the internet, he found another company, called Silver Orca Sensors, but it seemed they did more than just sensors. Frowning, Adam remembered the name from somewhere, they had made the first order of sensors from them without realising what else they offered!

Looking around the website, he realised they also did cameras, the management systems, the monitoring consoles, and screens... basically everything they needed to upgrade the security systems. He grinned when he noticed they also did door locks and the RFID systems, for in the future. All of it was designed to interconnect and mesh together, and even connect into the server systems he was setting up! They also did standards for everything, so if they wanted to change to a different brand, they could do so. No 'designed to work with our other parts' and nothing further. He smiled when he noticed it could all be set up locally, without any Public Cloud systems, where data was sent to others.

Calling them up, Adam asked about adding to the original order, listing off everything they were wanting.

"Usually, we send out an installation team," The saleswoman said after placing them on hold for a bit, "As the configuring of the system is very complex. But the manager is willing to offer it without the installation, if you are assuming all the risk to the equipment for any failure or damage from an incorrect installation." It was quickly agreed to accept the risk, as the wolves weren't too worried about the cost to replace anything which failed.

"Did you have a camera system already installed, as I noticed you didn't have it as part of your order." The saleswoman asked as there was a bit of a commission for upselling. She didn't worry about it, but she did make suggestions when she saw there might be a need or opportunity and was glad they didn't do sales targets.

"I had looked at yours, but it was more expensive than..." Adam replied, naming the one they had gone for, as they had gone with a different system from a competitor. The saleswoman asked for details on what they were ordering, and when they got the details, they were put on hold again. Adam grinned at his mate, who was listening to the call.

"I have good news for you," The saleswoman said, coming back on the call a couple minutes later, "Since you are ordering all the other parts, we can offer you..." she went on to offer some changes to the back end servers, to a more powerful one which had the ability to also link in the cameras and the door security, which they were not approved to change right now, and more easily tie into other security systems. "Adding on the order of cameras and their other parts..." She named a price for the items which was slightly more than the other, but not significantly. They wanted the business and were willing to offer a deal for the 'package' of everything. The fact everything interconnected was one thing which usually sold their equipment.

"We do plan on doing another order later, to deal with our outbuildings, but they are a lower priority." Adam added, fishing for a deal.

"We definitely can promise the same preferred price for any future orders from you." She answered without hesitation, having anticipated the request and the manager already having approved it. There was another voice and some shuffling of papers, "The order is large enough we do not have stock at any one warehouse, so it will be coming in several orders. Can I get your shipping address?"

Brook smiled, as it sounded like this would be a good addition to the pack's Preferred Vendor list of companies who were willing to work with them to find a solution to their needs and work with them on any limitations they had. She made a note to have them checked to see if they were trustworthy to be added to the list.

After getting the address, the saleswoman seemed to pause then get a little chatty, but "That sounds very wolfish," And another two keywords which Brook knew for humans who knew of them were to use to identify themselves was part of the discussion.

Tapping Adam on the hand which held the phone, she took it, and started chatting, using the counter phrases which were used. The saleswoman caught them quickly and after a couple more exchanges to be sure, Brook told her, "Please hold a minute." And placed her on hold at this end.

Martin, can you check for Wolf-Knowledge for Silver Orca Sensors, please? They were able to complete a secure code exchange with me. They are the ones for the cameras and sensors. Brook asked silently.

I see them on trusted list for a couple of other packs we deal with. I must check with the Alphas. Was Martin's reply after a short wait. Often, the friendly packs shared lists of companies they dealt with, the good and the bad, and especially those who knew what they were.

Adam and Brook shared a grin, "This is getting better and better!" He typed up an e-mail cancelling the order of the cameras which he had just made and signed for, saying they had found one which better met their needs. If he needed to, he would pay a penalty for cancelling it happily, as he hadn't liked the attitude of the seller. They were not interested in doing anything rush, nor willing to do any sort of package deal. They had stated it would be "two to four weeks" before they could send out anything and were not willing to send in several smaller orders.

I have full approval for escorted access to the pack's property for the installers. Martin replied after a wait. *Seems they have had access at other packs before. I will deal with them while they are here.*

Brook grinned and picked up the call, "Well, it seems your installers are approved, and will have escorted access here, so will need a new agreement with installation and to get our pack up to speed getting the gear out, when can you have them here? We *will* be interested in the installation services, and to add on..." While they waited, they had looked at the other items the upgraded server system could handle, and there were several classes of sensors they hadn't thought to add to the system but were available. They even ordered a larger, more advanced video table for the security office which would be integrated into the system, which would work much better than just static lights on the one they had. They did mention that while they weren't looking at the door security right now, they would likely be in the future.

They heard a loud thud from the speakerphone, before the Rep came back on, "Sorry, the phone slipped, I have never had such a large order. I assume you are wanting to integrate both the cameras and sensors fully?" they asked.

"Yes, if it's possible." Adam confirmed.

They discussed the amount of territory they were covering, and how they wanted it handled. They settled on a cost which was less than Adam expected for everything, not including the table, and included a service agreement, and even sensor buyback or recertification for resale when they were at the end of their useful life.

"I have placed the order on 'rush' with next day shipping–no charge. However, we only have stock for about a third of the sensors and half the cameras. My boss is on the phone with the manufacturer..." The rep trailed off, and they could hear them talking to another, "Second third of the order," They said, coming back on, "Will be shipped direct from them in two days, and the last in about a week." It wasn't often a pack contacted them for an entire new setup, so they didn't normally stock the amount they needed. Their manufacturer often could ramp production up if needed by offering extra shifts to get them done in reasonable time.

"Thanks!" Adam replied, grinning. Having to wait for part of the order was not an issue; they would not likely need them till then. They could get the core systems installed, then the first part installed while they waited.

"Thank you for dealing with Silver Orca Sensors," The rep responded, "I will get the invoice e-mailed to you, along with a direct contact information for any support, and links to all the documentation. You should have it later today. The manager has booked the installers for arriving Monday, and for your location, will be towards the middle of the day. You are being assigned to an account manager, and they will also be e-mailing you their contact information as well. They will be passing on the details of who the installers are as soon as they are assigned, in the next day or two. They will know all the information about your group and will be your contact for future orders." She advised before they ended the call. Part of the installation agreement they made with the wolves was to house the installers and provide the meals.

Adam and Brook were laughing, "Who would have thought we could find a company which does the sensors, cameras, and all the back-end equipment, *and* they'd be already cleared?" Adam commented.

Brook chuckled, "Now, I am very glad we decided not to go with the first company! It sounded like they didn't care as much." She sent a quick report about the other vendors they didn't like, "I almost wish we had asked other packs what they used first!"

They let Martin know the installers would be arriving mid-day Monday and be there for the week for installation and training.

*****

As they headed off to dinner, Adam realised the next afternoon was when his sister was coming. Mentioning it to Martin as he joined them for the meal, he smiled, "Way ahead of you; already have an ID for her., When you meet up, send me a picture and I'll get it printed by the time you get to the pack house."

Adam smiled in reply "Thanks."

He was pounced from both sides by Toby and Robin, and both clung to him, looking much better.

"Hi boys, ready for dinner?" Adam asked.

Both nodded and smiled.

"Well, lets head in." Adam urged, wrapping an arm around each of the two boys. He could feel a bit of a bond from both, start to form. He was happy he'd be able to keep an eye on his favourite pups.

Sitting down with one on each side, and Brook on the other side of Robin, they grabbed a plate, and filled it with the food, and started to eat.

Brook commented, *I checked with Toby's mother, and let her know they have formed bonds to us, so we will be having them come more often to us. She was surprised about it with Robin, as she has been trying, but he refused to open up to her even as much as he has to us.*

I like these two and would like to help them excel. They feel much more senior than Theta. I think we need to get them some training, maybe some time with Rein, too. Adam replied.

I agree, although I think we should sit down with them after dinner. From the way they are clinging to you, I think they will both be wanting to join us for the night.

I agree. We can discuss it when we are done.

CHAPTER 20

Changes

After dinner, it took no urging for both Toby and Robin to join Adam and Brook for a chat. Sitting down on the couch, with Adam between them, and Brook on Adam's lap. The two pups leaned in against them, to enjoy the attention.

Adam took a deep breath, not having had to deal with too many kids before joining the pack, he wasn't too sure about it, "First, did you two have fun this afternoon working on the computer gear?"

Both smiled and nodded their heads enthusiastically, "We got to show the elders how to use the new laptops when they came to pick them up." Robin commented.

Adam smiled, "I was wondering why you two didn't join in when I asked for some pups to help with the old equipment?"

Robin answered first, "I had training that day and didn't want to ask later. Also, my aunt doesn't want me to do it, so wouldn't let me change my training schedule." He had been disappointed to miss it but hadn't wanted to ask about joining later since Toby's mom frowned upon the changes the technology represented.

Toby looked down, "My mom thought it was a waste of time, but I have bugged her to let me do it. She wants me to learn more to fight and be a pack enforcer than computers."

Turning to Robin, "I know there are several who have other training and aren't there all the time. If you want to join in when you're not doing any training, you are welcome to do it. Just show up and ask to join in."

Robin's face lit up with a big smile, and he nodded.

Turning to Toby and wrapping an arm around his shoulders, "Did you want me to discuss it with your mother? There is nothing which says you can't do both. Much of the new stuff which will be coming in next week is security enhancements. New requirements for security, which Martin and I are discussing, will require the senior security to know both computers *and* how to fight well."

Toby's eyes lit with hope, "Yes, please! If I became Pack Security, she would be happy." He just wouldn't tell her about the additions to the skills needed.

Both pups were still snuggled tight to Adam, so he asked what movie they wanted to watch. Brook ended up sprawling across all three males' laps while they watched the movie.

After the movie, they both asked to spend the night. Jess or Joshua must have already caught the fact they were going to be there, as there were soft shorts for both boys on the bed. Adam smiled and nodded and threw on some shorts as Brook pulled on some shorts and a reasonably loose sports bra as the two boys got ready for bed.

Adam slid into the bed and snuggled up against Robin, who giggled and pushed back slightly, playfully. Toby slid in on the other side and laughed when Brook slid in to bracket the pups from the other side.

Charlie flopped against Adam's back, squeezing the four tighter together. Adam grinned, thinking they may need to get a bigger bed if they continued to do this.

The two pups quickly fell asleep, as they felt well protected by the two betas around them.

The two betas, as they fell asleep, felt their wolves prowl forward in their minds, and would remain aware, to keep a watch; they were protecting two pups. Both sniffed the boys, to remind themselves of their scents. They could doze the night, and if needed continue to doze when their human half was awake.

*****

In the morning Adam and Brook woke at nearly the same time, at their normal wakeup for early training. Sending a quick thought to Brook about having the two join them for their training, today, and getting her agreement, Adam reached his mind and found Jess already up.

Jess, you probably know we had Toby and Robin with us last night. We're going to take them to our training this morning. Could I get you to grab their training clothes, please? Adam asked.

I got the cutest pictures of you with pups the last couple of nights. Jess teased, **I love the 'quiet' mode on your camera.** Then her mental voice got serious and replied to his request, **I thought you might, so went to get them last night. For the training you two do, what they had would actually hamper them, so grabbed them outfits similar to yours for them from the Pack Stores in your name. They are in your closet; I hope it was all right.** She hoped he didn't consider it stepping over the bounds.

Excellent! I love your initiative. I hope you don't decide just because I didn't ask for it yet, you don't do it. Adam sent her a wordless affection and thanks for it. He would hold off on the pictures till the pups weren't around, as he could then surprise them with copies.

Jess was ahead of us, and had gone to get their stuff, but instead decided to get them new stuff. She put them in our closet already. I love our two helpers. Adam told Brook. He didn't like the idea of calling them servants, even though it was mostly their job; it just didn't feel right. Brook had suggested 'helpers', and he agreed with using the term.

Waking Charlie, so he could get out, he headed into the closet with Brook, and after getting his training clothes on, found where the pup's stuff was. Both sets had been put with his and had taken a faint scent of his already. It would show anyone around they were under his protection.

The two boys grumbled a bit when they were woken up, until they learned they were joining them for training. Both jumped out of the bed, and quickly changed into the new clothes. Both wore grins as they followed the two Betas to the gym. Brook worked them through their warmup, as Adam did his more intense one.

At breakfast, Toby's mother marched up to them and spoke in a loud, harsh voice, "Where were you yesterday and last night? You know you had studying to do, and training." She forgot that Brook had let her know, as the regular instructors had left her notes they hadn't attended their classes. Both pups cringed a bit, "Also where did you get those clothes? You know I can't afford to get you new clothes!"

Adam stood up and gave Brook a nod he'd take care of it. He walked her out of the dining room, and to a small meeting room closing the door, since neither the pups nor the pack in general needed to hear this scolding, "The two pups have been staying under Brook's and my eyes or with the supervision of those we trust. The clothes were supplied from my funds, so don't worry about them. Robin came to us the night after the attack and needed some comfort. He is under the impression you wouldn't give any?" He made the last a question to find out more from her side.

"That's right. Boy-pups need to be tough and strong. They need to learn to not worry about it, and to sleep in their own bed, especially if they want to advance." She answered, arrogantly.

Adam's wolf let out an audible growl to it, for all her bravado, sent her cringing in submission, "First I don't disagree with everyone–not just males–need to be tough and strong. But not letting them seek comfort when they are upset or scared is *wrong*. I do not agree, especially with the forcing them to stay to their beds. Brook and I would welcome any pup who wants to, or any wolf for the matter, regardless of their age." He paused for a moment to let it sink in before continuing, seeing her disbelieving expression, "Monday night, we curled up with both Jess and Joshua to give them comfort, and when it wasn't enough, spent the day with them. If Duncan and Keanna were not so scared they are sleeping in a safe area, they would be welcome too."

"Well, I expect them to be at their training today, and not playing with new-fangled *toys*." She told Adam, ignoring her wolf's wish to defer to the Beta, who clearly had the Alpha's approval for what he was doing. The technology wasn't needed, and they didn't need to know it to do patrols.

Adam shook his head, "Brook and I have already decided we are going to give them some training ourselves. Brook is a Pack Trainer, and I have enough skills to help at their level. We already had them out for some early training this morning. Toby said he wanted to get into security. Martin has told me any of the new recruits will have to know the 'new-fangled toys' as you called them, as we are going to be enhancing the security with them. There is a company installing them in the security office starting Monday. I am considering having them help with parts of it, as well." He stopped to take a breath, and worked to not laugh at her now blank expression, "Do you have a problem with that?"

She growled just shy of insubordination, not liking this change, "Fine! If you want to deal with the brats, who won't listen to me, they are all yours! You can be their protector and take care of them." She then stormed off.

Adam was stunned at her reply. It took him several minutes before he and his wolf could think straight. His wolf wanted to go and discipline her for the disrespect she showed to them, but the human part could see where she was still hurt from the loss of her mate, and didn't think a fight would change anything. He decided he need help with this, *Alpha, it seems Toby's mother has turned over both him and Robin to my care. What did we need to do?* He asked, pulling Brook into the link as well, since she needed to know. He shared his memories of the discussion. This was way outside of what he had been taught so far. All he got from his wolf was a savage satisfaction the two were out of the reach of one so disrespectful and set in their way now.

Adam got a sigh from Gareth, *I thought something like that would happen. She has not been the same since her mate was killed along with Robin's parents. She rejects any changes and thinks everything needs to stay the same. I take it you and Brook are wanting to take them?*

Yes. Came the reply from both as Adam walked back into the dining hall, still a bit upset, but seeing his mate, and now *his pups* helped calm him down. He sat down and started to eat his breakfast again.

In that case, after breakfast bring them to see me at my office. We'll see if they want to be with you or not, although from what I can see, they both would prefer you. Gareth could see the care his newest Beta was giving to the pups, and how the pups returned the affection.

"What happened," Toby asked, "What is going on."

Adam shook his head, just saying, "After breakfast."

Where would they stay? Adam asked his mate; he wasn't sure he wanted them to move into his room but did want them closer than the third-floor rooms they currently had.

The inner rooms, across from us are generally used for older pups of those in the wing; those who are old enough to be able to care for themselves, but need supervision, or for our helpers. Brook replied, affection in her mind-voice, *One would be perfect, as they are set up with bunk beds, so they can have the comfort of one close.* She was silent for a moment, *Jess and Joshua are going to make sure the room is clean and aired out after breakfast.*

Noticing the Alphas getting up, and nodding to them, as they headed out of the hall, Adam and Brook waited till the pups were done, before urging them up, and out the door, "We need to speak to the Alpha before we say anything. You two are *not* in trouble, but it does involve you."

They were still nervous, but were holding up, which made Wolf-Adam proud; he already considered the pups *his*. Sitting the boys down, Adam and Brook stood behind them, each with a hand on the shoulder of a pup, so they knew they were there.

Gareth nodded but didn't say anything. As was traditional, the female generally dealt with the pups. He could see Adam and Brook ignoring the tradition, as both were equally dominant and soft.

Maria looked at the pups, "This is unusual, but your current guardian wants to turn you over to Betas Adam and Brook. Since you are old enough to decide for yourself, do you two want this?"

Both Toby and Robin nodded, excited. The loss of her mate had really changed Toby's mother; she used to be kind and gentle, and now was very hard and set in her ways and ideas and hated any change. She still treated them like they were very young pups, and needed constant care, and for her to make all the decisions.

Maria smiled, "As they are Betas, you will have many more duties and responsibilities to deal with. You will be considered responsible to help other pups, especially those younger than you. You will also be expected to set an example for the other pups."

Both nodded, sitting straighter, each uttering a "Yes, sir".

Maria smiled, looking at the two Betas, "Then they are all yours. We'll announce formally to the pack at the full moon tomorrow night."

Walking out of the Alpha's office, they headed over to the room for them, as Jess walked out of it, "We'll move your stuff down here as this room you two will share." He had to stop, as both had pounced onto him with a hug in thanks. When they had calmed down, "You two need to decide which bunk to take."

"Top!" Toby called.

"Bottom!" Robin said at the same time. He preferred to be down lower.

Adam and Brook laughed, "That was easy." Brook commented, "Now let's get your stuff down here, and it will be part of the morning exercises."

Brook disappeared and returned with some friends and boxes to help them move by the time they made it to their rooms. Piling the boxes, Adam started to pack Toby's clothes.

"I see you're moving," Sneered a voice, "Getting put up with the Omegas, where you belong?" Adam placed it as one of the bullies he had disciplined.

Adam watched as Toby stood stronger, and answered for himself, "No. My mother decided *Betas* Adam and Brook can care for me better, so they will be my guardians now. I'm moving down to the first floor to a room near them."

"I don't believe you." Came the sneered reply, "You shouldn't lie. There's no way those two would want to deal with *you*."

Adam decided to make his presence known, "If you couldn't smell me on him, or the fact I was here, you should get your nose checked out."

The pup turned pale having the Beta who had just recently sent him for punishment catch him again. His wolf was whimpering and had flopped over submissively. This had been the last straw and had realised what they had been doing had been wrong and would work to change his human's mind. He didn't want to have another punishment like he had received at Rein's paws.

Adam commented mildly, standing behind Toby, "He was correct in what he said; the announcement to the pack will be at the full moon howl tomorrow. Now, are you here to help or just to be a nuisance?"

"Help," Came the oozing reply, the human-half still not getting the message, but didn't want to be punished more, and thought this might be a way to get in the Beta's good books.

"Here" Toby said, handing him a box he tried to make look light, with a mischievous smile to Adam.

He almost dropped it when he was handed it, "What's in here? Rocks?" he asked.

"Some, but mostly my classwork books. My new room is on the first door opposite Beta Adam's room as you get in the wing. Put it on my desk, please."

The bully decided he didn't want another punishment, so he just nodded and headed off to do so, walking slowly on the stairs. Just then Brook walked out of the elevator with the large cart to move everything looked at the two curiously, seeing the other pup carrying the box. Adam and Toby looked at each other and burst out laughing.

"I made the box as heavy as I could for him, I was going to split it with some light stuff on top," Toby confided to Adam, "It will help him exercise, and maybe teach him not to be a bully."

Adam smiled at the slight punishment and helped get the rest of the stuff packed up. They had all the stuff loaded on the cart for him and Robin, as both didn't have much other than books and some clothes.

They took the load to the elevator as the bully came back, puffing. Toby smiled and thanked him for his help, clearly dismissing the bully as he closed the door, took his name out of the slot, and helped move the cart to the elevator.

Jess had commented to them to not worry about cleaning the room, as they were going to be doing so maintenance to it. The paint was old, the light fixture needed to be replaced, and they were going to swap out the bed. She had also arranged for the networking to be done at the same time, so they would be doing a deep cleaning after the work, so it made no sense to do a cleaning first.

Once the elevator started moving down, Adam smiled at him, "Good for you! I like what you did with the bully. I don't think you'll have trouble with him. From his condition, I think he doesn't work out much."

Toby smiled back at the praise, "No, but I'll need to watch out for the other pups, so he doesn't go after them in retaliation."

Adam nodded with a grin, "Let an adult know and they will help, if you need."

Helping the two get their stuff organized in the space didn't take too long.

Adam then took them to the computer lab and let them choose a laptop from the ones which hadn't been assigned. He also let the other pups know the two would be joining them at times but had other duties as well.

Both were quite happy to be getting their *own* laptops.

When they got back to their rooms, Adam sat them down, "First off: the laptops are a privilege, not a right. Second, they are pack property, so you need to treat them well. After lunch, I will show you how to use them, before I must head off to get my sister." When he got a nod from both, Adam stood, "Well, it's time to do some training before lunch."

Adam ran behind the two with Brook staying beside him. Spending the hour left to train, both boys worked hard at learning the skills.

At lunch they shared the news with their friends that they now had the two pups in their care. They all were quite happy for the pups and very happy for their friends. Martin told them he'd get their access adjusted; being pups of Betas, they had a few more areas they could access, beyond it, Adam had requested the data centres, security, and the tech areas for their access.

Smiling, they all ate. Both Toby and Robin wanted to play with their laptops. Adam knew there needed to be ground rules for them and discussed them with Brook silently. He had already had Brook turn on the internet filtering for Adult Content on the two, so they were less likely to see it, and there was malware protection at that level as well.

Getting back, Adam helped them sign into the laptops, before giving them the ground rules, "You are allowed to play the games which are on them, *after* you have all your class work done. If you want to download something, you need to ask Brook or myself first." Thinking for a moment, "Same goes for signing up for a site." As wolves, they needed to keep a low profile, and not tell anyone what they were. As such, they tried to be regular teens online, but it was harder with them, as they were deep in what humans would consider back country.

Adam grinned, "Eventually, we will have other packs online, so you would be able to connect with other pups your age as well." Both looked excited for it and nodded. He laughed, "You can play with them for the afternoon, but you also need to make sure your class work is completed.

Looking at the clock, Adam realised it was time to run down to the warehouse. Adam stuffed his clothes, cell, and his ID into a special pack he had been given, which was designed to be comfortable for both a human and a wolf to carry, gave Brook a kiss, then shifted and opened the door to run down to the warehouse to meet up with his sister, so he could direct her to the parkade. He told Charlie to stay with the two pups; he didn't know if his sister had room for him too and didn't want to make him run back alone.

*****

A while later, Adam slipped through the hidden spot in the fence, and up to the door in the shadows only panting slightly. There had been an Enforcer resting in the shadows just inside the fence, who woofed a quiet greeting. Pulling off the pack, he shook the snow from his fur, before grabbing the pack in his mouth and slipping inside before dressing. He had grabbed some jeans and a long sleeve t-shirt. Pulling out a hair tie, and pulling his hair into a ponytail, to keep it out of the way.

He nodded a greeting at Shana, "We're going to be having large shipments of cameras, sensors and other gear starting Monday."

Shana nodded, "I expected stuff would be happening much faster now. Surprised your sister got cleared." The pack was still at heightened alert, so the security was tighter.

Adam smiled, "Her clearance was started when I joined the pack, so it would be ready before she came; Martin likes to be proactive like that. She does have restricted access, but enough to be here while heightened security is on, with the Alpha's approval." Which he had given.

Seeing Tara pull in, Adam smiled and headed out to her, "How was the drive?"

"Icy." Tara replied, stepping out, "Since you know the way, and I don't see your vehicle, I take it you're with me?" At his nod, "Good; you're driving." Tara replied, walking around to the passenger side, not having turned the vehicle off. She was relieved to not need to drive any more.

Adam laughed, "Fine with me, I was going to ask to do it, anyways. The parkade is quite hidden."

Adam pulled his phone out and snapped a nice shot and forwarded it to Martin.

"What was that for?" She asked, as she glared at her brother.

"Needed a picture for your ID card. They'll print it and meet us as we go in." Adam replied with a grin.

Tara hopped in the passenger seat and smiled as they headed out. They talked about how she had been for the last two weeks on the drive in. Adam pulled onto the access road then seemed to stop at a tree just before a little hill. Rolling the window down, he swiped his card in what appeared to be a crack in the bark. The tree seemed to beep twice, before the hill seemed to split in front of them and move sideways. In the gap, Tara could see a steel roll up door opening, "You're not kidding! Hidden is right."

Adam smiled and drove just inside before parking the vehicle as the doors closed behind them, "Mandatory car wash. You stay, I'll do it."

Tara smiled and sat back in the seat: free carwash and free heated parking; she liked it!

Adam quickly got her vehicle washed and typed the code to open the inner door.

Hopping in, he took them all the way down to the third and lowest level. Parking in a spot he turned it off and handed the keys over, "So no cats?"

"Nope. Didn't want to have them stuck in the car all day. My neighbour will check on them." She commented, hopping out, and grabbing one of her bags. Adam already had the other.

Adam led her up the stairs to the first level, then out into the tunnel, "Since it's already getting dark, thought I'd show the outside tomorrow, and take you through the tunnel."

"Fine with me. But slow down a bit!" Tara panted, having trouble keeping up with her brother.

"Sorry, I forget my strength a bit." Adam commented, slowing down.

The rest of the way Tara didn't have the breath to speak, so she just followed.

*****

Reaching the last door, Martin was waiting. "Hi Tara, I'm Martin. I'm the head of security for the Pack." He pulled her in for a hug which startled her, and she missed his sniff, then offered her the ID, "Here's your ID. Keep it with you, as it identifies you as being trusted by the pack, and you can't get into the parkade without it."

Tara said a quiet thanks, still catching her breath, and threw the lanyard over her head, as Adam led her to some more stairs. She groaned but climbed up them.

"Last stairs, I promise." Adam assured her.

Reaching the main floor, she gasped at the beautiful wood look and all the carvings, "No wonder you wanted to move in so fast!" It seemed they were in a giant log cabin, with warm wood posts and panelling all over the place.

Adam grinned, "I was the same the first time I came here. Come, we'll throw your bags in your room." He urged heading to the guest wing. Reaching the door, he nodded to the guard who was there whenever there was a guest present. He swiped his ID after tapping a button, then had Tara swipe hers, to identify her as a guest, before pulling the wooden door open, and leading her to the first room.

Tara stood in the doorway, mouth hanging open. "This is my room?" She asked; it seemed to be too much: a large bed, desk, and a couch facing a TV and wood fireplace. A closet stood open, and the door to the standard washroom was open too.

Adam laughed, "If you think this is plush, come see the room I share with Brook."

Tara shook her head in disbelief, "Let me get changed first?"

Adam nodded, and let himself out of her room, and waited in the hall. Tara was out of the room much faster than he had thought.

"First, I have to introduce you to the Alphas; they're waiting." Gently he guided her to the Alpha's office.

Knocking on the open doorframe, he walked in, "This is my sister Tara. Tara, this is Alpha Gareth and Alpha Maria. They are the leaders of the pack."

Tara held her hand out, but it was ignored by Maria who moved to wrap her in a good hug, "Welcome!" Maria replied, before Gareth wrapped her in a hug as well.

Adam could hear them sniffing to catch her scent, as he stood beside her, but wasn't sure if his sister would notice.

They chatted for a few minutes, mostly just exchanging pleasantries, before they were sent on their way.

Adam guided his sister out of the Alpha's office, and over to his suite. He silently tipped off his mate for them coming. Opening the door to it, he stepped to the side, to let her have her look.

Tara stepped into the room without looking any more than she had to, and once the door was closed, she started looking around, stunned as her jaw dropped more.

Brook grinned at her mate and snapped a photo of her stunned expression, as they had discussed.

Shaking her head, she came to and turned to Adam, "Wow. Just... Wow."

Adam smiled knowingly, "I know. It was almost my reaction too when I first came here. This, the closet, and bathroom is the suite for us. The rest of the place is shared with the rest of the pack."

Adam motioned Toby and Robin forward, who had been watching amused from behind Brook, "This is Toby and Robin. Toby's mother was taking care of both alone and was grieving the loss of her mate. She decided she could no longer take care of them, and with the Alpha's approval, I have taken guardianship of them."

Tara looked at the two boys neither were meeting her eyes shyly, before smiling at her brother, "I guess we can call them nephews?"

At Adam's nod she came forward and gave both a good hug, "Well, Mom was asking when you would be getting her grandkids!" She joked. Again, missing them sniffing to get her scent.

Both boys looked startled at Adam over the comment, he nodded in confirmation, "I'm thinking we will have it as a birthday surprise for her." Looking at the time and feeling a hole in his belly, "Well, it's dinner time; let's go. Tara, I'll introduce you to the chef who is on-duty. We have three full chefs, and four who are learning, along with several helpers. They know of your allergies and have prepared a special meal plan for you."

Remembering the lunch they shared, Tara got hungry, "I won't want to leave if it is as good as the last meal they made!"

Smiling Adam introduced her to the Chef on duty, who smiled, and grabbed her a covered plate staying warm in a tray, sitting on top of the oven, "It came out ten minutes ago. I hope you enjoy it."

Adam guided her to their usual seats. "Aunt Tara, come sit with us!" Toby called. He was already feeling better, now he had two parents who cared deeply, and it seems a human aunt and grandmother; he felt he could deal with anything.

Tara smiled and sat in the seat between them. When they commented about her eating something totally different than anyone else, she told them she had several food allergies. Since wolves didn't get them, she had to teach them what a food allergy was. She then moved onto other conditions which humans commonly got. Both pups were surprised at how fragile humans were.

After dinner, Tara had some paperwork to do, then wanted to sleep. Adam escorted her back to the guest wing. "Tara, if you need to leave the guest wing for any reason, have someone escort you."

"Why?" She asked; it seemed safe to her, everyone was friendly, if a little nosy. "I won't do it unless you tell me." Tara demanded.

"Fine. All I can tell you is we had an intruder in here. Another Wolf. Because of it, the pack is on heightened alert. The guest wing is one of the most secure areas."

Tara went a little pale, "OK, that is a good reason. I'll follow your rules."

Adam smiled, "Thanks; once you have a wolfdog, they will be considered escort enough for within sight of the pack house. So, what time do you plan on getting up in the morning?"

"Around nine."

"Then have the guard contact me. I'm up at seven and do some warmups in the gym before breakfast. I'll wait to have breakfast with you, then take you to see the wolfdogs after breakfast. Have a good night." Adam told her, as he gave her a hug, and held the door for her to enter the secured guest wing.

Adam's wolf knew she was safe there; the windows were thick and had bullet, and claw, resistant layering. The walls were even tougher.

Nothing readily available could breach them; it was one of the most secure areas outside of the emergency safe areas. He had learned the pack paid more than lip service to the customs surrounding Guests.

Adam headed off for his relaxing evening with his mate and pups.

CHAPTER 21

Tara's Visit

When Adam woke up, he was smiling, as he was nice and comfy, and his wolf was very content. He had woken up on his back, with Toby and Robin back in the bed with them. He had an arm curled around each and they were using his chest as pillow. Brook was curled up against Robin, and Charlie against Toby. When he went to bed, both Robin and Toby wanted to spend a night with him. He expected another night or two before they were comfortable enough to not sleep with them.

Since he was awake, he gave both his pups a good hug and kiss, getting them to start moving, also waking Brook up.

"Time for training," Adam reminded them, as they stretched. Both perked up and scampered to their room to get changed.

Brook shook her head, "Before, they were never wanting to learn, and would use any excuse to get out of training." She grinned as she tossed Adam his clothes, "Now? They are eager for it."

The two boys were waiting when Adam and Brook came out, and all four headed down to the training area. Brook kept an eye on them, as she worked with Adam. Both boys were showing a little improvement and pushed themselves harder than she had ever seen. Adam just stayed to the side, doing his own more intense warmup.

After they were warmed up, they had moved onto doing staffs, which all three were at a similar level, and worked together with Brook.

Heading back, the two boys were giggling, and refused to tell Adam what was so funny, when he asked. Adam shook his head and followed Brook into the shower, so they could be clean for breakfast.

The two boys followed them in, even though they had their own shower. Adam looked at Brook, a bit surprised.

For families, often pups shower together with parents, or siblings even as adults. It works as a way to have bonding time together. Brook offered, with a shrug. *It also allows for parents or their guardians to check on the pup's physical condition.*

*****

Tara was just coming out the door as they walked past on their own way to breakfast. Adam threw an arm across her shoulders, making her jump. Looking at all four, they looked well awake, and with the wet hair, must have had a shower as well.

"Are all wolves up early?" she asked, with a yawn. It was, for her, an early Saturday morning.

Adam shook his head as they headed for the dining room, "No, but most are. Those who are night owls tend to do our overnight shifts and will head to bed after a late breakfast." He didn't mention, with their wolf-mind in control, their human half could sleep while the body could still be active, as long as it wasn't physical exhaustion. That was a secret known only to wolves, and those mated to one,

The head chef himself came out with Tara's covered plate. He smiled and offered her some gluten free and dairy free pancakes, with some fresh berries and maple syrup from a fresh container which had her name on it, so there was no chance of contamination. Waving away her thanks, he got her choice for lunch and dinner. As it was a full moon, they had a large party, and as soon as the food for the breakfast was done, they'd be starting to prepare food for it. Making sure some food was put aside for her and making sure *nothing* which could harm her reached her plate was an interesting challenge, but one he had to deal with time to time.

Over breakfast, they chatted about some of the funny things the dogs had done.

She was into a second serving the chef had brought out for her when she saw how he was caring for the two young ones.

"I'm wondering what attracted you to them." Tara asked, curious.

"Well, Robin had lost both his parents, and Toby had lost his father in a rockslide." Adam replied quietly, hugging the two to his side.

Tara was shocked speechless, no idea on what to say. She had not expected that answer.

Adam nodded sadly, seeing her shock, "Toby's mother has tried to care for them–" he started.

"But she changed after losing her mate." Brook answered, as Adam wouldn't have known what happened. "With werewolves, we form tight bonds, and it is common if one dies, the other follows fairly quickly. His mother had changed a fair bit and became one who can't stand change for any reason. Being she was low ranked, she couldn't understand how the pups were getting our attention other than they tricked us somehow. When we had told her the changes we were doing, she just basically tossed them to us, not being able to handle the change."

Tara had tears on her face as she abandoned her food, to give both boys a good hug, which they returned. After a bit, and at Brook's urging, she returned to finish her food.

"You're coming to Mom's birthday, right?" She asked, changing the topic.

Adam nodded, "Yes, and we should have it at..." They discussed a couple places, but ended up going with Brook's first choice, of a steakhouse she told them had been recommended to her.

Toby and Robin were playing with the remains on their plates, not liking the idea of being left behind.

Tara caught the look before Adam and Brook, "You two will be there." She told them firmly, getting surprised looks, and looking at Adam for confirmation.

Adam nodded, "She has been bugging me *forever* to get her grandchildren." He gave his sister a sly grin, "Lets keep them a surprise," he told her.

Brook chuckled as Tara agreed happily to it.

The two boys were smiling, "But we don't know what to get her!" Toby complained.

Adam smiled, "Why not a nice, framed picture of our family?" he asked the boys, having some ideas for what to do. "You two could make the frame."

Both Toby and Robin nodded at the idea, knowing Adam had made the *awesome* picture of the Alphas hanging in the main hall, by the door, and the ones in their room. They started to chatter on the idea, and settled on a nice wood frame, and having a group shot, and then individual ones around it.

When the pups started planning out the layout, Adam turned to his sister, "I have the systems set up, so we can do video chats, and I will get Mom set up for it as well. It will keep us close." Even his wolf didn't want to have them drift off.

Tara grinned and nodded, "It would make it easier."

*****

"Can we go see the wolfdogs, now?" Toby asked. His mother hadn't let him see them, as they were kennelled outside of the inner pack area.

Tara shivered, as it was looking cold outside, and headed back to her room to grab her winter jacket, boots, gloves, and hat. When she got back, the four were wearing jackets, but they were what she'd call a spring jacket; it was much lighter than what she was wearing.

Once she was outside, Tara stopped and turned around to look at the outside of the building. Her jaw dropped, as she looked at the outside of the place. The wood and stone had it blending into the surrounding trees and the nearby cliff. It was done in a way which when looking at it close up, the building looked aesthetically pleasing, not just a jumble of nature. It also seemed to pull itself in and look smaller than it felt inside.

Adam reached over and put a hand under her chin and closed her mouth. She blinked and blushed in embarrassment. Adam smiled and led the way over to the dog area silently. As they walked in, the five of them were surrounded with dogs. Tara moved to give each a good pet and few words of greeting, and once she gave them some attention and they got a good sniff of her, they scampered away. The five wandered around and many of the dogs came for a sniff and got a head scratch for their trouble, before one, after sniffing, whined and nuzzled Tara's leg instead of heading off.

Brook smiled, "That's Sara. It seems she's chosen you. Let's go get you her gear." Again, she was happy with which one had decided to bond. There had been a few humans who had to come two or even three times before one would bond. Rarely, but it did happen, there were none who were interested in bonding. Often, later it was found they were not a good fit to be caring for an animal, and they had sensed it.

Tara bent down and gave *her* wolfdog a good hug around the neck. As she let go, Sara gave her a good nuzzle and a lick to the cheek. She had an almost typical husky colouration and shape but was nearly the size of a smaller mastiff; she looked to be about 55 kg, but due to muscle density from the werewolf blood, was closer to 75 kg. The look in her crystal blue eyes was one of intelligence and interest.

Charlie came over and sniffed Sara, wagging his tail; she was small compared to his size; the two were at the opposite ends of the typical size range. After their canine greeting, both moved to near their person to wait.

As they headed out, Sara wagged her tail and followed Tara closely, having been trained for this, knew where they were going.

Brook led the way, turning into the office which was beside the entrance to the dogs' yard. "Sara is going with Adam's sister, Tara." She told the wolf who was at the desk. They nodded and started to fill out the paperwork for the assignment. The Alpha would have passed on the approval and the fact they were going to be looking, so they didn't even need to ask.

Adam went with his sister to the board which had the gear: they picked out a collar and leash, and the other gear she would need for being in the human world.

Brook helped get the details down for the paperwork and made sure a copy of the contact information for Longview Pack was attached, as they were the closest for her, if there were issues.

The wolf handed Tara the pouch of papers with a smile as they finished up. "The paperwork will be filed with the support organizations on Monday, and if there are any issues, contact the pack." Longview would also be notified about it, and the fact any costs were to come to them.

As many of their wolfdogs were assigned to people out in the human world, they had set up the systems to have all of them accredited as service animals, so they could easily be registered to a person over a weekend. It did mean they did do charity cases for those who needed them but could not afford them. Usually where a child lost their sight. Others were assigned and specially trained for rare conditions they could scent, or as comfort animals.

"Thanks!" Tara replied taking the pouch and guiding Sara out the door.

"She should be a good fit." Brook mentioned, as they walked back to the main building, "Sara is one of the most laid back of the 'dogs. If you have any issues, you can call us directly, if needed, day or night."

"Thanks!" Tara replied.

Having some of their wolfdogs in the human world, gave them contacts if they needed something done which they couldn't. It was also a hedge against if the worst came, and werewolves were exposed to the general population, it allowed them to show their pack at least was one which cared about their neighbours and helped those most in need.

The work also brought in a good amount of money for the pack from the organizations who helped find those in need, and from government grants and tax deductions. Brook had worked with the pack's accountant at one point, and was surprised the program was basically self-sustaining, with any excess money given to charities to help those who couldn't afford a dog to be given one.

Giving a tour of the pack house, Tara could see wires hanging from the roof and asked the two about them.

"Security cameras. Going to start arriving on Monday." Adam commented curtly, his tone saying to not ask more. It was all everyone knew, other than the few who had a "need to know".

Showing her their medical facility, Tara was astonished; "You have a full emergency room!". All they lacked was the big diagnostic equipment from what a hospital would have.

Brook snickered, "We're geared to deal with both wolf and human shapes in all the rooms, so we can handle the wolfdogs easily as well." They didn't need the big diagnostic equipment because of the couple of healers on their staff who could sense the problems with better accuracy. If Tara asked about it, since she wasn't a pack member, they would have to try to not answer.

Taking her through another tunnel, Adam and Brook showed Tara the greenhouse, there were different bushes and trees at different cycles of the year.

"With the constant conditions," Brook explained, "It allows us to have fresh food year-round without issues of having to ship it in at a high price." Heading towards the leisure section Brook smiled, "We have hot pools, and you are welcome to use the pools at any time, day or night, but they are clothing optional, and we generally don't bother wearing anything."

It made Tara blush tomato red, and comment, "I am not going to be going near it, then." She glared at her smirking brother. They had been raised in a house which expected them to be dressed.

Heading back in, since they weren't going to get a pre-lunch soak, they took Tara to lunch.

As they waited in the line for the buffet, Adam let his sister know, "We're doing the formal adoption with the two tonight, at the start of the Moon Howl. After that, there is a party for dinner. Dress warm, as it is outside."

Tara was startled for a moment, then just nodded. Tara had got some information from Adam and Brook, so she knew they honoured the moon and the changes of the season, but mostly it was just an excuse to party and have fun. She did like the part about not getting drunk, unlike many of her friends, although getting a buzz was fun; having a hangover or getting sick later was not.

Brook helped her new sister pick out the food for her companion, explaining, "Almost all of this food they can eat, although some are picky eaters." Sitting down, they placed Sara's bowl under the table, so she was out of the way and wouldn't get stepped on.

After another delicious meal, Tara and her new companion headed back to her room for some well-deserved bonding time and a nap together, before the party.

*****

Adam knocked on the door to his sister's room shortly before it started. Tara smiled and pulled on her jacket and followed her brother out. Sara was wearing her collar, but being at the pack, she didn't technically even need it. "As a guest, and since you are my sister, you get to be at the front," he told her, as he led her to the front, before stepping up onto the deck, which was used as a stage, giving both nervous pups a touch of comfort as he joined Brook standing behind them.

It seemed the cue for the Alphas to step forward and gave a short howl of *Listen!* Getting everyone's attention. "Before we start the Moon Night," Gareth started, "There are a couple of things we have to deal with first." The pack knew what they were, and most were grinning or nodded in agreement.

"First, I would like to welcome Tara to this moon howl. She is Beta Adam's only sister. She is spending the weekend, partly to be chosen by one of the dogs, which happened this morning. I would like to congratulate her on being selected by Sara." When he paused, a general howl was heard in welcome. Tara was blushing, but it quickly moved on, since guests were not a big deal, not even if they were a human. All were greeted, usually at the first meal, unless there was a party, like that night.

"Adam and Brook have taken two pups into their care." Alpha Maria continued, "Will you four step up?"

Adam and Brook stepped forward with Toby and Robin, both boys nervous over this, but with their new parents standing behind them, they were dealing with it.

"Does anyone have any concerns or reasons why these pups cannot be taken in by them?" Alpha Maria called out to the pack, starting the ritual of adoption.

"They're Theta while Adam and Brook are Betas!" Called one voice.

"Adam is still Turning." Called another.

"Toby's mother is still alive." Called a third.

From somewhere in the mass, Toby's mother called out, nulling the last complaint, "Adam seems to want them, he can have them. I give up claim to them." She knew she hadn't been much of a parent since her mate died, but what Adam had told her had sunk in and she could feel the Truth in it; if the two Betas could give them more opportunities and skills, she would let them go.

Maria responded to the first, "Rank of the parent does not determine the rank of the child. We will be checking on all the pups tighter, as Adam brought a concern to our attention following a run with many pups of how they seem incorrectly ranked. We have decided we will be ranking them by ability, not by who their parents are. The idea of what rank their birth parents are to determine whom they can adopt is not an idea this pack will follow, nor has it ever followed it." She dismissed it with a hand.

"Adam's turn has progressed beyond the point it matters. His strength already meets or exceeds that of a Beta's requirement." Gareth answered to the second complaint, showing it was without any merit, since he had been keeping an eye on their training. The pack didn't need it announced Adam was already near Brook in skills, he was now learning some weapon skills Martin himself was guiding his training in hand to hand. It is nearly at the point he personally would need to help train him and was looking forward to it.

"Any other complaints?" Maria asked, looking out over the mass of pack members. Hearing none, "I call it closed, and accept they are suitable to be their parents."

Turning to Toby, Maria asked, "Do you wish to be bonded as a pup to Adam and Brook, to follow them as if they caused your body's creation?"

"Yes, I do." Toby answered strongly, "Ever since Adam was bound to the pack, I have been drawn to them."

"So be it." Maria answered and nodded to Adam and Brook to proceed.

Adam and Brook touched their forehead to his. All three felt a tight bond link them together. Gareth caught Toby as he nearly fainted, guiding him to a chair, and handing him an herbal remedy they used for this; he'd be totally fine within the hour.

Turning to Robin, they repeated the ceremony, and Gareth also helped him to the seat.

Adam and Brook smiled their thanks as they were handed similar remedies, making a face at the taste of the hot bitter herbal remedy. Brook had told the three about it during the afternoon, so they knew what they were feeling was natural. A howl broke out to show the pack's support of the new family.

Calling the pack's attention back to him, Gareth called, "A couple of announcements: First the new computers are pack property, so please treat them gently. If it is determined negligence or abuse caused damage, the cost will come out of your pack stipend to repair or replace them. Second, starting Monday there is a contractor who will be working on the security system. They are vetted by two other packs fully and know what we are. They will be staying at the pack house for the week, while they work to get all the security systems online. The cameras and sensors will start arriving Monday as well, for the most part. Some will be here for a bit longer. The elders and I are working on what caused the issue and have nothing to report at this time."

After a moment, Gareth stood tall, "Let the Moon Howl begin!" he called loudly, before letting out a long, loud howl which echoed off the mountains around the pack house. It was answered by all the wolves, and even the wolfdogs.

Tara cringed slightly at the volume, but then was caught up in the festive spirit. She congratulated her two new nephews, before Adam came and lead her to the Chef who had a plate set aside of the beef which was on offer but had used spices which were certified to not have anything she was allergic to. She noticed there were a couple other trays like hers, and asked about it, "Those are for a couple of human mates we have who still have food allergies; they tend to fade over time once a Mate has been Bitten. Till we have been told they no longer need them, as with you, we do special meals for them. We have a little more if you want it; just come see me or Lupita, my assistant, and we will get it."

Tara thanked her before she turned to Adam, "Bitten?" she asked with a frown; she hadn't heard the term.

Adam sat her down at a table, "Eat. I'll explain…" Adam started, explaining in broad terms about Mates and how the bonds are formed. By the end she was blushing. Adam had even shown her his mate mark at the base of his neck; the scarred mark Brook gave him; he was still honoured to wear it. Brook had only half teased when she told him it would keep the unmated females away from her mate if they didn't want to be hurt.

Soon Adam had to shake his head to Tara's questions, as they were getting into topics he couldn't answer, "I can't tell you anymore. First there are many secrets you would have to be a pack member to be permitted to be told, others if you have a wolf for a mate, as they would need to be the one to tell you." Tara nodded, a little disappointed, but she understood.

A couple of young single males had sat down at the table and had decided to listen in on the chat. They took over and started telling her some light, funny stories. Adam shot them a grateful look but told them silently she was off limits for any sort of encounter, and she was keeping herself for her mate. It was an old idea, but one which some did; they would respect the limitation on their interaction, although one offered to curl up with her and keep her warm. Everyone laughed at Tara's deep blush but sent the discussion off on what was normal for Weres. Curling up for cuddles was normal, and while it could lead to sex, other times it was just to be together, or to comfort the other and would stay platonic. They reassured her they had been told of her choice and would respect it.

*****

Once all the food was eaten, the young males happily escorted Tara to the firepit, in the stream of everyone else, leaving Adam and Brook to spend time with their pups.

Adam had arranged a thick blanket for Tara to wrap up in, to stay warm on the cold January night. Sitting her down, Sara flopped across her booted feet, keeping them warm. Toby and Robin had curled up on either side of her, as they enjoyed the evening. Towards midnight, Adam escorted her back to the pack house, a few others going with them, explaining, "We're going to shift and be running and playing for most of the night as wolves. Those who don't feel up to it are heading back now." Adam was excited, as this was his first chance to do it, as the last full moon was on Christmas eve, and he had to miss the run, due to the drive the next morning. That it was the Wolf Moon he considered to be a good omen.

Tara nodded, starting to see the differences, and the fact he was no longer even the same *species* as her. He was excited to spend the cold night outside. She planned on starting the gas for the fireplace in her room and sit beside it to warm up before curling up for the night. Snagging a mug of hot chocolate from the dining hall on their way by to warm up her hands. Adam had only a t-shirt and a light jacket on.

"There will be some up for breakfast, but it tends to be a buffet brunch in the morning. The morning chef promised a plate would be kept warm for you. I'll come get you early afternoon. I need some help with some pictures for our mom." Adam reminded her.

Smiling she remembered the chat at breakfast about photos and a frame, she nodded as she swiped the badge to get into the guest wing, Sara following at her heels, wishing her brother a good run.

Adam raced to his room to strip and shift, then pawed the doors open, and raced back, getting there just as Gareth and Maria howled the start of the run. His wolf joyfully joined in the chorus which called the stragglers to the hunt.

Adam easily kept pace with the Alpha pair who led them on a nice run, although he hung back from the hunt, watching, as his skills were not up to taking down the elk yet. Brook brought a piece of the flank for them to share, before they went for their own smaller hunt with their two pups and the others who looked to them; even Duncan and Keanna had been coaxed out for the run. They helped them catch some rabbits, and Adam finally caught his own without any help. The pups needed some help still from Brook; even Charlie had helped keep them from getting away.

*****

They played in the snow for a while, then headed back just as the sky was lightening up and everyone—as Brook told Adam was normal for a Moon Howl night—just flopped down by the kindled fire in their suite. A couple other waterproof pads had been laid out, for enough space. Brook and Adam snuggled together as wolves, then their pups used them as pillows, and the rest found space to curl up for a sleep around them.

*****

When Adam awoke, he stood with a stretch and a yawn. Looking around, all but the pups, himself, and Brook were already up and gone, and those left were starting to stir. He looked at the time, and it was already time for lunch. Heading into the shower, he shifted and was quickly followed by the other three. The run and hunt then long sleep helped wonders with his stress from the attack.

Hopping out, he quickly chose some good clothes, and when dressed, helped Toby and Robin choose some nice clothes, as they dressed, Brook plaited his hair into a nice braid, then he helped do hers into one as well.

Heading out, he grabbed his camera bag, and found his sister already in the dining hall, eating. Placing the bag beside her, he smiled and told her "Good Morning," Before going to fill his plate from the buffet table and joining her. Some of Brook's gifts was a couple of nice lenses, since he had heard some nice cameras were coming out soon, he was going to wait for them. He was quite happy with the upgrade in quality they had given him.

Chatting over breakfast, he told Tara what he was wanting to do for the photoshoot, and she was happy to help with it. Heading out when they were all done eating, they hiked along a cleared trail to a nearby slight ridge with a beautiful background of the mountains.

Adam set up the shots, and took the nice background shot for his stock shot.

Handing the camera over, he had Tara take a bunch of nice shots of them as a family and alone. Many of the other pieces they were going to do inside, where it was warmer for Tara. Adam even had Tara pose for some shots with the rest of his family, especially of some of her with Sara. Linking Jess, he had her find a nice sheet to use as a backdrop, and they used a small boardroom for the pictures and took them with the four of them together as human.

Tara still couldn't stand them naked, so turned her back as they disrobed and shifted to their wolf forms. They then took the shots again. Tara told them she'd meet them at his suite, taking the camera gear. They quickly shifted and dressed, grinning at how body-shy she was compared to the wolves.

Heading back, Adam quickly worked out what they were doing, and generated the photographs with the mountains in the background. They had a larger central shot with all four in it, with their wolves beside them. Around it, there was a headshot of each in half profile, and their wolf basically a mirror image.

Sending the shots to the printer, he also added the one Tara had requested at Christmas and looking at the one of the four of them sleeping together which Jess had taken, sent it for a few copies too.

The completed family one, he printed one which didn't need a special frame but used more of the mountain shot as a background, for Brook's parents. Knowing the shots would take a while to print, as the printer was nice, and did excellent reproductions, it did not do them very fast. For photos going on a wall, quality over speed was what he preferred anyways.

Tara used the time Adam was doing the photos to get to know the boys a bit more, knowing she'd not be able to take weekends like this very often.

Chatting with Lucas over e-mail, he had given them a good idea, of running as wolves then borrowing a vehicle from them to go the last bit as humans. It took a 5- to 6-hour drive compared to a 3-hour run and 90-minute drive. For a wolf, a three-hour run was normal workout. It just meant they would be limited to what they could carry on their backs or ship it ahead. Since their human minds could sleep and just let the wolf mind take control while on the run, it meant a day trip to visit family was possible. They forwarded it to their respective Alphas to hash out some of the logistics and approval. They had finally completed all the work, and had agreed to it, along with the occasional night there; their trial was going to be for his mother's birthday.

Adam was happy, it not only would allow him to see family more but would also bring both packs a bit closer together. It seemed nobody had thought about running as wolves to visit between the two packs, even though they could travel fast across the ridgelines, not needing to follow the roads around through the lowest passes. Looking it up, had shown they didn't have a pack between them, just lots of mountains, but there were a couple of passes they could use.

*****

All too soon, it was time for dinner, and everyone knew Tara was leaving right after breakfast the next morning. Leaning over, she commented the internet was much faster here than at her place.

Adam just laughed, "Of course it is." he said without elaboration. She just sighed when he refused to say why, just grinning at her.

It was a good meal, and everyone stayed up just to relax and enjoy each other's company. It was late by the time they ended up going to bed. This time, Robin and Toby decided to sleep in their room. Brook and Adam wondered if they would stay or would come in during the night. They hoped just by being in the room next door would let them sleep. Both Adam and Brook were missing their alone time to continue to bond, but the pack—and especially their pups—came first.

*****

The next day was Monday again. Due to all the work, they had cancelled the meeting with Alpha Gareth. Brook and Adam helped Tara pack up all the stuff and piled it on a cart. She had much more stuff now, with some being gifts, others being items for Sara. Adam was feeling much better now his sister was going to be protected. His mother flat out refused one of their wolfdogs when he offered. His wolf wanted to growl at her for it, but Brook soothed him.

Getting to the garage was fun, Adam decided to just use the elevator. Tara was surprised at the size of it, as they went down to the basement for the tunnel.

Tara went to turn in her ID to Adam who shook his head, "That ID is yours to keep. Keep it with you. It will identify you as having ties to this pack. Just having it would show any wolf you have been told about us, and if you were to end up at a pack's territory needing help, they would let us know where you are."

The pups had met them at the door to the tunnel and followed along to give their own goodbyes.

Adam smiled and loaded up her vehicle, and opened the back door for Sara, motioning for her to climb in, which she did, sprawling across the entire back seat.

Turning to his sister, he gave her a good hug. Then it was Brook's turn, then the pups.

After she left, they headed to the gym to spend the morning training till the first load of gear arrives.

Mid morning, Shana let them know it had arrived, and was moving it to their truck to deliver it to them and would have it stored in the data centre. Adam smiled and let Erin, Martin, and Rein know, so they could help organise getting the cameras connected and be ready for the other side to be installed. He was starting to learn to just delegate more and do less of the physical install work.

Honing his skills at fighting in both forms he had decided was what he needed to do more than anything and hoped he would have more skills before his next encounter with the white wolf.

CHAPTER 22

Installations

Just after lunch, the installers arrived and were escorted down to the security office to meet with Adam, Brook, and Martin, who were on hand to deal with the work, and having the notice, Adam and Brook had time to take a shower and change. Their two pups had begged to help with the cameras, and they had quickly scampered when they had permission to assist the installers.

Mostly Adam and Brook were there to help with the setup of the data centre equipment and monitor the access of the high security areas. The system used the network to connect to the servers in the data centres, although to separate it, they had their own switch on each floor. Once they figured out what they were doing, they called in Rein to help get the frame up for the monitor wall.

By the end of the day, everything was scheduled. The installers chatted with the wolves who were also heading to dinner—Including Adam and Brook—and mentioning they were very much looking forward to the meals; they had installed two other systems at packs, and they always had excellent food. Adam invited them to sit with him. Partly to get to know them, and partly to keep an eye on them.

There was much banter back and forth with the installers, as most wolves curious about them.

"So, what do you think of us?" One of the pack asked, at a lull of the conversation.

The lead installer smiled, "I have realised you are just normal people trying to live their lives. Yes, you like to get nude and grow fur at the drop of a hat, but it is just the way you are." Several laughed at his description of them shifting, as he intended before he continued, "But it doesn't make you evil as some would say; just different." Forking up the last of his steak and eating it, "I would ignore the differences just to get access to the food alone!"

Everyone laughed again and nodded; the food here was excellent, they agreed. The two junior installers were a bit nervous but were keeping an open mind. The wolves could smell it in their sweat, and gave them a bit of room, but also explained whatever they could for them.

One commented, "I always find it hard to leave a pack, as I love the openness, how we are made to feel welcome," He hugged the wolfess who was cuddled up against his side and smiled, having agreed to join her for the night. "I also love how close knit you are, but willing to make room for visitors. It's refreshing how everyone is willing to help out and watches out for everyone else." His friend was sitting across the table and nodded.

As they stood up, one of the installers stretched, popping his stiff back, "Is there a hot pool we can use?" he asked. He was stiff from all the bending over they had to do getting all the frames installed.

Adam sent a mental query to Alpha Gareth, who sent back an affirmative they were permitted he grinned, "We have something better! We have a natural hot spring which we have piped to pools which you are welcome to use." He had several wolves who piped up with offers to show them to it. Adam smiled and nodded his thanks.

As it was Monday night, they headed over to the fire. Adam had to bundle up, as the weather had turned frigid, and he couldn't shift to the hybrid shape to have a thick fur until the Turning was completed, which at the current rate, he and Brook expected it to be done before the next full moon. The annoying aches he had were getting less intense, and less often. Mostly they were after he shifted back now. The speed he shifted was faster too, even if it was a fair bit slower than Brook, still.

Getting to the fire, Joshua waved at them and smiled. The fire was again already going for them, and the trickle of people had already started. Brook had shifted to her hybrid for its warm fur in their room before they left as he pouted. Adam snuggled down in her warm lap as soon as she sat down, and Joshua shifted to his wolf and flopped across their feet.

As was normal, they had the Thetas come for short chats and to cuddle, many in their hybrid forms. Many teased him about him needing the protection of his mate. He just smiled, "She just makes a very nice, heated blanket here to keep me warm. And for my feet, Joshua is being kind enough to keep them warm." Many laughed. Brook growled mock-annoyed, but kept her arms wrapped around her mate as she sent him warm and loving thoughts.

Even the two Omegas came and cuddled for a bit but didn't say much. Neither wanted to talk about what happened before becoming Omegas although they did thank him for making sure they were included in the fire. They had been excused from working this one evening, so they could come, since Adam had explicitly invited them, their supervisors didn't want to have an angry Beta asking about it. He did coax out they did get one day a week off to do what they wanted, but they had duties the rest of the time, and although was hard, they didn't feel they were overworked.

Adam still didn't like what he had heard about what happened to Omegas and talking with his wolf felt death was kinder.

Many others just enjoyed the company. He was glad he hadn't had to ask anyone to leave after the first time. All four he had seen again, but as they were civil, nothing was said, even if they stayed away from him.

Many were concerned about the cameras being installed.

Adam smiled, "Security will need to be involved to view the video, as the only place to see it will be the security office. Even I will need to go down to see it! They will be the ones dealing with the maintenance and repair of them as well." He smiled at those who still were not happy,

"We are not planning on placing them in your private rooms, or shared bathrooms." he shook his head, "I would refuse to have them installed in either. Your rooms are your private space." Shuddering, "Bathrooms is just wrong. I will not do it."

Rein seconded the thoughts about where they would be from his spot across the fire. Both had the same idea, the Thetas stopped worrying about them, and Adam directed the talk to what it actually could do for them: Allow security to see if someone was trying to hide from sight; what had happened before would not happen again.

From investigation, they had found out the Scout had been spotted within the vicinity of the pack house over an hour before the attempted kidnapping. It concerned everyone the most, the fact he could have evaded the security and notice for so long. There were only five who knew the result: The Alphas, Brook, Martin, and Adam. There was no plan for it to be released, as the idea would scare many, and could undermine confidence in the leadership and throw the pack into chaos. So far, nobody had asked for details, either. They were already working to make sure it didn't happen again, and it seemed everyone was satisfied.

Even with the warmth of his mate behind him, Joshua on his feet and lower legs, and some warm clothes, the winter cold was starting to seep in after only a couple hours; he may have had better tolerance than any human, but still not the same as a wolf, yet. When he started to shiver, Brook decided it was time to head in, and Adam agreed. Nobody said anything when they said their goodbyes. Brook swung her mate to her back and gave him a fast ride on her back all the way back to their room. Arriving, Jess was waiting with nice warm mug of hot chocolate and the fireplace lit.

Smiling, he nodded his thanks and sat down on the mat before the fire, and relaxed. Joshua had followed them, and lay behind Adam, giving him a backrest. Brook shifted back to her human form and cuddled in on one side after pulling some clothes on. After passing out some hot chocolate to Brook, and picking up a mug for herself, and a warm bowl of water for Joshua, Jess cuddled Adam's free side.

"I am surprised you lasted *that* long out there, even with the fire." Brook commented.

Adam just shrugged and let the warmth from the fire and shared between them warm him up, "It was also the warmth of those who curled up with us, and the fact the Thetas *needed* the time. I know how to layer up to stay warm," Adam handed Brook his drink, then pulled off two layers, leaving a last one on. All were surprised at how much he had been wearing. Most wolves only wear a single layer, as if they got cold, they shifted, and their thick double-layered fur worked better to keep them warm.

After pulling off his excess layers, he sat back down in just some soft leggings and top he had used as the inner most layer and cuddled up, working to warm back up as he drank the warm drink.

Finishing the drink, he handed off the mug and wrapped an arm around both females, cuddling them close. Looking over his shoulder, Joshua had his head down, and appeared to be asleep.

"You and your brother doing better this week?" Adam asked Jess quietly.

Jess nodded, "I'm not sure why we broke down last week, it's not normal for us."

"You two haven't had much time to grieve for your parents," Brook murmured, "I looked it up; you were basically treated as adults and given duties and tasks to learn. You didn't have anyone's shoulder to cry on or to seek comfort from, other than each other." She sat up more and looked Jess in the eyes, "I want you two to come to us if you need *any* help. Even if it is another day to cry on our shoulders."

Jess nodded slightly, sighing softly, pulling a blanket over them.

Adam noticed they were all done, so he just slid down and used Joshua as a pillow, and pulled the women close to him, "Well, we can just sleep here. Get some comfort from being with us and cared for by us. Being close to so many was not something which humans tended to do, and his wolf had felt a bit of pity for them; comforting others of a Pack was a big thing for him.

Brook smiled as Jess snuggled down and quickly went to sleep, *I agree, and hope we can get them better. I'm going to get their training records and see if they are missing any skills we think they should have. I suspect they are missing some.* Not just their physical training, but also their book-learning and the other skills.

I agree, but let's just offer to help them with them. Don't force it on them, and make it clear we would not change or make them go elsewhere. I think the fact they have stability and a good future with us is helping them get over it too. They don't have to keep their heads down and live day to day. They have a future with us; my wolf has the thought they could advance farther than just Theta. He thought delta, but his wolf was feeling Beta, with the right care, attention, and their own drive to succeed; both were deciding to disagree. Adam commented, knowing they would rather stay unskilled but under their protection, if the other choice was to cause them to lose the protection.

Brook nodded agreement, and let the conversation end, as she curled up against her mate, *I love you.* She commented as she drifted off to sleep.

Adam's comment was mumbled, but the intent of "I love you too," was felt.

Charlie had abandoned them earlier in the evening and had been curled up on the bed waiting for them; seeing them curl up by the slowly dying fire, he grumbled as he jumped down and curled up against Brook's legs on top of the blanket.

*****

Waking up in the morning, Adam could hear two more breaths than he expected, and woke more, before his wolf mentioned it was just their pups. Opening his eyes, he smiled; both were curled up on the blanket as wolves; one along Brook's back, and the other against Jess's legs.

He smiled from the very content feel from his wolf having not just his pups, but also the other two he almost considered his pups as well. They were definitely *his* to protect. The other pups who worked on the tech were less his, but if they came to him for help, he would do all he could.

Hearing the others start to stir, Adam opened his eyes again, and smiled and gave Brook a kiss. She smiled and stretched, careful of the pup against her back.

Jess started to move and smiled, feeling much better today. She gave Adam a good hug and kiss before heading to start to get ready for work.

Adam reached back and petted Joshua, waking him up, "Thanks for being our pillow" he teased.

Thanks, you were nice. My wolf loved the fact you were so close. Joshua commented back, as he got up, stretched, then headed off to get ready for his duties for the day.

Brook petted Toby, to wake him up. Adam moved and did the same for Robin.

Toby woke up, and stretched out, laying on his side, enjoying the petting, *I hope you didn't mind... We were feeling a bit down, and just being with you helped.*

Robin did much the same as he woke under Adam's stroking, letting out a yawn as he stretched.

Adam nodded, "Well, we did say you could join us any time if you needed to. I am glad you decided to actually do it, and not just suffer. Being lonely is not a good feeling. I plan on leaving this mat here, so you would be welcome to come and use it to sleep on, if you need to just be in the room and don't want to disturb us."

"Well, it is time to get ready for breakfast." Brook told their two pups, "Go get ready, and meet us in the hall." Both nodded and scampered to their room, so their parents could get ready.

After a quick shower, they got changed into plain clothes, some jeans and t-shirts, before doing each other's hair in a braid to keep it out of the way while they worked on the security centre.

Heading out the door, both pups saw them, and looked surprised at what they were wearing as it wasn't normal for them; it was just some jeans and t-shirts, "Helping in the security centre today, since there's humans, we had to dress to not shock them, or we wouldn't get much work done. You two want to help?" Adam offered.

Both nodded and quickly changed from their training clothes to something a little stronger.

Both came out in similar outfits to them. Wrapping arm around Robin, Adam asked, "Are you wanting to be in security too?"

Robin shook his head, "No, I would get bored doing it. I'd rather learn your job with the technology."

Adam smiled, "OK. I can do that; you can be our assistant." Looking at Toby, which Brook had an arm around as they headed into the dining room, "By the way, I talked to Martin, and you can shadow him at his work when you're not training or with us." They had also had to get approval from the Alpha, since it was a restricted area, but he had not seen any issues as both pups rarely got in trouble.

The smile which lit up Toby's face was warming, and well worth the effort they were doing for them.

"Both of you want a fairly hard job, so you will need to work on your studies more and doing more physical training. My wolf keeps thinking you both could do the jobs, but you will need to really work at it. None of the other Betas have children right now, so you will need to set an example for the other pups in the pack. You may want to talk to Rein, as he would know how you feel, since he was born to Theta parents."

Toby spoke up, "We already have been talking to Rein when he's not busy. We try but it's hard when being bullied—" At Adam's low growl, he quickly added, "Haven't been bullied since under your protection. Nobody wants to get your punishment."

Adam had a bit of a satisfied grin on his face, "That is good." He could accept they didn't want the punishment, so would be good, even if they didn't change to wanting to be good.

Handing them some food, they went and joined their usual table, and chatted with their friends while they ate. The weather was still icy outside, so most were trying to do most of their tasks inside. With the ice, some of the outdoor work had slowed down. Luckily, they had the cables placed before the weather turned. Being in their hybrid shape, they had to be much more careful, as their strength was much more, and the paws, even though they had thumbs, were clumsier.

It may slow them down, but anything less than a blizzard would not stop them from getting the work done. It did mean the hot pools were in extensive use later in the evenings though, as they worked well to thaw out.

When they were done breakfast, Martin joined the four as they headed down to security centre to work on the equipment. Today they were working on getting the monitors installed, now the supports were all nice and secured. They also were getting the control servers installed.

Adam led his pups to help with the servers, making sure they had the earplugs in correctly before leading them through the doors into the data centre and over to the racks which had doors with steel mesh and keys in the locks. Right now, they were empty, but there were several carts with equipment beside them.

Both pups mentioned how noisy it still was in there.

Adam just sent back, "That's a data centre for you. You just must live with it. That's why you have earplugs in." The equipment had many fans, then the racks had more fans, and then was the heavy AC systems which brought cool air to the equipment—with it being very cold outside, was mostly just adjusting the humidity level of the intake air as it wasn't needing to be chilled—and the exhaust system pulled the hot air away to have much of the heat captured and used to heat the buildings.

After lifting the doors of the equipment racks off their pins and disconnecting the ground wire, and putting them aside, they started with installing the Access Layer switch for the cameras on this floor, and connected to the ones on the other floors and it to the distribution layer switch, showing them how to correctly handle the fibre optical cables; they had to be gentle with them, and no hard bends or tight straps, as it would damage them, and never look straight into the end; the light could damage their eyes, even if the wavelength wasn't one they could see.

Quickly, they had them installed, and after putting the doors back on, locked the cabinets, then putting on and recording the serialized seals over the lock holes, and then headed out, telling the pups, "That's the main room, now we have to do the same on the backup."

The Access Layer switches on each floor, and the one in the separate rack for the basement, had fibre lines going not only to a distribution layer switch in the main data centre, but they also had a second set of wires which went to a second set of distribution layer switches in the Backup Centre, so both would have to be damaged before they lost connection. Both large Distribution Switches had a linking wire between them as well.

Separately, each rack had an Access Layer switch, and each data centre had two distribution layer switches, to handle the server traffic, with those in their two "Core" rack, with those racks at each end of the room, and both centres had an even larger Core Layer switch. Right now, only the main data centre had a fibre link to the Wi-Fi, but once he added a second switch to the box in the cave and connected a second wire to the other network port the Wi-Fi router, he planned on using one of the spare pairs to run to the other switch, but also when they had the Fibre link, he would add that to both locations too.

Adam handed the keys to Martin as they passed, seeing they had one row of monitors installed. There were another three to go.

The pups were looking at the screens with wide eyes, and it took Adam to tap their shoulders for them to follow, so they could get the other servers done before lunch.

Brook smiled as they left, she was opening some of the floor tiles for routing the connections and cables for the monitors. The table had been wired, and one of the techs was programming it.

It was almost lunch time when they finished with the secondary servers. Adam passed the keys to the rack to Martin letting them know they were all done. If the equipment needed to be serviced, he would have to get the keys from Martin, but he doubted they would need to physically access it anytime soon.

Breaking for lunch, both pups smiled, as they got told they would help with the monitor wall after lunch! It took Adam threatening to have them not help, to get them to stop and enjoy lunch instead of gulping it down and wanting to hurry back.

With the addition of the three to helping, they were able to get the last two rows of the monitors installed and all the power cords connected. They were taking the next morning to connect the wires from the server room to the computers which controlled the monitors, and the three stations which had manual controls.

Dinner was an interesting meal, as Adam had invited the four installers to join him. They genuinely were shocked when invited again. They said he was the first wolf to invite them to share more than a single meal. Finding out he was also a Beta and had just been turned would have made them fall if they weren't already sitting down.

"I couldn't tell you weren't born a wolf!" Commented the senior installer. He was still shocked. One of the other packs refused to give those Turned senior positions.

Adam grinned amused as usual, "Thanks. I've had comments of that sort, or I have control which far exceeds what my actual time as a wolf is." Shrugging, he continued, "I just feel much more at home and comfortable here as a wolf than I ever did as a human. I never felt like I really fit in."

Eventually the meal ended, and all had fun, with Adam and Brook heading for their suite, talking about what they should do for the evening. Brook had thought the nearly full moon would allow for them to continue some tracking training, as they had eaten, they didn't want to hunt for food they didn't need.

Adam agreed, and his wolf was doing circles in his mind in joy, making him slightly dizzy. They dropped their clothes and were about to head out the door when Toby and Robin came and asked if they could come.

We're going to go do some tracking training, Adam commented, not knowing if they wanted to do it.

"Pleeeease can we go?" Begged Toby. They only had basic training on tracking; they were not the best. Robin just gave them puppy eyes.

It wouldn't hurt to have them along. We are just looking for scents and tracks, and following them. Brook commented, when she saw Adam's hesitation.

OK, you can come. Adam relented. His wolf wanted their pups to be the best they could; he wasn't sure how high their skills could be, but felt it was Beta if they put their minds to it.

Both quickly stripped and shifted, wagging their tails quite fast, happy to be learning more about tracking.

Brook led the way outside, trailed by the three male wolves and Charlie.

Heading into the forest Brook moved into instructor mode, and had them tracking, showing them the scents, and teaching them what they were. They followed many tracks, and the animals seemed to know the wolves were full and were not out hunting, so were not in hiding. Both pups were quite serious about the learning and worked hard to learn. Charlie trailed behind but kept back, as he was trained to do while the wolves tracked or hunted unless instructed to help.

Eventually it was time to head back, and the pups were quite happy to have spent the evening tracking but were quite tired now. Heading back in, all four wolves curled up on the pad near the fire in one big ball of fur, with Brook and Adam curling around their two pups protectively.

*****

Waking up in the morning from his light sleep, Wolf-Adam was in quite a good mood, having enjoyed the night curled up with his mate and pups. Yawning he nudged his human mind awake, it being time for him to wake up and get to work with the boring human stuff, and for him to sleep. Shifting back to human, he petted the other three, to wake them up, before heading to the shower. By the time it was warmed up and he stepped in, he was joined by the others, and they helped each other get clean.

Setting out the plans, the pups got to help them this morning, but had some classwork to do in the afternoon, so were not able to help.

Both groaned about the work, but knew they needed to do it, nor did their new parents allow them to skip it either.

Adam smiled when a couple of the installers asked to join him, and he nodded in agreement, not seeing a problem with it.

"I'm Chris and this is Steve." Chris introduced to those at the table, not knowing if they would know his name, and it was just polite.

Everyone around the table gave their names, even if they didn't expect the two humans to remember their names. By unspoken thought, they didn't talk about work at the meal.

"We are wondering outside of mates, if you allow humans to join the pack?" Chris asked politely, "And can they be Turned?" He had heard it was the term they used for when a human became a werewolf.

Brook quickly sent her thoughts to the Alpha, as they didn't usually talk about those things to outsiders. *Alpha? Chris and Steve are asking about humans joining the pack and turning. What should we say to them?* Most humans were offered a spot in the pack, but rarely did non-pack humans even have an opportunity to visit a pack, or even know of them.

I like how they have been acting so far, and how respectful they are to our beliefs. Especially those two. You and Adam can discuss it in broad strokes, but don't bother too much with details. Have them come to us if they are interested. The alpha sent to Brook and Adam.

Brook turned to the two humans to answer their questions, since she was the most senior, "We do permit humans to join, but it needs to be sponsored by pack members, usually a mate, but those mates sometimes ask to bring in siblings or other close relatives, usually ones they are supporting. In all cases, the Alphas make the decision for new pack members, usually with an interview."

Hey, I didn't have an interview! Adam commented to Brook silently, a bit amused.

Not a formal meeting, but the fact you were helping a stranger, and the way you acted at and with the Longview pack, including with the Alphas there, was yours. Alpha Grant and Alpha Louise felt you would do well and passed their thoughts to our Alphas. It is also mostly a formality *for mates.** Brook retorted. **Gareth would have accepted the views of Alpha Grant and Alpha Louise for you, was why he didn't ask any questions before accepting you.** It was also a thing positive he was willing to give up his life immediately, while there was support for his obligations and bills, which the pack was quite willing to assist with. The common thought was if someone was a mate of a member, they also should be able to handle being a member too, or their mate would be able to assist them to learn the skills needed to function in one.

Brook saw both looked like they were wanting to join, "If you want anything more on it, talk to Alpha Gareth and Alpha Maria. They prefer to discuss it with someone first."

Both Chris and Steve nodded in understanding about further details was between them and the Alphas. It was understandable to both the Alphas would be the ones to decide on if they were to join, and what they needed to say.

Brook smiled, "For the Turning, usually we only do mates, as having the mate bond and the changes which helps the Turning both with speed and lessening the severity. People have had severe reactions during being turned and have died, as their body couldn't handle the changes." Others had no control, and at worst went insane and had to be put down or be permanently confined to the pack and watched at best.

Adam took over, generally describing the turn, "Most are down and bedridden for the first two weeks following the Turning Bite. Often you are unconscious for the first few days, then you are in and out and barely move. The last few days you are little more mobile but need help even to get to the bathroom. Next, you start to recover, and you need to basically relearn your body, as everything will be different, from your senses to your strength and endurance. A few weeks later, is when your wolf first speaks to you, and you must learn to integrate them into your mind, as you will be two halves of a whole. A bit later is when you first shift. Then a few months of everything settling down. During all the stages aches and pains from stressed muscles to feeling like bone deep bruises, to muscle spasms, to muscle cramps."

Both humans were quite startled, not realising there was a cost, or it took so long, "But is it worth it?" Chris asked.

Adam paused for a moment before he shrugged, "I feel it is. Oh, and until you can show you have control of the shifting, you are not permitted near humans, and before shifting, you must always have an experienced wolf with you. After shifting, you still are required to have an experienced wolf till you show you know what you are doing. It got annoying a bit, even with it mostly being my mate with me."

They nodded, thinking on it.

They gathered up their dirty dishes and took them to the tubs of soapy water for them. Adam, Toby, Robin, and Brook walked with the two techs headed down to the security office. The two humans talked quietly on their thoughts, not realising the wolves could hear them clearly, and the wolves for their part, pretended to not hear them. Both deciding to talk to the Alpha farther about joining the pack. Both weren't sure on the turning, one wanted more details, the other more thinking he'd wait for a bit.

Brook quickly sends a thought to the Alpha letting him know to expect the two at some point. The morning passed quickly. They got all the equipment installed, including the mini-PCs which controlled the monitors, the two manual control stations, and a management station.

For the privacy, they locked it down to the security office for managing the system. They liked the auto-add features, as the sensors and cameras started to appear. Martin pulled out the list of serials and where they were located and started to add the details to the system. When most of the internal cameras came up, and were grouped by area, and they started to come up on the screens by area, instead of randomly.

They set up the operations table, with its large touch screen imbedded in the centre, and after loading in the satellite and topographical maps, they started tying in the sensor locations. By lunch time, all the critical areas had a sensor marked, and were starting to fill in many other areas. A couple of areas, they would have to send a wolf to scale up into avalanche areas but were waiting for conditions to improve. Martin wasn't worried, as it was unlikely to be needed until summer and likely wait till the snow was gone to place the sensor. Before then, the danger of an avalanche itself would be enough of a deterrent for travel that way.

Heading out to lunch, they decided the afternoon would be on training them to use the systems, so they could teach the others.

Steve shook his head, "We haven't had an install go this fast and smoothly, ever." He commented, "But we haven't had the support and help of a pack to get the work done. Usually, the mounting rails took two days, alone. The other packs just watched us work. The servers another day and identifying the sensors the other two if not more; most didn't keep records as good as yours on the locations of each and every sensor." He sighed, "One didn't even record which sensor was where... so had to have someone visit and relay each sensor."

The head installer tasked the two who sat with Brook and Adam in the morning with doing the training, as he had seen they were getting along quite well with the pack. Since the pack was dealing with the rest of the installations and didn't need any oversight or instruction, the other two installers were going to head out that afternoon. There wasn't a need for all four to be there.

Smiling, the Lead installer told Steve and Chris not to leave till they were scheduled, on Friday afternoon. He had seen they were making some friends, which would make it easier. Both were happily willing to do so. Since the pack was well connected, they might be able to get some more large contracts with other packs. This was the largest contract in the last few years and was only slightly less than the largest in parts ever according to his manager, but with the urgency, they had been able to get a higher price for the services even with giving them a bundle discount, so it was the largest in value. Everyone involved had been promised bonuses.

Both Steve and Chris turned and asked Adam to pass on a request to see the Alpha after dinner. They almost immediately had a reply he'd see them then. Neither asked how he had passed it on, as they had thought from not only this pack, they might be telepathic, but they were not asking, as it wasn't their place to know.

So far everyone who had interacted with them had nothing bad to say about them. They had asked questions, some a bit personal, but when an answer was refused, they asked a less personal question, or asked for general information. They had quite happily followed pack customs, as much as they could.

CHAPTER 23

New Members

Thinking of an idea as they finished lunch, he asked the Alpha for permission, *Alpha, looks like we will be up and running for all the sensors, other than some of the ones on the cliffs by the end of the week. I'm thinking if we have them done by Thursday, we should have some bison steaks for everyone in the pack. It would help with morale.*

I love the idea! I'll arrange the food, have it passed to the installers. We'll have it on Saturday if they don't, anyways. Good food always helps with morale, just don't tell them that.

His wolf was nearly drooling in his mind over the thought of the bison meat, as he passed it onto Martin, who knew who the installer leads were, if not the installers they were watching. They thought if they bustled, they could get it done the next day, with a few more hands. They sent out a few more pack members, mostly older pups, to help with the recording and fetching of equipment. Adam grinned, as it was many of those who had helped with the tech or played the computer games.

Heading back down with only the two installers, Adam and Martin were the first to get the full training. Adam from an IT/management side, and Martin from a management and support side. They watched as the last of the interior cameras were installed and detected. It would take them a bit before they got the outside ones done, but they should all be up and running by the end of the next day.

Evan had even climbed up to the Wi-Fi-cave, and had installed one hiding in the back, to watch the cave, and a wide-angle one at the edge looking over the valley and connected them to the switch already up there, at the same time wiring up the second switch he planned. He was glad the enclosure had plenty of space for expansion. The exterior one covered the town, the approach road, and a fair bit of the land, even if most of it just showed trees.

Cameras which were inside service areas – wiring cabinets, server room, etc. – were set to alarm if they detected movement.

The sensors were still popping up, but they passed the notes from the wolves installing them for the morning, they were able to register those, as the helpers had placed them out where they were to be installed in the forest. The number of units still available to install was dwindling. The lead installer had already checked, and the rest were to be there the next Monday, or Tuesday at the latest.

The new sensors were now coming online so fast they were being detected in clumps. They slowed the rate the system scanned for new devices, as it was putting too much load on the systems and causing the system to pop up service-level warnings.

"Wow, I didn't realise how fast you wolves could work! You sure have them going hard!" Commented Chris, grinning in amusement.

Steve laughed, "They promised Bison steaks if they finished the ones they have by tomorrow. Even that would get me to work double time!"

Adam smiled, "If they finish on time, we won't exclude you, you get to taste the treat. To make you eat something else while the pack eats bison is not very nice. You are guests, so should be treated well."

That lit up both of their faces. "I knew I always thought werewolves were better as clients! They like to feed their guests well! Unlike some companies which just give you a loaf of bread and cold cuts and call it supplying food." Commented Chris with a shudder, "At least our manager was able to expense our meals for us."

Just before supper a teen-wolf ran in with the updated reports of where the sensors were for the afternoon, before scampering up to have dinner.

Brook joined them in the dining room, as she had gone to help get the exterior cameras online.

Adam smiled as Toby and Robin came up grinning, "Guess what, Dad?" Robin asked.

"What?" Adam replied. *Robin called me 'Dad'* Adam commented to Brook as she sat down beside him, feeling the proud father.

"We both got perfect on our Pack History exam today!"

"Great! I'm proud of you both!" Adam exclaimed, as he gave them a hug, "Now you can teach me some of it." And laughed at the scared look in their faces, "OK, you don't have to." Brook moved to give them a hug to congratulate them on their test.

The others at the table congratulated them. Brook commented to Adam, *I just got their education records this morning, and seemed they were barely passing the class and a couple others, although there are notes they are doing much better now. I am now very happy we have them, as their bump in seniority seems to have motivated them quite well, or maybe just having a couple of caring parents care about their scores.*

Sitting down, the two humans asked some questions, quite interested in the pack's history. They were surprised they had moved out here as early as any of the first colonists in North America. They were impressed with the pack all over again. They had helped with the rail line then the highway which went through. They had purchased some of the land which backed onto the parks and helped lobby for the parks, as it helped protect them, and give them the space they needed to run.

All too soon for the two humans, dinner finished, and it was time for their meeting with the Alphas.

They had talked about it between themselves, and both were wanting to apply to join the pack.

Identifying themselves to the guard outside the wing, Chris and Steve were guided to the Alpha's office. Both Maria and Gareth stood and gave them a greeting hug.

"Well, what did you want to speak with me about. I have some inklings from the questions you have asked my wolves, but I want to hear it directly from you." Gareth asked, sitting down on one couch with his mate, motioning the two humans to the other one. Unless he had to, he preferred to be informal.

"We would like to learn more about being able to join your pack." Stated Chris, "I have worked at three packs, and it seems yours is the most welcoming. You have given us a large amount of freedom to be here, and talking with those here, most were very friendly, and treated us as friends." He enjoyed with curling up with the female, which was a first for him. He had only ever had casual girlfriends, and never had they invited him for more than a single night. Crystal had even had his security adjusted so he could go into her room without her.

"You shared your food, and we even had some invite us to sit and eat with them. Neither of the other two packs we went to did it. One had us very much segregated from them, the other had us staying in a hotel and had to commute in. You treat us as respected guests."

Gareth and Maria shared a pleased look, before Gareth continued, "But why do you want to join this pack? Steve?"

After thinking for a bit, Steve answered, "I'm not sure why, but since the first pack visit, even though we barely had any glimpses, I felt a connection with the way you live. Your pack is basically a large family and work together for the greater good of all. You don't work to put others down just to get ahead or ignore those around you."

Gareth looked to Chris, and nodded for him to have his say, "I too felt a connection. After leaving the first pack, I felt like I had a knife in my heart. I had several nights I couldn't sleep at all. I ended up needing to take sleeping pills for the month. Since then, if I don't get out to nature at least once a week, it seems to come back. I too missed the way you live and care for each other. I am wanting to *become* a wolf but know what we were told was only the edge. I think the risks are well worth what the gain would be."

Gareth nodded sagely, "I have already had several wolves who, when they heard about this meeting, also thought you would be petitioning to join and offered to sponsor you. With what you are saying, and how you work, I am willing to accept you two into the pack. What sort of work would you do? We don't have enough work to hold you into an installer role, but if there is interest, we may have you work with other packs."

Both looked relieved, and much happier. Steve answered the Alpha, "Well, I am from a security background, and would be interested in working with Martin in your security. There are other ideas I could do but would require me to know the details much more, including stuff you wouldn't want others outside the pack to know."

Chris added, "I'm from an IT security background, and know much on that side. I haven't investigated it much, but it does seem like you have a good start here, as from what I have seen, your network is fairly secure. Adam refused to go into details on it, which was understandable. I could work with him to get it even more secure."

Gareth smiled, "Both of them, and Rein were the three most senior of those who offered to sponsor you. All three were impressed. Many of the other wolves you worked with handed in good reports about you, and several had said they would support you joining." He reached into a drawer in the table beside him and pulled out new permanent IDs for them with 'Prospective Member' across the bottom, "We are accepting you as possible members of the pack."

Pulling two thick binders off the desk, Alpha Maria handed one to each of them, "These are the Pack Laws, and what you would be agreeing to be bound to for your life, if you formally decide to join. One thing, the Pack Bonds are telepathic, and will lay you out for a day or two since you don't have a mate's bond to help reduce the impact. Review them. If you have questions Adam, Brook, or Martin would be able to answer them, or find the answer for you. You will need to agree to the Pack Laws and give an oath to it to join; the oath is in there. There is also the basic information on being Turned in there. Further details can be given later once you are settled in as pack members."

Both nodded happily clutching the binders.

Gareth smiled and sat back, "Those notes cannot leave the pack house, as they contain some information we don't want to spread around. Now what are we going to do about your current job? Did you want to have a discussion with them with us involved, or did you just want to quit?"

Steve sighed, from the look on the Lead's face as he told them to stay for the last time, he suspected he knew, "I think we should call Jason, our lead, and see what he says. We'll do it in the morning. I want to get a start on the laws tonight."

Nodding Gareth and Maria stood, which had the other two standing too, "It probably is a good idea. Enjoy your evening."

Both Alphas gave them hugs as they left. Getting more members was always a happy time. Even if they didn't find a mate soon, having new views is always good. These two looked like they would be a good fit to the changes which were happening.

*****

Both Adam and Brook smiled as they were curled up with their pups, enjoying a movie when the alphas advised them, *Sounds like we're getting a couple of experienced helpers! It is going to help both Martin and us help the pack immeasurably.* Adam commented.

I'm glad; I really like those two, they were curious but were also very respectful of the pack. The knowledge on not just the equipment they installed, but how to use it well and security in general will be a big asset. From the comments, I am betting Chris will ask to be turned. Brook replied, *Not sure about Steve. I do hope both find mates here.*

Adam gave her a mental snort, *No bet; I think the same way. With him going to be under us, I do suspect we will be asked to do it, but not for a while. Spring or summer at the earliest.*

Brook was amused, *I suspect fall. But spending the time between learning all he can to do it. If they are accepted, I suspect they will get our 'dogs assigned. In testing, I suspect they will be Deltas.*

Adam looked down as the movie ended, turning off the TV, he noticed their pups were asleep between them, *Put them in our bed?* he asked.

Brook nodded and picked up Robin who had been curled up against her. Adam did the same with Toby. Brook had Charlie pull the blanket back, and they slid them in the middle of the bed, before stripping them. Slipping out of their clothes, they snuggled their pups, pulling the blanket up, and Charlie flopped on the bed to sleep as well.

*****

The next morning, it was Toby who woke first. At his first sniff, he could tell he was in his parent's bed. The thought made him stop; he smiled, when he realised he already felt loved, and Adam and Brook were his parents. Since his father had died, his mother had mostly given up, and had gone to not wanting any surprises or changes in her life. He was glad to now be where he was.

Rolling over, he snuggled into his new father's chest, and dozed waiting for the rest to wake up. He was happy his cousin was now his brother.

Before he could fall back asleep, he was woken by a squeal from Robin, and when he tried to roll over, was grabbed in a hug by Adam.

"Time to get up, we're doing some training today, as it is going to just be waiting for the sensors to come online." Adam said before letting him go.

Both scampered off to their room, grabbing their clothes as they went.

Both grabbed clean training clothes and slipping them on. "Our parents are much better trainers than the ones we had before." Toby commented as they dressed.

"Naw, it's because they have only us two, instead of the ten who were in our group." Robin retorted, before pausing for a minute, "I think it is also we are working harder as we don't want to disappoint them."

Running a brush through his growing hair, Toby agreed, "That too. I'm just glad they have no rules about having to keep hair short, and can afford to get us clothes, rather than just nearly used up stuff."

Robin smiled, "I agree. I love the training clothes; they are nice and light. Let's not keep them waiting!" he called, opening the door after doing his own hair.

Adam and Brook stepped out their door as they waited and both pounced their parents for a hug, before heading down together for some training before breakfast.

*****

At breakfast, Adam smiled as Chris and Steve again came towards them, Adam just nodded before they could ask, and he noticed their upgraded IDs on lanyards commented, "Congratulations on being accepted. What are your plans for today? I'm needing to get back to training some more, so will be in the gym with my pups."

Chris smiled, "Thanks, even the tentative accepting let me have the best sleep I have had in years. We're going to need to call Jason this morning and figure out what the options for our current job are going to be. I don't know if we could keep our job, but stay here, or if we have to quit."

Nodding, Adam continued to eat his breakfast, "I noticed you got the Big Binders last night. Any questions?"

Chris shook his head, "Not yet. I'm writing them down, but most are being answered later in the information, so I'll wait till I'm done before asking them. One question, what are the rules about..." He looked at Toby and Robin sitting beside Adam, changed his words, "—Female companionship?"

Adam laughed, "As long as they are willing, you are free to do whatever you want with other pack members; sex is talked about openly here. If you have noticed, there is no nudity taboo here, so we are open about it. Same goes for same-sex relationships. Just remember, all relationships are considered over when either side finds a mate, and No means No."

Chris blushed, and nodded, watching a couple females as they walked by, who smiled back.

Picking up his plate, Adam smiled, "As long as you get your work done, nobody is going to say a thing about any companionship, as long as they are cleared for the area."

Brook and the pups followed him, and they headed down to the gym for some training. Alpha Gareth was there, and they nodded in respect to him, "I thought I'd come join you, and work with Adam, since

Martin isn't available, for some advanced training." Gareth offered. Adam nodded and joined the Alpha, as Brook worked with the pups.

*****

By the time lunch came around, Gareth was frowning; not only was Adam able to show an increase of skills which was astonishing, but he had the same thought as Martin; his movements reminded him of another; he had been able to tell who it was, unlike Martin: his own grandfather, who had died sixty years before and had stepped down as Alpha to be their main trainer forty years before that, after spending the fifty years before working with him to transfer powers and duties slowly to him.

The whole pack mourned his passing for several years as he had been well loved. Gareth had been trying to follow in his paw prints. He decided he needed to talk to the elders, and maybe have some of the older members who had worked with him confirm what he was seeing. Until then he'd only tell his mate and keep an eye on Adam. He wondered what other skills he may have inherited, and if he — and his mate — had the skills to be Alpha. If so, they might be perfect for a project of his, one which nobody but his mate knew of; not even his pups, the presumptive next-alphas, knew of it.

*****

After lunch, the four came back down, Adam was a bit stiff from the hard workout the Alpha put him through, but still worked on his Bow skills for a good couple of hours.

Later, they took their pups for a run as wolves. Adam and Brook had decided they were going to show them their private spot, after getting a promise to not tell anyone about the spot.

They decided to use it as hunt training for the pups as well, and they were able to each grab a rabbit. Adam was able to get one for each himself and Brook, which really made his wolf feel good. Charlie also grabbed one too, and fed, they headed up into the hidden fissure which led to the pools. The pups understood the secrecy when they saw how fragile the place was and felt very honoured they were being entrusted with it. All four shifted to human when they were at the hot pools, as even the cool one was too warm for their winter-coated wolves to be in for more than a few minutes.

Relaxing in the water, they enjoyed being a family. Adam told some stories of his being human, and his family which he remembered. They asked how the two met, as they had heard rumours but not the actual story.

"I had some free time and went for a good run." Brook started, blushing a little. "My wolf kept getting whiffs of his scent on the wind, then it would be gone, then it would be back much closer. It happened three or four times, but on the last time, my wolf took over and set us running full out. She didn't want to be like Lazy Jack." Both pups nodded while Adam looked a little confused, not knowing who they were referring to. "When I got close, I tried to climb the cliff, instead of trying to find a trail around, but started a rockslide..." She stopped there and hugged the two pups who were remembering what happened to their birth parents. "I was very, very, very lucky." She added to them, "And it was tiny compared to the one which took your parents." The two looked a little more relieved, as rockslides and avalanches were the leading cause of death for werewolves. In the last century, it had over-taken fights as the leading reason for wolves dying.

"I was taking pictures at various lookouts, so I kept driving between them. I seemed to have been travelling in the same way as the wind was blowing." Adam told them, giving his side, "Up to that point I had never seen a wild wolf, just the few in the zoo, so when I saw her running, I just turned my camera and started taking pictures. Not sure why, but something urged me to go down off the ridge and rescue her." He smirked, "Not sure if it was Luna, or just the mating bond, but I did get her up to the ridge, unconscious. I still have no idea how I lifted her up as a wolf, since I wasn't in good shape!"

Brook nodded, "Not sure why I shifted back, but I did, and when I woke up, he was standing over me. The fact I was taken to a healer right away also helped."

Adam grinned, "The next week, with her trying to pretend to be human was partly stressful and partly amusing." One of his former roommates almost didn't live out the week, since he refused to think about anyone other than himself, and both had agreed if it had been longer, he wouldn't have survived. He often didn't bother worrying about cleaning up after himself, leaving out items on the counter, or a sink full of dishes, so nobody else could use it, Adam was glad he had nothing to do with him anymore. "Once I had released my work obligations, I moved into the pack, instead of the big city."

Brook took over, seeing the pups were still a bit stressed, and told them some funny stories of her growing up. They soon just relaxed and enjoyed the hot water. They watched the sun set, and the stars come out. With a groan, they got up and headed out of the water, shifting to wolves for the run back to the pack house to sleep. Again, they curled up together, this time as wolves, feeling no need to shift back.

Brook commented to Adam, as she settled down wrapped around the pups, *All the running and work we are putting in, they are getting much better. I think they are ahead of their year-mates, now. Maybe we should let them invite their friends, and make sure they have time to be pups and hang with them.*

Adam gave a wordless agreement, already nearly asleep.

*****

The next morning at breakfast, Martin announced all of the sensors were installed, and as a reward, they were having some special food at lunch: Bison Steaks! The howls of celebration were loud.

Adam chuckled at the surprised look on Chris and Steve's face, "Us wolves love our meat. If you want to make friends, take them for a good meal." He replied with a wink as they picked their selection and headed for a seat.

Both smiled and nodded, catching his meaning.

He and Brook were keeping half an eye on their pups, who they had sent to sit with some of the other pups instead of them this meal. He could already see they were getting some deference, and both had a female pup curled into their side. He didn't know if they were happy about it or if the females were just attracted to them since they were senior. He made a mental note to have a talk about it, and how he expected them to treat any companions they wished to have.

Chris shook his head, "Why am I not surprised when it's put that way." Thinking for a moment, "I heard you had an issue which was why this was pushed so much forward; the special food also is a morale boost for the pack."

Adam grinned, "Yup! You can see just the anticipation is already helping it improve. Are you two heading back after lunch as was initially planned?"

Chris sighed, "Unfortunately, yes. Both of us need to file the official paperwork. We're going to be kept as 'consultants' to deal with the packs. We will be back in a week; I need to sell off most of my stuff, and the pack is dealing with the bill to ship my stuff here; it's going to mostly be clothes." Taking a breath, he asked, "Any chance of getting a pack computer when I get back? My current computer is old and was looking at replacing it."

"Oh, joining the pack just to get some new tech goodies?" Adam teased.

Everyone laughed, knowing it wasn't the case at all.

"PC or laptop?" Adam asked when it settled down.

"Laptop should be enough power for what I need."

Adam looked at Steve, "You want one too?"

Steve shook his head, "I've got my own computers. I'm good. I assume you have network in the rooms?"

Erin piped up, "We're working on them. Betas are done; the Deltas are on hold, as we're working to get the cameras done. The rooms you are moving into are done, though. We got all the empty rooms done before starting on those in use. There is Wi-Fi up there too."

Breaking up they went to their jobs, Erin to work with Rein to make sure all the cameras outside were done and operational, before working on the outbuildings. Chris and Steve to help get the remaining sensors registered in the system and answer any last questions before needing to pack up their stuff for heading out. All were looking forward to the lunch.

Adam and Brook were doing some advanced training with the Alpha. It seemed after the morning before, he decided they needed his personal attention. Adam had commented they must have either done something wrong and this was punishment, or they were being groomed for something from the way he was working them. Even Brook had wanted to crawl away when they were finished.

While they were doing unarmed today, they both picked up a selection of training bruises. It made a quick shower before lunch a bit painful. After lunch, they both were being worked as wolves by Martin.

The lunch was a big hit and most just sat in the chairs and had satisfied looks on their faces at the end. Quite a few had even taken to licking their plates, as the sauce they used was excellent, too. Adam and Brook decided they needed to talk to their pups for sure that evening, seeing them eating with the female pups again.

Peter led the two humans off to grab their bags, as he was taking them the nearly three-hour drive to the airport, so they needed to get moving, if he was to make it back for dinner. Many wolves wished them a safe trip, knowing they would be back in a week's time. Both had left some stuff behind and were going to be moved to their new rooms on the third floor once they had been fully cleaned and aired out.

When Adam had heard about what Chris' skills were, he nearly danced. He was planning on having him take over the security, and would officially be reporting to Martin, so even he couldn't bypass the security systems to get into something he shouldn't. Over the next week, he would arrange it with Martin to have it done.

Adam and Brook changed in their rooms then had a playful game of tag as they headed to the training meadow. Martin was waiting, and they immediately went into training. Both Adam and Brook wanted to be in top shape to go after the white wolf. Wolf-Adam's feelings of being violated by the attack on the two under his care and how scared they were now. The fact they still only left the security centre in the company of an Enforcer or a Beta, had started the feeling to be shared with his other half, and had also gone across the bond to Brook. The wolf would not have a chance to submit to them.

*****

All three limped back, having minor bites and scrapes, as was normal after the training, but Martin was satisfied how they were coming along. Their injuries would be no more than scars by morning and be gone within a couple days.

Changing for dinner, they smiled and sat down with their friends, and they all chatted about the lunch meal. Most were still savoring the taste of the lean meat from lunch. The Chefs had made food which was completely different; it being a nice meat and cheese lasagna, with some salads and other sides instead of trying to live up to the lunch. Slices of warm home-made garlic bread was already spread out across the tables; more was piled on the serving table.

CHAPTER 24

The Talk

After an enjoyable meal, Adam and Brook gathered up their pups and headed into their suite for a chat.

The pups were a little nervous, as they didn't know what they needed a talk about, but from the way they sat, they knew it wasn't trouble, which relieved some of their stress, but their wolves were cringing in their minds trying to figure out what they wanted to talk about.

Adam took a deep breath, "We noticed you had some female pups with you at breakfast and lunch today." Noticing the blushes and looking down, he continued, "There is nothing wrong with it, it is normal for pups your age to start being interested. We are not going to interfere, and just wanted to give you a few pointers."

Both Toby and Robin looked startled, "My mother said boy-pups needed to stay away from girl-pups till of-age," Toby commented. "She would yell at us whenever she saw us together."

"This pack doesn't think that way and most don't follow a separation of genders. We are not expecting it of the two of you." Brook corrected, "I know there are some in the pack who have followed that part of Christianity, but we will not." She didn't like pushing one way or other onto someone and would help their pups however she could.

After letting them think on it for a little bit, Brook continued, "I do expect you to treat any you are with, regardless of if they are male or female, with respect and care. Also, they should be doing the same. There are some who would only want to be with you for your rank; you need to be careful about them."

Toby smiled, "Sam and Lea were friends before we came to you. They are pups of a couple Deltas. Their parents didn't like them hanging with us as we were Thetas, but now we are Beta, they are nearly pushed at us. We had to keep quiet and stay hidden when we hung out. I know of other girls who tried to move in, but they... were not ones we, or our wolves, wanted to deal with."

Adam smiled, "I guess trusting your wolves would be the best. Your wolves like them?"

Robin blushed red, "Mine whines and wants to curl up with Lea often."

Human-Adam chuckled softly, his wolf wanted to meet these pups and see if they were worthy of his pups. *They were willing to defy their parents to be with them and didn't care they were some of the lowest in the pack. It shows they are likely be good for them; could even be mates, for all they are too young to start to know what their mate smells like.*

Wolf-Adam sighed and had to agree with his human. He still wanted to meet the pups; if they were acceptable, he'd keep an eye on them as well.

"In that case, we would like to meet them this weekend. Invite them here, and we will have a private meal together. Find out which meal works best for them." Brook requested.

Both pups turned pale, not sure how to get out of it. Robin had a glazed look as he asked them silently, and got an instant response, "Saturday evening would be best."

Adam nodded, "I'll have Jess and Joshua arrange to get us our food for then. We won't bite, we just want to get to know them."

After making sure they knew the mechanics of sex, not a fun discussion for any of them, they went into the even more embarrassing, how to treat a partner well, and the fact each had control of their body. They knew at their age, they might become active, especially if their wolf urged it. As the risk of any sort of illness is non-existent, and pregnancy was not possible till they were older, they didn't bother worrying about them having fun; just it had to be mutually consensual.

Eventually Adam and Brook decided to release the pups and end the discussion. They could provide advice, but some things everyone had to learn for themselves.

*****

The next day Adam and Brook spent working with the Alpha. All morning he put them through some training, and they broke for lunch. Both were sore and wondered what the afternoon would bring.

They had fun exchanging some teasing with their friends. They both had quite a few training bruises, but most were light, and were on their forearms from doing the blocks. Brook knew how much training the others did, and it was no where near how much they did; so far Adam had continued to advance as fast as he had before; Even Brook had taken up the challenge and worked to improve her skills.

Looking over at their two pups, they both gave a mental smile, as they were sitting as close to the two girls as they could, and their mental feeling was very content knowing their parents were not going to try to separate them. Adam smiled, and his wolf was watching them, head tilted.

The afternoon was some more work, but with just Adam and Brook. Adam was extremely surprised at how much his endurance had increased; he could easily do eight hours of solid training and not be more than a reasonably tired.

They headed back early to have a good wash, and once ready, helped Jess and Joshua get the table ready; they added one of the leaf's in to make sure they had the room, as Jess headed out with a cart to get the food from the kitchen. They had decided to just get the normal food, and just have the private dinner with the four pups.

The four showed up all together, with Lea in a nice knee length dress, and Sam in a blouse and pants.

"Welcome you two." Adam greeted them. Both him and Brook gave them a good hug as they introduced themselves. His wolf was forward and made sure they got a good smell of them, so they would be able to remember their scent.

Jess quickly arrived with the selection of the food, and showing his wolf manners, Adam let the four pups make their selection first. Toby and Robin smiled and made sure their friends went first. They sat with Toby and Sam on one side, and Robin and Lea on the other, with Adam and Brook taking the ends of the table.

Chatting, they had fun learning about the two their pups liked. They both had been somewhat interested in the tech, but not to the point of the work the other pups were doing with the old technology. Both had joined in with the working on the new stuff, though.

"I'm more interested in working on the security stuff with Toby," Sam commented shyly, "But I don't have the contacts to do so. My parents told me if I can get in, they would support me."

Adam linked Martin, *It seems Toby has found a girl with similar interests to him and wants to work with him in the security. Would you mind another pup?*

Martin replied immediately, sounding excited, *Yes, please! I never have enough willing to learn the security centre. Most of the people in there are older. More we have, the shorter the shifts we can do. What's her name?*

Adam was amused, *Sam. I'll tell her you'll see her on Toby's next shift.*

Getting a wordless agreement, Adam grinned, "If you had said something to Martin, he would have worked to get you in."

"Didn't want to abuse my access," Toby muttered, blushing.

"Didn't know there were openings," Sam commented softly, but eyes wide.

"Well, you don't need to think about it anymore; I contacted Martin for you. You get to stay with Toby when he goes for his next shift, and Martin will teach you both." Brook replied, smiling. "Most of the people who are in the security office are older, and most of the ones under Martin can't stand the security centre, so he lacks many who can or will do shifts in there. He has no problem teaching anyone interested in learning, so if anyone else you know wants to try it out, have them talk to him."

Both Toby and Sam stared at him for a long minute before breaking out in smiles.

Adam looked mock stern, "It does mean you both will need to work hard at your skills, especially the fighting and leadership. Being the person in the security centre is a big responsibility: you are responsible to watch out for any threat and to alert the Alpha and follow his directions on how to respond. From what I have seen, you can handle it, Toby."

Toby sat straighter, "Yes, sir."

Giving him a final smile turned to Robin and Lea, "Robin is wanting to be my assistant, and help me with the tech. I'm wondering what you are interested in, Lea?"

"I like technology, and using the latest stuff, but I don't like fixing other people's problems. Most of the time it is because they don't want to think it through for themselves!" Lea started. Or don't bother reading the error message.

Adam broke out in laughter, "I totally agree. I spent many years as a computer tech. Overseeing the technology and those who support it is much nicer."

"I also enjoy teaching. I loved helping give out the new computers and teaching them how to work on it." Lea continued.

Adam and Brook traded a smile, "Well it works for me. Talk to Erin, and we'll see about getting you some training so you can do it even better."

Lea looked startled, "What?" she exclaimed.

Adam nodded, "I've been looking for pups who are interested in the tech, as the adults all have jobs to do, and none who have put in requests for a change are interested in working on the computers. It leaves me finding pups around your age to be my first helpers."

Lea looked eager, "You mean you would have it as my job?"

Adam laughed, "Yes. It would let you have a job as soon as you are of age, and part time till then. With Robin working as my assistant, you would both be working closely with me and Brook."

Lea had the deer in the headlights look, which made Adam laugh, "So you wanting to start being the official trainer? As I am in charge of all the Tech, as long as Brook and my wolf don't have a problem, I can make assignments without asking the Alpha. But since you are still a pup, it would have to be run by your parents first."

Lea nodded, "Yes, I would love to have it as a job, and be paid to do it."

Brook commented, "I just linked to your parents, and they would be happy to let you do it." She knew them, and had worked with them for a bit, but not in a few years.

Lea grinned and nodded.

Adam laughed, "Well, in that case, let Erin know, and start working on what you would want to do to train the pack."

Lea nodded and looked eager to start.

Adam smiled at the girls, "Do you two have laptops?"

Sam shook her head, "I'd have to buy one myself."

Lea also shook her head, "My parents think I don't need one."

"Come see me tomorrow right after breakfast. We'll get you each one. I still have a bunch unassigned. Lea, you definitely will need one, as a trainer you will need to know how to do more than the basics." Adam was surprised more of the pack hadn't signed out a computer. The Alphas, Seconds, Elders, and most of the Betas had picked up one. Questioning the two, it seemed many of the lower members didn't want one or didn't think they were eligible for one. It was one thing he planned on discussing at the fire that week.

Although if it was any colder than the last one, he was going to take over one of the living rooms, or just invite everyone to his room, until his Turning finished, or it warmed up instead of going out to the firepit.

Both pups were working at their physical training, and right now, were helping those in their classes, as they were ahead of them, but they moved the classes ahead all at once.

"They could join us!" Toby exclaimed, "I have been showing them some of the moves, but I'm not good enough to teach them yet."

"Hmmm... It isn't a bad idea." Brook commented, thoughtfully. "Anyone else you'd want to include in the training?"

"Ummm..." Toby commented slowly, "I'm thinking Jess and Joshua may be interested?" As he looked over at the two who were cleaning off the plates and putting the dessert on the table.

Both stopped for a moment and looked startled, but with a wishful look.

Adam smiled, "I like the idea too. What do you two say?" he asked Jess and Joshua.

"We would love to, but we don't have any training clothes..." Commented Jess, before shaking her head, "But you're just going to say get some under your name, right?"

Both Brook and Adam laughed, "Yup. May as well get some for Sam and Lea at the same time." Turning to them, "We wear some close fitted but stretchy clothes when training, so it doesn't hamper your movements, but allows the trainer, usually Brook, to see how your muscles move, to make sure you are doing the movement correctly. Does it sound good?"

Adam could feel the agreement from Brook in his head and smiled at the four heads nodding.

Brook looked at Jess and Joshua, "Meet us here after we have breakfast for a wolf-run."

Both nodded in agreement.

"After Adam gets your laptops signed out, we're going to go for a nice long morning run. I want to see how strong you are in wolf form as well." Brook told Lea and Sam, "Monday mornings, we do some training after our weekly meeting with the Alpha, if we have time, but meet us for the first session after lunch on Monday, in the training gear." She got six nods of agreement, "Bring your work schedule, so we can work out the schedule for when we will meet for training. Mostly Adam and I have been just fitting it in around all our other commitments."

They moved into other lighter topics, to learn more about their interests. Both girls were interested in reading and were quite surprised at how many books Adam had collected. Finding out his eBook collection was several times the size of his physical one, they were quite astonished.

Eventually they sent the pups off to bed, with theirs walking them to the door to the Beta wings, as their parents helped Jess and Joshua with collecting the dishes.

"If you two would like to get any training or learning, let us know. I don't want you to think you're too old for any learning." Adam said quietly to their two servants, "I want you happy."

"We're fine now. Been reading your photography books, since you said I could." Jess replied, "Your offer of physical training though is nice. I had been considering asking. Think Duncan and Keanna would be interested?"

Adam shook his head, "Martin is already taking care of them. They are getting some specialised training, especially with what has happened to them."

Stretching, he smiled as his pups came back in. "I like your girl-friends; they seem very nice. I especially like the fact they had realistic wishes for jobs, and interests which we could help them with." Adam commented, while they blushed.

Brook hugged them both, "I guess our talk a couple nights ago was worth it, and right on time. Don't worry too much, just keep them happy, and learn to have fun. Now it is time for bed; Adam and I are going to be taking you two for a good run with your girlfriends in the morning, so you need a good sleep."

After giving both their parents a hug and kiss, they headed off to their room. Following them out was Jess and Joshua who also got a hug and kiss goodnight as they took the dishes with them.

When they were alone, Brook smiled over at Adam, "My wolf thinks Sam is Toby's mate but isn't sure about Lea and Robin."

Adam nodded, "My wolf is the same, but thinks the other two could be mates, from the way Robin's wolf treats Lea's. We have a few years before they will be able to tell, so there is no rush right now to have them together. I did ask to have the other kids' room which shares the bathroom with Robin and Toby's room cleaned and made ready, so if they do want to pair off, there is space for them to do so under our eyes."

Brook laughed, "I wondered what you whispered into Joshua's ear."

Adam pulled his mate close, and gave her a kiss, "Finally alone…" he commented as he led her to the bed and smiled, holding her close before they spent an enjoyable evening just the two of them. Even Charlie had taken himself elsewhere.

*****

The next morning all four pups sat at their usual table. He could see all four of the girls' parents glancing over. Catching their eyes, Adam gave them a small nod. He was keeping an eye on them. He didn't know them specifically but hoped to chat with them at some point. The girls were even more eager for the run than the boys, since they knew it was going to push them, even if it was going to be fun.

Doing the quick stop to get the laptops for the girls, they stopped in their suite, and stripped before shifting to their wolves. Jess and Joshua had already shifted and were waiting for them. After some wolf greetings, Wolf-Adam led the way out the patio door, and once outside, Brook took the lead, as she knew the best route for a nice long run. Adam slipped back to run at the back, so they could keep an eye on their six. As they suspected, their pups were already faster than the rest, but Lea and Sam were just having to stretch a little.

Joshua and Jess were a bit slower, and Adam ran with them for a bit to give them some encouragement and kept an eye on them. They decided as they got up, if needed, he'd run at a slower pace with them, while Brook ran faster with the pups.

They both hung in quite well, and never lost sight of the rest of their group. Wolf-Adam was quite proud of them as they came back into sight of the pack house. They did some slow jogs around the place to cool down before heading inside. Charlie had been left behind, as there was no way he could have kept up with their training pace. He was quite happy to see them all. Brook had already put out bowls of some tepid water, as having cold water could cause cramps with their hot bodies. They all were panting as their wolves lapped up the water, but it was a nice run.

Brook and Adam had stayed in close mental contact the entire run, so they could make sure the pace was a good workout but was not too punishing.

All four pups shifted back and were chattering together. They seemed to enjoy their time together. They had just enough time to take a shower and get rid of the perspiration which came with them after shifting from their wolves while still hot before lunch, which was what they planned.

After having lunch, all four pups came back. Adam and Brook helped them get their laptops up and running, then all four did some homework. They all wanted to finish off their assignments. Adam gave them a little bit of help, but mostly they did it themselves.

The pups were released mid afternoon, as they had finished all their work.

Adam and Brook curled up on the couch to watch a couple of movies and enjoy their time together. They just barely made it to dinner —after a hasty shower, so they didn't announce their activities to the entire pack, and quickly resumed their fun before getting to bed at a respectable time.

*****

In the morning, they had got up early, and gathered their various notes for the meeting with the Alpha. When they arrived after breakfast, both Gareth and Maria were there.

Exchanging hugs in greetings, they quickly sat down for the meeting.

"We have one more shipment of sensors expected today. Martin says all which can be installed will be done by Wednesday. There are some which are on top of cliffs, but they can't be accessed due to avalanche conditions. They will be installed when we can, but some are likely going to have to wait till the snow is gone. All the cameras are online." Adam reported.

"Martin advised me there were four rogues who were found lairing at the southern extreme, where we rarely patrol. Since they were peaceful, and hadn't caused problems, we came to an agreement to let them stay there, especially since from the facts found they had been there for over two years. Sadly, they are also from Shadowed River Pack." Gareth commented with a sigh, "I have put through the paperwork to have them reclassified as Lone Wolves and have offered them our protection. They declined the offer to officially join the pack, but I'm going to leave the offer open." He added. He had liked them, it was a strong-looking warrior, his mate, who looked just as tough, and their two pups. All had been wary of him, but were respectful, and surprised they were on the property they claimed as the pack's, even more so they were being permitted to stay. They had been grateful for the protection extended over them, even if they had never expected a pack would do so. "I'm thinking they are a bit burned on packs for right now, but now there are patrols which will visit them once every other week and give them help if we can. I want to show other packs are not like Shadowed River and am thinking on inviting them to the moon night, in a month or two."

Both Betas nodded their heads in accepting the ruling.

"How are the computers and network going?" Gareth asked, changing the topic.

"The network installs for the Deltas are being done; they were put on hold for the security work, but now the close stuff is all complete, they have the time. Erin is handling it all at this point, as it is just labour intensive." Adam provided. "The computers: the seniors all have them but recently realised not many of the Deltas or Thetas are getting them. I am thinking many don't realise they are entitled to have them. I am going to discuss it with those who are at the fire tonight."

The cold snap had ended, and they had got a bit of warm weather to bring it up warm enough he didn't need to layer up as much as he did the week before, so his other idea didn't have to go into work.

"I found our two pups have found girlfriends and found out they had some good aspirations within the pack. Sam was interested in working with Security. I arranged for her to shadow Martin with Toby. Lea is interested in being the Tech Trainer for the pack. I never wanted to do it, so I am going to help her get the training for it." Adam offered, quite proud of the pups, "I am having Robin do some shadowing of me, as he likes being on top of all the tech."

"I noticed yesterday morning you took all four, and Jess and Joshua out for a long run." Maria commented.

Brook smiled, "Yes. Took them on the Delta classification speed run. I haven't told them, but all six passed. Jess and Joshua just barely did. I think if we challenge them, they will be able to cleanly pass it."

"What!" Both Alphas exclaimed, surprised.

"Well, we didn't officially time it, so it wouldn't be a valid trial, but we checked the time when we left and returned. Also, since we are connected to all of them, we also can't be involved. I would like to offer them the chance to train to see how well they can qualify in the Spring Trials." Brook elaborated, amused at their reaction.

"Both Jess and Joshua have expressed they would still want to stay with us and take care of us. I don't know if they would want to complete the Delta qualifications, due to their passive nature. We will assure them even if they qualify, their position with us will be secure." Adam commented, "My wolf watches them almost as much as they do for our pups. He considers them our pups as well, so wants them to have some skills, if only for self defence, so we don't have to worry about them if we have to fight."

"That is interesting. Some wolves refuse to accept pups who are not of their body, yet yours not only accepts your official pups, but your helpers as your pups." Maria commented. "I take it that it is mutual?"

Adam thought for a minute, "I think it is, they have come to us several times for comfort and care. I am certain they at least know we are there as a source of comfort if nothing more. Their bonds in my mind are as strong as Toby's and Robin's." He sighed, "They are stronger than Duncan and Keanna's bonds have been since their attack. The attack seems to have greatly shaken their faith in the security of the pack. I'm not sure on what to do about them. Martin has been letting them stay in the security centre's dorm for the time being. They refuse to go anywhere alone."

Gareth and Maria traded a look, as Brook wrapped an arm around her mate, and his perceived failure with the two to protect them. Looking up at them, Brook commented, "This is hitting him hard, it's the first time he feels he has failed those under his protection."

Maria reached across the table, taking his hand in hers, "You didn't fail them. You were there so fast all the attacker could do is escape and run for their life. If they had been any slower, they would have been caught. I'm thinking you are the fastest wolf we have. Your pleas have gotten the security to prevent it from happening ever again. I don't think those two will feel better until the white wolf is caught. Duncan and Keanna were not physically harmed at all."

Adam nodded, "Yes, I know. It just upsets my wolf so much, and it just passes over." It was such a new feeling for him, it was hitting hard.

Brook rubbed his back, "It happens to all of us." Her care was also very nice too.

Gareth nodded, "You're just going to need to work through it. If we catch the white wolf, he's yours to deal with."

Adam nodded, with a feral look in his eyes as his wolf looked out.

Gareth smiled, "Back to Jess and Joshua, since they are orphans, if you wished to ask them if you could adopt them, you can. Giving them some family ties may be something they want."

Adam smiled, and felt the agreement from Brook, "Well, I think we might. Although I think they would prefer to stay helping us than take on any different duties, at this point. I would help them in any way I can."

Gareth replied, "I have no problems with that."

They spent the next couple of hours discussing some other topics, and ideas for more income for the pack. Their idea of opening a small computer repair shop or to offer internet to the people in the area. With everything going on, they were putting them off till stuff calmed down.

Just before they left, the Alpha commented, "We are trying to contact the Shadowed River Pack but so far, they refuse to answer or return our calls. Even the elders haven't got a response. Keep a good watch out."

Adam and Brook nodded. They would keep a good eye out, especially when their pups were with them.

As they walked out of the Alpha's wing, Adam turned to Brook, "I need a good hot soak before lunch, join me?" He stretched his arms up, feeling stiff.

Brook smiled and nodded, "I could do with one too." She agreed, needing some time to relax.

CHAPTER 25

Questions

Heading into the suite, since they wanted privacy not a shared soak with the pack, they found Jess and Joshua cleaning, not wanting to interrupt, they just waved as they headed into their bathroom to have a soak. They started the water, and made sure they had towels, then climbed in while it filled. Brook added a little aromatic oil to the water, as they lay back together.

"That looks nice. Mind if we join you?" Jess commented, standing at the door.

Adam grinned, "Feel free. Plenty of space in the tub!"

Jess and Joshua came in to join them, letting out a sigh as they relaxed in the large tub.

"We were doing a benchmark test yesterday for the run." Brook commented, "How fast did you think you ran?"

Jess shrugged, "Not sure... Average?"

Brook shook her head failing to hide her grin, "The route we took was a Delta certification test course. From what I saw on the clocks when we left, and you got back, I think you ran it just within the 'pass' time."

"What!" Both exclaimed. Jess sat up fast, sending a wave sloshing around the tub. Both were shocked. They didn't realise they were that fast. Adam had been mostly just jogging the course beside them, it made both feel slow.

"If you want, I can take you on more runs, and we can see how fast we can get you before the spring trials." Adam added. Seeing the alarm in their face, he quickly added, "Even if you pass the Delta qualifications, you can stay being our assistants. We would never make you leave."

"What would we get if we qualify?" Joshua asked. His wolf really wanted to excel and running fast was fun. He could sense both were for the idea.

"Well, you would normally get a better room, but since you're already down here, that wouldn't change. You would get the Delta Stipend and the seniority which comes with the increase in rank. It also opens more options for training if you want to take them farther." Brook answered, "It also means if you need more to help keep us and any who look to us cared for, you can have others who will report to you."

"I would like to try." Joshua answered, after thinking about it, "At worst I get to learn some skills and test myself against other pack members. Our job is secure."

"I think I would like to at least get the training; not sure I want to do the testing," came Jess' quiet reply.

"Well, we will integrate it into the schedule of testing we're starting with you this afternoon." Adam replied.

This is a perfect time to ask them, Brook commented to Adam. She knew he had been considering it for weeks, since he had found out adoptions within the pack happened and were very much easier to do than for the humans, and they had no other close family. She was all for it and would give the two even more security.

"I have been thinking on this for a while," Adam started, "I know you two have no close relatives to go to, so was wondering if you wanted to formalize our bonds, and join Toby and Robin as our pups—"

"Yes!" both yelled out, interrupting him.

Jess threw herself at Adam, and if it wasn't for the water slowing her down and his wolf-reflexes, he would have been pushed into the water. He gathered her up in his arms and held her, as she had tears running down her face, "I thought you'd never ask." She sobbed, happily. He held her close, and smiled, as he noticed Brook had pulled Joshua close to her. He was smiling broadly, even though his eyes were dripping tears. "We had approval from the Alphas as of this morning to ask. We will formalize it at the next Howl. We already have a good bond, so I don't mind waiting."

They stayed cuddled close as they relaxed together. Quickly, they sent notice to the alphas and to their other two pups, as they deserved to know right away.

"We may need a bigger tub." Adam commented, getting a laugh from everyone. With four it was a little bit of a close fit and wouldn't fit the other two, but they didn't mind.

Getting out, they quickly dried off, with Jess and Joshua running off to their rooms to get the new training clothes, they had already picked up, while Adam and Brook got dressed. They headed off to the lunch together.

Reaching the dining room, Adam and Brook guided them to sit with them and their friends, instead of the end table they normally did with other Thetas.

Their friends knew of them if they didn't know them. Both were a bit shy, being with the senior wolves. They were surprised at the greeting they were given, which was quite enthusiastic. Especially when they were told they were adopting them.

After lunch, they headed to the training, meeting up with the four young pups. Jess and Joshua got some more good hugs from all four, especially their new brothers.

Looking at everyone's various schedules, Monday afternoons and Thursday mornings looked like the best fit for the training sessions, for now. Once they were done, Brook told the pups about the run the day before. They were not too surprised they had done it but were surprised to hear all six had completed it in time. They decided they were going to go for a run on Friday evenings too, to get their wolf endurance up higher.

They were expected to work on the training other times as well.

Adam and Brook had fun teaching. They went over their current skills, and just started a new move when it was time to head off to dinner. All four of the young pups were bouncy still. Jess and Joshua went off to visit with their usual Theta friends a bit sore from the hard workout.

After dinner, Adam smiled as he and Brook headed off to the fire pit. They both had started to enjoy the time to relax at the gathering with the lower wolves and give them a chance to find out their thoughts.

Jess had made it out ahead of them and had started the fire. He pulled her in beside him and smiled. Both Jess and Joshua had grins on their faces all afternoon.

"Are you trying to take a second mate?" One voice called, teasingly.

Adam grinned and shook his head, "Nope. I'm adopting both Jess and Joshua as some more pups. I've found I really care about them, and when I found out they had no close relatives, I offered." At the stunned silence broken only by the crackle of the fire, he continued to grin, "It becomes official at the next Full Moon Howl."

There were quite a few wolves who howled happily for them. Many congratulated Jess, and Joshua, who had shown up just as he announced it. Both were startled at how many were happy for them, and blushed.

When they had finished giving them the congratulations, Adam decided it was time to ask the question which had been bothering him.

"We bought the pack computers, and so far, very few Thetas have come to get any. I've been wondering it you wolves are just not wanting them?" Adam asked. Working to not be judgemental, and more just curious. He had just bought the laptops, as they were easier to deal with, and frankly could do almost everything someone could want. PCs could be ordered in if someone wanted one, so far most had just wanted larger monitors to use with the laptop, which they had, along with docks.

Many of the replies were questions about how much they were: nothing; they were just owned by the pack instead of them personally.

He fielded quite a few questions, including many about the fact they didn't know how to use them. Adam smiled at the comment, "I found out Lea was interested in being a Pack Trainer. She's starting to develop stuff for training courses. I'm already going to have her start at the basics, which will include basic handling expectations, how to get help, and how to do the basic navigation. If you have pups, they may already know a little, and the techs can do a little training while you pick the computers up."

Quite a few commented they were going to take a look at picking one up; they hadn't realised they weren't paying for them—well, unless they broke them, as was the general policy for pack equipment—and several almost ran to get them, if he hadn't said they weren't giving them out in the evenings.

They went onto lighter topics, and jokes. There were even some songs they sung. Those who were there as wolves howled accompaniment, giving the songs a depth to the sound, as their good hearing heard slight echoes off the trees around them. By the end, most had joined in the singing, as the songs were ones they had grown up hearing. Adam and Brook used their mate bonds to share the words, so he could sing along with them, as some of them he had never heard.

As a human, Adam didn't care much about music, but as a werewolf, his wolf half was helping him along, giving him the skills of a trained singer, and he was happy to sing out with the rest, and enjoy the evening with nobody judging how others were singing. As was usual, he had many packmates coming up to curl against him for a bit, before leaving and another took their place. Brook stayed on one side, as was normal.

Since the weather was nice, most stayed late. Eventually the fire was allowed to go out and everyone headed out as many had to be up in the morning. Brook, Adam, Jess, and Joshua walked back slowly enjoying the evening.

Not much was said, as all four walked into the room. Adam and Brook stripped, tossing their clothes in the hamper. Turning to the other two, it seemed they didn't want to leave.

"You are welcome to stay and spend the night with us," Adam commented, as he climbed into the bed, making the decision for them.

Jess smiled, and stripped, hopping in to curl up on the side of Adam which Charlie hadn't already claimed, putting her back to him. Joshua was right behind her in hopping onto the bed, with Brook grinning at Adam, and pulling the blanket up over the four of them as she climbed in and snuggling against Joshua.

*****

The rest of the week went by fairly well, with Adam and Brook meeting with the Alpha on Tuesday and Wednesday morning for some training. Both afternoons they took Jess and Joshua, as they had the time the other four didn't, for some wolf-training, under the watchful eye of Martin. Adam excelled, and Martin had to step in and train with him for part of the afternoon, teaching him some tricks of how to force an enemy to disengage who had a friendly in their jaws, while causing the least damage to the packmate.

After the dinner, they had some family bonding time with their four pups. The older two, knowing they were being accepted and wouldn't think of rejecting them now, were starting to come out of their shell. They took all six for a short evening run after their younger pups, and the two girls finished their classroom work, getting back just in time for dinner.

Thursday morning all six pups were waiting for them in the training room when Adam and Brook arrived. They started them on the warm-ups, stretching their muscles. They helped all six work on their skills, and they were showing more confidence in how they were doing it. By the time they sent them for showers before lunch, Adam and Brook also had had a workout, working the six hard, sometimes having them two on one against them.

Lunch revived all six pups a bit, with Jess and Joshua checking on rooms they now covered for cleaning. They had been moved to super-vising several of their Theta friends, but they still took care of Adam and Brook's suite personally, refusing to let anyone else take care of it. Their friends had teased them gently about the promotion, but all seemed to enjoy the change. They had both talked to Adam and Brook about their issues with the staff they now had, and their suggestions gave them the skills to deal with it. Their old supervisor had moved to a recently opened position and with them working to be Delta-qualified, Rein had given them the responsibilities, showing his support.

With the changes Adam started, there were quite a few vacancies, and when they were filled, it left others. It had started to cascade, but it happened at times, and the pack used it to move around on jobs, so they weren't stuck doing the same thing for decades, unless they wanted to stay. All the changes and position shifting could take a year or two to work out, as usually the outgoing wolf trained their replacement; they went from the new wolf just shadowing to them starting with the easy tasks and as they learned the duties more were added, till the outgoing wolf was just sitting back giving advice before moving onto their new position and being the trainee.

With Adam and Brook taking in the two, and being able to mentor them as needed, Rein and Mikan had decided to bump the two to the supervisor role, and reorganised the reporting for the Thetas, as he liked to do at least once a decade, and had found those who wouldn't mind reporting to a couple who were just shy of their majority; it didn't hurt many were already friends with them as well. It would get them good leadership skills for the future, and confided to Adam and Brook he felt the two could even eventually have skills to go even higher.

The four younger split up, with Toby and Sam heading to the Security Centre to help with getting the last of the sensors online and registered. Robin and Lea headed with Adam and Brook to their suite. Lea had been working hard all week to get the basic training course ready, and she was going to do a mock presentation for it.

Leading them into the room, Adam and Brook sat back. Lea was giving off a strong scent of nerves, it could almost be considered fear. Adam's wolf growled and was wanting to tear something to bits, but the human half had him firmly in control. *You would need to tear yourself apart, as it is nerves over giving a presentation, even if it is just a trial of it. Calm down and let me deal with her. Having you upset just gets in the way of helping her,* Human-Adam told his other half.

I guess you're right sighed Wolf-Adam, after thinking about it for a moment.

Adam smiled at Lea, "Come here for a minute, before you start, please?" When she came up, he pulled her in his lap. He knew the scent of a Beta holding her would calm her down the fastest, "This presentation is so we can see how well you did on your first task. I am not expecting perfection, nor does this have a grade you have to meet. Presenting in front of family is harder than anything. For me, it's harder than presenting in front of my peers, which is much harder than doing it to strangers." Giving her a few minutes to cuddle and take it in before continuing, "We will work with you to make the training as good as we can, since we don't have a team of trainers, although we might eventually get there."

Eventually Lea hopped off his lap after a final hug and a quiet thanks. As they were just sitting at the table, they had her use her laptop for the training. The boardroom had been retrofitted to double as a training room, and Adam had the plans to expand some of the controls to the other rooms too. It had a presenter's podium with controls for the lights, and the projector, along with a screen to see what is being presented behind them. The table had power and network ports for a dozen students to be on their own laptops.

By the end of the presentation of the training, Adam was smiling, "If it was a class project, you would have gotten an 'A' on it." He saw her nearly limp with relief she had gotten it right, "I did see some places you could improve..." he went on to work with her on how to make it better. Robin had taken his own notes for any changes he thought the presentation needed, and they worked on a second set when they were done, to make it more for the pups. Most had taken to the new technology much faster than the older members, most of whom had been born before the computer was even thought of, let alone the internet.

It was supper time by the time they had finished. To help her polish her presentation, they had arranged Jess to bring food to them, as Adam was trying to discourage people from using the laptops in the dining room, as from the large amount of food and drink and the limited space, it would put the equipment at risk, much more than with them working and there only being the five of them, and them knowing how to work around food. Not only that, but he didn't want it to get to the point people ignored everyone else around them.

Even Robin was feeling stressed by the time they were done, soon after dinner was done. Conferring silently with Brook, they decided they needed a time to relax. They called the other two pups, and headed to the hot springs in greenhouse, for a relaxing soak.

Adam and Brook slipped into the water and relaxed. Quickly Lea curled up in Adam's lap and cuddled. Wrapping his arms around her, Robin curled up against them watching her with concern.

"It's OK. It's just the nerves coming out after the presentation and the work. I had them too when I started out doing them in college classes. It gets easier with time. Eventually you won't have an issue doing them at all." Adam reassured both pups.

Brook and Adam had discussed it, and although they were too young to know who their mate was, it seems both may have found them, they had several years to let them grow before they would know for certain. If it was the case, all four looked to be ranked fairly senior and they were working to have them learn the skills they needed.

They relaxed and chatted with the pups about how their classwork was going. With technology being available, some of them had started to use it, and an additional class had been started, like what Lea was doing. Quietly she did comment she had gotten the instructor's help, and they together had worked on the two courses, hers more as a training course for the adults, and the teacher integrating it into a classroom for the pups.

Adam looked at her, "That was actually a smart idea!" He praised, alleviating her fears of censure, "It allows for a uniform training of the pups, while you deal with the adults. Eventually, the basics would only be needing to be taught to those who join the pack, not all the members. Then you can do more advanced courses. Monday, we are going to have you do the presentation to the Alphas."

"Th-th-the A-a-a-alphas?" Lea stuttered, going pale.

Adam stroked her back, reassuringly, "Yes, the Alphas. They want to see it, before you start offering the classes. They are scary at times, I agree, but they are looking forward to it. Brook and I will come get you after breakfast. We have you first, so you can leave right after."

Lea didn't see any way out, and it was doing something she enjoyed. Her parents would be happy *she* got to train the alpha. They had been very happy when she had taken the position, as they had said it was a step up. She ended up just nodding, and relaxing from the hot water, and Adam's musky scent of a Beta protecting her. She closed her eyes, as the stress drained away.

*****

Adam smiled a bit later, as Toby was against Brook, and Sam in her lap, as he had the other two. All four were at least dozing, but he though Lea was asleep in his arms. Jess and Joshua sat near them talking quietly with some of their friends.

Let's take them to bed. We can put the two girls in the other bedroom beside Toby and Robin's Adam linked to Brook, Jess, and Joshua. All three gave a wordless agreement.

Jess and Joshua moved to take their two sibs, who were asleep. Grabbing towels, they dried them off, and didn't bother with the clothes, one of their friends had grabbed them saying they'd take them for a wash. They just grabbed their IDs from the pocket, throwing the lanyard around their necks, the four of them took the young pups with them through the tunnel, and up to the first floor. Taking them to their room, they didn't bother putting Toby in the top bunk, but put them both in the bottom bunk. They rolled together to cuddle, without even waking up.

They met Adam and Brook as they came out, and they could see they had done the same thing.

"Time for bed, I think." Adam yawned. He gave both Jess and Joshua a good hug before heading to their room.

Jess grabbed her twin's hand and tugged him to their room, "I think it is a good idea. Want some cuddles?"

Joshua smiled tiredly, and nodded, "You know you don't have to ask, sis."

They ended up curling up in her bed and quickly fell asleep, knowing they had to be up early.

*****

The next morning Adam and Brook woke up refreshed. Adam smiled and rolled over to kiss Brook, "Time to get up. I think we need to go wake the four pups. I'll do the boys you do the girls."

Brook smiled as she woke up and nodded.

After quickly getting dressed, Brook headed into the room Sam and Lea were still sleeping in. Jess, she suspected, had already brought them some clean clothes and were on the desk.

Both were curled up with arms around the other. She gently shook their shoulders to wake them up. Both jumped as if Brook had struck a large gong.

"Time to get up. Breakfast is in thirty minutes. Clothes are on the desk." Hearing the shower turn on, and knowing it was big enough to fit all four, "If you hurry, you can grab a shower with Toby and Robin."

It seemed to work as they were nearly instantly stepping into the shared shower. Group showers were one way they could bond at their young age. Meeting Adam out in the hall, she cuddled against him, her wolf purring in her mind as he wrapped his arms around her.

All four pups came out with smiles, and giggles. Adam and Brook quickly corralled them and took them off to breakfast. Adam gave Brook a look which said 'I don't even want to know' about their giggles. His wolf was relaxing in the back of his mind, and happy the four pups were healthy and happy.

Once they reached the dining hall, the pups headed off to their friends leaving Adam and Brook to head off to their seats. Grabbing some food, and some for Charlie, they headed over to their usual seats for breakfast.

Adam and Brook used the morning to check up on their various techs. The pups had moved back to dealing with the old computers, and the storage room they had moved the equipment to was starting to show how hard they were working. It was comical how much was stuff in the room; he was surprised the first time he had opened the door at how many the pack had accumulated. They had gotten through less than half the stuff stacked on the floor and not yet into the stuff on the racks. It looked like it would keep the pups out of trouble for a few months yet. The groups who were receiving the repaired machines were happy to accept them, as there was always more demand than equipment donated. A few of the oldest had been sold to collectors, and both were happy. The money was handed out to the pups doing work, as getting them sold, when they otherwise would be going to an e-cycler would make sure they were doing their best.

Erin was working her team to get the wired ports in, although some wolves were refusing to have them put in.

Adam shrugged when she told him, "Just making notes about what rooms they are, but not pushing the install. If they change their mind, they can book a time your crew is available." He told her, to her relief. "Worst-case, when they moved out of the room, they can finally be wired."

All the spare rooms were the first done, so they could see how minimally it changed. The wireless phones seemed a hit, but once the novelty wore off, the techs had stopped using them, as their mind-talk was easier, and didn't need any external pieces, although they tended to use them rather than the wired phones for the most part. As such, they had brought in more of the wireless handsets too.

Checking into the security centre, the first thing Adam and Brook did was have a chat with Duncan and Keanna. Both were still badly withdrawn and worse than when he first met them. He had to sigh and pull Brook tight into his arms when they left.

"I think until the white wolf is gone, they won't be able to live normally." Adam commented, sadly.

Brook let out a sigh, "As much as I hate the idea, I think you're right."

Chatting with Martin was fun, as he was acting like a kid with a new toy over all the stuff the sensors and cameras could do. He had set the system to track on one screen a specific patrol. It was jumping camera to camera to follow them as they did the patrol. The big map had all the patrols lit up on it, as known. At times Martin was giggling like a pup at how easy they could now track the patrols.

Heading to lunch brought the surprise: Steve and Chris were back. Both looked like they hadn't had a good sleep in several days but had faint smiles on their faces. Adam waved them to their seats, and grabbed them plates of the food, "You two look wrung out, so I won't ask how the trip was."

Chris sighed, "It was the same as before; even with sleeping pills every little sound of humans woke me up. I am glad to be back. I plan on sleeping this afternoon. Tonight, at midnight the Alpha is having us sworn in." Looking at Steve, "We both decided we're joining the pack."

Adam grinned, "Excellent! Did anyone tell you about the duties we have planned for you?"

Both perked up, waiting patiently for him to continue, silently telling him he was the first.

"Chris, since you have an IT security background much more than I do, you will be officially reporting to Martin but working with me to secure it as much as possible. I have already set up your laptop with the management consoles and information, it is in your room. You will be handling the security audits."

Chris grinned, "Awesome! Just what I was hoping for but didn't know if you wanted anyone stepping on your toes."

Adam shook his head, "I would rather have my paws stepped on to keep the pack safe and secure, than have us hacked, especially by a government. I have tried to get some basic security policies and best practices going, but I am sure you know it better. Let me know of any changes you want."

Turning to the other human, "Steve, since you have a security background, for right now Martin is just having you as a security controller."

Steve nodded; not sure what else he would do.

After eating a bit, "Those jobs are yours as long as you can do them, but if you want to change and be trained for another duty or skill, even if it is wildly different, let Martin know, as he's your supervisor. If he doesn't know who to ask, he'll pass it to the Alphas who will."

Steve nodded, "What about the costs for training?"

Brook answered the question so Adam could eat, "The pack has an education investment which we use for it. At most, you will have some of your stipend used for it, but usually the pack covers the total cost, as long as you pass. You won't have to pay for it out of pocket."

"Stipend?" Steve asked.

"Everyone in the pack is paid a weekly stipend, for any luxury items. Your basic housing and food are covered, as are reasonable clothing costs from the Pack Stores. It's about three-quarters of the pack living here, with others in small cabins in the forest. A few live in the town. The amount you are paid is determined by the skills and rank you have; I don't know how much yours will be."

Steve thought about it, and nodded; it was totally reasonable, as making everyone pay for housing, food, and such out of pocket after being given the money just set up for issues; was better to use it before.

Adam sat back and nodded, taking back over so Brook could finish too, "One thing you will be expected to know is how to fight. Both hand-to-hand and with weapons. Martin will test your current skills and set up your training course. We will be taking you tomorrow to meet our unchosen wolfdogs, like Charlie," Charlie was under the table, asleep against Adam and Brook's feet, "They will bond with you, and will be a protector and companion for you. They have Service Dog designations, so they stay with you all the time. Martin will work them into your training, too."

Seeing them done, and starting to fade, Adam smiled, "I think both of you need a nap." Jess had come at his mental request and was leaning against Adam, "Jess made sure your rooms were all ready this morning. You two have a Delta room, and the bathroom is shared between you. They are shared rooms, but currently there are extra rooms, so each have an entire room. I'll have someone wake you in time to have a shower before supper."

Both nodded and stood, following Jess, as Adam and Brook gathered the dishes; both helped with it most meals, as the kitchen helpers had enough to do without picking up everyone's plates.

They headed for a nap too, as they were standing in as the witness for their oaths and to help them to their rooms after. Saturday was going to be fun; the chefs were already starting work on the food for the Introduction feast. They were also taking the pups for a run after dinner. They had worked out a three-hour trail for them to run.

As they curled up, Jess padded in and slid in behind Brook. All three wolves enjoyed an afternoon nap.

CHAPTER 26

Pack Bonds

Joshua lightly shook Jess awake, *Dinner will be in half an hour. You need to wake our parents up. I'll go wake the two humans.*

Once he got an agreement and knew she was awake, he left as she started stroking Adam and Brook's cheeks to wake them up.

"Time to get up. We need to get ready for dinner."

Adam and Brook stretch as they wake up, and all three head off to the shower.

Coming out, Adam brushed Jess's hair out and put it in a braid while Brook did the same for him, and then while Adam got some clothes for the three of them, since Jess was also about the same size as them, Jess did Brook's hair.

Once ready, Adam put an arm around both and they headed out to the dining room.

As the humans came in Adam smiled, "I see you two are looking much better now."

Both smiled back in greeting. Steve answered, "I feel much better. That sleep was the best I've had... well since we were last here. I'm glad to be back."

"I was the same," Adam said with a reply, "If it wasn't for my mate, I too wouldn't have slept well after meeting her and learning werewolves exist."

Chris smiled, having heard the story of how the two met. He noticed both of them were nearly inseparable, and there was lots of love between them. He hoped he could find a mate like her. He noticed this pack didn't have any stigma against human mates, but he did know some others which did.

Adam smiled as the six pups they were taking for a run all came up, wanting to get out and run as they finished their dinner. Quickly he introduced the pups to Chris and Steve, before excusing himself, to get them ready for the run. Brook got up with him and helped. They had worked out a route to run for today, and since they knew the time a Delta could run it, they were expecting to be that fast. The route was about 150 km, with an expected time of under three hours to meet the qualification.

After stripping, they all shifted to their wolves and followed Brook out, for the warmup. The last one out, Adam pawed at a stopwatch, to start the timer. He'd stop it when they got back.

After starting the pace slow, to warm everyone's muscles up, Brook sped up to the running pace. The younger pups soon caught up to her and were running right behind her.

Adam stayed back with Jess and Joshua, as he and Brook discussed; this wasn't much of a workout for his wolf, the pace was way too slow. Setting a bit slower pace, but one which still challenged the two. He didn't want to hurt them, but he did want to increase their stamina and strength. Charlie was already panting, as this would be a hard pace to maintain, he just didn't want to be left behind.

Staying just in front of the two, to guide them on the path, Wolf-Adam enjoyed the leisurely run, keeping an eye on the two, making them work for the pace, but not having one which would feel like a punishment.

They passed some other wolves on the trails, also out for some exercise, only once were they passed themselves. Jess and Joshua didn't even have the energy to call out to anyone or respond. All their attention was on the run. Adam, on the other hand was able to call out and exchange greetings with those around them. Martin teased Adam he was getting slow when he passed the three, and Adam gave a burst of speed to nip the other Beta, before dropping back to the other two.

Eventually, they made it back to the pack house.

Heading inside, Brook was waiting, sipping on a glass of water, as the four young pups were all still in wolf shape, and lapping up bowls of water, looking tired. Jess and Joshua headed over to the water as well, lapping up some, before doing some cool-down stretches.

Brook handed the stopwatch to Adam after he shifted to human, "Stopped it as you three came in. We were at two hours fifteen minutes."

Adam nodded and accepted a glass of water, looking at the time on the stopwatch: just under the three-hour time they needed to be. Looking at the twins, who were watching him, *Well, how'd we do?* Jess asked.

"Just under the three-hour time, which is what Deltas need to run. I want you two to do a run at that pace at least once a day. Your pace needs to be at fifty kilometres per hour. Or get a Delta to train with you."

Both nodded but were surprised to be able to maintain the pace; if it wasn't for the icy patches in the trail, they would have been even faster.

"OK, bedtime for you four." Brook called to the four pups once they had finished drinking the water.

Jess and Joshua also headed out when they finished their drink.

As they got dressed for witnessing the two humans being sworn into the pack, Brook commented, "Well it was a little workout for me. You get to take them next time, and I'll take the slower ones. They might have been able to get down to the two-hour mark."

Adam smiled, "OK. My wolf would enjoy a faster pace. Be able to get them to go faster."

Giving Brook a kiss before wrapping an arm around her and leading her out the door. They started over to the Alpha's wing, heading into his office, meeting with Alpha Gareth and Maria.

"How was the run?" Gareth asked as he gave both a hug, "The pups go any faster?"

Maria just gave them a smile and a hug, before standing beside her mate.

Brook nodded, "All of them did better. Adam started a stopwatch as we left. Jess and Joshua just under three hours for the hundred fifty kilometres. The four young pups made me work a little and took two hours fifteen minutes. I am going to have Adam work them to make them even faster while I work on the older two."

Gareth nodded, with a broad grin, "I am getting used to them surprising me on their advances. They seem to be very much excelling with the right motivation."

Maria just shook her head, as she had watched them come in, and the pups had still looked eager, even having been run a stiff course.

Adam grinned in reply, "Use positive encouragement instead of negative and it lasts longer. They get a family who cares about them and helps them push to be better. I also tell them *why* I want them to do it, and when they have the skills, what they would be able to do."

There was a knock at the door, as Chris and Steve came in, "Are we late?" Chris asked, seeing the four chatting.

Gareth shook his head, "Not at all, I was just catching up on Adam and Brook's pups," he shared as he gave them both a hug. Adam and Brook got up and gave them hugs after Maria's greeting hug, before standing off to the side, since they were just there as witnesses.

"Are you two ready to join the pack?" Gareth asked.

"Yes." Chris affirmed.

"Yes." Steve replied.

Gareth moved to stand before Chris, "Chris, do you wish to join the Pack?"

"Yes, I do." It seemed his whole life was for this point.

"Will you uphold the Pack Laws?" Gareth asked, holding his eyes.

"Yes, I will." The laws were much more straight forward than the human's which got more restrictive each year. Once he got the idea the Pack was more important than the individual, it was easier to understand them.

"Will you protect all those who are weaker than you, even if it means laying down your life for them?"

Yes, I will, without hesitation." Although currently he was one of the weakest currently, being human.

"Will you guard the pack secrets which are entrusted to you with your life?"

"Yes, with my life." For the pack, he would protect them, as they were becoming more his family than the few actual relatives he still talked to.

"Will you obey those in the pack who are senior to you, to the best of your ability?"

"Yes, I will."

"Will you help your packmates to the best of your ability, whenever possible?"

"Yes, I will." They would also help him, he just had to ask, was also a nice way to live; much better than the humans of each for themselves.

With a grin, "Welcome to the MacLaren Pack, Chris." Gareth leaned forward and placed his head against Chris'. Adam and Brook could feel Chris in their heads, and joined the pack in sending the welcome, as well as hear the howl of welcome the pack gave out. The adding of new members to the pack was always a joyful experience.

Adam stepped forward as Chris winced in pain, moving him to a nearby seat, "Just sit there while Steve is Joined, then we will put you to bed."

Chris gave a slight nod, as Adam stepped back to beside Brook, his head feeling like it had been cracked open.

Gareth nodded at Adam, before turning to Steve, "Steve, do you wish to join the Pack?" he started. The oath was the same for all members. The pups all gave it on their twentieth birthday as part of them moving from being a pup to being an adult member, but they were already part of the pack mind, so the forehead touch was more symbolic, and didn't give a headache as the bond was created.

Steve got the pack's welcome before gasping in pain from the bonding headache.

Brook moved to support him, as Adam got Chris to stand.

Gareth nodded, "Put them to bed, they should be good in the morning. Their minds just need to get over the shock to their systems." He picked up a mug of a tea which would help, as the Alpha also had to deal with the slight change to the bonds too.

Walking them out of the Alpha's wing, they headed away from the stairs, "Going to take you in the cargo elevator; don't want you to trip on the stairs." Adam informed them.

They quickly took them to their rooms. As Adam helped Chris out of his clothes and into the bed, he informed him, "No drugs, not that they would be of any use for it, and they could actually harm the bonding."

Adam picked up the wet cloth and put it over Chris' forehead getting a sigh, "I didn't think it was going to be this bad," Chris commented.

"It should be gone by morning. I'll have someone check on you then. Don't bother getting up until it fades. Your mind just needs the downtime to let the abilities and bond settle in. Try to sleep."

Chris sighed, "OK."

Adam quietly let himself out, and joined Brook, who sighed, "He kept asking for pills; I had to go into detail of what it is doing before he'd lay down. He stopped complaining and accepted the wet cloth after that. How was yours?"

Adam smiled as they went down the stairs, "Down nice and easy. I did tell him to not take anything, and he seemed to accept it."

Brook shook her head, "I wonder if Steve will listen, or be one of those who tries and ends up having the pain for longer."

Adam laughed, "Well if he does, he's just going to make it worse for himself." He thought of something he wasn't sure about, *I never asked, but do they get some wolf-ish abilities by joining the pack without a Mate?* Adam was curious about it, as he skipped that part in his notes, since it didn't pertain to him.

Well, they get the ability to speak mind-to-mind with any packmate, and those within sight. They will need some training on using it. Eventually, they might gain stronger skills for it. Usually, their immune system gets a bit of a bump, as the pack bonds can give some extra energy, and their lifespan is a little longer. It's not even close to what happens with the mate bonds. In some, their senses are a bit enhanced as well, or they just learn to use them better. Brook replied, she knew them from her schooling, but had never thought about them since. *Any other parts of the Pack Manual you skipped?* She teased her mate but was wondering if they needed to review anything else. As a Beta, he had to know, as he could be expected to answer the hard questions.

I glanced over the changing without a mate; I know it was longer than mine, and the Alpha, the Elders had to agree to let them be turned before being opened to the pack for comment. Also, it is more dangerous, as the mate bond does some of the changes, so the body is already a bit accepting to it. Adam answered, truthfully, *I also didn't look too much at the rules for the lower wolves, I spent most of the time on the Pack Laws, and the rules and information for Betas. I know there is a pup who works with the pack lawyer typing them up, so all members can access it when on the network and be able to review it whenever they want. They are also adding in all the amendments, removing all the parts which no longer apply, and are going to take it to the Alpha for approval before I make it available for all pack members. Once it is up, I know I will be reviewing it myself, as with some experience, some parts will now make sense which didn't before.*

Brook smiled as they went in the door to their room, "That is the way of most members. I didn't realise you had done that in the meeting with the lawyer."

Adam shook his head, "It was more of a suggestion on my side, to a comment about needing more copies of the binder, as they kept getting lost. They liked the idea, and it gets rid of the copying copies, and making parts hard to read. I'm glad I don't have to do the typing of the over five hundred pages." He grinned, "It will also make it easier to search for the various parts." He had also suggested to have them make notes of any parts they felt were old and not needed. He suspected there were a great many.

Climbing into the bed, he pulled his mate tight in his arms, "I love you so much," Adam said, as he sent the feelings over their mate bonds which he couldn't put into words.

Brook just kissed him hard, while wrapping her arms around him in a crushing hug, letting her feelings be shared with him too. The edge of their minds seemed to blur as they shared their thoughts and feelings. They could even feel their wolf-halves sharing their own love too. They knew they had a very strong bond and realised without the other, their life would not be worth living.

*****

The next morning, they got up and headed up to wake up the humans. Knocking on the door before entering Chris' room, he groaned as he woke up, "I don't think I moved all night. I'm so stiff!"

Adam laughed, "I know how you feel. A hot shower would be good for the aches, then a good breakfast. We need to go see if Steve followed the instructions; he was really wanting to take drugs." They helped him into the shower to ease the stiffness.

They headed to the next door and knocked, entering Steve groaned, with a hand over his head, the cloth on the bedside table, "Just kill me now. My head is hurting worse than ever."

Brook growled not sympathetic at all, as she could see a bottle of over-the-counter pills on the table, "You took some painkillers after all, I see . The headache is caused by the new mental abilities forming, along with the pack bonds. Painkillers can't stop it, but it slows them down, causing the pain to stick around *longer*. They also make the bonds not form as well as they should." She didn't bother going into the worst parts, as they were very rare.

Adam brought the cloth back, with fresh cold water and placed it on his head, "If you had followed the directions, like Chris did, your headache would have disappeared over night and already be just a nasty memory. Here is an order from someone senior to you, since you didn't take the suggestion: you are to stay in this bed and try to sleep. No painkillers or any other drugs are you to take. If you do so, your pain should be gone by lunchtime, and your Pack Introduction. Take the extra pain as your punishment for failing to heed us in the first place." He sent some disapproval and disappointment over the pack bonds to him, which would help reinforce the lesson.

Steve's eyes got wide as he *felt* the disapproval, which brought tears to his eyes. These two had supported him joining and already he wasn't doing it right. Before he could gather his thoughts to apologise, they had left him in the dark room. This time, he would follow their order.

Adam closed the door quietly behind them, with a shake of his head, "I hope he learns better, soon." He commented to his mate, sadly.

They headed down to breakfast, sitting with their friends, "Don't expect Steve to be down. He decided to take some painkillers." Brook commented, annoyed. She would have to teach him a suggestion from a senior wolf was usually an order. A good trouncing in a training session would do it.

They all shook their heads, "He should have listened." Martin said. Looking at Brook's face, "Want him for a training session trouncing I assume?"

"Yes. Monday afternoon." Was the clipped response.

"You got him." Was the amused response, "I want to watch it!"

Brook gave a feral grin and nod.

Chris came and dropped in a seat, putting his plate down on the table. He was passed a glass with some juice. There was plenty of greetings for him, welcoming him unofficially to the pack. Martin traded him his ID for the permanent one, showing his dual Security and IT designations, with the order to report to him Monday morning for orientation.

Chris turned to Adam, "Steve going to be down?"

"Hopefully for lunch." Adam replied with a growl.

Chris winced, "Ouch. Last night was enough for me."

Brook smiled, "Only would have to go through it again if you change packs." Even then, since the body was used to the bonds, it was much less, usually.

Chris winced and started to eat for a bit, enjoying the company, "Anything planned for the weekend?"

Adam smiled, "Well, for you, there is the wolfdog this morning, then at lunch the formal Pack Introduction, and the meet and greet this afternoon, and a bonfire in the evening. Tomorrow is all free, you'll be able to hang out all you want."

Chris nodded, "And Monday morning is orientation with Martin."

"Have any training clothes?" Martin asked.

Chris nodded, "I think I do; what sort of training?"

"Wear them on Monday; if they don't work, I will get you something else. Hand to hand and staff. I want to see what skills you have." Was the answer.

Chris shook his head, "None at all. I think Steve had some though."

Martin grinned, "Excellent, nothing to unlearn. As you are technically security, you have a certain skill level you must meet. We will get you to the level you need."

After an enjoyable meal, Adam and Brook took Chris off to see their 'dogs.

"I still don't see why I need one; it's not like I'm going anywhere." Chris complained.

Brook laughed, "Well, for one thing: you lack teeth and claws. These are not normal dogs."

Adam had worked out an allegory, "These are to normal dogs, what werewolves are to humans. I can't tell you everything, but the fact they are much smarter than a dog, and they have been known to match a Delta in a fight. Also, unless you know what to look for, they smell like a werewolf, which has deterred rogues from attacking."

Chris nodded, "So they are companion, attack deterrent, and body-guard all in one."

Adam nodded, "And if you get lost, they can get you back."

Chris though about it, "OK, I can see why you give them out to the humans. I take it that is why you have Charlie?"

Adam nodded, "Yes, as when I first came, it was as just a mate to Brook. I didn't start the Turn for two weeks—normally it is even longer; the moment I could be Turned, I took it. I didn't shift for another three weeks. They have a much longer lifespan, so will be around for a long time. They have almost the lifespan of a human." Adam refused to think about the day in the future he would lose his buddy. Even his wolf thought of him as more than a pet.

Leading Chris into the dog area, there was many who sniffed and wandered off. They were around for a good while before one timidly came up and sniffed before whining at him.

Adam bent down, "This is Mika. The name means Intelligent Racoon to the natives." Her colours were greys and blacks, in a wolfish shape, but seemed to have a Racoon mask across her face. Her eyes had startling intelligence to them. "She is fairly shy but is fiercely loyal. She is one of the more intelligent ones we have seen." Many of the most intelligent ones worked with the Enforcers, and as such, often stayed with some of the werewolves in their rooms, going with them on patrols as well.

Chris was stroking her head fur, and both were watching each other.

After a bit, Adam stood up. Mika's shyness vanished, and she was on guard for a moment, as the movement seemed to have startled her. Adam smiled at her, as Charlie came up and gave a wolfy introduction of sniffing noses.

Chris smiled, "I like her. Now what?"

Brook smiled, "We get her registered to you, and get you the gear for when you are off the property."

They quickly registered her, and got the gear, and the information for the papers.

Adam smiled at how Mika stayed as close to Chris as she could, "I think you should head up to your room and spend some time together. It will help the bonding. We'll let you know when lunch is."

Chris nodded, "Is there anywhere I'd have to leave her behind? How about food?"

Adam shook his head, "No, she stays with you all the time. Occasionally I have Charlie stay behind, as when I'm a wolf, he can't keep up with me when I run full out; for you it wouldn't be a problem taking her on a run. For food, she'll eat what we eat. Their digestion is much better than a dog's. There are metal bowls at the end of the serving tables for the bonded 'dogs."

Adam watched as the two headed off to his room up on the third floor.

They walked over to the Alpha's wing, knowing he usually spent his time working on the paperwork. Today, they found him in his lounge reading a novel. Looking at the cover he saw "Dog Got Your Tongue" and laughed at the title. He had happened to have read the story and loved it. He didn't mention he had a copy of it, and the others in the series, in his books. It was more of a sci-fi romance, but it had been written very well.

"How do you like it?" Adam asked.

Gareth, "I love it, so far. Its fun seeing the issues Ray is having; I suspect a Turn would have resolved the issues too. Haven't looked if there is a sequel."

Adam nodded, "I know there are several. I'll show you where to find them tomorrow."

"Steve still had a headache this morning. He tried to relieve it with drugs. I had told him not to." Brook advised with a growl. "Hopefully he listens this time, or he will be introduced to the pack with a splitting headache as part of his punishment!"

Gareth chuckled, "The pain should teach him to listen. If not, he'll have to answer to me."

Adam smiled, "Chris has been chosen by Mika."

"Mika?" Gareth said, surprised. "I am surprised she even had the courage to come scent him."

Adam nodded and grinned, "I'm hoping having a bond-mate to protect will have Mika getting her courage. I startled her, and she was immediately on her guard of him."

Gareth nodded, "It is good. Sounds like it's started." Her shyness was why she had not been used for patrolling.

Looking at the clock, "Well, it is time to go see if Steve is going to miss his own introduction."

Both laughed, "He will make it, if I have to carry him over a shoulder." Brook promised, as she and Adam stood. Charlie nuzzled the Alpha's leg before following them. They headed up, and again knocked on Steve's door before entering.

This time they saw the cloth still on his forehead, and him just starting to move.

"How's the head?" Adam asked.

Groaning as he moved, dislodging the now dry cloth from his head, "The headache is mostly gone. But now I'm very stiff."

Adam smiled, "Then time to go for a shower before the Introduction. We'll wait outside for you. Dress warmly."

Stepping outside the room, Adam headed and knocked on Chris' door, and when it opened, "Time to get ready to head out for the Introduction. Dress warmly." He informed Chris.

Mika was right beside him, as he nodded and closed the door again, to get ready.

Adam and Brook cuddled, as they stood in the hall waiting for the humans. Charlie sat at their feet.

Not much later, they both came out, wearing comfortable but warm clothes, and had their jackets with them.

Steve saw the new dog following Chris, "Who's this?" he asked, crouching down, with a hand extended for her to sniff.

Chris looked down, "This is Mika. She chose to bond with me. She's very shy." Mika had moved like a small child presented with someone she didn't know, hiding behind Chris' leg, and peaking her head out. She had half tucked her tail and lowered her ears as well.

Steve looked at Adam and Brook, "Where's mine?" he asked, half in jest.

Adam smiled ferally, "You decided to take the drugs, when we told you not to, otherwise you'd already have your own. You will have to wait till tomorrow to be taken over to be chosen."

Steve stood up with a sigh, "I guess so." His own actions caused the issues, so he had nobody to blame but himself. The disappointment and disapproval of his actions still stung.

Adam smiled and led the way down the stairs then out the door to the back deck, placing them on the deck, as the pack gathered below them.

The Alphas came up and howled to get everyone's attention. This was the first time Steve and Chris had seen exactly how large the pack was. They knew the number but seeing the pack as faces—well other than those who were providing security. Seeing almost three hundred werewolves together was quite intimidating. Chris had the advantage of Mika, who was pressed against his leg, to reassure him he was safe.

"We are here to welcome two new members to the pack!" Gareth started. They knew they had been helping with the sensors and securing the pack. He didn't need to introduce what they were going to be doing. The humans were given as rousing a howl of welcome they gave Adam. "This is Chris!" Another pause, "And this is Steve!" and a third howl was given.

Once they calmed down Gareth smiled, "Show our newest members how we are thankful of them joining us! Show them how we party!" A louder howl echoed off the mountains as they started the music and the food, which had been started driving those downwind to distraction, was started to be handed out.

The Alpha had the two new ones eat with him, introducing them to the Elders. When they were done eating, Martin came over to introduce them to some of the other members. Adam was glad he didn't have to do it.

He used the time to mingle with the pack, and chat with those he didn't often get to see. Being a Beta, meant to use this time to chat and get a feel of the pack. He and Brook were keeping an eye out. He had seen Toby and Robin curled up with Sam and Lea, with other pups around them. Jess and Joshua were hanging with some young Deltas and some Thetas.

Adam's wolf was forward, and sniffing to get more packmates' scents, committing them to memory.

"You!" called Rein, a glare in his eyes, but his mouth was failing to hold it and going to a smile, "I'm very annoyed with you!"

"Me?" Adam asked, not sure what was going on.

"I'm losing my best woodworker because of you!" Rein mock-accused.

"What did I do?" Adam asked, even more confused. He didn't know of accepting anyone from Rein's team.

"He starts Monday doing programming for a company. He could only do it because of your network enhancements!" Rein glared.

Adam smiled and shrugged, "Sorry, not my fault. Maybe bring on some pups as apprentices? I have been working to avoid making waves so didn't recruit from those who hadn't already posted they wanted a change."

Rein lost it and started to laugh, "Guess I can't scare you. You didn't ask him, and he's going to be starting to work for a human company, remotely." He was a bit annoyed at loosing the worker and with almost no notice, too; he would have to train the replacement himself. "I already have three pups, one of which was from the four you sent for punishment. He had asked to stay on and work with the wood. He seems to have a knack for it. I also have ten wolves applying for the one position. Change is good, as are new ideas. I have already been able to streamline several tasks which each took me all day and now I finish them all in a morning due to newer computers, a fast connection, and some updated software."

Both smiled and hugged him, "I'm glad it is the case." Adam commented.

The pack didn't limit the member's employment, nor did it force them to live even in the territory, although Adam had learned, some changed packs when they moved near another pack for work. There was some industrial work near the pack's territory, so they had quite a few labourers who worked there; their wolf-strength and stamina made the hard tasks easier to do. Others worked and lived in the towns, not wanting the long commute and stayed at the pack on their days off.

The rest of the day and evening was like Adam's own introduction, although he had arranged for some warm blankets for the two humans, since he knew how fast humans could get cold. His own turning bite scar had started to fade, showing the changes were nearly complete. Until it did, it was unlikely he could shift to the were shape. At the same time, he would have to be careful of who he bit, as he could turn someone, which was one downside he would deal with.

CHAPTER 27

Chosen

The next morning when Adam and Brook met Steve at breakfast he complained, "I'm glad the headache is finally gone." Everyone at the table laughed, as his indiscretion had made the rounds of the pack already.

"One of the reasons we do it at midnight, where you can sleep for several hours, is so it can disappear," Brook commented. "Unless you disregard what you are told, and try to use drugs, it's usually gone before the next morning." She commented with a bit of a disgruntled growl.

"Sorry," Steve commented, not wanting another dose of the disapproval or disappointment. He didn't know those could cut his mind so deep. He was going to work to not feel them from those he respected in the pack again. He had realised he nearly broken his pack oath within hours of giving it. He had made a mental vow to work on honouring it, but since he had been living alone, he was going to need to work on it.

He had not got much sleep over night, as he had been one of the last to head off from the fire, only about three hours before, as he had been very much enjoying himself. As nothing was planned for today, if his stomach wasn't trying to gnaw his spine, he'd still be in bed.

"Ready to get your wolfdog?" Adam asked pointedly, seeing his plate empty. Adam refused to give Steve any sympathy for what was self-inflicted. Brook's annoyance was shared, along with a feeling he'd disrespected her.

Steve nodded, deciding sleep could wait; he had seen what Adam and Charlie, and now Chris and Mika's bonds were, and was envious. He had dogs growing up but hadn't been able to find a place he could afford to have one in the five years since moving out. He had read the chapter on them several times and knew they would have almost the same lifespan as him, unless he was Turned, which he was gratefully looking forward to. The worst part of owning dogs was of them being shorter lived.

Steve raced to his room to get his jacket and came back, knowing they were going outside. He panted a little as he got back down to Adam and Brook, waiting at the door. Both nodded, but it seemed they were still annoyed at him; he hoped his good behaviour would help get their relationship back to the friendly terms it was before his mistake.

As they headed out, Steve decided the best would be to take the first step and apologise, "Ummm, I'm sorry I disregarded your comments about not taking any drugs for the headache," he said quietly.

Brook and Adam stopped, and turned to face him, "You were reckless in taking them." Brook stated, a little pleased he decided to apologise, "The decision could have harmed you much worse."

Steve was taken aback, "How much worse?"

"You could have been out with the pain for a month, or more. Or it could have affected your brain, you could have even had seizures." Brook elaborated, going over what he would have read in the details provided, "Since you had been bonded to the pack, if the seizures had caused your death, it would have hurt everyone in the pack. Having a death is hard on a pack; having an unexpected one is much harder. When there is fighting, your mind can be ready for it, so it hurts less. On one so newly bonded, where everyone is in anticipation of greeting new members, and the official welcoming, it feels like a knife in your head."

Adam wrapped an arm around her, picking up the train of thought from her, "Just after she became an adult, ten years ago, they had one do that. From what she remembers, many of the pack were down for a week."

Steve got paler the more she described, not wanting any of those complications, "Then I am very sorry for putting everyone at risk."

Brook gave a feral grin, "I'll forgive you tomorrow."

Steve knew he was in for something and was feeling doom was coming, "What's tomorrow?"

Brook's grin grew feral, "I get to see how much physical training you've had. And I will be seeing if we can use you as a nail."

Steve shuddered at the smile since it promised pain in his future, and muttered quietly to himself, "I sooo deserve it, but it's going to be painful."

Adam and Brook heard it and laughed before they led the way to the kennel area.

Just outside it, Steve realised one thing, "Wait... you became an adult ten years ago, but it would put you at thirty!"

Brook smiled, "Yup, thirty-one, end of February."

"But you look twenty!"

Brook grinned, "Thanks!" She sobered a bit, "Wolves age at a slower rate; even those turned. How old would you say Adam is?"

"Twenty or Twenty-One?" Steve guessed.

"Thirty-Two." Adam answered, getting into the teasing. He grinned at Steve's stunned look and explained, "From the time a Wolf is about Twenty, they age at a fifth of the rate of a human. Those turned, their body slowly regenerates till they are in line with the wolf aging."

Turning and heading into the kennel area, the wolfdogs started to come up and sniff Steve. Unlike Chris, Steve was chosen after only about a half hour.

This one was a solid dark stone-grey colour, but also had an intelligent look. If they were on a rock, you'd be hard pressed to see him. He had nearly pushed Steve over when he crouched down and was head-butted playfully.

"This is Dunstan. His name is an old Anglo-Saxon name meaning dark stone." Brook informed them. She liked to know the history behind names.

Steve grinned up at her, as he wrapped his arms around Dunstan, "I can see why. He's perfect."

Adam grinned, "Come let's get your gear for him, and then you can go bond." Seeing the dark circles under his eyes, "And maybe have a nap. I know you were up most of the night."

Steve stood, and Dunstan came and gave Charlie a sniff, before going to lean against the back of Steve's knees, while wagging his tail. Steve just flicked Dunstan's ear hard, and he stood beside him and looked up, returning Steve's glare with a canine-innocent face.

Adam and Brook grinned at each other, and shared their amusement silently, *He's going to be a handful for Steve. He's almost been renamed 'Mischief' several times. He's one of those who likes to get into trouble, but in a crisis he's one of the most solid and reliable.* Brook commented.

Picking up the collar and leash was fun as Dunstan insisted on carrying it and started to gnaw on it. So it didn't get damaged, Steve put the collar around Dunstan's neck, and the leash balled up at the back of his neck. The papers he signed, Steve noted Dunstan was five, but he still acted like a pup.

Seeing dog packs on the shelf behind the counter, he inquired, and after a discussion on which to get, Dunstan ended up outfitted with a reasonably sized pack as well. Heading away, after getting a wave from Adam, the two headed up to their room for a nap and some bonding time together.

Adam had become intrigued on getting a pack for Charlie. After a bit of a discussion, he was outfitted with a larger one. It was so when they did the running trips to Longview Pack, he could help carry. Adam and Brook had packs which were designed so they could be worn comfortably in human, were, or wolf shape, and easily removed in any form by themselves. Getting them on when they lacked thumbs as wolves was a different matter. While difficult, it wasn't impossible, although having another put it on you was usually what happened.

Heading off to their place to relax, as they still had most of the morning free. Brook ended up challenging Adam to run the route they took the pups on last. The Alpha speed was to do it in an hour and half. She wanted to see how fast he could run; the last Alpha had set the record at seventy-five minutes.

After some grumbling, Adam admitted his wolf wanted to see how fast he could be. After having Charlie stay with Brook, even though he was fast for a wolfdog, he was still much slower than a werewolf.

After shifting in their room, he did some stretches and warmup, before getting ready. Brook shouted "Go!" and he was off.

Wolves on the trail were spreading the word there was a speed trial being run, and to get clear. Some miscalculated on how fast he was moving, and nearly were run over, even with the warning, forcing him to nearly stop several times, and a few others to slow down. Using every fibre of his wolf's ability to run the course, they skidded around hairpin turns and bounded over the boulders. His tail was also used a fair amount to counterbalance. The last bit he dug his claws into the hard-packed snow and ice and sprinted.

Brook was astonished how fast he ran: ninety-five minutes. Five minutes short of the Alpha speed trial. Adam slowed down and did some jogging around the pack house, and the fields close by to cool down, stopping to stretch at periods. Gareth had caught wind of it and had been standing beside Brook as Adam finished. He plucked the stopwatch out of Brook's hand and stared at it. Some colour drained out of his face. If he had pushed it a little more, or had better surfaces and nobody interrupting his stride, he would have passed his own personal best of eighty-four minutes.

Adam finally came in, panting. Brook tossed a blanket over him, so he didn't get chilled, as Adam came up and lapped up a big bowl of water, *Well? How did I do?*

That was fun! I want to do it again! Wolf-Adam commented to Brook and Gareth, while sending some pleasure of the run to his other half.

"Ninety-five minutes. Five minutes off the Alpha Standard for the route they took, *on clear ground*." Alpha Gareth commented. "You took the whole track, no shortcuts?" He asked, still not sure how Adam could be Alpha fast; he hadn't even finished Turning. Brook was currently the fastest after himself and Maria and had run it in ten minutes faster than Adam had at a spring trial, with clear ground. If the ground was clear, ten minutes faster likely would be easy.

Brook just laughed at Wolf-Adam's comment.

Once Adam had cooled down, he shifted back, pulling a dry blanket around himself, "Yes, this was just a test to see how fast I really am, not one to pretend to be faster than I am." Seeing the shock on the Alpha's face, he quickly reassured him, "I am not looking at replacing you. I do not have the skills or experience to do your job, nor do I want it. I may want to in a couple hundred years, but not any time soon. I have so much to learn first." He decided to flop down on a sofa and relax. His wolf was very satisfied with the run, but since the Alpha was there, he was alert and listening, even as their mate flopped down on the sofa beside him.

Gareth smiled as he sat on the sofa facing Adam and Brook, "Well, it is a relief. I wish I knew you were running this, as there is some information I need to tell you."

Both Brook and Adam sat there, giving him their undivided attention.

"When you sparred with me, you used moves and a style I last saw with my grandfather, Ralph. I took over as Alpha when he stepped down about a hundred years ago, and he became our head trainer. He died about sixty years ago, to the pack's great loss." Gareth had to stop, for a moment, as it was bringing back memories.

Both Brook and Adam were riveted, as much was not in the pack's history, just oral stories.

After a few deep breaths, Gareth continued, "What I am telling you here cannot be spread around. You can tell your pups, but only when they are of age." Gareth waited for agreement and got a nod from them both. "I have discussed it with the Elders, and it is more than just your fighting skills, Adam; you seem to have many of his mannerisms, and forward thinking. He had designed this place to last, but still be able to accept changes, and enhancements. He saw the rail line, highway, and electric grid coming in, and urged me to work with them, and get us connected. He lived just long enough to see us get power into here, instead of having to use oil lamps." There were still a few rooms which had them on the walls, but they no longer had the piping full of oil, it had been cleared once they no longer used them, as a fire hazard, so had required installation of the electrical system.

Gareth held up the stopwatch, "And it looks like you also have his speed." He turned and looked at Brook, "If you worked hard, you too would be able to get down to the Alpha standard. You are off by only five minutes."

Brook gasped, "You think so?" She hadn't bothered trying to go faster, as she already outpaced almost everyone. She last did the Spring Trials when she was twenty-five, as she didn't like to rub it to the rest of the pack on her skills.

Gareth nodded, and decided to share his thought, "We are almost too big here. I am considering before I step down, it is likely we will need to split the pack in half. I think you may be the Alpha for the other half. I want you to study hard and work on the fighting skills. I know my Seconds are wanting to retire, and they deserve to. They have served both myself and my grandfather well. In a few years, we can look at having you start to step down and slip someone to take over the IT stuff, or at least day to day, and start having you train as my Seconds."

Both were astonished at the honour being placed before them, even Brook was stunned. Her wolf wasn't and just preened at the chance to shine. Adam's wolf was just thinking it was his due.

After blinking for a bit, they nodded.

Gareth smiled, "Right now, lets keep it quiet. There are enough changes even some of those who aren't opposed to changes are starting to grumble. You two just train to get to the peak of your skills. Due to the age of my Seconds, I am going to discuss it with the other Betas and the Elders, to see if there is much opposition to you two taking over some of the traditional roles they cannot do, like leading the pack if myself or Maria can't. You basically will be placed in third position of the pack. This change will be gradual, and over several years to decades. We have no need to be hasty on this."

Adam nodded, "I already have learned to delegate much of my duties. Could we have permission to let some of my staff know, so they can know why I am delegating much of what people would see as my duties? I am thinking of just saying we're being groomed for being future Seconds would be enough."

Gareth thought about it, then nodded, "It would satisfy them enough they wouldn't see beyond that. Do think about who would be relieving you. Also, keep an eye out for good Seconds. They are very hard to find; they seem to only be there when you are needing them."

Adam and Brook nodded in agreement.

Looking at the clock, Adam smiled, "No wonder I'm hungry, it is time for lunch."

Gareth laughed, "In that case, let's go eat!"

Lunch was a nice, tasty chicken dish. Adam and Brook discussed the details silently for their training. They were at the point they more of just needed to work on their skills. Mostly, they were working on hand-to-hand; they were planning on learning weapons later.

After lunch they decided they needed some private time and headed for their hot spring. Shifting, Adam and Brook played a bit of tag on the way there, with Charlie following along as well. Arriving, they shifted, as when in wolf, thinking complex things was a little harder, as their wolf was more forefront and tended to think more in the *now*.

Laying back in the hot water, Adam pulled Brook so she was laying in his lap. For a while they just lay there and enjoyed being together, up to their necks in the hot water; the only sound being the trickle of the water.

"It sounds like I would really have liked the old Alpha." Adam started, into the quiet.

Brook didn't bother moving or even opening her eyes when she commented, "Yes, I always thought it too. My parents said the pack lost much of its drive to change when he died. He became the Alpha for this part, when the pack last split, back in Scotland in the late 1500s. He helped the pack move here and designed the original pack house, and the concept for this one was his vision."

"My wolf wasn't surprised at Alpha Gareth's offer of being Second, the feeling I was getting was 'it's about time'. How about yours?" Adam asked.

Brook chuckled at how he described his wolf's thought, "Mine wasn't surprised either and thought it would be a good challenge but thinks we would be good."

Adam kissed her head, "I'm just getting used to being a wolf and waiting for the final changes, so I can start learning the more advanced abilities. Now we have the addition of being offered the Second." The last part was almost a whine. "I wasn't wanting to give too many more ripples to the pack, and just learn and settle in." He had no interest in leading a pack. He had a mate, and it is all he had ever wanted. That he had pups already was just even more enjoyment. He would be happy if he had just been a tech or working with the network. The fact he was being pushed higher and higher was making him nervous, but other than to his mate, he would never tell anyone.

Brook smiled, and sent some love, "Changes like the one we are being offered tend to be slow and gradual. With our long lifespan, we prefer to have stability at the top. For an Alpha, they spend nearly a century learning from the current one and slowly taking on duties. It also allows the pack to relax and know if the worst happened, and the Alphas died, there was another to take their place."

Adam hugged her tight, not liking the morbid though, "We don't officially have one, right? From the pack laws, then the Seconds take over and become the Alphas, if there isn't Next-Alphas already trained, but with how much older they are, would put the pack in a bad way."

Brook nodded, "Yes, they should have had their replacements trained and taken over a couple of decades ago and be retired to being Elders. Next Alpha? We have two, but they are off training, so haven't been formally given the position, and haven't any experience for the role. From the discussions with the Betas and Deltas, there has been concern about who would lead the pack; the seconds can't, their wolves no longer have the strength. Rein has no interest, and flatly refused to move higher. Martin is the same. Usually, one who wasn't born a Wolf doesn't get the opportunity to even be as high up as we are; most are like Chris and Steve, at best a Delta."

Adam sighed, "And it causes some issues within the pack, as I have not been raised with the abilities and knowledge, there are gaps and stuff I don't quite get."

Brook smiled, "Yes, you are doing quite well for only being a wolf for a couple months. It usually takes up to a century of living as a wolf before some who are turned 'get' being a wolf and stop trying to over-lay human concepts on the pack. You are past that point already and working to just think as one of us."

Adam chuckled, "I love reading werewolf stories, and had thought about what and how they lived. Most stories just had them being human with the ability to change shape, but with all the human morals and ideas. I always chuckled at the idea of one who was body-shy and need-ing to go behind a tree to change, and being all embarrassed when one changes back to human to do something which needs hands. Or even more so, ones where the old Alpha would just dump the title on their child when they turned eighteen and had just found a human mate."

Brook laughed, "Those always cracked me up. An eighteen-year-old has no life experience. Unless they had a good support behind them, and listened to them, the pack would likely fail quickly, as most pack members would not feel safe and would move to another pack. Espe-cially with how they seem to ignore or worse bully the low members of the pack." Sobering up, "Even us, would be some of the youngest, so I think it is why Alpha is wanting to keep it quiet, as from what I heard, he was fifty before he got tapped to start to learn the Second's role, and learned it for several decades, before starting to learn the Alpha's with his approval for several more decades before they spit the pack."

Adam hugged Brook, "I was expecting to not even get what I have here and now, for a very long time. Just having you in my life was more than I expected. Everything else is just bonus."

Brook moved, leaning her head back and kissed her mate, "I love you too."

Adam held Brook close, "Back to the Second role, I'm thinking we should accept it."

Brook smiled, "I agree, but keep it low key, and allow us to learn the skills needed. Both of us need to qualify at the Alpha level, as the Seconds take over while the Alphas are unable to lead."

Adam nodded, "Well, my wolf is eager to excel, and help the pack to the best of their abilities. He has been pulling me more into a leadership role. As a human, I hadn't ever had a leadership position and didn't really want one. I was always too worried about being left without any position from a minor issue, or the number of decisions which were politically decided, not what was the best for those who were needed. Here, there are much less issues and I'm much more interested in leading. Here, everyone works together for the pack, instead of just for themselves to get ahead. It's a much better feeling."

Brook grinned at her mate, "And you have been excelling at being a leader; you seem to attract loyalty, and a drive to perform. You also can understand when someone is having issues and needs to have a break. You expect lots, but you provide the support for the person to excel."

Adam blushed, "You say the sweetest things!"

Brook laughed, after a moment Adam joined in.

When they calmed down, "Now, who should we tell, and how much?" Adam asked.

Brook thought for a minute, "Erin for sure, and our pups. Erin, as she would probably start taking on more duties, and eventually take over. Our pups, as they would be most impacted. Erin, for now, just needs to know she will be taking on more work and starting to make the decisions." It took a minute to think, "Jess and Joshua should know more, but most should wait till after their birthday. I'm thinking once we have confirmation we are going to be moving to be trained as

Seconds, we can let all four of our pups and Erin know we are being groomed for a senior position, but they can't say anything till its official." She knew there were only three positions which were more senior than their own. So, the fact they were being trained for it, likely would be known fairly quickly, even if they asked them to not pass it on.

Adam nodded, "Once they have been sworn in as adults, I think we should take Jess and Joshua into our confidences and be fairly open with them, then if we have to do something which can't be told to the pack, we would be able to have them cover for us." Stopping for a moment, he thought hard, "I think we should offer them the option to be our personal assistants for when it is known. It typically is a Delta role for the Alphas and Seconds, isn't it?"

Brook grinned, "I like it; gives them a promotion while keeping them close. What about Toby and Robin?"

Adam shook his head, "Not sure we could tell them what we are being groomed for; it would be a question for the Alpha. Since Toby is having a leaning for security, we could have Martin groom him to be eventual Security Lead, and have him as his assistant, if he can pass the tests to qualify. Robin, I would want to keep close."

Brook smiled knowingly, "You see yourself in him, right?"

Adam nodded, "Yes, I do. I think when he's older, he may be able to take our place. I want to make sure we raise him right, and make sure he has the skills to be a good leader, even if he doesn't become a Second, and stays as a Beta. But also, to make sure he doesn't become spoilt. He's going to have to work and earn his privileges. And we will make sure Toby does too."

Brook smiled and nodded, laying back to just relax against her mate before they headed back for bed. Monday morning was going to come far too soon.

CHAPTER 28

The Attack

The calm before morning was split by noise, as both Adam and Brook were awoken by a loud alarm going off. Brook rolled out of bed, hitting the ground in her wolf shape. *Get up, and shift! That is the attack alarm!* she yelled into Adam's mind.

The pack hadn't had the attack alarm sounded when Duncan and Keanna were attacked, as it was only a single wolf, who was already retreating. There was no need to have all the non-combatants evacuated to the shelter.

Adam tugged clear of the sheets, before shifting. Thinking about the humans, he realised they were supposed to have their orientation this morning, so wouldn't know what the alarm meant. He had only heard recordings of it and made a mental note to re-record it better, as it didn't sound anything like the recording. *Steve, Chris. Pack is under attack. Get to the Security Centre immediately.*

Getting a sleepy grumble from Steve as he bounded after his mate and Charlie out the door before steel shutters slammed shut over the windows and the doorway, *This is an order. Pack is under attack; you aren't trained. Get to the Security Centre.* he ordered, putting the full weight of his seniority behind it, so he would get moving.

Already on my way with Mika, Chris sent.

Jess, Joshua: Check to make sure Steve and Chris make it to the Security Centre immediately. If they are still in bed, you drag them out and down there. Then you stay there with them; tell Martin you are under his orders for now. Adam ordered bounding after his mate, since she seemed to have some orders on where to go and be. They were running directly north and were being joined by other wolves. He got a wordless savage agreement to the order.

Robin and I are securing the pups and Thetas in the saferoom with Lea and Sam; we have our staffs and will be the last ones in. Toby called.

All Techs and the tech-pups are secured or in their stations. All four of your pups are secured; Toby and Robin were a big help and are guarding from inside the saferoom. Pack house is now confirmed locked down. Erin called a couple minutes later. As they reported to him, he was their point of contact. Erin oversaw the securing of the pack house and managing the Deltas who guarded it.

Both halves of Adam were relieved the pups were already doing their new job: being senior pups. He sent a wordless acknowledgement, but as he could smell the attackers, if not see them, turned his mind to the Alpha who was giving out orders.

Thanks Adam replied to Erin. *All of mine are secured. Pack house is now confirmed in Lockdown.* Adam called to the Alpha. Adam knew the procedure, and as he had worked with Brook, he would deal with any communication out they needed, and Brook would get their position and orders then lead to their spot, and he'd just follow. There was a quick broadcast from the Alpha that everyone was secured and the Pack house was in full lockdown, so everyone knew their pups and loved ones were safe and could keep their minds on the attackers.

Now Adam could pull his attention close; he was getting a little angry about the intruders. He worked to control it; anger he could temper and use, but not mindless rage. He worked with his wolf to control their anger, wanting their thoughts to mesh, as they would need to work together.

Head North-East, we're going to bracket them. Brook called.

Thanks for the security; we had notice just as they stepped on the territory before they had even started to prepare. The scouts who are watching them, see them preparing to attack, not ready for it. The Alpha said just to Adam and Brook, a savage pleasure felt in it. *We get to turn a stealth attack on its head and take away the element of surprise.*

Glad to help, Adam called back, *Maybe even get to have a surprise counter-attack?* he added with a false innocence as he followed Brook to the North-East, with some others following them. Getting into position, Adam crouched down right beside his mate, opening his mind to her, so she'd know his moves, as he felt her do the same. That way they could work as one and know each other's moves before they did them. Charlie was crouched on his other side, keeping watch. He would stay as close he could and watch his back; it was what he was trained to do in this situation. He would attack any wolf who wasn't a packmate who got too close, unless he was ordered not to, or to override his training with other orders.

You two are to make sure the white wolf doesn't escape, if you see them. Alpha Maria ordered them. As they were not human, deadly force was always authorized, unless they surrendered, Adam remembered from the Pack Laws. Surrender was by showing belly and neck. He wanted to capture the white wolf, and to capture the Delta who had attacked Keanna. He had gotten them to give him a mental image of them, and of their scents, but they didn't have one of them in wolf form.

Ready, Brook called out, as their group was in position. Since she had experience with doing the groups like this, Adam had instantly let her take control. He was there to help her, and protect her back, this time, as he also learned how to do so. It also freed him up, for if he needed to suddenly go after the white wolf.

The wind was a cold arctic wind from the north, so until they moved the group behind the pack, they were all downwind, and were getting fairly close without being detected. Even Adam knew how the wind could change direction, and steal their element of surprise, so was ready to spring into action if it did.

Sentry, ten metres ahead, Adam told their group. They were hidden in some bushes, and with his dark colours, Adam was hiding in some shadows. The stars were just starting to fade with first light.

This is the Shadowed River Pack who is attacking us. Alpha Gareth told everyone, *In contravention of the Inter-Pack treaty by this unprovoked attacking us, their pack is now considered Rogue. The elders have contacted three other packs, and they have confirmed it. Take any who surrender, but I want none escaping. The Alpha is mine.* The last was underlaid by a nasty growl, which promised pain before they died.

That part of the laws, and the treaty, had interested Adam: Three packs had to agree unanimously the pack had gone rogue and have three documented cases: The unlawful calling Duncan and Keanna Rogues when they weren't, the attack of the white wolf on them, and now this attack. Adam knew they had been looking to see if they could find any other pack who would go on record for it, but none would; they feared retribution. Now they had the third case, they could get the other packs to agree they were the ones attacking, triggering the fight condition. There was a part in there about other packs supporting them in their fight, but with the number of wolves they had, he doubted they were using it. It was also how they were already ready to fight, and not fighting a defensive battle, but were taking it to the aggressors. At best, the reinforcements were an hour away.

Now they were considered Rogue, their lands were now forfeit, any who participated or supported in any of the attacks were now Rogues, and could be killed on sight, and nobody could support them in any way, as it would risk them personally being labelled rogue too. Single wolves could challenge the designation and beg for leniency, but it was up to the Alpha to give it. The non-attackers would be folded into other packs, and the Rogue Pack would cease to exist.

Brook gave a mental gasp, *The last pack which was made Rogue was in the sixteenth century!* She whispered to Adam. It was totally under different laws, as this inter-pack treaty didn't exist then. This is the first use of the rules in the Inter-Pack Treaty to make a rogue. It was not often an Alpha—or the pack as a whole—would willingly open themselves to that sort of action, as it was basically the death of the pack, and an Alpha normally thinks of the pack more than himself. The help from the others in the Treaty would likely be helping with the fight, but it was for the future; they had an attack force here and now.

The last group moved in at the alpha's order cutting off the pack's retreat, but also letting them know they had been found.

Moments later, the two scouts they could see went on alert and started scanning around. They both had a sword out but were still in human form. All of their pack were in Wolf or Were forms, for the better senses and abilities.

They quickly overwhelmed the sentries they had spotted, and flushed two more out, as they tried to bring a gun to bear, they were knocked flat from behind. A third saw them and threw away his weapons and threw himself on his back with his neck exposed; he surrendered. You could see he wanted to get out of this alive. He was one which may get leniency.

Two other sentries were taken alive, one had given up when he had Adam land on him as he fell backwards, realising he'd be dead before he could aim his gun, let it fall from his hand before interlacing them on top of his head and baring his throat. The third hit his head as he was taken down, knocking him senseless enough for the Were in their team to take control of him.

Several had packs of gear, first aid and were-strength cuffs and plenty of rope. They quickly secured the ones they captured to a tree, cuffed, leaving a wolf behind to guard them, till some Deltas could come to take them to the secured lockup cave.

Moving on, they encountered several more sentries and overwhelmed them with their numbers. Two had gotten off shots but had missed when the wolves dodged. Two of the pack got deep knife wounds when they failed to dodge enough when attacking, but they were not too bad, it just took them out of being able to use the limb, and after a quick pressure bandage to close it, were sent to guard their prisoners, and go to Medical when they went back. One of the healthy wolves who was guarding the prisoners would be sent out when they arrived.

Adam was growling lowly, not liking having *his* wolves injured. The two who had knifed them had died, as their group mobbed them following the yelp. Wolf-Adam was savagely pleased. His human half was a bit stunned, as this was his first experience with this side of the wolves, but he was trying to understand, and get rid of the human notion of every life had to be saved, even those who were unable or unwilling to live by the rules. When the lifespan was on average of four-hundred years, it was not feasible to incarcerate offenders for the time; the only option was to kill them. Saving the offenders, he had read, would also force a rift between the two halves, and make the wolf side harder to control, as they would continue to consider the attacker an enemy and threat to be destroyed. He hadn't really understood that part, but feeling his wolf, he could feel it was true; his wolf would never give up trying to bring what he felt was justice to the other.

The human half had decided to not think about it, so he could focus on dealing with the threat; he would have to deal with it afterwards, but it could be done in the privacy of their suite. He slipped back, letting the wolf take more control, while the human side kept watch for the white wolf they had scented.

Brook was watching him with concern, as she dealt with an attacker. Adam saw another sneaking up on her other side while she was distracted. Catching his current attacker in the neck, he gave a quick snap and broke his spine, before leaping over his mate and quickly tearing strips off the wolf who was trying to sneak attack his mate, while she was busy with another attacker.

Before long, their group had broken through, and more were starting to reach the core group gathered around the Alpha. Seeing the white wolf, Adam and Brook moved to attack them. Charlie and the rest of their group, which had attracted several other wolfdogs to them, followed their lead.

The white wolf saw them and moved to bolt. Their Alpha grabbed his arm and slowed him for a split second before he bolted for the trees as he shifted. He evaded the perimeter by dodging the wolves using his speed and feints. Several left gouges and just got bloody fangs and a mouthful of fur. Adam and Brook were off as if shot from a cannon and were catching up.

Adam snarled when they got close, which startled the wolf. Looking over his shoulder, the white wolf blundered into a tree, and yelped as his shoulder bounced off it. Getting his stride back, a little slower allowed Brook to catch up as well, and they started snapping at his tail and hind legs.

Brook caught his tail and bit the tip hard, making the white wolf yelp. Again, he slammed into a tree, this time with the other shoulder. He now was slowed down enough Adam was now flanking him, as Brook stayed behind him, nipping at his heels, in an attempt to hamstring him. Adam used all his power to body-slam flanks their together, causing the white wolf to stagger sideways and slam headfirst into a tree.

Brook skidded to a stop beside the now red and white wolf. Adam had to circle back as he panted from the run. Adam could hear his breath and heartbeat, so the wolf was just knocked out. Looking at the Tree, there was a dent in the bark, starting to ooze sap.

He must really have a very hard head! Adam commented, amused to Brook, as they caught their breath, watching over the wolf who was still knocked out.

They stood guard over the wolf, neither having any restraints on them. Brook shifted to her Were shape, to have the additional muscle power, at the trade-off of being slower and less manoeuvrable.

The white wolf was starting to wake up and Wolf-Adam moved to grab his throat letting out a chest-deep growl. The white wolf struggled trying to free his neck, until Brook placed a heavy paw on his side pressing the injured shoulder. He subsided, although neither moved off.

Finally, two wolves came panting up, and seeing they had restraints, *Get him tied up while he's dazed. Then I want two guards on him till he's in a cell.* Adam ordered, not taking any chances. *He's mine to deal with, later. I want him alive, so make sure he doesn't take the coward's way out.* Suicide was not seen as a bad thing by werewolves, as they understood sometimes life became unlivable, but to do so to escape punishment was frowned upon, and often considered an admission of guilt and of cowardice.

He struggled a bit as one shifted to Were and slipped cuffs on all four paws, before securing a nylon muzzle on, so there was no way he could bite. Seeing him up close, he was about the same size as Adam, and if it was a challenge fight, it would have been equal.

He started to thrash when Adam and Brook released him, but a savage growl from Adam had him laying still as the Were picked him up and carried him back the way they came; he could tell they would instantly kill him, if he did start to get free.

It took them nearly an hour to trot back to where the main group was, the Alphas were there, and were fighting the intruder's Alpha. As one, Brook and Adam gave out orders to have the trussed up wolves taken to their lock up, while keeping many of the others still here to work on capturing the rest of the Rogue Pack. Unless asked, they were not going to interrupt the fight between the Alphas.

Other wolves of the *former* Shadowed River Pack were trying to intervene and help their alpha, but Maria was working to keep them back and many came away with painful injuries from her teeth and claws. Adam and Brook moved to help her.

Gareth eventually was able to pin the other Alpha down, and when called, they came to help secure him. They were capturing as many as they could, so they could find out details. The Alpha refused to stop fighting, trying to get away from the jaws around his neck, ignoring the savage growls Gareth gave in warning and the damage the teeth were doing to it. The wolves with the restraints couldn't get close enough to use them. Gareth was forced to just bite down harder to control and crushed the rogue alpha's throat, ending his life.

Most of the Shadowed River wolves just gave up then, letting out a mournful howl for their Alpha. They knew they were beat. Many were in tears, and others screaming, as they felt their bonds to the alpha break with his death. The pack bonds were starting to fade too; the Alpha didn't have a Second or Next-Alpha to have the bonds and loyalty move to, nor was there even a Beta they were loyal to. A few seemed to go feral and attack those close enough to them from the pain of loneliness. Most were put down by former packmates they were attacking. A couple were put down by MacLaren wolves when they attacked. Adam had thought it was one downside to werewolves; the lack of a Pack, especially if the loss was sudden, could make one dangerously insane, where death was a mercy kill.

Once all the living wolves were secured and they started marching them back to the secured lockups, Alpha Gareth came over to Adam; both the worse for wear with several nasty bites in their pelts which were just starting to be felt.

Even Charlie was looking quite red and favouring a paw which had a nasty looking bite.

Your security ideas allowed us to capture most of the pack, and with minimal loss of life. Gareth commented, heart heavy with the loss of their pack members. The noise in the pack bonds didn't let anyone know yet who was dead and was just knocked out for all the pain from injuries. From experience, he did know there had only been a few deaths. *It also gave us enough warning they didn't even get organized. We caught them in the middle of their briefing. It seems most of the pack didn't even know what pack they were attacking and many still didn't have their orders yet.* Seeing a couple of Deltas come to start to collect the dead, *Bury the Alpha. I want him in a deep unmarked grave. He caused his pack to be declared Rogue and attacked another pack without provocation. The rest of the dead rogues can be burned. Their ashes will be scattered to the wind.* The two wolves turned pale but nodded; Burial was the worst sort of punishment. To have their ashes scattered was a loss of Pack, as they would not be part of the Urn of Remembrance. *Bring our dead and injured back to the pack house. Let me know who has left us.*

Adam, Brook, and Charlie fell in behind the Alpha at the end of the line of their prisoners, to head back, none moving very fast. *Since we're together, was there anything of note for our weekly meeting?* Gareth asked, trying to get his mind off the loss of the members.

Adam thought back over the week, and realised how much had happened in just the one week, *Talked to Jess and Joshua; they want to be our pups, so we will do the official stuff on the next Howl, I don't see a point to do it before, as we already have strong bonds with them.* Adam commented, *Once they are of age, we would like permission to have them fully briefed on what you told us, not just basics. I plan on keeping them as our assistants and have them qualified as Deltas. Then we could bring in some of their Theta friends as our support staff.*

Gareth liked the happy news, although it wasn't anything unexpected, *Congratulations. I never liked forcing them into an adult role early, and definitely not giving them any support of some older wolves. I hadn't realised they didn't have anyone to turn to. I am glad they worked out well.* He had thought they had the support but seems they hadn't received it, and the elders were discretely looking into why and how it happened. Changes would be made to prevent it from happening again while he was around, and he was going to make a record, to make sure it didn't happen again after he was gone. On the second half, he had to think about it for a bit, *I don't see why not. Your other two can also be briefed you two are being groomed for Seconds at any time, and the rest when they are of age. I suspect they both will be qualified at the Spring Trials; Betas often have Deltas as their support staff, so it isn't a problem. Since you are handling the techs and both data centres, I can see you needing more support staff, so it is approved. I know they have been promoted to monitoring those who did the cleaning for the rest of your group. I'll have them officially moved to your group when they are qualified.*

Wolf-Adam wagged his tail, as the more who would report to him, the more experience he would have leading, and the more status they would get with other packs. *Found out the Thetas and Deltas haven't gotten computers because they had thought they were for seniors or had to pay for them. What we had in stock has now been taken, and I have ordered the next batch. They should be here before the end of the week.* Adam let out a sigh when he remembered one thing, *Lea was supposed to do her presentation this morning about the tech training to you. I know she has been hyping herself up for it.*

Excellent. Gareth didn't like the idea of having the lower wolves excluded from the technology. *Well, I think we could spare some time this afternoon. Nobody is going to be doing any training for the next couple of days, and none of us are hurt enough to need a stay in Medical.*

Steve's trouncing will have to wait till I'm healed. Brook commented, still very annoyed with how he had ignored her. She suspected it would take the trouncing before her wolf would allow the issue to drop.

Steve got Dunstan, not sure if you heard. Adam commented with a laugh. Dunstan was nicknamed Mischief for a reason.

The alpha panted his laugher, which the other two joined in on, *Yes, I heard; I still think it is a perfect bonding, as he's going to have his hands full with that one. He's even a paw-full for a wolf who has teeth to keep him in line! Hopefully working to keep Dunstan out of trouble will settle him.* All three shared some amusement over it before continuing to have their meeting silently as they headed back.

*****

It was mid afternoon by the time they made it back to the Pack house and were checked out in medical. All four needed several injuries stitched together, but they would be healed within the week. They got the report as they were treated, very few of their wolves needed to stay in Medical, although there were many with broken bones or dislocated joints which would be on bedrest for several days.

As most had missed breakfast and now lunch, the kitchen had not ended the lunch serving at the normal time, and had gone all out and had made extras, in addition to the hearty beef stew which had been cooking all night. Venison meatloaf, some fresh breads, and sausages were out on the serving tables along with other foods which wouldn't get hurt sitting out for hours. The pancakes and French toast were also still in their serving warmers, although a little dry, along with lots of bacon.

Entering the room, Gareth was amused, "I guess the Chefs decided to come out of the saferoom and cook as a way to relive stress, since the pack house wasn't under attack, and was still locked down tight, as usual." He commented to the two, he was already considering them his Acting-Seconds, "I had given up on reprimanding or trying to stop them early on. I just required them to qualify as Deltas and to have a Beta with them as a compromise. Scott—the head chef—and Lupita—his second—had gone further and both qualified as Beta, so it met my requirements. Both maintain their training regularly." He told them, "The kitchen has also been reinforced to the point it could almost function as a saferoom, as it would take a battering ram to get in, nor would I want to have to fight with the number of sharp knives at their disposal!" They flashed a tired smile, before heading to their usual table.

The few times he had watched the two chefs train... he supressed a shudder. Both had been armed with an armful of the various knives. They had started with tossing them into a target, and almost all of them hit where they wanted. The sound of a cleaver hitting was like that of an axe and caused similar damage. They had done some knife fighting with Martin, and Martin had come out of it with many more knife wounds than the Chef. They had done more, and both trained at least two or three times a week. He made sure he didn't see it, knowing the kitchen wasn't a soft spot in their security.

As Adam and Brook sat at their table, their pups quickly came to curl into their sides. Lea was looking down as Sam and her came over as well, Lea just picking at her meal. "We're not doing training this afternoon." Adam winced as a wound pulled painfully, "Lea, the Alpha is making some time after we eat for your presentation, since we missed this morning."

Lea nodded, before she started to eat; she had come to look forward to doing the presentation and showing the Alpha she was right for being a trainer. The attack had made her upset for missing it, but they were willing to make time for her? It made it all better.

The rest sat and chattered around the adults. All the adults were exhausted; not only were they up at least two hours early, but most spent much of the morning fighting. It also was starting to be felt, the three holes in the pack bonds from death.

Steve and Chris had red faces from crying. Steve sighed, "Does it always hurt this much when packmates die or are injured?" he asked as the slumped down in some seats.

Brook sighed, "It hurts much more when it is unexpected. Everyone knew there was an attack, so expected there would be some death. There are two still in the hospital in critical condition, but hopefully they got help in time. We should know shortly if they will survive. This evening we will be holding last rites for those who died. You feel the hurt, as you weren't fighting, and those fighting were using your strength, so they could do their job. Now we mourn."

Chris sighed, "How often are there attacks?"

As this was the first time it hadn't been a drill, Adam wasn't sure and looked to his mate.

"Not very often. We get maybe one in a year; and it is usually a single wolf, or a pair. This sort of attack of a pack coming in, when not actively at war between them: very rare. Wars between packs are also very rare." Brook answered.

One of the older Thetas was refilling the pitchers of drink, "Last time I heard of pack wars, was over a hundred years ago and was on the other side of the continent. It was a pack which had just emigrated and wanted the lush land of a pack who was already there. Both packs were decimated with the leadership of both dead or permanently incapacitated. They were taken over by another pack in the area."

Brook continued, "From the two unprovoked attacks and one item I can't talk about, the Shadowed River Pack was declared Rogue." All the wolves who heard made shocked sounds. The two humans glanced around confused, waiting for an explanation. "The last time it happened was in the sixteenth century. When it happens, the pack ceases to exist. The only place they will exist is in history books, and very rarely are they mentioned; they will have seemed to die off a few hundred years ago, or even never existed." Any records would be updated to blot out their pack name. The pack would become nameless, which was worse than death; it was that they as a pack had no future and would be forgotten. "All the attackers have a death sentence unless they can talk an

Alpha into giving them a new start. All the Thetas and pups who stayed behind will be given new lives in another pack. Some may be brought here, if they can be retrained."

Both Steve and Chris were pale from the statement, "But we don't have a death penalty—" Steve started.

"*Human laws* don't have a death penalty." Brook interrupted, "*Weres* do; never do we recognise the *human laws* for Were-on-Were fights. It's also not feasible to lock up a wolf, as our lifespan is much longer. A life sentence could be three or four hundred years. Humans are lucky for seventy." Brook corrected, "Our crime rate is much lower than humans, as if they are caught, the serious offenders are killed. It works as a much stronger deterrent. Also, there is very little mitigation, except in some cases the person was attacked has a say and can request leniency to be considered."

Chris nodded, "Like the laws around a forced turn?"

Brook smiled, "Yes. If a person gets turned, and the rules were not followed, the one turned can decide if the one which turned them gets to live, and if the person is OK with it, to be their mentor for the new world they are in. It allows for mitigation while not having such a drawn-out decisions, the way human legal systems are, and keeps it more fair for the one who was offended. Sentences are usually handed down in days, or weeks at the longest, not years and years as the human system has."

Once they were all done eating, Adam noticed the rest were not loosening their grip, *I'm bringing a few extras to the meeting, my pups are still very clingy and upset; I hope you don't mind?* Adam asked the Alpha.

No, it's OK, under the circumstances. Let's use my boardroom; it'll be quiet and calm in there. Came the reply.

CHAPTER 29

Aftermath

Sitting down in the boardroom, Adam showed Lea how to connect the laptop up to the projector system they had installed, and how to use the controls. It was a nice change from the fighting and death of earlier.

Alpha Gareth sat back in his seat and looked satisfied as they got the system working, "The system looks great, Adam. I'm glad you talked me into getting it installed."

Adam laughed, "This is only the basic function. I have it connected for video streaming from the cable, and if we get Longview set up, you would be able to do video conferencing with them."

"But how would it work? Just show everyone?"

"There are two cameras, one shows the room, the other picks up whoever is speaking for a closer view. The screen will show both, plus the view of what it's sending like a picture-in-picture."

Gareth nodded. It would make conferences easier, "What if there is more than two?"

Adam smiled, "Then the main view is whoever is speaking, with up to eight views along the bottom. If there are more than eight cameras, it displays the last eight to speak." Seeing Lea was ready to go, he nodded to her and stepped to the side, sitting down to let her begin.

*****

Gareth smiled as Lea wrapped up the presentation, "Excellent! I like how you made it interactive, not just a lecture. I have had some courses which were less interesting! You can do others, and not need to involve me, except as a student. Once you are done the main schooling, and have your high school diploma, I am going to make notes for you to get some training as an educator and trainer. You have an ability to be a good one. Any questions for me?"

Lea shook her head. All training which was approved was paid for out of pack funds, for the most part. Rarely, the training was paid by the wolf, then reimbursed when they completed the training successfully. Part of it was to allow the pack to learn more, but also to make sure they worked hard. If a course was failed, they would have to pay back the costs or pay for the costs to retake the class and pass it. Most had to show some skill or ability in the field or a related one or get permission to change from the Alpha. A few wanted to take a chance on a wildly different field, and while the pack paid for it, it had an agreement for working in something related to the training for two years after finishing. Now with Lea approved, she would be able to get whichever she wanted as long as she could say how it would help her.

Gareth looked around, the other pups had curled up in the corner after shifting to their wolves and were napping in a pile together, napping as a wolf would let them be a bit aware, and was much more comfortable than as human on a floor. He had no problem with them, as a major attack like this one was so very rare even he didn't want to be alone. Clapping his hands woke them up, and they were quickly looking at him.

"Time to go get changed for dinner. We have three packmates to send on their way to their next life."

They nodded, and followed Adam, Brook, and Lea out the door. Robin brushed his side against Lea's leg and paced beside her.

Lea and Sam headed up the stairs and to their rooms to get something a bit nicer on, for respect. They grabbed a change of clothes and headed down. They put the change in Robin and Toby's room, as they wanted some comfort, since they didn't think they could sleep without it.

The four headed out for dinner and met up with Adam and Brook, again sitting close to him, enjoying their comfortably dominant scents. Their wolves could relax with having the two Betas nearby to protect them.

The dinner was some steaks, only flash-seared, a comfort food for the wolves. Most were feeling the affects on the pack bonds, and those who fought, their healing injuries.

After dinner, they headed outside. There were three pyres set up; one for each of the three they lost.

The two who had been in critical condition, were now stable enough, and although they were on hospital beds, with IVs, and medical staff hovering around them, they were there too. Gareth had worked with the Healers when he took over, for whenever it was able to do so, the patients were brought out for the ceremonies. It helped them with mental health, so the healers usually agreed, as long as they didn't need any machines, but with most now having internal batteries to allow them to work while not plugged in, and small enough to be moved easily, it was rare for a wolf who was awake to be denied the right to be there.

There were some missing, as they were still at a "watch" status, so the security was still tight, and there were some patrols out, but due to all the security tech which had been installed, there were fewer wolves actually out doing patrols. Adam and Martin, along with the two humans had even been able to develop a remote tablet to monitor any alerts, so the security office didn't need to be manned; they were monitoring discretely as they paid their respects to the fallen.

The teams still patrolling were volunteers and would be relieved in an hour by another set, so they could come for part of it to pay their respects, if they wished.

The Alphas came up on the small step which had been set out so he could see everyone. As Alpha Gareth stepped up, everyone was immediately silent. He had discussed it with Duncan and Keanna about more of their story being told to the pack. It was part of the reasoning for the attack from the preliminary reports from their prisoners. Both had been offered the white wolf's life, but had turned it down, so once they were done with the interrogation, Adam had his shot. So far, he had not even told them his name.

Gareth took a breath and let his eyes glance over the pack, and to give the *why* of the attack first, "Today we were victorious in defeating a pack who decided, for taking in a pair who left before they could have been stripped of everything and tossed out for a false statement. The alpha decided they would take over the pack and kill those who resisted. They were planning on using hollowed out bullets filled with liquid Wolfsbane."

The Alpha had to hold up a hand to quiet the mutterings, "As we all know, use of that poison has been outlawed by all packs, prides, and other groups for the last millennia. Sadly, they decided to ignore the long-standing decision, even with the instant death sentence we still have for having it. They had already been declared a Rogue Pack. One: for the unlawful declaring of members who left of their free will as Rogue, to prevent them from joining another pack. Two: having a pack member enter a territory of another pack for a malicious act *and* without permission; namely the attempted kidnapping or murder of the two who left. Three: the unprovoked and undeclared attack of another pack."

Again, he had to hold up his hand, "The requisite elders of three packs shared the proof and had declared the three separate incidents as valid and declared the pack Rogue. As we are the closest, we will be taking control of the Rogue Pack's territory and finding out about the members they had still there. We start on Wednesday." Stopping there, he let it sink in for the wolves.

Holding out a hand, he was handed the lit torch, "Now, we had three wolves who died giving their lives to fulfil their pack oaths to protect the pack. We are gathered to say farewell to their life, and to speed them onto their next one. Kyle, James, and Jason." He paused, as the names were not known widely as there hadn't been time to pass them around, "You will be missed, but not forgotten. Their names and stories will be added to the list of those fallen in the service of the pack."

Stepping down, he stepped into the gathering, moving slowly, greeting, and sharing a touch with those on the way. Lighting the torches of the families who wished to help send them on their way, he lit the first pyre, then moved to the second, then the third. The enemy dead were planned on being lit out of respect for the dead the next day. It was large enough they needed a burn permit to keep curious humans away, and they hadn't got it issued yet. Those found with wolfbane on them had been buried, as had their Alpha.

Gareth kept his torch, while the rest tossed them into the fires. He would light the firepit with it, a symbol they were not forgotten, even if they were not there. He let out a mournful howl which was picked up by all the wolves in the gathering, then by those still out on patrol. They howled out the grief of those lost, and their wish of a better life on the next time.

As they finished howling, many had tears on their faces. The Alpha took the stand again, the torch still in his hand, "Beta Adam had started one custom, which I should have started long ago. The firepit is open to all, lets just be packmates together; leave your rank outside the circle and just be respectful to all. All are welcome; come." He handed the torch to Adam and let him lead the pack to the firepit for the traditional wake, but with the new twist of just being rank-less packmates. The elders and some volunteer helpers would make sure the three pyres burned totally to ash. Today was for the fallen, tomorrow was for looking to the future and the living. Talking about it, the Alphas and Elders decided all future wakes would be rank-less out of respect of the fallen; it would show they valued all the pack equally and it didn't matter the rank, all grieved equally.

As was the pack tradition, the ash would be collected once it cooled, some would be scattered where they died, some at any favourite places, and the rest in the memorial garden, with some added to the Urn of Remembrance, which contained part of all the members who had come before. When the packs split, each got half of the contents.

*****

Reaching the firepit, Adam waited till everyone was there, before lighting it with Gareth's torch. Once lit, he stepped back as he joined the Alphas and Brook, starting the traditional wake song, to help the lost ones on their way. The song started quiet and sad but ended upbeat and with hope. Adam had learned it as part of his Pack education. The fact he was being honoured with the leading of it touched him, and if he had tears in his eyes, it was not commented on. They sang it three times, for their three lost members.

One song moved onto another then another, as some started handing out some non-alcoholic apple cider, passing it down the line till everyone had some who wanted it. An insulated and heated urn was plugged into a hidden outlet which was hiding in a hole at the base of the tree. It was one of the side-effects of all the networking of the forest: some places they wired with power.

It amused the wolves to have 'power trees' to plug into. For areas close to the pack house, they had scattered the waterproof and camouflaged outlets. They liked to leave the areas looking natural and unspoiled, but they also had grown to enjoy some of the human 'creature comforts' like entertainment systems, and the ability to communicate with others. Able to brighten up places with lights was less of an issue, due to their wolf-vision, and the fact they liked to see the stars. But able to have an urn stay hot with electricity was one idea they liked. They were working on waterproofing and painting a mini fridge to put out here for 'roastables' once it was ready.

After a bit, they started remembering stories about the three who's lives they were celebrating. The Alphas and Betas were scattered around the fire and were giving comfort to the lower wolves who came to them. Being very tactile, many were curling up in laps or against friends. The fact they were together and sharing their grief was what mattered.

Chris and Steve had come out, and they were all bundled up against the cold. Adam had some extra clothes on as well, as his body was still changing, and all three were close to the fire. Those who had shifted to Were worked to keep the three warm. Adam had snuggled down into Brook's furry lap and right now was reasonably warm.

Adam smiled as he felt along the bonds to Duncan and Keanna they were less scared and more content, knowing the white wolf was in the lockup. They were staying close to Martin and a few others from security. Looking inside himself, he could feel no special bond with them, but probing with the help of his wolf, could tell they had one with Martin now.

It was very late—or early, depending how you looked at it—when Adam and Brook headed back. Adam was surprised Toby and Robin weren't there too, only having seen them early in the evening. Checking on their room, found them and their girlfriends curled up all together, asleep. He quietly closed the door, heading to bed as well. Adam dropped into their bed, snuggling up to Brook, who mumbled, half asleep. Jess, Joshua, and Charlie were already curled up asleep in it. With a large yawn on Adam's part, they fell asleep.

*****

When they finally woke up, it was almost time for lunch, which was not surprising due to the time they went to bed. Adam smiled and stretched. He nudged the rest in his bed to start them waking up and headed for a shower. Looking at his face, he smiled. If he didn't want a beard, his face was staying smooth and hairless, as if he had just done a good shave. It sure saved on buying razors.

His wolf snorted at him, ***Skin for human, fur for me!*** he commented, agreeing with staying smooth.

Stepping into the shower, he was soon joined by the three. Jess and Joshua helped wash around Adam and Brook's healing injuries, being especially careful of the stitches. When they were clean, both helped wash the other two, their wolves forward to check on their pups; making sure they were all good and had come to no harm.

Heading out for lunch, they came up behind the four younger pups also heading for food. Putting an arm around Robin and Lea, he felt them jump. Chuckling in his mind he didn't show he was trying to startle them, he commented innocently, "You sleep alright?"

Both nodded, as they worked to calm down from having been startled.

All four pups came and sat with Adam again. Sharing a look with Brook, she commented, *I expect it to take a while before they are comfortable again. Today is for pack relaxing and to calm down. Tomorrow we're going to be trying to get back into the schedule. Are we still heading to your mother's birthday on the weekend?*

Adam realised with a start it was the next weekend, *We need to. We're taking Robin and Toby with us. I'm thinking Joshua and Jess should be there as well.*

I agree. Your sister making the dinner appointment? Have you let her know how many wolves will be there? Brook asked.

Pulling out his phone, quickly texted Tara he was bringing a couple more with him. He then used it to e-mail Longview there was six wolves and Charlie coming but knowing the four pups wouldn't want to be in another room so soon after the attack and at a strange place, advised they would be sleeping together. Sharing the humour with Brook over what any human would say to the message, had Brook laughing out loud.

Chatting in private messages was not unusual, so most just looked curious, at the sudden laugh. Brook just shook her head; she wasn't going to pass out the private information.

Getting a quick reply from Tara, *Thanks for the reminder to call the booking in! 2 more pups, I assume?* Adam chuckled.

Yes. Jess and Joshua. Found out they had no close family at all. Brook and I decided to give them one. He replied.

Good for you! I liked them when I met them. It's sad they have no other family.

They were going to run between the two packs, since when they looked at the route, it was a four-hour run, which was a good workout, but not more than that for them. They were heading out after lunch on Saturday, then spending the night at the Longview Pack. Borrowing one of Longview Pack's vehicles to head in to see his mother for the afternoon, and evening, then spend a second night with the pack, before heading home.

Adam and Brook spent the afternoon, hanging out in the pack's common areas, curling up with those wolves who felt down, and giving hugs to all who wanted them. This day was for everyone to recover and be together. Adam had seen both Alphas, all the Elders, the two official Seconds, and even Rein and Mikan also making the rounds as well.

Dinner that night was more of a buffet of smaller pieces than of larger mains, as had lunch, which was continually renewed. There was many who weren't feeling too hungry and more of nibbled at it. Adam and Brook, as were many other senior wolves, were starving from the amount of work they were doing to comfort the pack. Both ended up going back for a third helping in the evening before the food was finally taken away and fresh over-night food was placed out.

Adam and Brook checked on Toby and Robin, and they again had the girls curled up with them. Once they closed the door, they smiled at each other.

"I'm going to talk to the girl's parents' tomorrow, see if they would be willing to have them move into the other room. From the way they are acting, both of us are feeling they have found their mates." Brook commented as they got ready for bed themselves; they had spent lots of energy during the day helping with the pack. Both were yawning widely.

Adam felt his wolf growl in agreement, and promise to protect the girls, as if they were his own pups. He nodded in agreement, "Add in our agreement, and my wolf's promise to protect them as if they were our own. If we do become the Seconds, I hope the personal suite is big enough for us."

Brook grinned shyly, "It should be, as long as we don't gather many more pups." As they curled up together to sleep.

Soon after they crawled in, Jess and Joshua came as well, but they curled up on the pad by the fireplace. To Wolf-Adam, they needed the comfort of them nearby, but not as much as the night before, where they needed to curl up with them.

*****

The next morning, Adam woke Brook with a kiss. Smiling they both got up and winced as they stretched. Adam moved to check his com-puter, quickly getting through his addressed e-mail, and making a start at the backlog of his mailing lists. Quite a few he just deleted unread or clicked the remove link to unsubscribe to many of them, and most with just a quick glance. There were status updates and reports from the wolves who reported to him, but most were just everything was good and could just be filed.

There was a reply from Hank in the Longview Pack, showing everything was in order for them to come over Saturday. He was having the patrols advised they were coming in, but they'd likely be challenged, as they were unknown, and just to have them contact him.

There had also been a couple IMs from those friends who knew him before he found Brook. Most were just generic messages, but he thought several times before replying, as he had started to do. Most of his contacts had slowly stopped chatting, and he let those go, as he had many more friends in his packmates. Since many of his old friends were 'furry' many would understand way too much, and some would beg to join and be turned, even with the risks. He had to be very careful on how much information about his new life he gave out. Most times, he just didn't bother sending them messages and they didn't bother contacting him. He was slowly weeding out his contact list in that way. He planned on every three months, those who hadn't said hi to just remove them, so the status no longer showed up.

Finishing up his email, he smiled. After breakfast they had their appointment in medical. Everyone who was fighting had an appointment over the next few days, even if they didn't get hurt, as the Healers also checked on their mental and emotional health, not just their physical.

"I think we should see how fast you are today if we get cleared by Medical. It would let us know how much we need to push ourselves to reach the Alpha standard, for the Spring Trials." Adam commented. He had still not seen exactly how fast she could go in relation to him, other than the chase of the white wolf, there she was nearly keeping up with him going flat out. When he got to the wolf, she was only four or five body lengths behind him.

"I'll deal with the stopwatch, if you want." Came Jess' voice behind them. Jess and Joshua had followed them off for breakfast.

Brook nodded, "I think it would be good. I haven't tried to push myself in a few years. My wolf likes the idea of a challenge." She commented. Turning to Jess, "We have our medical appointment after breakfast. We'll see if they have any issues, and we'll let you know when we're back."

Jess nodded taking a bite of her French Toast.

The others dug in as wolves started trickling in for breakfast. Most looked tired, and although the official time was over, some wolves he knew had requested additional time. Erin had commented Aurora was still on bed rest, as she had a shattered leg from the fighting; it had been broken in several places with several bites on top of it. She had been in the group who had prevented the escape, and although she helped, it was where the worst injuries had been. She should be up and healed by Monday.

The security wolves were dealing with interrogating the prisoners. Adam was glad, as he didn't like the idea of the hard tactics they were having to use. He did know with the white wolf he'd get the chance to deal with them. They had found out he was the highest-ranking wolf left in that pack. From some of the others, he already knew they were breaking up as a pack. Many were giving up every secret they could when confronted with what had happened, and in exchange many were just not wanting to be killed.

Some of the pack this weekend was going to deal with the remains of the Shadowed River Pack, and start finding them new homes, or dealing with the remaining fighters. Duncan and Keanna were going, as they had plenty of knowledge about the pack. He would be helping out a bit at the start, so they could secure any computers they had. They were heading out that afternoon.

Finishing up breakfast Adam and Brook headed down for their checkup, and probably their stitches to be removed.

*****

Adam sighed and sniffed the air as they left, "The one thing I hate, is the medical smell, it clings to you as you leave. I want a shower before we do anything else," He complained.

Brook laughed, "That is the same for most wolves I know. The smell of all the pain, illness, injury, then add in all the blood and cleaners and strong disinfectants; it really makes for unpleasantness. I'm just glad we are cleared. A good scrub would be good. We just have to watch the healing scabs, as they said. Personally, I can do without any scarring."

They bantered a bit as they took a quick wash and waiting for Jess to arrive. They shifted when she did and did some warmups, including a couple warmup laps around the pack house.

Brook and I are doing an informal Alpha speed trial on the one-fifty trail momentarily. Keep a watch out. Adam sent to the pack in general, as it was a very popular training and exercise trail. With it having a mix of all the types of terrain in the territory to deal with, it allowed for a good workout as well.

"Ready! I'll start it when you're ready." Jess called out.

Adam looked at Brook, and she send a wordless affirmative as they started for the track, *Now* he called out to Jess, as they took off.

They raced each other. There was ten centimetres of fresh powder of snow which fell the night before, but with their snowshoe-like paws, they just scampered over it, not sinking in. It hid all the ice under enough they would have great traction in most areas. There had been enough traffic already so the bad spots would have safe paths marked out.

The wolves were setting up a rolling announcement ahead of them, so the trail was clear, but with many standing to the sides watching. Those in wolf form howled and barked encouragement. With the handing of the torch over to them, and them leading part of the fight, there were many rumours going around; from the idea of them breaking off to start their own pack, to them being groomed as next alphas over the Alpha's pups who were off training, to being named Seconds.

Both were going full out and wanted the bragging rights. They did keep it clean, and didn't try to disrupt each other, as they both wanted to pass the time. In some spots, they went single file, but being nice, they alternated who was first. They panted as they climbed the steep hills, and nearly flew down the other side. They did controlled skids around the hairpin turns and where switchbacks swapped direction.

Their wolves loved being pushed hard to be the best, and both minds worked together to keep them running at the best pace.

The Alphas stepped out an hour after the announcement and stood with Jess watching the stopwatch. It may not be an official trial, but with the announcement, and the watchers, there were enough watching it would count if they completed it within the ninety minutes. Within the pack bonds, Gareth could hear the chatter about where they were, and how fast they were going.

The two wolves sprinted the last bit of the trail, and there was a large number of the pack, including several of the elders out waiting for them to finish. Jess hit the time, as both Adam and Brook passed the end point at the same time, side by side. She blinked a few times at the stopwatch before passing it to the Alpha.

He had to blink at it, before he announced it, as Adam and Brook panted heavily, as they had trotted a couple of laps around the building, and then did some stretches. "Eighty-five minutes!" he called out. The gathered wolves erupted in a howl.

Eighty-five minutes? Brook asked, not thinking she heard right as she started to lap up some warm water Joshua put in front of her.

Gareth nodded, "Yes. And from all the wolves watching, there were enough who are qualified as track monitors the Elders have agreed it will count as an official run, as one of them was also timing it, since they had the warning of the start in time. Congratulations." He told the both of them, speaking aloud for everyone to hear. *Come see us in our office when you are cooled down.* He and his mate had plans for them, they could now start to put in motion, even if they would take years to be complete.

Epilogue

Adam and Brook were promoted to Acting-Seconds, and when the time came, both had no trouble qualifying for the Seconds, and at the end of the Spring Trials, in front of the pack, they both were officially promoted and sworn in as Seconds and became the Alpha's trusted right hands.

Adam soon had his Were form, and knowing the differences, and remembering what happened when he was first turned, and how much his strength increased, learned carefully what his new form's strengths and weaknesses were.

Adam and Brook lead a counterattack at the now nameless pack as their Leadership and Fighting Trials, and Adam took down the remaining lead wolves, and even recovered the one who had attacked Keanna and had lied about what Duncan did. They return victorious, and with no packmates lost, and had found out they had several more violations. If he hadn't already been killed, the Alpha would have had a very slow and painful death as a warning for other Alphas to heed the Inter-Pack Laws; they were very few and were there to keep the peace between the packs.

Those recovered in the fight were treated fairly and given new packs and new homes for those who were innocent of the issues with the pack, while those who had fought and never surrendered were treated harshly, especially those who used Wolfsbane.

The picture frame with the pictures of Adam's family for his mother was a hit, and although there were tears, they were tears of joy. It hung on her wall, with her pride of her son's place in the world.

Adam's new life with his werewolf mate had just begun, but where it led was many more stories, and it took both Brook and him where they never expected to go, and in ways neither had ever really dreamed could happen.

FROM THE AUTHOR

I hope everyone enjoyed this first book. I have spent much time reviewing and editing it to get it ready for being published. For those who encouraged me, when I posted the first couple of chapters, on Wattpad and have stuck around, a great big thanks! I would not have gotten to this point without your support.

I am Very grateful for Brian's support (MaxD01 on Wattpad), as I would not have posted even one chapter, as I didn't think it was good enough to let anyone see, let alone to get to this point of being published.

There are many people on Wattpad who pointed out mistakes and corrections for this story, and I am grateful for your help with the editing. It allowed me to crowd-source my editing, even if I did a fair amount of work. Their suggestions and corrections have been integrated into this final version. Any errors which remain are my own.

This story started as a daydream, but quickly morphed into its own life. By the time chapter seven came around, it was not my life, but that of its own; as the character I had made had to make decisions I did not have to make at all. My life since then has had some ups and downs and has changed much from it too. I have a totally different life than I did in 2015. There have been a great many changes in the real world as well since then.

The saddest part is we have lost Brian, with him passing away in June 2019. He is greatly going to be missed. I wish he could see how far this has gone, and how we can proceed further. This book is dedicated to his memory. Since his passing, it has been a bit harder to get back into the stories, especially since I had one sequel which was to almost be Why Us 3, as it would centre on Zane and his changes further on than I have gone. While that one may not be coming out for quite a while, it is one I have been working on for over 2 years, very slowly... almost sentence by sentence at times. I haven't decided if it will just be going straight to publishing. Wolves in Space and Folican Wolf Pack had been ones which were being co-authored when he had passed and have not had much done since then. They are going to be hard to finish.

I can be reached at books-interact@adamwebster.ca if you want to interact with me.